THE
DEADENING

To Sheri,
What a journey you've been
on! So blessed to have
been a part of it. The best
days are ahead!
In Him,
Kerry Peresta

THE
DEADENING

OLIVIA CALLAHAN SUSPENSE

BOOK ONE

LEVEL
BEST BOOKS

ISBN (Hardback): 978-1-953789-37-2

First edition

ISBN: 978-1-953789-35-8

Cover art by Level Best Designs

This book was professionally typeset on Reedsy.
Find out more at reedsy.com

This book is dedicated to my mom, Sarah Ann Smith, deceased, 2014. No one was more excited about my first book's release than this tiny, fierce, feisty woman. She'd be on the front row cheering for the second, too. Mom, this one's for you.

Death is not the greatest loss in life. The greatest loss in life is what dies inside us while we live.

NORMAN COUSINS

Praise for THE DEADENING

"A gripping read populated by likable characters. Peresta draws us into a colorful, detailed world and makes us care what happens to the people living in it. We root for Olivia as she struggles to regain her memory, her bearings, and the identity she lost long before her injury. Excellent!"—Susan Crawford, Internationally bestselling author of *The Pocket Wife* and *The Other Widow.*

Prologue

The stiff bristles of the brush grew coppery as he scrubbed back and forth, back and forth. Wrinkling his nose at the smell, he groped for the mask he'd bought, looped it over his head, and snugged it into place.

He dipped the brush in the red-tinged solution in a blue, plastic bowl beside him on the floor, and continued scrubbing. Fifteen minutes later, he emptied the bowl down the toilet and shoved everything he'd used into a trash bag. He fought to staunch the bile creeping up his windpipe, but his throat constricted and he gagged. After retching into the sink, he turned on the faucet and splashed water on his face, pausing to take deep breaths. He could do this. He had to do this. He gripped the edge of the counter and stared out the bathroom window.

She'd not told anyone. Thank God for that. No one could know. No one would ever know. He'd make sure.

He walked to his garage, opened his car trunk, tossed in the latest trash bag. His hands felt icy. He rubbed them together, wiggled his fingers, and slammed the trunk shut.

Admittedly, her terror had excited him. *Confusion. Dawning realization in her expression.* His lips curved upward into a smile, then disintegrated. Reliving it didn't change anything. He needed to move forward.

He returned and studied the carpet. In spite of his efforts, the stain still needed work. He cursed, dropped to his knees, and pounded the dampness with a fist.

Through a veil of fatigue, he watched in horror as the kidney-shaped stain stood and pointed an accusatory finger at him. He blinked, hard. Was he hallucinating? How long had he been without sleep? He crabbed backwards, leaned against the wall, pulled his knees to his chest and squeezed his eyes shut. When he opened them some moments later, the blood-apparition had disappeared.

He groaned.

He stared at the ceiling until his brain spit out a solution.

The problem lay in the other room. That's how he looked at her now.

A problem to solve.

He rose from the floor and walked out.

His eyes slid from her pale face, down her form, to her feet. He no longer thought of her as warm, soft, desirable. *She had been so scared...eyes wide and unblinking as she fell.* He shook his head and pushed the image away.

Nesting her in towels so her blood wouldn't pool on the couch, her bronze-sandaled feet with their shiny, pink toenails hung over the edge. He looked away. "Get a grip, man. Just do it."

The towels fell away when he picked her up. He wound them back around her, careful to tuck in the edges. His heartbeat slammed his ribs.

She was fragile, a little bit of a thing, like a bird. He drew his index finger across her lips. "I'm sorry," he whispered. "If you had just...if you had only..." His voice trailed away. Jaw clenched, he carried her to his car.

Chapter One

Nathan ambled along sidewalks that wound through the manicured hospital grounds, fishing in his pocket for a lighter. He lit the cigarette dangling from his lips and inhaled deeply, his smile saturated with nicotine's unholy bliss.

"Thank God," he mumbled around the cigarette, and withdrew it from his lips, stretching. He glanced over his shoulder at the brightly lit ER entrance to Mercy Hospital, rubbing his neck. He rolled his shoulders, inhaled several deep drags from the cigarette, dropped it, and ground it beneath his shoe. "These night shifts are killing me." He groaned and gazed at the sky. Clouds hid a full moon. He'd been grateful to get the med tech job, but after two months of bodily fluid testing and storage, he was bored. He needed a challenge.

Nathan followed his typical route through the hedged lawn, almost on auto-pilot, so when he stumbled and sprawled onto the grass face-first, he was stunned. What had tripped him? Cursing softly, he explored his cheeks, nose, forehead. No damage done that he could tell. "Klutz," he berated himself, pushing up to hands and knees.

Something soft and warm lay beneath his palms. His breathing sped up. He looked down, but it was too dark to see. Trembling, his fingers inched their way to lips, nose, eyes, stiff knots of hair. His mouth dropped in horror. The clouds obligingly slid off the moon and revealed a woman's body, her hair blood-matted, her face ghostly white. The grass around her head was rusty with blood. He edged his head toward her lips to check her breathing. Shallow, but at least she was alive.

He scrambled to his feet, fighting nausea and staring at his palms, sticky with the woman's blood. Shrieking for help, he raced into the hospital and skidded to a stop in front of the desk. The ER nurses behind the reception desk squinted at him like he was deranged.

"Possible head injury!" He flailed an arm at the entrance. "Someone, anyone, come quick!"

A male nurse and two aides followed him outside, shoes pounding the sidewalk at full gallop. The tech stopped, turned, and signaled them to tread carefully as they parted ways with the sidewalk and navigated the shrubbery in the dark. Single file, panting, they tiptoed through the shadows until the tech raised a palm for them to stop.

"Here," he hissed at the nurse, and held a point like a bird dog.

The nurse dropped to the ground and clicked a flashlight on. "Ohmigosh," he whispered. He lifted the woman's thin, pale wrist and glanced at his watch. Satisfied that she had a pulse, he slapped the flashlight into Nathan's bloodied palm. "Stay with her!" He rushed inside.

Within minutes, looky-loos poured from the ER and clustered around the limp form.

"Move back!" Nathan stretched out his arms like a cop directing traffic. "She's barely breathing!" His glanced nervously at the ER entrance.

The crowd didn't yield an inch. The ER doors whooshed open. A stretcher clattered down the sidewalk and onto the dew-damp grass. Chills shivered up the tech's spine as the ashen pallor of death climbed from the woman's neck to her face. He dropped to the ground and picked up her hand. The paramedic team drew closer, their flashlights piercing the darkness with slivers of light. The crowd eased apart to let them through.

Nathan bent closer to the woman, and whispered, "Hang in there. Help is on the way."

The stretcher slid to a stop beside him. The paramedics dropped to their knees, stabilized the woman's head with a brace, staunched the bleeding, and wrapped the wound. They eased her onto the stretcher and rumbled away. The aides shared nervous smiles of relief. They looked at Nathan, then followed the paramedic team back inside.

Nathan, his heartbeat finally slowing, called, "Thanks for the assist, guys!" as they walked away.

The crowd dispersed with curious glances at Nathan, who watched until the group disappeared behind the ER's double glass doors. He heaved a sigh of relief and swiped perspiration off his forehead. He patted his scrubs pocket for a cigarette, reconsidered, and trotted toward the ER entrance.

After the automatic doors parted, he jogged past two closed-door exam rooms and paused at a third, wide open. He looked inside.

The paramedics shared their observations with the ER doctor on call as he deftly explored the woman's wounds. When he finished, he nodded, barked instructions, and pointed at the bed. In seconds, the woman's transfer from stretcher to bed was complete. One of the nurses whisked a blood pressure cuff around her arm. Another hooked an IV bag to a chrome stand, pierced the skin on the back of the woman's hand, slid in a needle, and taped it down.

The tech stepped back from the door to allow the paramedics to exit. Holding his breath, he stole into the room and crept past a floor-to-ceiling supply cabinet. He planted both palms onto the smooth, white walls behind him and inched sideways, melting into the corner next to a shelf holding tongue depressors, a box of plastic gloves, and a sanitizer dispenser.

"Pulse one-fifteen." The nurse studied the blood pressure cuff. "Blood pressure eight-five over fifty."

"Need a trach," the doctor barked. "She's bleeding out. Get some O neg in here."

A blur of motion, two nurses and the ER doctor huddled around the woman's body. When they stepped back, a laryngoscope, an endotracheal tube, and four sticky electric nodes leading to a cardiac monitor had been secured.

The medical team stilled, their eyes riveted to the monitors. The nurses wore sage green scrubs. Both had pink stethoscopes around their necks. The ER doctor had on a crisp, white jacket with his name scripted in black on the pocket. Nathan fidgeted and stuck his head out from the corner to focus on the screens.

The readings sputtered, stalled, plummeted.

"Code Blue!" The doctor spun around. A nurse jumped to the wall and slapped a flat, white square on the wall.

"*Code Blue!*" echoed through the ER's intercom system. Frantic footsteps in the hall. Shouted instructions. Clanging metal. Squealing wheels. Nathan squeezed farther into the corner as the cart bearing life-saving electronic shock equipment exploded through the door.

"Brain must be swelling," the doctor mumbled. He grabbed two paddles and swiped them together. "Clear!"

The woman's body jolted. The doctor's head jerked to the cardiac monitor. Flat.

"Clear!" He placed the paddles on the woman's chest.

Her frail torso arced. The machine blipped an erratic cadence, then droned a steady hum.

The doctor cursed. "Clear!"

Another jolt. The monitor surged, sagged, then settled into a reassuring metronome blip. Tense faces relaxed. Applause spattered around the room.

The doctor blew out a long breath. "Okay, people, good job." He smiled.

Within minutes, more lines snaked from the woman's form. An orogastric tube drooped from the corner of her mouth, behind the intubation tube. A lead to measure brain waves clung to her forehead. The doctor studied each monitor in turn. Nathan let out the breath he'd been holding, slid down the wall into a crouch, and balanced on the balls of his feet.

"Any additional instructions, Doctor Bradford?" Brows raised, the nurse waited.

He rubbed his head thoughtfully. "Think she's stable for now. CAT scan already ordered?"

She nodded. "Of course."

"Tell them to expedite." He cocked his head at the woman. "May be a long night. Watch her closely." The doctor strode to the door, paused, and turned. He glanced at the tech huddled in the corner. "Good job, son."

Nathan grinned and rose from his crouch, his chest puffed out a little. He'd never saved a life before. After a sympathetic glance at Mercy Hospital's latest Jane Doe, he returned to the lab.

Chapter Two

Olivia Callahan

The back of my head felt like someone had used it for batting practice.

Why was it so dark?

My body floated like a balloon tethered to the relentless pounding in my head. I opened my mouth to speak, but my lips refused to budge. I instructed my arm to move, but it lay stubbornly still. I puzzled over this a few seconds and tried again. As if my efforts had pricked the balloon, a falling sensation plunged me into an odd, suffocating heaviness that pinned me down. Panic gurgled up my chest and bubbled into my throat. I focused, desperate, on *calm*.

I sensed a presence and struggled to open my eyes. Nothing happened. Tried to blink. My eyelids remained glued shut. Hinges squeaked, steps shuffled, paper rustled. The steps drew close.

A soft click, the scantest illusion of light in one eye. Another soft click. The light moved to the other eye. A pleasant scent. Clean, masculine. Strong fingers poked and prodded.

"No change," a silky baritone voice murmured. "A shame."

No change? Change in what?

A pen scratched on paper. A sigh. The same strong hands unwound something from my hair and turned my head to one side. The fingers softly explored, setting off little explosions of pain. The smallest pressure drove a spike through my skull.

My ears pricked at a different set of footsteps, springy and light.

"Morning, Sarah. Any news about who she is?"

Sarah? Who is Sarah?

"No. So sad, isn't it?"

What is sad? I clawed at the bars of my paralysis.

"What happened to her?"

A pause. More scribbles.

"Dropped off at Emergency last night with a head injury. Blood every-where, according to the trauma team. Nobody saw a thing. No ID, nothing. A tech on a smoke break found her in the bushes around the ER."

The blood froze in my veins. *I'm in a hospital!*

"She's so pretty. Like an angel,"

No ID? But my name is...my name is...my name is.... What is my name?

My hand lifted, held in a larger one.

"Healthy, mid-to-late thirties, probably." I decided the baritone voice belonged to a doctor. He released my hand and laid it on the bed. "She almost bled out last night. Cranial injury, no surgery planned at this time. No movement or response to stimulation."

A sweet scent, feminine and fruity, curled up my nose. Soft hands adjusted my arm.

Sarah...is a nurse.

Cool palms stroked my forehead, touched my hair, turned my head, and parted the strands. I held on to consciousness by a thread.

"Stitches okay for now?"

"Yeah," the baritone voice responded. "I know it's kind of a mess back there."

"I'll clean her up today."

The heavier steps receded. A door squealed open.

"Pretty nasty injury. We'll know more after the current batch of test results. Advise me of any change."

"Will do, Dr. Sturgis."

His steps faded into the distance. Metallic sounds chimed beside me. A slight pinch on the back of my hand.

"You'll wake up soon. I have a feelin' about you." Sarah patted my arm. The light steps squished around the room. "I'll be back in a bit, honey," she said.

I heard the door squeal again, then the soft click of it closing.

Wake up? Ohmigod. Ohmigod!

The batter escalated his pounding on the back of my skull. I strained to clap my palms on either side of my head and squeeze, but my arms lay still. The truth of my situation weighed heavy, disbelief caving in my chest. I howled. Terror leaked from me in droplets of sweat tracing down my cheeks, dropping off my chin, pooling on my bedclothes. I screamed and screamed, but my useless lips refused to utter a sound.

Oblivion swooped in, a dark savior, and took me.

Chapter Three

Sophie stared at the kettle on the stove, willing her tea water to boil. The haphazard bun she'd knotted at the nape of her neck that morning had loosened, and a few reddish-gray tendrils grazed her shoulders. Her call to Monty, her son-in-law, had been no help at all. She frowned at her cell as if it held an answer to her daughter's whereabouts.

When Olivia had asked her to babysit while she traveled to Richmond, Sophie had been delighted to accommodate. But she hadn't heard a peep from Olivia the entire weekend. The stack of brightly colored bracelets she wore jangled as she pressed her daughter's number again. Voicemail.

"Probably nothing," she reassured herself. She'd been so busy with the girls, she hadn't thought too much about it, but now—she glanced at the time: two p.m. Hadn't Olivia said something about coffee around three, when she got back? She tried another text, then slipped her phone into the back pocket of her white capris, poured the boiling water over a fresh tea bag, and walked to the front porch.

The antique screen door banged shut behind her. Riot, Olivia's cat, growled. She'd disturbed his nap in the midafternoon sun.

"Sorry, Riot."

Riot lifted his comical, flat face to hers. He arched his back, stretched, circled twice, and curled up on the foyer rug with a wary eye on the door.

The wicker rocker creaked as she sat. She smoothed her turquoise and orange sleeveless tunic and crossed her legs. Her gaze swept across the yard. Her daughter's house was a half-mile from the nearest paved road, nestled in the lovely, manicured Maryland horse-country hills. Birds darted to

Olivia's feeders, then flew to a far branch with a piece of fruit or a sunflower seed. Riot's ears flicked with every chirp.

Sophie sipped her tea. *It's such a haven here. What a tragedy if Olivia loses this house in the divorce.*

She drained her teacup and replaced it in its saucer with the gentle clink of good china.

"She's lost track of time, that's all. I'll hear something shortly," she reassured herself.

A breeze whipped through the massive trees. Dark clouds chased and caught the sun. The brightness deteriorated. Sophie shivered, picked up the teacup and saucer, and went inside.

* * *

Later that day, her granddaughters exploded into the house looking for her.

"Grammy? Grammy, where are you?"

Sophie smiled, closed her book, and rose from the couch.

"What are you doing reading?" Serena demanded. "We thought you'd be on the porch, ready to go. Weren't we supposed to—" Serena, the taller, slimmer of the two, glanced at her younger sister for confirmation.

Lilly's head bobbed, auburn curls bouncing. "Yeah, weren't we supposed to go for a Starbucks with Mom after we got off work?"

Serena fastened startlingly green eyes on Sophie and flipped her long, sun-streaked hair over tanned shoulders. Lilly waited, her forehead furrowing above eyes the color of molasses.

"Wasn't Mom supposed to be back by now?" Lilly jerked her phone from her back pocket.

Sophie forced a smile. "Let's go to Starbucks without her, okay? I'm sure we'll hear from her soon."

Both girls ran to their rooms to change. Sophie pulled out her phone. Five o'clock. Olivia had said she'd be back by three, and it was so unlike her not to check in! While the girls were busy, she trotted upstairs to Olivia's bedroom and paused beside her prized antique dresser, placing both palms on its marbled top. *Olivia, honey, what were you thinking before you left?*

At the right edge of her splayed fingers, she noticed a business card. Simple black letters on a white background. Niles Peterson. *Richmond?* She touched the card to her lips thoughtfully. Visiting a girlfriend in *Richmond*, that's what her daughter had said when she left. Would a girlfriend have a name like Niles?

"Girls," she called, "ready to go?"

"Yeah, just about," they chorused.

Sophie slipped the card into her back pocket.

* * *

The Starbucks visit proved stressful as Sophie tried to steer the conversation more toward Serena's upcoming status as a high school senior and less toward the fact that her mom was MIA. The drive home was marked by a tense quiet.

Sophie sat on the porch and tried her daughter a few more times with no success. She staunched the niggling suspicion that Olivia could be in trouble and walked into the den where the girls sprawled on a couch watching TV and checking their phones.

Serena looked up. "You heard from Mom yet?"

Sophie smiled. "Not yet. Maybe she lost her phone. Don't worry."

Each girl's face immediately radiated worry.

Sophie sighed and went to fix dinner. The girls wouldn't eat, they just sat and stared at the TV. When was it appropriate to call in a missing person report?

She needed to unravel possible scenarios. Sophie returned to the kitchen with untouched plates of food, thinking she might focus better if she made some notes. Kept a timeline. She jiggled the drawer in which Olivia kept pens and notepads, but it wouldn't open. She jerked hard. It fell out and upturned itself on the hardwood floor.

A thick, white, legal-sized envelope was taped to the bottom.

She knelt to put everything back into the drawer, staring at the envelope.

Her fingers nudged the envelope and began to peel away the tape, but she thought better of it and withdrew her hand. "None of my business."

"What the heck was that, Grammy?" Serena's voice was an octave higher than usual.

"It's okay, girls. Just an old, warped drawer that wouldn't pull out." *Olivia, where are you? We're all getting jittery. Please let us hear from you.*

Sophie found a tablet and a pen in the stack that had dropped out of the drawer. She scraped the remainder into a pile, flipped the drawer right side up, and replaced the contents. As she wrestled the drawer back into place, her mind nagged her. What if this envelope held a clue? She jerked the drawer back out.

Lilly stepped into the kitchen. "Grammy, what are you doing?" She nibbled a fingernail. Sophie had a brief flashback of Lilly sucking her thumb as a baby. It had taken Olivia a long time to break her of the habit. Sophie still had a hard time believing her youngest grandchild was fourteen.

"Nothing, honey," she said. "Just trying to fix this cranky, old drawer."

Lilly gave her an uncertain look, then left.

Sophie drew in a breath, slid her fingers along the underside of the drawer, and tried to unstick the tape. It had been taped awhile and wouldn't give up the envelope easily. She found a butter knife and pried the envelope loose. It fell to the floor. She picked it up and laid it on the kitchen counter while she decided what to do.

The hell with privacy, my daughter is missing!

Then she thumbed open the flap, unsealed but tucked. The rich smell of ripe hundred-dollar bills floated from the envelope. A lot of them.

Easily fifty grand. A home savings account? Olivia's stash? No. Olivia had never been involved in the finances. Monty handled all that. She stared at the cash and wished her daughter was less trusting.

A little paranoia can be a good thing. Two divorces had taught her. She grunted in disgust, an instant reflex when her exes crossed her mind.

She took a deep breath, blew it out. Surprising to find that much cash, but nothing exactly...nefarious, she thought. Promising herself she would discuss this discovery with her daughter when she returned, she taped it back onto the bottom of the drawer.

A tiny slip of paper floated to the floor from the envelope.

Her gut churned. She lit a cigarette. Olivia would kill her for smoking inside the house.

She nudged the piece of paper with the toe of her shoe.

Don't read it.

She picked it up.

A phone number. No name.

Don't call.

She longed for the peace and quiet of her tidy beachfront condo in West Palm. Her book club would be sitting down to discuss the latest mystery novel about this time of the evening. She'd had enough drama to last her the rest of her life, and now...

She chewed on a fingernail and studied the scrap of paper in her hand.

Where was her daughter? Why was fifty thousand in cash taped to a drawer?

With a sigh, she replaced the slip of paper inside the envelope.

Chapter Four

Olivia

The lostness scared me the most.

I'd decided I'd be better off under the ground than in my blind-and-paralyzed bubble of torment. My whole world was Sarah. Her prayers buoyed me, sparked tiny flickers of hope. But the flickers died a quick death when she left the room.

The first three days, it was a toss-up as to whether I would survive, apparently, and now, my survival was cause for everyone's celebration but mine. Would my survival mean existing as a vegetable in the dark? To never see the light of day again or wash my own hair?

Oblivion had become a close friend. I welcomed the fresh IV surges that took me to it and hoped they would make a mistake and pump me so full I could embrace it forever.

I longed for quiet.

There must be a memo somewhere: Make sure TV blares at all times—especially if patient is comatose.

Periodically, a news program caught my attention and helped me keep track of time, or gave a weather report, but mostly, information went in and slid right off me. Bizarre, jumbled thoughts jumped around in my head. Nothing made sense. I existed in a hellish dream until the drugs blurred me out of it.

"Good mornin', sugar! How'd we do last night?"

Thank God. Sarah.

She squished to the bed. A random image floated through my mind. A cartoon character—SpongeBob. He squished when he walked. I zigzagged to the logical conclusion that I must have *children*. The thought sent me spiraling to a deeper, darker gloom. I strained to speak.

Nothing.

"Here, honey, let's change your position."

Sarah put her arms under my armpits—lift, shift, drop. She plumped my pillows, cranked my bed up, brushed my hair with gentle strokes.

If I come out of this, Sarah, I'll tell you how much your kindness meant to me.

The TV droned on and on, like the buzz of mosquitoes. Big mosquitoes. Sarah's brush became erratic, then paused. Another brief stroke through my hair, then a shriek. The brush thumped to the floor.

She screamed. "It's *you*! It's you, honey!" Her voice rose octaves. I heard several squish-steps in rapid succession. Either she needed to go to the bathroom or she was doing the hokey-pokey in my room.

The volume on the TV rose. "...and she's been missing since this past Sunday."

I counted the days. Six days I'd been here.

"If anyone has any information about this woman, or has seen her, please call the number on the screen."

Sarah's scent wafted under my nose as she leaned in close. "Your name is *Olivia*, honey. You live in Maryland. And your family must be worried sick about you."

She clasped both my hands in hers. A tingling sensation started at the top of my head, raced through my limbs. A tear trickled down my cheek.

Sarah gasped and put a finger on my cheek. "You can hear. You can *hear*!"

More squishing, this time accompanied by hand claps.

"Stay right here, honey. Oh, um, I guess you can't..." She chuckled. "Anyway, I gotta get the doctor. I gotta tell somebody. Right now!"

She ran out of the room. I mustered all my effort into a solitary move. Just. One. More. Time. I wasn't sure, but I think my little finger shifted. I couldn't even wipe the tears off my cheeks, but I had a family, and they were worried about me. They would be here soon.

The darkness parted a little.

* * *

Long after Sarah had gone and the night crew had checked on me twice, the squeal of the door opening woke me. Its slow, cautious closing put me on alert. The staff bustled and hurried, but this was different. Plus, visiting hours were over.

Slow, deliberate steps approached my bed.

Someone from the intern team that had visited me earlier? After Sarah's screamed announcement to the entire fourteenth floor, interns had descended on me like a flock of buzzards. Prodding, scraping, plucking. They'd clicked their little flashlights into my sightless eyes. After comparing notes, they'd agreed the patient should make rapid strides. At that pronouncement, I'd graced them with a tiny uplift of one corner of my mouth. They had laughed.

The steps paused. Male, I thought, from the weight of them. As if my paralysis had broadened my senses to include emotion, I smelled tension. I wriggled my toes. This did not encourage him to speak. I waited, mute, paralyzed, and blind, but not deaf. My ears strained for every sound.

I kept my breathing even and shallow, as if I were asleep. The steps resumed. His smell intensified. The distinctive scent of an unwashed body or cheap antiperspirant that had worn off.

"Olivia?" He poked my hand with his finger. "Olivia, can you hear me?"

I tried to identify the voice, but couldn't. And something was going on out in the hallway that involved clattering and running, so I had to strain to hear his words, but no. I didn't think I knew this man. Did I?

"Reports are true, I guess." He walked to the other side of the bed, scraped a chair close. "Came to see how you're doing. Looks like not too well."

I heard him shift in the chair. I didn't trust this voice.

The sour scent hovered closer. "I guess I'll have to figure out what to do when and if your memory comes back, Olivia." He stroked my hair. "A shame," he said.

My mind spun. *A shame? Is that what he said?* His voice chafed. I wanted him to leave.

He began to sniffle. "Olivia, I'm sorry. I'm so sorry. I never should have—never should have insisted..." he whined.

Insisted? On what? I slowed my breathing. *Just play possum and listen hard.* The noise in the hall had intensified, and I strained to hear his words. After a few minutes, he stopped sniffling. Had he been crying? I felt him hover above me. My pulse raced.

His lips brushed against my cheek. Beard stubble scratched my face. I desperately wanted to move my head, rub him off. *Who was he?*

His whisper rasped into my ear. "It'll be bad for you if you remember."

He poked my arm, my hand. I tried to lie still but jerked anyway, a reflex. His hand stroked my arm. Fear snaked through me. I had no way to fight back. If he put a pillow over my nose and mouth, bye-bye, Olivia. Sweat trickled down my cheek to my chin and dripped. He touched its trail with a fingertip.

My mind withdrew into a soft, velvety cocoon. I slid down the dark tunnel where my good friend, Oblivion, waited with outstretched arms. At the end of the tunnel, a cliff. I stood on the edge and spread my arms...prepared to push off...waiting and hoping that my arms would sprout feathers...

Brightness stabbed my eyelids.

"Sir? Sir! Visiting hours are over." The voice of the night nurse, a critical, complaining woman I didn't like, but right now I would have smothered her in hugs if I could.

The distasteful odor withdrew. The chair scraped back. He told her he was getting ready to leave, his voice a chirp instead of the threatening tone he'd used ten seconds ago. One last scratch on my cheek as he planted a token kiss. I longed for the woman to wash my face. *Please.*

* * *

Twenty-four hours had worked wonders.

"Okay, missy, lean your head up now." Sarah lifted my chin, and this time, I was able to help. I'd graduated from paralyzed to semi-paralyzed.

I leaned my torso forward so that she could slide my hospital gown off and replace it with a fresh one.

"There, that's better. So how'd it go with your company yesterday? The night nurse said he was a friend of yours and he'd read about you online. She was none too happy about his being here too late, though. You know how she is about the rules."

I jerked my arm up in response. I waved it around, trying my best to communicate distress. I was sure I looked like a surprised, spastic manikin, since my blinking reflex had been thrown out of whack. The blink reflex would come, they'd assured me.

"What in the world?" Sarah sat on my bed and held the hand that had been careening through the air. "The visit didn't go well?"

I moved my head side to side.

"Oh dear," she said. "I'd ask you what happened, but we know that probably wouldn't work very well right now." She smiled sadly. "In time, honey, all in good time. Just be patient." She broke out a bag and unzipped. "Got a surprise."

She held up a gold necklace with a delicate gold heart. "You had this on when they brought you in. Recognize it?"

I carefully swiveled my head right and left. No.

Sarah sighed. "Didn't think you would, but it's time you wear it, anyway." She fastened it around my neck and stood back, considering. "Very nice." She dug around in the bag. "And furthermore, ta-daaa." She produced a few small items in her hand. "Makeup. I'm gonna help you look nice."

I groaned and croaked. My head fell to one shoulder. She gently lifted it back to center as I observed her, thinking she looked so much like I had imagined. Black, close-cropped, tight curls framed a round, ageless face with startling blue eyes. Generous, upcurved lips exposed small, perfect, snow-white teeth. Sarah's skin was the color of coffee with just the right amount of cream. She was the most beautiful thing I'd ever seen.

She selected a makeup pencil and started on my eyebrows. Then applied eyeliner, powder, and lipstick and held up a mirror. Empty, unblinking, hazel eyes. Anemic-looking, hollow cheeks. I studied myself at length, pawing at my reflection with clumsy fingers. Sarah laughed through the whole thing.

"Sugar, you remind me of a six-week-old kitten just realizin' it has a tail."

I croaked at her.

Sarah laid the mirror aside and sat on the bed, which sank with her considerable bulk. She held my chin in one hand and carefully applied mascara. She grabbed the mirror again.

"There. All finished. What do you think?"

One side of my mouth lifted, my best attempt at a smile. Much better than the face I'd first seen upon waking two days ago, which had looked like a corpse. Color dotted my cheeks, and my full lips had a nice shape. A smattering of freckles across my nose. I lifted my chin and turned my head side to side, relieved that with makeup I was almost—well, *pretty*. I studied the furrow between my eyebrows, the slight lines on my forehead and around my mouth, and wondered how old I was. I dipped my head down and stared at my red hair—clean, but lifeless and flat. I fluffed it awkwardly, wincing as I touched my head wound.

Sarah laid the mirror in my lap and busied herself with stashing the cosmetics back into the bag. The bed squeaked as she stood to tidy up the room and check my IV and various mysterious tubes that invaded my body.

"They said we might try feeding you normally soon, so I'm sure you won't miss this guy," she said, pointing to the feeding tube.

I swiveled my head right and left in full agreement.

It was getting easier.

Sarah walked around the bed and took my hands in hers.

"Look, honey," she said, her tone serious, "I know you can understand more than you're lettin' on."

My eyes filled with tears.

She smiled at me, let go of my hands, and patted them. "It's gonna be all right. Everything may spring back the minute you see your family." She shrugged. "Really never know. It's always different."

The tears spilled over.

She plucked a tissue from the aluminum table and daubed my tears. "Your mom's name is Sophie, and your girls' names are Serena and Lilly. They wanted to come right off, but the doctor told them to wait a little. They should be here in a day or two."

I grunted like a Neanderthal, all I could manage.

"You may want to remember what you look like," she said, pointing to the mirror in my lap. She told me she'd be back later and left.

After a few feeble attempts, I clutched the mirror and studied my face. *Who was this person?*

Chapter Five

Three months earlier

"Well, do you think that's wise?" my mom asked. "What research has your lawyer done? Have you been given information about Monty's financials?"

I raked my hand through my hair and stared at my lap in an attempt to stop this interrogation. My mom had a way of plunging me into reality when all I wanted to do was avoid it.

I'd managed to avoid it for months, now.

I clutched the cell phone tighter, rolled my eyes and sighed.

"Mom, you know my lawyer is not exactly communicative. Besides, I don't understand what he means most of the time. If he says uncontested is the best way to go, I should do what he says. Right?"

Sophie snorted. "Honey, you *have* to learn to be more aggressive. It's been three months since this thing started! Why aren't you more informed? Do you want me to go with you next time?"

I could think of nothing worse. My mom, the Bible-wielding champion of all things conservative. The most non-politically correct and misconstrued woman on the planet.

"No, of course not, Mom. You don't live right next door, anyway."

"No problem to hop a flight on short notice. Nonstop flights from West Palm. Not a big deal."

I shook my head and looked away. "I'm just not handling this very well,

Mom. I still don't understand what happened. Or how it could happen."

"Monty *told* you. You're going to have to assimilate his screwed-up viewpoint into some kind of productive result." Her voice gentled. "I know it's complicated."

I waited for the obligatory biblical scripture. It didn't come. "I am so tired of trying to figure things out," I whispered.

"What's Monty want this time?"

"The house. The *house* in exchange for child support until they're eighteen, then he'd split college expenses and provide alimony."

"How much?"

I told her. She gasped, then took a drag on her cigarette. "That's ridiculous, honey. You can't live on that." Exhale.

"Well, what do *you* think would be a good amount?" I sputtered, exasperated. "He handled all the finances. I don't know how to negotiate this stuff."

"Your lawyer is supposed to do that for you. What the heck is he doing, anyway?"

"I've called him twice this week," I said. "No response."

Thoughtful drag. "Gotta be some way to get him moving. Be persistent. Call. A lot."

I cringed. I didn't want to bother anyone. I wanted to hibernate. "Okay."

"You aren't going to let him have the house, are you?"

"How do you fight someone like Monty, Mom? I'm not *letting* him do anything—he just does it. He has connections everywhere. He's a man that gets his way."

"You don't just roll over, for one thing. I never figured Monty would pull this kind of stuff." She spat the words. "Olivia Rosemary, this is *not* something you can stick your head in the sand about. Be specific. Give your attorney a list of what you need." She pulled on the cigarette. "What *you* need."

After a few more minutes, we ended the call.

I walked out to my front porch, where white wicker chairs with pink, green, and white plaid cushions nestled against matching wicker tables. A fan sliced the midmorning air in lazy circles overhead. Each vintage board of this porch had been sanded, waterproofed, painted with my own hands. Wisteria draped a trellis on one side. Each year the lovely purple clusters bloomed in spring and lasted well into summer. I had a good two months yet to enjoy them. I sank into a chair to think, my hand sliding over the fabric. I'd spent a long time picking out this furniture.

Mom was right. I somehow had to fight my way to independence, and I'd been languishing like Alice in Wonderland. I took a deep breath.

Life as I'd known it was over. I needed to accept it.

My gaze rested on my overgrown, shaggy front yard that Monty had mowed and trimmed every Saturday. He had told me he would hire someone to help me, but hadn't. "Time to tackle stuff like this, Olivia," I muttered.

I walked the fifteen paces to the shed and pulled the door open, my arms over my face to guard against spiders. I considered both the riding mower and the push mower. I yanked out the push mower to at least take a run at the front yard. Mowing the rest of our two acres with the riding lawnmower would have to wait.

I'd watched Monty mow thousands of times with this thing, a green and yellow monster with huge wheels on the back, but I had no clue how to operate it. With a clench of my fist, I pulled the starter with all the force my one hundred twenty pounds could muster. Nothing. Pulled again. A sputter. Again. A growl. One more time. When the monster came to life, I almost fell over.

After a few loops around the yard, the lawn began to look respectable. I smiled. The mower coughed, then roared back. *Mom had asked me to figure out what I wanted and make a list for my attorney. Why was that so hard for me?*

The beast gurgled and sputtered to a stop. I frowned at it. I could do this. I yanked the pull cord, and it roared to life again. After a few more laps around the yard, I rolled the mower back to the shed. Then I sat on my porch with a bottle of water and admired my handiwork.

* * *

Later that afternoon, Lilly and Serena walked in through the back screen door—an old-fashioned, wooden affair Monty and I had picked up at a flea market, restored, painted red, and hung. It shut with a muffled bang. I heard their footsteps marching through the house, backpacks plopping on the kitchen table, voices yelling for me. I smiled. They loved to find me and talk after their part-time summer shifts at the YMCA.

The front door squealed open.

"Hey!" Lilly said. "There you are." She dropped into the wicker chair beside me. "Hot today. Pool was crammed."

"Yeah." Serena sat on the front steps. "Crazy day. Everybody's finally realized school's out, I guess." She laughed. "You wouldn't believe what I heard today."

My eyebrows lifted. "I wouldn't? What?"

I saw Lilly shoot Serena a warning glance. Since Lilly worked inside in the nursery, her pale, freckled skin was mostly untouched by the sun. As a lifeguard, Serena spent hours in the sun and looked like a native islander next to her sister.

I set aside the list I'd been working on for two hours and crossed my arms. "What?" I repeated.

Serena widened her eyes at Lilly and said, "She'd find out anyway."

I sighed. I wanted new revelations to stop.

"Tell me," I said, looking at Serena.

"Well, you know, Dad's, um…Dad's girlfriend is really young, right? As in *really*. Young."

I looked at the ceiling of the front porch, at the beadboard Monty and I had picked out and painted together.

I frowned.

"Seems her *sister* comes to our pool all the time. Their mom lives just a few miles from us."

I was silent, wondering where this was going.

Serena deliberated. "Don't you think that's weird?"

My gaze rested on the mown lawn, a tribute to my burgeoning independence.

I shrugged. "Doesn't bother me," I lied. "I'm getting used to this stuff."

No anger, no sadness at this news, I realized. *Numb.* Maybe that was why I couldn't exactly...feel. Plus, I wanted to blunt my reactions to make sure the girls weren't worrying about me.

Serena gawked at Lilly, who, in turn, gawked at me. "You are?"

"Yeah," I said, studying their body language.

They had been furious with their dad for leaving and scared to death for me. The relationship they had with him post-exit was strained and touchy. Our anger had exhausted all of us. We'd talked endlessly about the girlfriend which just made it worse. ""Girls, all of us have to start getting used to this new...this new *normal.* I think the shock is over, and I, for one, don't really want to talk about his girlfriend's sister." I cocked my head at the yard. "Look."

Both sweet faces turned.

"What?" Serena asked.

"The yard."

"You mowed?"

"I mowed."

"Thought you said you'd *never* touch a lawnmower," Serena quipped, twisting her hair into a bun and wrapping a band around it.

"It's a new day." I pointed to the list I'd been working on. "Want to see what I've been thinking about?"

"Maybe later. We've, um, got stuff to do." Serena glanced at her sister and cocked her head.

"Sure, go ahead. Just let me know what's going on, okay?"

They galloped from porch to stairs to bedrooms. I traced a finger down my list. Maybe it wasn't a good idea to share it with them. Why should they have to think about divorce negotiations?

They shouldn't.

The crumpled bits of paper that marked failed list attempts were piled beside me like super-sized popcorn. I studied what I had finally decided were the most important issues: the house, alimony, child support, and custody.

I gazed at the yard, the bird feeders I'd carefully placed, the Rose of Sharon bushes I'd pruned last year starting to sprout fresh green. It was unthinkable that I could lose all this. *You jerk, Monty. How could you desert us? What happened?*

A deep moan rumbled out of me. I refocused and studied my questions:

1. *How much money do we have? Should I ~~ask for~~ insist on access to all bank accounts?*
2. *Find out if I can stay in the house. Can he force me to leave? Why?*
3. *Custody? What are the options?*
4. *A wife's legal rights in Maryland. What are they? Alimony?*

My hand swept away tears that had straggled down my cheeks. The weight of my situation seemed suffocating. I stared at my rose bushes, my lovely fence, the one Monty and I had chosen together. The trees we'd planted, grown now to twenty feet or more. I squared my shoulders and added a fifth item:

5. *Counseling: Refuse to finalize until we've seen someone.*

I circled this the last item and drew stars around it. *Do I want to spend more time trying to repair a broken marriage?* I colored in one of the stars with black ink. *Do I want to live with his exacting habits, criticism, and condescension in exchange for homemaker status? Do I think he is tired of his young nymphet?* I colored in another star. *What if she is the first in a long line of nymphets?*

I colored in all the stars. The paper tore beneath the point of my pen.

I went inside.

* * *

The next day, I sat in front of my attorney, Earl M. Sorenson III, my hands twisting in my lap as I waited for him to get off the phone. I patted my wavy hair, which felt stiff from the gallon of hairspray I'd used to force it to submit; dug into my purse and found the list I'd worked on. My heart felt like it might beat right out of my chest, a familiar reaction when I asked for something, which explained why I tried never to ask for anything. I was surprised I'd not chickened out and thrown the list in the trash.

I straightened my shoulders and plucked imaginary lint off my navy slacks. Would this man never get off the phone? His office looked like something out of the seventies: olive-green shag carpet, dark wood paneling, ponderous bookcases. Ancient metal file cabinets, three of them, took up most of one wall. At least they covered up the paneling.

"Yes. Absolutely." Earl glanced at me and held up a finger to indicate he was winding up the conversation. "Don't worry, Mrs. Pendleton. I have every confidence we will prevail," he said, his jowls shaking in lawyerly determination.

I looked away.

The walls held numerous diplomas and award certificates, all from the 1960s, all yellowed with age. The office smelled vaguely of tobacco. I squinted at him. A formidable presence when he was younger, certainly, but if this went to court, I sure hoped he'd pull a rabbit out of his aging hat. I clutched the list I'd worked so hard on. He dropped the receiver into place and grinned, his teeth horse-big. They matched the color of the diplomas on his wall.

"Olivia! It is, ahh, Olivia, isn't it?"

I nodded.

"So what can I do for you? I've filed the appropriate paperwork with the court clerk, of course, and we're waiting on their response. Has something come up in the interim?" His mahogany-colored leather chair creaked as he rocked. He peered at me over reading glasses. Bushy eyebrows bloomed from his forehead like twin caterpillars.

"I have a few questions." I leaned forward and gave him the list, now crumpled from my sweaty grasp. He adjusted his glasses and ran a thick finger down the page.

"Well, Olivia, this changes things." He grunted.

I thought about all the retainer money my mother had poured into this guy.

"Look, um, Earl." I paused, staring into his watery, brown eyes.

He crossed his arms and frowned.

I continued, "I thought about this, and I think these are valid questions. I need to know what my options are. I'm not sure I should agree to a, um... an *uncontested* divorce, as you suggested." I contemplated the watercolor prints of downtown Baltimore on the wall behind him. "I'm not sure..." I mumbled, my confidence faltering, "...what he wants is good for the kids."

Earl leaned back in his chair and put his readers on top of his head, pulled at his jowls, and lowered the readers back to his nose. "I'll get something drafted for you to look over, then we'll file our own motions. Let's see if a settlement is an option. If not, we'll set a court date."

"Good." I stood and draped my purse on my shoulder.

"I'll have my assistant get some things together and email you after I've done a little research to answer these questions," he said, raising my list in the air, releasing it, and watching its descent as it dropped to his desk. "We will do our best to address each question specifically." Earl smiled at me then, his eyes lost under the shrubbery of his eyebrows. "I must say, you seem a bit more...*determined* today than the last time we got together."

I shrugged. "I have no idea what I'm doing. After twenty years of marriage, I'm still in shock about the whole thing."

"Warning you, it may be a long haul with a contested divorce." He leaned back in his chair, crossed his arms, and winked. "Best thing you could've done is leave the details to me. I already had a good settlement fleshed out, but now..." He shrugged, and repositioned his glasses on the end of his nose. "Now it's gonna be a free-for-all." He waved his hand at me in dismissal as if I were an errant child.

I left his office, stepped past his assistant's desk, and closed the door behind me. I walked down a long narrow hall bordered on each side by offices with gold lettering embossed on ancient oak doors. The building smelled of ammonia and dreams that had passed their expiration dates.

Chapter Six

Monty ran his fingers through his straight, coarse, black hair, coaxing it into shape with hair wax. He flexed his knees, dipped, and checked the end result in the mirror. It looked okay. He walked from the bathroom to the living room in his small apartment located on the perimeter of Baltimore's suburban sprawl. The television—his white noise of choice—droned its comforting stream of background drivel as he walked to the kitchen. He pulled a mug from mostly bare cabinets, set it on the counter, and poured a cup of coffee.

He cursed as he tried to find cream and sugar. He finally located packets of sugar in the silverware drawer and creamer in the refrigerator crisper bin. He closed the refrigerator with an impatient shove, and stirred two tablespoons of sugar and a generous amount of cream into his coffee. He took a tentative sip, winced, and added more sugar.

As he stirred, his thoughts drifted to the short conversation with Olivia's mother when she'd called to ask if he'd known who Olivia had visited in Richmond. How would he know, he'd said, and further, why would he care? Disgusted, he'd hung up before Sophie had a chance to launch into one of her sermons. Yet another perk of being separated from Olivia was not having to subject himself to her mother.

He shook his head and chuckled. The call only increased his determination to get Olivia to sign a final decree. Monty sipped his coffee and glanced at his watch. Fifteen minutes before he needed to get on the road to his office in downtown Baltimore. He poured the coffee into a travel mug and left it on the kitchen counter.

Jogging through the living room to the single bedroom, Monty slipped a gray sport coat from a hanger and shrugged into it, tugged at the cuffs of his pale yellow shirt, and looked in the mirror one last time. He patted his pockets for keys, sunglasses, wallet. *Check, check, and check.*

As he picked up the remote to turn off the TV, he blinked at the sound of his wife's name. He stared at the image displayed on the screen, groped his way to a tired-looking recliner and sank into it.

"...local woman, Olivia Callahan, has been located at a hospital in Richmond, Virginia. After a weeklong search for the missing woman, the communications director at Mercy Hospital in Richmond had these words to say."

A different face popped onto the screen—a young woman in a sleeveless red dress and matching lipstick, her black hair pulled back so severely her eyes slanted. "Yes, Chad, we are very encouraged here at Mercy. We are delighted to finally be able to identify this woman." She paused to consult her notes. "Um, her mother and her daughters are reported to be on the way...she is separated from her husband, so we are not sure if he has been contacted. Olivia's prognosis is uncertain at this time, but we are hopeful the family's presence will have a positive impact. It's a waiting game at this point."

The woman disappeared, replaced by the local news team that promised, cross their hearts, to keep everyone posted.

Monty squinted at the woman pictured in a small square in the upper right of the screen. Pale and thin, but definitely Olivia.

He stared at the ceiling and groaned. What should his response be? Fat chance *his* presence in Olivia's hospital room would make a positive impact. Their separation had not been exactly warm and fuzzy. Other than his weekly visits with their daughters, he'd had very little contact. His choice, not hers. He scowled. Was this some kind of sick attempt to increase the allowance he gave her? Rethink the divorce, maybe? She'd dragged it out over the past few months, and when she called to get help with something she needed around the house, she sounded pathetic. Needy. Couple this with her crazy, Scripture-spouting mom, and...he was better off without them. *Much* better off.

He punched the remote with his thumb. The screen went dead.

Chapter Seven

"But...what happened? Why is she in a hospital?" Serena's almond-shaped face was a queer mix of elation and puzzlement.

Sophie tucked her hair, worn loose today, behind her ear, adjusted the bright orange tunic she wore over skinny jeans, and sighed. "Don't know yet, honey, we'll just take it one step at a time. The police told me she'd been brought in with an injury and had no identification." She paused to absorb the ramification of this information, but pushed it off, and forced a smile for her granddaughters. "Important thing is your mom is going to be okay." She slapped away fresh tears. She'd been crying all week, and it was getting old.

Lilly sat on the steps, arms snugged around her, and rocked back and forth. "What happened to you, Mom?" she whispered. "Be okay, Mom, be okay."

Sophie cursed herself a thousand times for not insisting on specifics from her daughter. She'd felt so helpless when the detective from Richmond had called. Sophie fingered the business card in her pocket. She'd called the name on the card a few days before. Five attempts before the man answered. Yes, he'd met Olivia on the beach once. It had been a while. No, he hadn't seen her since, why? He was very sorry that she'd been reported missing but hadn't any idea about what happened. Yes, he'd call if he heard anything.

A dead end, she'd told the detective when she'd given him the man's name and number.

Lilly sniffled and looked from Sophie to Serena and back again. They clung to each other, bunched together in the wicker loveseat like puppies in a basket, as Sophie prayed for their trip to Richmond to see Olivia.

Serena lifted her deep green eyes to Sophie's. "She's going to get better, right, Grammy?"

"Absolutely, Serena. Now, you girls get packed. We're leaving bright and early tomorrow." They scrambled off the porch, the screen door banging shut behind them.

Sophie grabbed her cigarettes and walked into the house. Riot curled in and out of her legs as she bent to pet him. "You're worried, too, aren't you, buddy?" He arched his back and purred.

Chapter Eight

"**O**livia, I think we may be able to release you soon." Dr. Sturgis patted my arm. His eyes, a chocolate brown, were kind, and I glimpsed a blue and green plaid shirt underneath his white medical jacket.

I tried to speak, but the sounds I made were still unintelligible. I slapped the bed in frustration. He took my hand and said, "Listen, you really *are* making progress. The words will come." I nodded and sighed.

He straightened and put his hands in his pockets. "You have company in the hallway." I stared at him, unblinking. "Are you ready?" I couldn't move. Dr. Sturgis stroked his chin. "I'll take that as a yes. They've been worried, Olivia. They love you."

He walked to the door and stepped into the hall. I strained to hear the conversation.

"...talked to us yesterday...Richmond Police...told him not yet...investigation... she needs more time..."

"...Detective Faraday said he needs to talk to her as soon as...I gave him as much as I knew...yes, Doctor, we understand...he's going to contact her husband..."

My breathing accelerated. *Detective? Husband?*

The door eased open. Three female heads appeared around the door, one atop the other. The first, a young girl, maybe fourteen or so, curly, shoulder-length, reddish hair. Behind her, a gangly, taller teenager with wild green eyes, a deep tan, and long, straight blond hair. Hovering above them, a woman with graying hair smiled uncertainly and plucked at the silver earrings that fell to her shoulders. From the looks on their faces, my inability to blink had freaked them out.

I croaked and raised both arms. They lunged. "Mom! Mom!" I thought how beautiful the girls were, how stately the older woman appeared. Her eyes had closed, and her mouth moved silently in what I thought must be prayers.

I didn't recognize a single thing about them.

* * *

When the shrieking and hugging subsided, they pulled chairs up close. The youngest sat on the bed. Tears had leaked down my face, but I didn't know if it was because I didn't remember them or because I was glad I had a family.

"Mom, we were so worried about you." The one on the bed—Lilly, I thought, from what Sarah had told me—picked up my hand and held it.

The other—Serena?—added, "We're glad you're safe, Mom."

The mother-stranger sat quietly observing me from her chair. After the girls' voices drifted into an awkward silence, she said, "It's so wonderful to have you back, but it's obvious you don't...can't...this may be a little much for you." Her voice trailed away.

She rose and gently hugged me. I tried to lift one of my arms, but it refused. I lay against the inclined top of my bed, staring and still. Like an agitated turtle, my body had retreated into its cave.

Sarah bustled into the room with practiced ease.

"Well, hi there, everybody. Olivia is so happy to see you, aren't you, honey?" She gave me a piercing look. I obliged her with the merest nod. She turned toward my mother and daughters. "We on staff here at Mercy are just tickled pink that you're here. It always helps if family's around."

Sophie cleared her throat. "It doesn't...she doesn't..." She contemplated the window.

My gaze slanted in the same direction. Thunderclouds darkened the sky. Sarah glanced at me. I silently pleaded with her. *I don't know them.*

"Maybe not yet, but we're pretty confident that she will. We just never know, with a brain injury, how long it'll take." She walked to Sophie and patted her on the shoulder. "Don't you girls worry, now." She smiled toward the girls. "Your mom has some healin' to do. Her brain has had a nasty shock, and it'll take time for it to get back to normal. It's only been a couple of weeks, and wakin' up is the main thing. And she's got some movement back already. That's somethin' to celebrate." She smiled.

Disappointment evident from their expressions, they group-hugged and tried to regain a semblance of calm for my sake. My mind couldn't wrap itself around these three strangers, and I wasn't prepared to deal with feelings. Mine or anyone else's.

Sarah crossed her arms over her chest and cocked her head at me. She walked over to the emotional knot that was my family and gently patted their backs.

"Now, ladies, it'll take your mom a while to regain her ability to process. Right now, her brain doesn't know what to do with y'all, so I can tell she's pulled back a little. That doesn't mean she doesn't love you. It means she's tryin' so hard, she's exhausted from the effort."

Sophie straightened, extricated her arms from around the girls. "I understand. A little of this family goes a long way, even under normal circumstances."

Sarah grinned. Sophie glanced at me. I ignored her and watched a plane emerging from the dark clouds outside the window. I focused on breathing. In. Out. In. Out.

All business, Sarah shepherded them to the door. "Okay, ladies, first visit needs to conclude. I know it wasn't much, but tomorrow will be better, or maybe later today." She studied me. "Yeah, later today will be okay. Try to bring your emotions down a notch, and I think she'll do better. You agree, honey?"

I continued staring out the window. The plane disappeared into the clouds.

Sarah moved the group to the hall. I heard low, excited voices as they talked outside the door. All I wanted to do was sleep.

Chapter Nine

Later that day, Sophie and the girls hurried from Mercy Hospital's parking lot to the elevator, exited on the fourteenth floor, and skidded to a halt in front of Dr. Grayson Sturgis, who waited for them outside Olivia's door.

He smiled. "I'm Olivia's neurologist, Dr. Sturgis. I thought we might talk a bit before you go in?"

He extended his right hand to the seating area in the waiting room. They followed, eyeing each other.

Dr. Sturgis and Sophie sat on an uncomfortable simulated-leather couch, and the girls settled in across from them, on a couple of tan chairs. Sophie glanced at the magazines piled high on the coffee table that separated the couch from the chairs. The area was deserted, except for an elderly man sleeping in a chair on the far side of the room.

Dr. Sturgis sat back, crossed his legs, lowered his voice, and directed his remarks to Sophie. "An investigator from the Richmond PD dropped by yesterday. I gave him approval—reluctantly—to ask Olivia a few questions. She became distressed."

Sophie crossed her arms and frowned. "Yes, I know him. Faraday. He called. It's much too soon to upset Olivia with—"

Dr. Sturgis interrupted with the wave of his hand. "I completely agree. Told him to come back in a few days. He keeps in touch with me on her progress." After a glance at the girls, he whispered, "Didn't know if you knew that her injury might be the result of an assault." Sophie nodded in understanding.

Dr. Sturgis cleared his throat and continued, his voice louder. "So, after you've spent a little time with Olivia, how do you think she is doing?"

Sophie crossed one leg over the other and splayed her fingers on the couch. Her bracelets clanked. The girls studied the floor.

"We weren't totally ready for..." Sophie paused, choosing her words. "...She had *no idea* who we were. How serious is her injury? Can you predict how long her..." she put her hand on her chest and closed her eyes, continuing in a whisper, "if she recovers...how long that will take?"

Dr. Sturgis sighed. "May I call you Sophie?" She nodded, taking in his short, gray hair and stubborn jaw; the large hands that never seemed to stop moving. "Sophie, your daughter has sustained a blow or blows that affect both frontal and temporal lobes. This is the area that controls personality, motor function, intelligence, and touch, also speech, smell. The swelling is slowly receding, but until it is back to normal, we don't know the extent of the damage."

Serena blurted, "You'll fix her, right?" Tears spilled down her cheeks.

Lilly listened, silent, her small hands clasped so tight her fingers were bloodless-white.

Dr. Sturgis's eyes held theirs.

This is a kind man, Sophie thought. *Thank God for that.*

"Girls, I wish I could answer that question," he said. "We are never sure exactly how a comatose patient will respond when they wake up. It usually takes weeks or months for them to recover a full range of motion or full mental capacities. Sometimes motor skills are affected. Sometimes it takes them a while to learn to talk again. In a few cases, memory is permanently impaired. For instance, they can remember some things, but others have been blocked." Dr. Sturgis shrugged an apology. "We can only predict so much. The brain is complex."

Sophie bit her lip.

"On the bright side," he continued, a grin transforming his face, "the brain can regenerate, create new neuron paths. In some cases, recovery is miraculous." He looked at Lilly and Serena, adding, "Your mom is a miracle around here, you know. We call her 'Mercy's Miracle.'"

Sophie's frustration crept into her voice. "So...we just...wait?"

Dr. Sturgis nodded.

"We don't know how long?"

Sophie watched him process the question.

"In this case, because we've uncovered no significant bleeds into the brain and the swelling is going down, I'd anticipate a relatively fast recovery. Brain scans and an intensive MRI showed no remarkable discoveries. Add to that going from paralyzed and unconscious to awake, trying to talk, and movement in less than a week..." He spread his hands. "Pretty optimistic indicators, but..." he paused, and continued softly, "...no guarantees. If you pray, this would be a good time."

Lilly quipped, "Oh, we got that covered," and pointed to her grandmother.

He smiled in Sophie's direction. "We are doing all we can for Olivia," he reassured them. "You need to understand that your mom's brain... the part responsible for emotions and perceptions—how she processes information—that part has been damaged. If it's overstimulated, the brain shuts down. It's a protective measure."

They shot anxious glances at each other.

"What that means is, less is more, okay? Try not to get too emotional. Calm and peaceful, that's all she can process right now."

Lilly took a deep breath. "Has she forgotten us?"

"Most of the time, victims of cerebral concussion come all the way back. Sometimes, they've had to start over. Make new memories. Sorry, but we don't know yet."

Serena slid over the side of the chair to put her arm around her sister.

Dr. Sturgis reached into one of the pockets of his white jacket—crisp with starch—and pulled out a card.

"Call me with further questions. Anytime." He smiled. "The best thing for Olivia is your presence. You should see a little more progress every day, if all goes well." As he turned and walked away, the words 'if all goes well' repeated on a loop in Sophie's mind. "It has to go well," she stated aloud. "It has to," she repeated, her voice a whisper.

* * *

Sophie smiled at the two heads she watched in her rear-view mirror, one covered in red ringlets, the other in sheaves of honey-gold, lolling together in the back seat. They deserve to sleep, she thought as she drove her granddaughters back to where they would spend the night. Another glance in the mirror revealed deep circles under her eyes, pronounced wrinkles and lipstick that had faded into non-existence. She frowned.

As she drove, she tried to weave together the gaping holes in Olivia's story. For instance, she hadn't answered her cell, not once, and it was missing. Where was it? And for that matter, where was her purse? Her car? Sophie blew out a frustrated breath. The thought had occurred that her daughter might know the person who had done this to her. But she had been *dumped* and left at the hospital. Had that someone been responsible for the injury? Could this have happened on her way home?

She groaned softly, hoping Detective Faraday would put the business card she'd found on Olivia's dresser and all the other information she'd managed to find for his investigation to good use. Was there anything else she could do? And what about the money she'd found underneath the drawer? The phone number? Was that involved? She pounded the steering wheel. The bangles on her arm clinked a merry tune.

Chapter Ten

Monty strode into his place after work, and opened the refrigerator to behold two Coronas, a jar of mayonnaise, and leftover takeout Chinese in a small, square, white carton. He thought about the overstocked refrigerator in his house in Glyndon. He sighed and shut the door, wondered where his girlfriend, Kirsten, was and why she hadn't returned his call. His shoulder ached in a familiar spot—the spot Olivia had known exactly how to rub. Monty took off his sport coat, hung it carefully on the back of a chair, and rubbed his own shoulder.

In disgust, he looked around the tiny apartment, as nondescript as a hotel room. Worse than a hotel room. Naked, white walls held one calendar he'd tacked up. Rented furniture populated the bedroom, and he'd rescued his old recliner from the Goodwill pile Olivia had stashed in the garage for the living room, plus an ancient end table and lamp. All temporary, he reassured himself, until he and Kirsten could firm up where they would live after the divorce had finalized.

He frowned. Where was she, anyway? Striding to the refrigerator, he pulled out a Corona. *Damn. No limes.* He slammed the refrigerator door and chugged half the beer as he walked to the bedroom, loosening his tie.

Five minutes later, garbed in gray athletic shorts and a Baltimore Orioles T-shirt, he sank into the recliner, grabbed the remote, and punched the TV to life. His cell blurped. He squinted at the number, then pulled out reading glasses. Kirsten's number, thank God, and not the idiots that believed he owed them money from an unfortunate weekend a few months back.

"Hey," he said, his voice softening.

"Hey. What's up, baby," Kirsten purred.

Monty's eyes narrowed. "Why didn't you call me back?"

Slight pause. "I texted you…"

Monty's irritation rose. "You know I don't like to text! Why the hell didn't you call?"

Longer pause. "Thought you'd see my text."

He put a hand over his face. *She's twenty-five, remember.* "No problem. So where are you?"

"We-e-ll," she drawled, "that's why I called. Friends want to hang out and I—"

"Cool," Monty said, "works for me. Where should I meet you guys?"

"They want to hang out with *me*, a girls' night."

Monty's face fell. "Sure, yeah…I get it." He forced his voice to sound pleasant. "You go ahead."

Her voice perked. "Great. You're the best!"

"Right, talk to you then, call me when—"

But she'd already ended the call.

Chapter Eleven

Olivia

Asmell of spices curled up my nose, the taste of a luscious wine lingered
on my tongue. Rapt eyes stared into mine. The color red. Deep, deep red.
Yes, that's it—the wine, it was a beautiful, deep red. I'd felt wonderful,
but so...woozy. Dizzy. His fingers locked around my arms, hard. So hard. An
angry face, inches from mine...no, no!

My racing pulse jarred me out of the dream. With some effort, I drew
my hand to my chest, then pulled it away wet. My pink nightgown was
drenched. I moved my arm to the buzzer on the bed. Sarah popped in two
minutes later.

"Good morning. You rang, Your Highness?"

I shifted and struggled to a sitting position. Sarah clasped her hands
behind her back and waited on purpose. I understood. She wanted me to do
as much as possible on my own. One thing I'd learned about Sarah, though.
She could not stand un-plumped pillows. Eventually, she squished to the
bed and plumped.

"What in the name of goodness...?" Her palm came away damp with
my perspiration. "Are you havin' hot flashes, honey?" She stood back and
cocked her head. I blinked, raised one arm and waved it. "That don't tell
me nothin', Olivia. Try to make a word for me."

"Mmmph."

Sarah shook her head and crossed her arms.

I sighed, tried again. "Dooph."

"Better," Sarah said. "Keep goin', honey."

"Dreash, dreash!" I waved both arms.

"Good! C'mon, girl!"

"Dreeeeeeem." I lay back, a crooked smile on my face. "Dream," I repeated.

Sarah clapped, then walked over and hugged me. "Good girl, Olivia! You are startin' to get your speech back!"

I nodded and blinked up at her.

"So, dream?"

I nodded again.

Sarah thought a minute, a finger twisting on her cheek. "Dream," she murmured. Her eyes widened. "Maybe you are startin' to have memories, honey. Memories of what happened."

I struggled for words, waving one hand around and wiggling my toes. Tossing my head in frustration, I eventually blurted out, "Scar."

"Scar?" Sarah leaned in.

I slapped the bed. "Scare. Scare!"

"A scary dream?"

Like a playful puppy, I wiggled every part of me that could wiggle.

"A *scary* dream. Hmph." She crossed her arms over an ample bosom. Her pink scrubs crinkled in the middle of her chest with the movement. "Scary dream," she muttered. "That don't sound good," she said, contemplating my face. "That don't sound good at all." She stroked my hair. "Honey, we need to write down some of this stuff, or record it or somethin'." She pulled out her cell and waved it back and forth. "Work on gettin' those words back. Then I'll record what you say and send the video to that nice detective that's been comin' around."

I nodded and waved my arms in frustration, my IV line perilously close to detaching.

"I bet you are good and tired of this, honey." She carefully peeled away the tape that held in the needle and pulled it out.

I rewarded her with a "Greesh!" and sat with arms held high as she pulled my drenched gown off, patted me down with a towel, and put a clean one on. I sighed in relief.

"'Bout time you got outta bed now, honey. You up for sittin' in a chair while I change the sheets?"

I nodded and struggled upright.

"Wait, now." She laughed. "Not so fast! You're still pretty weak."

I clutched the edge of the bed. Sarah put one arm under my legs and the other behind my back and lifted. She smelled like oranges.

"You're no heavier than a feather, honey," she said as she helped me into a chair.

The door opened. Dr. Sturgis stood in the doorway, a clipboard under his arm. I felt my cheeks pop up and my lips pull across my teeth in an attempt to smile.

"How's our celebrity today?" He shuffled through the pages attached to the clipboard.

I clutched the heart on the chain around my neck. It had become my good luck charm.

Dr. Sturgis turned to me. His eyes were soft. "Try to stand, Olivia." He retrieved a pen from his jacket pocket.

I blinked at him and clutched the arms of the chair.

"Did you understand me?"

I nodded.

"Try," he repeated.

I gawked at Sarah. She shrugged.

I let my breath out, long and slow. Pushed off the chair. Two inches, four. *Easy does it.* My legs trembled. Six inches. I collapsed back into the chair.

"Take your time," he said. He planted his feet, crossed his arms, and waited.

I took a breath and gripped the arms of the chair once more. One inch, two. My stomach threatened nausea. Three inches, four. I panted. Five inches. *So dizzy.*

I turned my attention to my legs and concentrated. Six, seven. My knees straightened, and I stood! I held my arms out to my sides for balance.

"Um-hmm," he said. "Touch your nose."

I drew in a hand to my face and touched my nose after a couple of misses.

45

"Now the other one."

I repeated it on the other side. He scribbled on his clipboard.

"Can you take a few steps?"

"Shampff," I grunted.

I slid one foot forward, then the other. My hands curled in determined knots, my fingernails digging into my palms. Another step. Another. Perspiration trickled into my eyes. I lifted a hand to wipe it away. Sarah plucked a tissue and stretched out an arm. I clutched the tissue, swung my arm around, and swiped at my face.

Then I held my hand in the air and made a shaky "V" for victory.

Dr. Sturgis laughed. "Well done."

I felt like I'd just won the lottery.

Chapter Twelve

Afternoon shadows draped the corridor, elongating Dr. Sturgis's shadow as he walked. Detective Faraday stood outside the door waiting for him, feet planted wide. Glancing at his watch, he hoped he wouldn't regret agreeing to Sturgis accompanying the interview, but he'd been told that was the only way to see her. He adjusted his red and blue tie and light-blue oxford button-down.

The men shook hands. "Thanks for making the time for this. I know I'm back sooner than anticipated."

The doctor held Detective Faraday's eyes a beat longer than necessary. "I hope you get some answers, but as we discussed last time you tried—"

"Don't worry, Doctor, I won't push too hard. But her case climbed up the ladder of priority the minute you alerted us to the fact that her urine sample had been compromised."

Dr. Sturgis' forehead knotted. "Some new tech mislabeled a batch of samples. All we can figure is that hers was among them. Dr. Sturgis raised his palms. "We took more samples, but it might've been too late to detect, in her case. For instance, Rohypnol stays in a person's system approximately two to three days. We didn't even find out about a problem with her urine sample until after that. Blood work is only effective for about 24 hours. Plus, we had no evidence of sexual assault. No trauma to the body except the injury we've treated. So initial treatment did not include a rape kit."

"Have you given us the lab tech list yet?"

"My assistant should've gotten that to you by now. Look, Mercy gets around two hundred Jane or John Does a year. We simply don't have the time

47

or resources to ID them all, and when we get the social workers involved, they have to jump through a lot of hoops and privacy laws to even find out who they are." He shook his head and frowned. "I know that's not what you want to hear, but the reality is, with an unidentified victim, we're told to do the minimum because usually they do not have insurance. I'm sorry I don't have more for you to work with."

Detective Faraday nodded, stuck his hands in his pockets, and rocked on his feet. "Okay. I'll check with my assistant."

"Let me go in first." Dr. Sturgis eased the door open after a gentle knock and walked to the bed. Olivia napped restlessly on her side, frail arms snugged around her torso. He tapped her on the shoulder. She stirred, rubbed her eyes, made soft waking noises, and smiled at him. Dr. Sturgis elevated her bed to a sitting position.

"How are you?" he asked, his voice low.

Olivia croaked, cleared her throat, and said, "Poosh. Greep."

Dr. Sturgis grinned. "Let me translate that. You're doing great, right?" Olivia nodded.

"Feel up to a few questions? Remember Detective Faraday?"

Olivia frowned, blinked her eyes twice, and nodded.

Dr. Sturgis walked to the door and opened it. "No promises," he said to the detective, "but she is okay with trying again."

He gave Dr. Sturgis a curt nod, entered the room, and pulled a chair beside the bed.

"This is not a test," Dr. Sturgis reassured Olivia. "It's just a few questions, okay?" He patted her on the back. "Go ahead, Detective," he said.

His voice soft, he said, "Hi, Olivia, I'm Detective Faraday with the Richmond Police Department. I don't know if you remember, but we spoke briefly a few days ago."

Olivia stuck out an arm and groped for Dr. Sturgis. He took her hand.

"I'm going to make this as easy as possible, okay?" Detective Faraday continued, "First, do you remember driving to Richmond?"

Olivia stared at him.

Detective Faraday jotted a note in the notebook he'd extracted from his overcoat pocket, then laid it aside. He pulled out his phone and started scrolling. He held the phone in front of Olivia's face. "Do you remember if this is the person you went to see?"

Olivia stared at a man's face on the phone. Seconds passed. A minute.

"Olivia?" Dr. Sturgis prodded.

Detective Faraday repeated the question.

She shook her head. "NO," she blurted. "No, no, no."

Detective Faraday scribbled on his pad. "Do you remember what you told your mother?"

Tears suddenly slicked her eyes. "No. Mooosh."

Dr. Sturgis shot Detective Faraday a warning glance.

"Good job, Olivia." The detective's tone soothed. "Just a few more questions." He consulted his notes. "Olivia, do you know who did this to you?"

Olivia twisted on the bed and tried feverishly to crawl into Dr. Sturgis's arms, moaning. Frantic, her limbs thrashed. "No, no, NO!"

Dr. Sturgis held on to Olivia and muttered, "Wasn't sure how it would go, Detective." He frowned. "Let's put this off."

Detective Faraday closed his notebook and returned it to his inside pocket. "Thanks for trying, Doc. I'll be in touch."

He held out a hand to Olivia, but she drew back and stared out the window. Dr. Sturgis murmured to Olivia, then followed Detective Faraday into the hallway.

"She withdraws. Her emotions are still all over the place. She's probably shut out what happened to her." Dr. Sturgis shrugged. "All we can do is wait."

"No problem. Sorry for upsetting her." Detective Faraday referred to his notes. "The lab tech that found her, Nathan...he didn't find anything in the area around her? No ID, no purse?"

Dr. Sturgis shook his head.

"Feels like an assault at this point, but," he shrugged, "we need evidence."

Dr. Sturgis sighed. "If we'd had her samples, we'd know more by now."

"Don't beat yourself up about it. Let me know if anything turns up, okay?"

"I will. You have my word on that."

"Thanks." Detective Faraday dipped his head and left.

* * *

The following morning, Detective Faraday got a surprise call from Mercy Hospital, and pulled into the hospital's parking lot gulping the last of his Starbucks triple-shot grande latte, thinking about the major news network that had contacted him requesting a follow-up on "Mercy's Miracle." He'd asked for a reprieve. The publicity wouldn't help the case, and he didn't think Olivia needed the hassle.

He drained the rest of the coffee, tossed his cup into the waste bin at the entrance, and entered the reception area. Like yesterday, he walked up three flights of stairs, but this time his goal was Dr. Sturgis' office to check out an alleged break-in. He'd instructed everyone to clear out and wait until he arrived before cleaning anything up, then he contacted a couple of patrol cops to secure the scene.

The door was ajar, the office dimly lit. He pulled on gloves and booties, then reached inside and patted the wall for the overhead light switch.

His eyes widened. "What the hell?" he muttered, taking in the scene. The desk looked like it had taken a grenade, and spread-eagled file folders littered the gray carpeting. Detective Faraday slowly moved around the office. Drawers had been pulled out and overturned, the desk lamp placed on the floor. It created a tight circle of light on one of the files. Whoever had been in here had left quickly. Interrupted? He squinted at Sturgis's desk. No electronic device observable.

Out of habit, he ran potential scenarios through his mind. *Some tabloid rag reporter desperate for a story? Could this be related to Olivia? Does Sturgis have something to hide? Could this be another issue? What about an assistant? Someone chasing information about their condition?* Twenty-two years with Richmond PD had taught him patience. He stood quiet and still, taking everything in.

The drawers to twin metal filing cabinets against one wall were mostly open. He sorted through the drawers that looked as if files were gone. A, B, C...*Callahan, Olivia.* Olivia's file was missing. *Damn.* He dropped to the floor and methodically searched through the clutter. Her file wasn't there. He leaned back on his heels with a long sigh.

Outside Dr. Sturgis' office, in the reception area, he heard panicked female voices. Quick, light steps. Then the shout of a male voice. Security, probably.

Detective Faraday rose, flashed his badge. The uniformed man relaxed. "Boy, you guys are fast." He laughed weakly. "It was like this when I was doing my rounds this morning. Got any ideas?"

Before Faraday could answer, an attractive young woman burst into the room. "Ohmigod, what is this?" Her face paled as she scanned the office. Her palms flew to her mouth in dismay. "Bennie, what's going on?" she asked the guard.

The badge came out again. "That's what I'm here to figure out," Detective Faraday said drily.

"Found it this way on rounds, Andrea. I tried to secure the office after I called it in."

The color returned to Andrea's face. She fisted her hands on her hips and glared at Detective Faraday. "My gosh, we've been cooperative with the media. They wouldn't steal her file." A few beats of silence. "Would they?"

"So you think this is about Olivia Callahan," Detective Faraday stated. "And you are...?"

She stuck out her hand. "Andrea, Dr. Sturgis's assistant." She looked around uncertainly. "Maybe I shouldn't touch anything."

"Maybe step out until we get our investigative team in here." He squinted at the large worktable that Dr. Sturgis used for a desk. Faraday cocked his head. "Usually a laptop there? Or does he take it home?"

Andrea gasped. "He never takes it. He uses his tablet everywhere but in here."

Faraday wrote in his notebook. "You have a backup, I assume?"

She jutted an index finger in the air. "Everything is backed up. Don't worry, I can retrieve." She patted her cheek. "I'll call the tech guys and get another computer."

"Did you happen to need Olivia's file for anything?"

Andrea concentrated for a few seconds. "No, everything I would need is on my computer. I can't think of any reason I would—" Suddenly stricken, her lips parted, but she couldn't complete her thought. She raced into the reception area. "My computer's still here, thank God," she called, relief in her voice.

Detective Faraday exited the trashed office and joined her. "Doesn't mean they couldn't have used a flash drive to get what they wanted." He shrugged. "Olivia's file is gone. Pretty obvious to me that Olivia's status was their objective—but you never know. You got a cell number?"

"Well, yes, but—"

"In case I need to ask a few questions." Andrea gave him the number.

"Dr. Sturgis comin' in today?"

She looked as if she might cry. "Yeah. So he doesn't know yet?"

Faraday glanced at the security guard to answer the question. "Not yet. We wanted the police to check it out before we said anything."

"Get him set up in another area, or whatever you need to do. Crime scene folks are on the way. Make sure no one goes in there. I'll be in touch," Faraday said.

Cell phone tucked against his ear, he strode down the corridor and disappeared into the elevator.

Chapter Thirteen

Sophie shepherded the girls down the gleaming corridor that smelled of the morning cleaning crew's fresh mopping. As they drew closer to their Mom's room, Lilly and Serena ran ahead like puppies off the leash. She laughed, dipped into her purse for a mirror and re-applied red Chanel lipstick and checked her hair. The mid-calf, tie-dyed skirt she'd worn made little swooshing sounds as she walked.

"Mornin' everyone," Sarah chirped as she opened the door. "This who you're lookin' for?"

Sophie gasped in surprise as Olivia swung her legs over the side of her bed and slid to the floor. Serena and Lilly ran to help.

Sarah smiled and lifted her arm in a 'stop right there' motion. "Not yet, ladies. Just watch."

With a massive grunt, Olivia wobbled upright, hanging onto her balance.

Lilly squealed with delight and Serena whistled through her teeth, a loud, long tone that echoed around the small room, and probably the entire floor.

Dr. Sturgis slipped in and watched as the girls helped their mother walk a few paces. Turning toward Sophie, he cocked his head toward the hall in mute invitation to a private conversation. Wiping happy tears off her cheeks at the sight of her daughter taking her first hesitant steps since the injury, she agreed.

* * *

In the waiting room, a platinum-haired little girl played with monster Legos at a kids' table against the wall. Her mother sat beside her, leafing through a magazine. The latest weather report blared from the TV affixed high on the facing wall. Sophie and Dr. Sturgis sat in tan armchairs as far as possible from the TV. He leaned forward, elbows on knees, fingers tenting and un-tenting. Sophie waited silently for him to say something.

"I'm not sure I should tell you this. I'm trying to figure it out myself, but you probably need to know."

Sophie squared her shoulders. "Okay."

He sighed. "This morning, or last night, someone ransacked my office. Olivia's file is missing."

"What on earth?"

"Not sure what it means, but you should be aware."

"Why would someone want her file?"

"Your daughter's the feel-good story of the year here in Richmond." He paused and glanced around the room. "With that kind of media exposure, you never know. I don't want to speculate until the police have done their thing."

Sophie stared at the floor, thinking.

"I believe you've met the detective assigned to Olivia's case?" Sturgis asked.

"I haven't."

Sturgis nodded. "I have a meeting with the head of Mercy to discuss." His beeper chirped. He pulled it from his belt. "That's them now." He clipped it back in place and rolled his eyes. "I'll be glad when they figure out how to get us our reminders on our cell phones like the rest of the world." He chuckled. "I'll keep you updated, but I think it might be premature to tell Olivia and the girls."

"I agree," Sophie said.

His eyes searched hers. "Or anyone else, for now."

"But do you think…" She covered her mouth with her palm. "Oh gosh, do you think the person that did this to her…"

"I wouldn't rule it out."

"But why?" Sophie pinned earnest eyes on Dr. Sturgis, waiting.

He held her gaze. "That's the problem. We don't *know* why. I've consulted with the admitting doctor several times about Olivia's condition when she was brought in. Typically, a rape kit is performed in situations like hers, but they found no vaginal bruising or tears—"

Sophie moaned and looked away.

"I'm sorry," he murmured. "My point is, they had no evidence that she'd been sexually violated. So a general investigation into possible assault and ID'ing her was the MO." He paused, ran a hand through his thick hair. "Now, though...they may dig a little deeper. Although it's been too long for a urine sample to be accurate, we could do a hair sample." He shrugged. "Takes longer, but traces of a drug may still be there. Just wanted you to know, in light of what happened today, we've now got the go-ahead to do more testing. But hair follicle tests are often inconclusive, and accuracy would depend on the amount of the drug—if she was drugged—in her system."

Sophie inhaled, then exhaled. "I need a cigarette." Her mouth twisted. "Politically incorrect, I know."

Dr. Sturgis chuckled. "I smoke too, but I *will* quit." He paused. "I have a good feeling about this Faraday investigator. I think he's somewhat of a pit bull, from what I've heard." He rose from the chair. "I'm sorry, but I have about a thousand appointments today—"

"I understand," Sophie said, touching his arm. "Thank you so much for your kindness. Will you—"

"I'll keep you posted."

Sophie stood and watched Dr. Sturgis walk away, dark thoughts swimming through her mind, all of them congealing around a central theme: Was Olivia safe?

Chapter Fourteen

Monty strode down the hall to his office after a difficult meeting with the stakeholders of his current project. The frown on his face turned into a smile as he watched Kirsten lean over her desk and give him a purposeful view of her cleavage. One hand smoothing his tie, he playfully reached for her with the other.

Scooting away, Kirsten chuckled. "Here," she said, pushing three pink pieces of paper into his palm. "Guy's been pretty insistent. A Detective Faraday. Aren't you checking voicemail?"

Monty ignored the question. Studied the phone messages. Not a Maryland area code.

"No idea," he said.

"Yeah, he wouldn't tell me what it was about. How was the meeting?"

"Don't ask." He sighed. "I cannot believe they won't move out the deadline."

Kirsten shrugged. "Sorry, baby."

Monty grimaced. "Don't call—"

"I know, I know...don't call you that at the office," she whispered. She leaned over her desk and looked one way, then the other. "But no one is around."

"Don't care." He scowled. "Just don't, okay?"

Kirsten crossed her arms and pouted.

Monty thought she looked adorable when she pouted, but resisted pulling her into his arms. Decorum. Especially since his wife had gotten herself in such a public mess, and his reputation might be splashed all over the media if things didn't settle down. He couldn't afford to take any chances in a professional environment. In a sudden epiphany, Monty threw his arm in the air and flapped the messages in his hand. "This is about Olivia," he stated flatly.

Kirsten's waxed eyebrows drew together in perfect arches. "What have you found out? Is she okay?"

Monty shrugged. "Not exactly in her inner circle lately."

"Well, your daughters—surely they would say something."

He stared at her. "Do we really need to have this conversation?"

"Um, no." She paused. "All I meant was—"

"Let's just not go there, okay? Got enough going on without wading through all that." Monty glared at the pink slips. "And now I have to talk to this guy. I wondered if they'd get me involved."

Kirsten studied her new manicure.

"I've been separated from the woman six months. We hardly talk."

"Yeah," she muttered. "I get it." She walked out.

He cursed under his breath and shoved his office door shut. Could Olivia not take care of one single thing by herself?

The minute he sat at his desk, Kirsten's line lit up. He snatched his landline. "What?" he snapped.

"Him again."

Monty sighed. "Okay, thanks." He switched to the other line and forced a smile he hoped would translate to his voice. "Monty Callahan."

"Mr. Callahan, this is Detective Faraday from Richmond PD. Do you have a few minutes?"

Monty cleared his throat. "Yes, of course, Detective."

"For the record, this is purely routine. We interview everyone close to the victim—"

"Victim? How have you determined that my wife, ahh...estranged wife, is a victim?"

"We haven't got anything conclusive yet, but we're pretty sure she didn't show up at the Mercy Hospital ER with a nasty head injury and hide in the landscaping all by herself," Faraday quipped.

Monty chuckled awkwardly and loosened his tie. "Detective, I'm sure you realize my, um, wife and I are in the middle of a divorce. It's been months since we've been involved in each other's lives."

"I understand. Just need answers to a few questions. Where were you on Saturday, June twelfth?"

Monty paused. "I'll have to check my calendar."

"I'll hold."

Monty quickly checked the calendar on his cell. He cursed under his breath. He had nothing noted on that date. Ad-libbing, he said, "I was with my girlfriend that night."

"So, she's willing to corroborate that?"

"Of course." *I'm with her every weekend*, he thought. Maybe she remembered what they did, but he didn't.

"Did Olivia happen to mention her trip to Richmond? Or did your daughters say anything?"

Monty thought about that. Had his daughters said something? Maybe they had. "I'm not sure. If the girls said something, I don't remember it, and Olivia and I...we don't talk."

"Why?"

Monty's brow furrowed. "Do you think that's any of your business?"

"Simple question, Mr. Callahan."

He sighed. "Because it's uncomfortable. She didn't want the divorce."

"So, there's animosity between the two of you?"

Monty blanched. "No. No, of course not. I just meant...we live separate lives now."

"Okay."

Monty wiped his forehead where sweat had beaded. "Look, I knew nothing about this until I saw it on TV. I don't keep up with her, and she doesn't keep up with me."

"Okay." Pause. "That's all for now, Mr. Callahan. I'll be in touch."

Monty replaced the receiver, rocked his desk chair back and forth, and stared at the ceiling. How could Olivia's accident—or whatever they were calling it—be traced back to him? It was ludicrous. But still, he needed to firm up his alibi.

After a few minutes, he decided not to think about it anymore.

"Kirsten," he yelled.

She scurried in immediately.

"Close the door." He smiled.

Chapter Fifteen

Olivia

My flowers had wilted. Papery petals littered the floor. Outside my window, fog had shrouded the morning in a gray veil. A glance at the clock told me Sarah was due any minute. I swung my legs over the side of the bed, tilted out of it, balanced, walked to the door, and stood to one side.

Sixty seconds later, soft steps halted outside my door. I tensed, grinning, plastering my body against the wall. I heard Sarah study the chart, the flick of pages turning. Then the door opened, and she walked in, head swiveling in confusion as she noted the empty bed. She went to the bathroom, calling my name. My throat hurt from the effort of trying not to laugh. I slammed the door shut and popped out. "Good. Morning. Shaah!"

Sarah scuffled around in a crazy circle, her eyes wild. "Sweet Jesus!" she howled.

I held my arms out to each side. "Ta-daaaa."

She shook a fist at me, laughing. "I'll get you for this." She patted her heaving bosom and blew out a breath. "Well, you got my blood pumping this mornin', girl."

I slid my feet across the floor to the chair beside my bed and sat. "Good. Fun."

"I just can't believe it, honey. Your progress this week is amazing." Sarah walked to the dry erase board tacked to one wall. "Seems you are goin' home soon. They tell you yet?"

"No." I thought about this a minute, staring at hazy tendrils of fog snaking past the window outside.

"Well, didn't mean to spoil nothin', but thought it was good news." She studied my face. "You got mixed feelin's. I can see that."

She squished on her cushy nurse's shoes to the computer and logged on. "Three more days of evaluation and that's it."

I studied the tiny yellow and pink flowers on her blue scrubs, the small gold cross she always wore, sighed, and got up out of the chair. I walked six steps, slapped both palms on the wall, turned, walked back six steps.

Bed, window, chair, Sarah's sweet face. Good and solid and familiar. Home would *not* be familiar. The thought of it panicked me. I counted my steps out loud. "One, two, three, four..."

"That's real fine, Olivia. But I know what you're doin'."

I ignored her. "Five, six." Slap. Turn. "One, two, three, four..."

"Olivia, you knew you had to go home sometime. You've been here almost five weeks. It's time. You've got speech back, you have most of your motor skills." She harrumphed. "You are nothin' short of a miracle!"

"Five, six." Slap. Turn. "One, two, three, four, five..."

"Olivia!" She pointed to the chair. "Sit."

I folded myself carefully into the chair like a bendable Barbie. I would be glad when my flexibility returned.

"Now, what's goin' on in that head of yours?"

I studied the ceiling.

"I've had dreams—nightmares—about a man. Cannot remember." I bobbled my head. "And smells...and I'm on the floor...carpet...white."

Sarah's eyes bugged, blue agates in their white orbs. "You have all these memories and you haven't told anyone? My gosh, honey, you need to at least tell that detective." Sarah walked to the dresser, picked up a business card and gave it to me. "This is the guy, honey. Remember, he was here just a few weeks ago? You should tell *him*."

I took the card from her plump fingers. Detective Hunter Faraday, Richmond PD. Email address and phone number. The man who had visited my room a few times, but I'd not been much help with his questions.

"I'll keep this," I said, and placed the card onto the metal cart beside my bed.

"You do that. Or I'll call him for you, whatever you want." She cleared her throat. "Now, you got company comin', so let's get you dressed."

Sarah pulled out jeans, a T-shirt, and sandals my mother and the girls had brought for me. I took them out of her hands and smiled. "I can do this now, remember?"

She cocked her head at me. "It's high time you showered by yourself, too. Think you can manage?"

"Yep." I clutched the clothes to my chest, walked to the bathroom, and shut the door.

I stared at the tiny shower with its white plastic curtain. After a deep breath, I reached in and turned the chrome faucet. Clumsy with enthusiasm, I lost my balance and stumbled in. I carefully stepped back and groped for a towel.

I heard three hard knocks. "Honey? You okay in there?"

"Sure you don't need me?"

"YES."

"Well, okay, then." Sarah laughed.

I stepped out of my pajamas and threw them on the floor.

"You can do this," I muttered to myself.

Gritting my teeth and holding onto the grab bar, I stepped in. Finally, a private shower! Slowly, I rotated under the showerhead, letting the delicious warmth reach every part of my body. I picked up the soap and tried to move it back and forth across a washcloth. A few arm spasms, then, success.

Enveloped in the steamy water and relishing the privacy, my reluctant, traumatized lump of a brain calved an image. I sucked in a breath, held the washcloth and soap to my chest and tried to focus.

* * *

My fingers trailed in the water. I was in a chair, a beach chair, reading. A lemony, early morning sun warmed my face. A man hovered over me, scowling. His lips moved, and as if from a distance, I heard him say, "Olivia, you want to look like an old hag before your time?" He snatched my book from me. "C'mon, get up. See that volleyball game down there?" He clapped his hands, impatient. "Hurry up. We want to get on the best team. And put on sunscreen, for God's sake."

The soap slipped from my grasp. I tried to squat, but my body wouldn't obey. After a deep breath, I clutched the grab bar and forged ahead.

A man pedaled toward me on a bicycle.

The man's grin beamed. "I see you're takin' life easy today. Good for you."

I watched myself tilt my head back and smile. "My favorite things. Reading and the beach."

The man shrugged. "Hilton Head beaches are so solid." He thumped the sand with one foot. "Where else can you ride a bicycle on the beach?" His gaze dropped suggestively from my face to my swimsuit. I pulled my knees to my chest and wrapped my arms around my legs.

I swiped at my arms with the washcloth and slid cautiously down the wall of the shower to get the soap, grabbed it, and rose an inch at a time. I experimented with gentle scrubbing. Two different men. Who were they? Were they even real?

I soaped and scoured from head to toe. It took a while, but I was determined. Just as I'd squeezed out a palmful of shampoo and plastered it awkwardly on my hair, my strength evaporated.

My hair a tangled mass of shampoo, my arms dangling and useless, the suds trickled from the top of my head into my eyes. I frantically reached for a towel but couldn't find one. My balance teetered on the slippery floor.

"Sarah!" The soap stung like mad. "Sha-aah!"

In seconds, the door flew open. Sarah jerked the curtain aside. I pointed at my face in desperation. The next thing I felt was relief as she rubbed the soap from my eyes with a towel. I heaved out a breath and opened my eyes. Still clutching the towel, Sarah took in my bright-red eyes that must surely match my scrubbed-red naked hide, the still-sudsy mane.

"Honey, if you ain't a sight." She gently turned me around and finished my shampoo. "It's all right," she cooed. "All in good time."

Chapter Sixteen

Olivia

The girls had staked out their positions. Serena sat in a chair, arms and legs crossed, regarding me quietly, and Lilly perched on the bed like a Jack Russell terrier, bouncing up and down and barking out past situations that she hoped I would remember. Serena's long, blond hair and somber face and Lilly's curly mop and cute pug nose sprinkled with freckles stirred a deep motherly instinct that felt familiar and protective, but my blank look when they talked about the past upset them. I desperately hoped my memory would return as a huge one-time event, and not piecemeal over years.

At least I could communicate now.

"Want…good news?" I asked, pushing myself to an upright position in my bed.

"You're going *home*," they squealed.

I laughed. "Pretty soon, I think."

"Mom, that is so great!" Lilly bounced on my bed until I felt seasick. I put both hands on her shoulders to stop her.

"It *is* great," I agreed, "but I will…relearning everything at, ahh, *home*."

"No problem, Mom. Piece of cake," Serena assured me. "We'll get you through it. Besides, your memory's coming back any day now."

"Hope so." I shrugged. "So, I…don't know…about my life."

I motioned them both in for a big hug. They smelled of soap and hair conditioner.

"Just need...patient. What did I do? Before the, um, divorce?"

Lilly crossed her arms. "Well, you worked in the yard a lot. You really love flowers."

I glanced around the room at the flowers that I refused to throw away even though they were like pale, withered ghosts on stalks.

I smiled. "What else?"

The girls warmed up to my questions. A game.

Lilly groaned. "You spent *hours* painting stuff or polishing stuff or sanding stuff."

My eyebrows rose. "I did? Why?"

Serena laughed. "Mom! You were always working on the house."

I straightened my blue-and-white-plaid pajamas, threw off the blanket, stretched my legs out, and fluffed my hair, which had grown out and looked a lot like Lilly's now. "Tell me about the house."

"It's *old*." Serena laughed.

"Okay," I said. "Is that bad?"

"*Good* old, Mom," Serena added. "It's an eighteen-hundred-something Maryland farmhouse that's two stories with restored everything."

"Mo-omm," Lilly drew out the word as if speaking to a young child. "We showed you pictures."

I shook my head. "I'm sorry, girls, some of that stuff just didn't stick. I don't think I...um...aware." I shrugged. "Hard to explain. Let me see pictures again."

Both girls dove into their pockets for their phones.

Serena's phone emerged first—a glittery, pink, slender rectangle. She thumbed through photos, a smile lighting her face when she found an appropriate one. "Here!" She shoved the phone under my nose.

I studied the photo. A traditional two-story house with a porch surrounded by flowers and trees. A happy contentment crept into my mind. Lilly carefully studied my face with eyes more honey than brown.

"Do you remember something?" Her curls bobbed with excitement.

I contemplated the picture again. "Maybe." I gave the phone back to

Serena. "Show me more."

I rejoiced that I felt *something* when I studied the pictures. I felt joy. My house. Home. Flowers. Birds. All these words ran through my mind. I tried to grab each one and make out of them some kind of sense. Future. Hope. Together. The words *down payment* echoed in my mind—a needle stuck on a vinyl record. *Down payment. Down payment. That's just a down payment, Olivia.*

I grabbed the pen and notepad beside my bed and jotted the words. Every snippet was important—pieces to a puzzle my mind would reassemble.

I just didn't know when.

* * *

Sleep would not come. I threw my pillow against the wall. When would I ever get a full night's sleep? I tossed off the blanket and pressed my button for a nurse. When she came in, I asked for some meds. Ten minutes later, my body relaxed but, as usual, my mind did not. The vivid, confusing memories played in my mind like a movie.

The steamy, morning air blasted my face when I stepped out of the condo and walked to the beach, each hair on my head writhing in tiny ringlet seizures because of the humidity. The waves, lazy and low, drifted to the beach.

I warmed up my sleepy muscles, windmilled my arms forward and back, then folded at the waist and dipped to the ground. I put one foot in front of the other and began to run, my legs like pistons, imagining I could outrun the fear and pain of the past few months. Maybe, I thought, the tide would wash it all away with my footprints.

I ran until I feared my heart would burst through my chest. Panting from exertion, I finally stopped and bent forward, hands on hips, elbows splayed like chicken wings. In mid-pant, two very brown, very male bare feet appeared under my nose. I gasped out a final breath, straightened, and pushed my sodden curls off my face. The possessor of the feet had a nice face, and an even nicer bottle of cold water extended.

I snatched the water like a dying fish. "Thanks," I managed between gulps.

His eyes matched the sky. "You're welcome. You a short-distance runner? You were really burnin' up the sand."

"No," I said, wiping my mouth. "Just like a good, fast run once in a while."

He wore running shorts and an armband for his phone. Curly brown hair, great smile.

"You on vacation?" His accent sounded slightly southern.

"Yes." I gasped the word, still trying to get my breathing under control.

He pointed over his shoulder and turned slightly. "Stayin' at the Pines. You?"

I pointed down the beach, vague on purpose. I hadn't watched all those murder mysteries for nothing. Who gives up their location to a perfect stranger? "I'm here for a week, um, my husband and I...aaah...well, we come here every year."

"Me too."

* * *

Sunrise winked through my window as I woke, my nightgown wet from yet another hot-flash-laden, pre-dawn excursion down memory lane. I groaned and stretched my arms high above my head.

A thousand questions haunted me. What would I feel when I walked over the threshold into a house I did not recognize after living in it for twelve years? Would I remember my favorite spots to relax, the tedious restoration? Would I still want to tend flowers like the girls said I always had? Would the yard be overgrown and neglected? Would the cat—Riot, I think they told me his name was—recognize me, or hiss and snarl and run away?

The clink of my mother's jewelry arrived before she did, and when she inched open the door, I motioned her in, enjoying her latest ensemble: yellow, button-front, collared shirt and palm-tree-patterned capris, platform sandals. Her nail polish matched her lipstick. She was always so well put together that I couldn't imagine why I wasn't. Had I been? Somehow, I didn't think I'd been a fashion diva. I smiled at her, wondering what I had called her. Mom? Mother? Mama?

"Here. Early," I said, swinging my legs over the side of the bed and letting them dangle.

"Wanted to get here before the girls. I'll pick them up in a bit." She sat on the bed beside me. She started to put her arms around me, but I instinctively pulled back. She clasped her hands in her lap.

"Honey, I just wanted to talk a little, before, well…before we take you home. I know you're nervous about it." She paused, and began to recite a scripture, a habit of hers I was getting used to. "The steps of a good man are ordered by the Lord—"

"And though he falls," I filled in, automatically. My mouth dropped in shock. So did my mother's.

She grabbed my arm and squeezed it tight. "The Lord upholds him with His hand. Olivia Rosemary, you are remembering. I must've used that one thousands of times while you were growing up." She laughed.

I frowned. "Why?"

She crossed her arms and cocked her head. "I think I was a little concerned about you."

I waited.

"You were my only child, and I wanted so much for you to participate in sports activities…or take violin lessons. I don't know—whatever felt right, but you were content with your nose in a book. You read more than any child I've ever seen." She shifted her gaze from me toward the drawers that held my clothes. "Always wondered if that was your way of hiding, of holding life at arm's length."

I chewed on my lower lip. *What did that mean? Hiding from what?*

She patted my shoulder. "Let's just say I am very happy you remembered that particular verse. I'll put your clothes in a duffel bag I brought. You can take care of getting yourself together now, right?"

I nodded that I could, but in truth, I was unprepared to get much of anything together, including myself. My mother handed me jeans and a top. I took them and scuffled across the linoleum to the tiny bathroom to shower. At least I'd learned to take a shower by myself.

I'd buried my head in books? Had I buried my marriage, too? My life? The girls had told me their father had called them a couple of times, but they were less than complimentary of his efforts. What was I facing when I went home? What had preceded the divorce? And why did I feel angry when I thought about…what was his name…*Monty*? The man in my latest dream had been nice. I had liked him. He couldn't have been Monty. Could he?

I rotated under the water in the small shower stall and managed to soap up a washcloth and awkwardly wash myself without major incident. *Progress.*

As I toweled off, I studied my reflection. I still didn't recognize the face in the mirror, but at least my expression held a glimmer of hope, now. I re-centered my heart necklace on my chest, then pulled a pink shirt over my head and tied the tail of it into a loose knot at my waist. Then, with careful precision, I rolled my sleeves above my elbows. My arms looked like toothpicks. Had I always been thin?

I took one last look at the stranger in the mirror, opened the door, and walked out.

Sophie was folding clothes and laying them inside a suitcase she'd brought.

"Need this?" She handed me an assortment of makeup.

"Yeah, thanks."

"Do you need help with it?"

I shrugged. "Not sure."

My mother watched as I hesitantly applied foundation. "You know, you seem different."

I paused. "How?"

"More direct. Less self-conscious." She scanned me, top to bottom. "Even the clothes I brought you, the way you put them together."

I chuckled. "Wonder if I got kind of a new…um…life on lease?" The words came easier now, but I struggled to put them together correctly.

"Maybe so," she said, her voice soft as she folded one of my shirts.

"Whatever," I said, returning to my makeup. "Maybe I had…kinks."

"See?" She raised her palms. "You would've never put something that way before. It's kind of fun hearing what pops out of your mouth."

I finished applying lipstick with a loud smack and turned. "You live by beach, um…coast…right? Not close."

She nodded and put the shirt she'd folded in the suitcase.

Maybe I *had* changed. I still didn't remember anything but the vaguest details. But the dreams…I was pretty sure all the loose ends flapping around in my mind would tie themselves together at some point. Right now, though, my thoughts were a jumbled, inarticulate mess that I couldn't quite speak forth.

"Done," she said, closing the suitcase and zipping. "Gonna go get the girls. Be back in twenty minutes, okay?"

I nodded. She left the room, her soles tapping on the linoleum as she walked down the hall. I listened until the tapping paused and the elevator doors opened and closed. The air in my room pressed against me. I experienced slight panic as the walls, too, pressed in. I sank into a chair and focused on my breathing. In slow, out slow. Repeat.

I glanced around my room, which had been restored to its original state. Dead flowers removed, spaces cleared, empty cartons and food trays disposed of. Uniform and impersonal—as if I had not lingered between life and death, slowly regained movement and sight, taken cautious first steps, or experienced dreadful, exhausting nightmares here.

It seemed incomprehensible that a tiny slice of sheet-rocked cement on the fourteenth floor with a single window had been my whole world for five weeks. I thought about the first few days, panicked and breathless; the second week, when I'd begun to see flickers of light, the third week, when my fingers twitched and hope sprang to life. Sarah and her light steps, cheery manner; Dr. Sturgis, my rock, and steady source of encouragement. Neurology interns stealing in and out of my room at odd hours, whispering. I'd learned a lot about medical minds, especially when the personnel thought I could not hear them. Sophie and the girls—the first tentative visit, the celebrations as my condition improved.

My brow furrowed. But that man—the mystery guy who'd visited me—who was he? What had he said? He lurked around my edges like a shadow. I didn't think he'd been a dream. Dreams didn't smell, did they? He'd smelled like fear.

I got up and walked to the window.

What the heck?

Far below, television crews grappled with lighting and people waved microphones as if they were orchestra batons. As I watched, a car pulled in and parked, and thanks to her neon-yellow shirt, I recognized the driver as Sophie. She got out of the car and herded my daughters toward the entrance. Reporters quickly surrounded them, shoving microphones into their faces. My mother's arms shot out and swept the girls behind her back.

With a start, I realized the hubbub was about *me*. My mother shook her head at the reporters and continued walking, then stopped and turned. The group closed ranks around her, a film crew capturing every second. Emphatically gesturing as she talked, she jerked an arm toward my room. I knew they could not see me, but I shrank back, anyway.

A dark-haired man in a light-gray suit ran to the group and edged in beside my mother. She turned away from him, motioning the girls to follow. The girls waved to the man but huddled behind Sophie. I frowned. Who was this guy? As I watched, the gaggle of reporters clustered around the man, who seemed at ease with all the attention.

I was still watching when my mother and the girls exploded into the room.

"Mom! Reporters want to talk to you. Get ready." Lilly's eyes shone.

"Yeah," her sister added, "you are a huge deal now." She fell into the chair beside the bed.

"Who was that man—"

"Monty," my mother spat. "He has the nerve to come *now*? What is he thinking?"

The girls glanced at each other. I wondered if my mother had always felt this way about my ex. Wait—was he my ex? Did we get divorced?

I shrugged. "Guess it's as good a time as any to meet him, right?"

They went quiet. I studied their faces. "What?"

Serena found her voice first. "Um, you're just different, Mom."

"I keep hearing that," I groaned and peered out the window. "He is…still… there." I threw them a hopeful look. "Maybe he won't come up?"

The girls walked to the window and pressed their noses against the pane. "We have no clue why he's here, Mom."

"I know why he came," my mother interjected. "He wants the publicity. He's a big mover and shaker for the State of Maryland government contracts. He can't afford to distance himself from this." She pushed her hair from her face. "And I know that detective interviewed him already." Her earrings jingled, and her scent sailed through the air as she waved her arms. Unlike Sarah's fresh, fruity perfume, hers was earthy, floral. "I tried to delete Monty from this whole thing, but that detective insisted."

I sighed. "Not the best time for…reunion?"

My mother grunted.

I shrugged. "Doesn't matter. I don't remember."

"Mom! He was your husband for twenty years. At least act interested." Serena's indignation ignited her sister, who glared at me.

"Girls, be…patient with me. I'll do…best, okay?"

Sarah knocked and walked into my room. Dr. Sturgis entered next. Nurses and orderlies formed a tight knot behind them, bearing a large sheet cake.

"SURPRISE!"

Dr. Sturgis walked over and bear-hugged me. His medical jacket smelled of starch and bleach. "I think I speak for the group when I say we'll miss you, Olivia." Soft murmurs of agreement bounced around the room and in a matter of minutes, everyone had a piece of cake on a paper plate.

I'd never been hugged so many times in my life.

At least I didn't think so, I couldn't remember.

I figured south of the Mason-Dixon Line, hugs are required, so I did my best. Sarah lingered behind, cleaning up after everyone had gone back to work. I offered to help, but she wouldn't allow it. Mom had gone to take care of any checkout paperwork. Serena and Lilly chatted in the corner.

"So, how'd you like the party, sugar?" She stuffed the last of the paper plates and plastic forks into a packed trash can.

I struggled with what to say to the woman that had shepherded me from aching despair to blessed hope. Sarah's compassionate, soft, blue eyes twinkled. She put out her arms. "C'mon for a hug, honey."

I did.

Chapter Seventeen

A loud knock startled Sarah and I apart. Larger than life, the dark-haired man I'd seen outside stood at the door. His head reached almost to the top of the doorway.

"Anybody home?" he boomed.

"Hi, Dad." Serena glanced at my mother, then me. She shifted her weight back and forth.

I pushed my shoulders back and thrust out my chin. Sarah crossed her arms and stood closely beside me like a protective lioness.

"Olivia! You look great." He spread his arms as if expecting me to run into them.

I stepped a pace back. He dropped his arms. Was it my imagination, or did a scowl flit across his face before he focused his beaming smile on the girls? So, this was *Monty*. Tall, on the chunky side, hair black as a raven's wing, teeth so white he must have had them professionally done. Eyes shiny and dark, like smooth pebbles in a creek. Deep dimples. Already showing a five o'clock shadow, though it was barely eleven in the morning. I examined him as a scientist might examine an interesting specimen under a microscope.

He walked to my side and put a companionable hand on my shoulder.

I blinked and shrugged it away. "Um, Monty, right?"

His expression narrowed into a squinty question mark. "So it's true? You really don't remember anything?"

Sophie moved closer to me. Monty ignored her. This was a man used to being in charge, I thought, with a little squinty-eyed assessment of my own. I cursed my lingering inability to form coherent sentences.

"But you remember the girls?"

"Not yet. Working...on it."

The girls smiled at me, then glanced at each other.

"So, I guess you do not remember, uh, our..."

Ah. The underlying reason for crashing the party. The separation? Divorce?

"I've been, um, told. But it would be good...to know why." I glanced at the girls and my mother. "*Later*," I emphasized, "after."

Monty's face reddened. He stuffed his hands in his pockets.

I addressed Sophie and the girls, "Ready?"

"More than ready," my mother said, shooting Monty a scorched-earth glare.

He frowned.

Serena and Lilly grabbed my bags. We cackled like a flock of hens on our way down the hall. Monty trailed behind. When we got onto the elevator, we held it for him, but he had vanished.

Okay with me.

* * *

"Olivia! Olivia, over here!" Voices clamored and fingers clutched at my arms. Mics hovered an inch from my nose.

"Not now," my mother implored, muscling through the cluster of mics.

The girls and I trailed behind her as she did her best to shield us, but the frantic reporters were determined to get at me. I tugged at her arm. She turned toward me.

"I might as well," I said, shrugging.

She sighed and pulled the girls out of the way.

"Okay, guys," I said, "questions?" I stood straight and tall, proud of my restored physical ability, infused with a confidence I could not explain. My mother had told me I'd always been introverted and shy, but I couldn't find an introverted bone in my body. I clapped and smiled. "Let's go. I don't have all...day."

The cameras clicked and whirred. Mics inched ever closer to my mouth.

"Olivia, how does celebrity status feel?"

"If this is how…it's done, I'm…against it," I quipped.

The group roared with laughter. The hospital's public relations director stepped into the fray, with arms outstretched, creating a wide swath toward me. Her dark hair had been slicked back in a bun, and bright red lipstick framed a perfect smile. She was so thin a decent breeze could blow her over. She embraced me as if we were lifelong friends.

"Olivia, we here at Mercy want to congratulate you on your stunning recovery."

The reporters spatter-clapped politely.

One arm draped over my shoulders, she continued, "This Jane Doe, landing on our doorstep five weeks ago, is a wonderful example of how the staff here at Mercy does everything they can to accomplish miracles." She paused for effect, then locked eyes with me for the cameras. "And you, Olivia, are one of our miracles."

Applause picked up. A few curious pedestrians drifted by. They joined in the applause. My mother shook her head and winked. I grinned at her.

"Maybe," I told the woman, interrupting her prepared speech. "But now need…to remember how I got here in the first place." The words marched out before I could stop them. The reporters closed ranks—all I saw were lips, teeth, and a bristle of microphones.

"What do you think happened, Olivia?"

"Are the police involved, Olivia?"

"What are the next steps? Are you planning to prosecute?"

"Do you remember, Olivia? Do you know what happened?"

"We were told you lost your memory, Olivia. Not true?"

"Tell us what you remember, Olivia."

"What about your husband? Aren't you in the middle of a divorce?"

I put both palms up. The reporters edged back.

"I don't remember much. Might…come back…might not. The Richmond police are doing everything they can. I shrugged. "I cannot…remember… I've tried."

A disembodied voice yelled, "Olivia, isn't it true you were away for the weekend, visiting someone here in Richmond? Who was it?"

"I've been...I'm not, I don't know—"

A sudden dizziness buckled my knees. I heard shoes pounding the ground, saw strong arms reach out and shake me so hard the ground swayed beneath me. I groped for the red-lipsticked woman, unsure if what I saw was real or imaginary. She held me up. The images faded in wispy rainbow colors. Not real, I thought in relief.

"That's all, guys," she said. "As you can see, she's ready for a break."

My mother jogged to my side. I leaned on her and walked, shaky but upright, to the car, and sank into the passenger seat. The girls scrambled into the back, staring down the reporters as we skidded out of the parking lot. I slid down the window for some air.

Sophie glanced at me. "What happened back there?"

I reclined my seat.

"I...I've been having these weird dreams, and—"

"And what?"

"Visuals come from nowhere and I have to try to...hang on. I just had... a really strange..." I took some deep breaths. "I think I am starting to remember."

Chapter Eighteen

Detective Hunter Faraday pressed the phone tight against his ear, listening intently.

"From what you've told me," Detective Shiloh Kennedy responded, "this is a tough one."

Hunter sighed and rubbed his beard stubble. He hadn't shaved in a couple of days, and the cream-colored dress shirt he wore had a coffee stain on the front. "Yeah, I get that. I figured that last case you were on—"

"The one with the stalker and the notes?"

"Yeah, that was a similar thing, right? Only you caught the guy before he could do major damage."

"We did," she said. "But we had a lot to go on. You got nothin'." She sniffed. "Don't envy what you got ahead of you."

"Tell me about it." Hunter chuckled. "I just wanted to see if you'd be available to consult, okay? If we run into a dead end?"

"I'm always available for you, McFaraday. Have you ruled out the husband?"

He smiled at the nickname, a nod to his obsession with Big Macs. Shiloh had become his go-to person for thorny cases. They'd almost made a relationship work twenty years ago when they were just kids in the police academy, but decided not to ruin a perfectly good friendship. She eventually married, had a baby, and moved to Savannah. Hunter got married too, but no babies, and his marriage ended eight years ago.

"Once. He has an alibi, but I need to check it out. It took a while to get the interviews started. They delayed getting her name out, and when her doctor finally let me see her, she was not in the best mental state. She's home now, so I'll follow up soon. Talked to her mother a couple times and her doctor several times."

"Yeah? What's the mother say?"

"Same thing the news says—weekend in Richmond with a girlfriend. Doesn't know the name of the friend, which is strange. She gave me some guy's business card she found in Olivia's house, and he lives in Richmond. I ran him through the system. Minor jail time for tax evasion, some insider trading, but that's it. No violent stuff. He's on my follow-up list."

Shiloh was silent a few seconds. "Interesting, though. Did her mom recognize this guy's name?"

"Nope," Hunter said. "I showed Olivia his picture, but she's, well…she's still working on regaining her memory and couldn't give me anything to go on. Feels like it wasn't a *girlfriend* she visited in Richmond, though—just a hunch."

"Well, of course it wasn't a girlfriend. She single?"

"Kind of. Middle of a divorce."

Shiloh snapped her fingers. "That's right, I heard that on the news. Obviously—"

"Yeah, I know, always the husband. I didn't want to spook him. Went easy on the first interview. Watching him, though."

"Good. Hold your cards and wait."

After the call, Hunter leaned back in his chair and rocked. He intertwined his fingers behind his head and studied the ceiling, thinking about his sun-drenched, happy childhood in Virginia Beach, and his college days in Charlottesville at the University of Virginia. His framed bachelor's diploma in psychology hung on the wall beside his master's in criminal justice and a framed photo of his graduation. He smiled at the thought of how proud his parents and brother had been. He'd talked to his dad recently, as he did once a week, a practice he'd started after his mom died two years ago. Still in Virginia Beach, his dad insisted he take some time off and come visit.

He dropped his gaze to his desk and stared at the business card he'd gotten from Olivia's mother. He checked the cheesy calendar on his wall that displayed twelve photos of awkward family portraits, a gift from his brother's wife. He walked the squares with his eyes and landed on a date to visit his dad and a date to travel back to Glyndon for another interview with Olivia.

* * *

The woman who answered Niles Peterson's work number put him on hold.

Hunter drummed his fingers on his desk.

"Niles here."

"Mr. Peterson? Detective Faraday, Richmond PD. Is this a good time?"

"What is this about?"

Hunter cleared his throat. "I guess you know about the woman dropped at Mercy several weeks ago? The Jane Doe?"

The silence stretched.

"Mr. Peterson?"

The man coughed. "Yes, of course. I met her at the beach a month or so ago. Horrible what happened. Have you...are you investigating?"

"Can we set up a meeting? I've got a few questions."

Niles tried to answer, but the words sounded stuck in his throat. He tried again.

"Pardon?"

"Sorry. Let me just grab a drink of water."

Hunter waited. His fingers resumed drumming his desk. After a few minutes, Niles returned to the phone.

"Of course I'll tell you what I know, which is nothing, but...whatever. I'm willing to help."

They set a time and ended the call.

Hunter lay his cell on his desk and crossed his arms.

Something definitely off about the guy.

Chapter Nineteen

Olivia

The road trip from Richmond to my house in Glyndon took three hours, give or take. Three hours stuck in a car together with virtual strangers who insisted they were my family. I struggled with their barrage of well-intended jaunts down memory lane that meant nothing to me. Not yet, anyway. Little snippets of memory flashed through me as they talked, ethereal glimmers of light, like fireflies.

This did not keep me from freaking out inside.

Serena and Lilly chattered nonstop, hoping to blast me back to their past: school days, road trips, vacations. Within these memories, geography stood out bright and clear to me—a palm tree or a bright blue sky or an iguana sunning itself on a rock. I tried to picture my daughters as younger versions, laughing and digging in the sand on a beach or running off to catch a school bus, but couldn't bring up the actual memory. I hoped photos would jog me back to my life. Sophie and the girls were sure of it. I was not.

Strangely, other than the cloudy shadow of men talking in some of my dreams, I couldn't pull in a specific memory of me with my husband. Like a wet knot my fingers could not pry apart, my brain kept working at it.

"We're here, honey," my mother said, patting my arm.

My hand gripped hers.

"Don't worry, Olivia, if you don't remember yet. Give it time."

She turned right onto a beautiful curved lane. The tires made crunchy noises as they rolled over gravel. Ancient trees rimmed each side, their branches touching to form a leafy arch. My heart rammed my ribs.

We stopped in front of a well-preserved, older, detached garage with an annex to a two-story brick house surrounded by split-rail fencing and a yard populated with ornamental trees: Bradford pear, eastern redbud, Japanese maples. A few locust trees. Azaleas framed the steps to the front porch.

I glanced at my mother. "The names of all those trees just popped into my mind."

She laughed. "Of course they did, honey, you planted almost all of them."

I stared at the front porch. Wicker furniture with floral cushions. Porch swing. Flower boxes on the railings around the porch.

"It's lovely," I said.

But I didn't remember living here.

My mother got out and trotted to the trunk to get the luggage. The girls tried to pull me out of the car. I stalled, preparing myself emotionally for re-entry. I suggested the girls help Sophie so I could take the first baby steps back to my life alone.

A sidewalk led to an old wooden gate. It creaked when I pushed it open. The sheer joy of the simple act of walking still melted me inside. I stepped inside the gate, tilted my head back and closed my eyes, reveling in the smell of flowers, the warmth of the sun on my face.

"This place looks like an English garden," I whispered to myself as I wandered around the perimeter of the yard, touching things. Rosebushes that had yet to bloom, and hydrangea that had already started. A butterfly bush, heavy with butterflies. Drooping stalks of forsythia that had surrendered brilliant spring plumage to leafy summer green.

The girls had said I'd spent time digging, sanding, and restoring. I marveled at the work of my hands. I held them in front of me. Short and square and small. I made a quick mental note to paint my nails the minute I found polish. I walked up the stairs to the porch and chose a chair. The cushion wheezed as I sat.

Lilly, her face beaming, ran up the stairs, an overnight bag swinging from her shoulder. "So, what about it, Mom? Remember?" She pointed at the yard. "And you had just mowed for the first time, remember that? For the first time."

I considered the shaggy lawn. "Do I not mow, usually?"

Lilly shook her head. "Dad did everything. You've had a hard time figuring out what to do since…" She looked away.

I wondered if I had understood the divorce had been hard on them as well. I wondered if we had talked about it. Now they dealt with double tragedies: pending divorce, a lost mom.

"Since you guys have lived apart," she finished.

I nodded. "I see."

Serena clunked up the four wooden stairs with a suitcase. "Man, it's good to be home." She pushed her hair behind her shoulders and clutched the bag. "Be right back. Going to put this in your room, Mom."

I smiled my thanks. They treated me like an invalid, but for now, since I needed to get my bearings, it was okay.

My mother pulled up one of the cozy wicker chairs and sat beside me. "You're home, honey." She patted my leg, bracelets jangling away, then leaned back into her chair and studied the yard. "So beautiful here. Always thought so."

"It is."

"Feel anything? Familiarity, sparks…anything?"

I shook my head. "Sorry."

She shrugged. "That's okay. You're safe, and you're *home*, that's what matters. In the mood for tea?"

I thought about that. "I guess I like tea?"

My mother laughed. "Yes, you *love* tea." She cocked her head. "In the afternoon. You drink coffee in the morning."

The screen closed with a bang behind her as she walked inside. The sound struck a chord. At the foot of the door, a huge, yellow cat had slid away to allow her to enter and now reclaimed his spot on the rug, his steady gaze studying me. He dropped his head and licked a paw. At least he hadn't snarled and run in the opposite direction. I wondered if I'd been a cat person or a dog person. Then I wondered if my personality change would encompass a pet preference. It was clear, from what I'd been told, that I'd emerged with a different slant on life.

Or something.

I sighed, rubbed my neck and rotated my head. The door banging, the cat, the trees, the porch. Should be familiar, and yet...*wait.* I jumped up. Was that someone behind a tree?

My mother appeared with a teapot, two china cups, honey, and cream. She put the tray on the table between us.

"There." She brushed her palms together. "Just like we used to."

A shadow darted from one tree to the next. I blinked and pointed. "Do you see someone out there?"

She shaded her eyes and looked at the front yard. "Don't think so. Did you?"

I stared. Nothing moved. Still. I had a feeling. A dark feeling. "Guess not," I said, and sat. "Thanks for...tea." With a last glance at imagined interlopers, I picked up the pot, held the top, poured hers, then mine. It felt familiar. "We did this a lot?"

"When I came to visit, we did. We've had quite a lot of tea on this porch, and long talks."

I plopped honey in my tea, added cream, and stirred. We sat quietly for a few minutes. The birds flitted to the empty feeders chirping accusatory chirps. I grinned. "Guess the birds missed me."

"We *all* missed you." The china cup chimed as she stirred. "You cannot imagine the terror we felt when you didn't show up when you were supposed to. I was already concerned because you hadn't called, and I had no address or phone number for where you'd be!" Sophie shook her head. "And your phone just went to voicemail over and finally...nothing." She took a sip of her tea. "And what happened to your car? Your purse?"

I blurted out, "Why would someone do this to me?"

"We don't want to jump to conclusions."

"But...motivation? My purse? Robbed?" I swallowed hard. "...my car?" I shook my head in frustration. When would speech become easier?

My mother raised her cup to her lips, then put it back on its saucer. "You don't have to think about this right now, honey."

I groaned. "I don't want to think about it, but I *have* to." I stared at my lap.

My mother chewed on her lower lip for a few seconds. "Well, you probably need to know something. We didn't want to tell you about it until you were strong enough."

"We?"

"Gray and I. He told me his office was ransacked."

"Ransacked?"

She crossed her arms. "Someone wanted your medical information. They stole your file and Gray's laptop."

"But...but that means—"

"That means it was definitely a crime, in my book," she finished my thought. "They're still investigating."

Like the start of an avalanche, my fragile composure fell off me in chunks.

My mother continued, her voice soft, "They'll find out who did this, Olivia."

Panic slid up my back. I gripped the arms of my chair. "Why didn't you tell me?"

Sophie sighed. "Well, we didn't want you worrying with all that. But now..." her voice trailed away. She stared at the floorboards, thinking. "But now," she continued, "you need to know so that you can be careful."

I examined my teacup. White with gold trim and pink roses. I refused to believe that what happened three hours away and a lifetime ago could touch me here.

"Lock doors and windows and keep outside lights on until all of this is resolved. Be aware of your surroundings. Just a few extra precautions, honey."

I agreed, but held on to the hope the world would right itself without too much effort on my part. I took a deep breath and let it out slow.

Gray?

"Did you call Dr. Sturgis...Gray?"

Sophie blushed. "He asked me to call him by his first name."

I smiled. "He's single?"

84

"Change the subject."

"Why?" I asked, "you're looking, right?"

"Olivia Rosemary! I've never heard you say something like that in my life."

"Well, maybe it's time for a change."

We laughed.

It was good to be home.

Chapter Twenty

My body begged for sleep after unpacking and trying in vain to remember my life, but I missed my hospital room. I missed Sarah. My shoulders slumped.

Eyeing the bed I'd purportedly shared with Monty for twenty-odd years as if it were a slimy alien, I padded across the carpet and wondered which side I'd slept on. One side seemed lower than the other, and since Monty was a huge guy, I figured my side had been the other one. I sighed and drew back the comforter. Through the window, a breeze whispered. Tree frogs and sounds of the night filled the bedroom. I had a near-irresistible urge to fix a cup of tea and take it to my front porch and watch the moonrise. A memory? Or reluctance to sleep in the same bed Monty and I had shared?

I snugged my arms around my shoulders and squeezed. *It's now or never, Olivia,* I thought. *What other choice do you have? The floor?* Cautiously, I turned and sat. The bed whooshed slightly with my weight. In a rush, I pulled my legs onto the bed and lay back, my arms splayed to each side, chest heaving a little. Like a little girl, I had a fleeting pang of need for my mom, relieved she was sleeping in the guest bedroom just down the hall, glad she had made herself available to drive me home from the hospital and stay a few days. *This is ridiculous, Olivia. Turn off your brain and go to sleep.* I rolled over, pushed my hair out of my face, and pulled up the comforter. Then I was dead to the world.

* * *

Serena's long, straight, flaxen hair lifted in the breeze as she flounced out of the car. Lilly squinched her auburn curls into a semblance of order, but the unruly mop sprang back to its original state the minute she dropped her hands. Serena stalked inside Coligny Beach's Piggly Wiggly with a toss of her head and her younger sister looked back toward me, rolled her eyes, and followed.

I paused to lay my head back and scan the heavens through the open sunroof. Gulls circled high overhead, screeching to brethren gulls the latest fishing report. I imagined the walk on the beach later, watching them dive with the pelicans. The Spanish moss swayed lush and lazy in the breeze. I gulped in great draughts of Hilton Head Island's coastal air, grabbed my purse, and eased out of the car to join the girls.

My steps grew slower as I approached the entrance—the first time since Monty's exit from our marriage—to enter Piggly Wiggly alone. I had paused, staring at the glass double doors, my fists clenching and unclenching at my sides, unable to move.

Like lightning strikes, the memories seared my mind—me behind the cart, Monty and the girls charging the aisles, picking up items, holding them aloft. Monty tossing things into the basket or replacing them on the shelf. Laughter. Me struggling with the cart and its mountain of accumulation, Monty leading the parade like a Banty rooster with his brood.

I had depended on him, trusted him. My shoulders sagged with the weight of a hundred anxieties.

I forced myself to approach the doors. They slid open with a whisper. Wading through unwelcome memories like déjà vu in reverse, I pulled out a shopping cart and helplessly stared at my knuckles turning white on the handle, my feet glued to the floor.

"Olivia?"

I turned to the voice calling my name from across the checkouts, blinking the wet away. "Lorrie! Hi."

Fragile, age-spotted hands waved me over. Since we'd always made a gazillion trips to this store during our vacations, the store's general manager had become more than a casual acquaintance.

"Get on over here, gal," she said, her head swiveling. "Where are those girls of

yours?"

I attempted a smile. "Around here somewhere. I'll find them, eventually."

"Probably around the ice cream," she joked, laugh-crinkles fanning her eyes. "I remember those girls love their ice cream." She put an index finger on her chin. "Let's see, Serena's probably a senior in high school this year, and Lilly's a, um... sophomore?"

"Almost," I said, motioning her to join me as I pushed the cart out into the aisle and away from other cart-seekers. "Serena's a senior and Lilly's fourteen, so she'll be in ninth grade."

Lorrie clapped in delight. "For gosh sakes, time sure passes. I remember when those girls were this high." She extended her arms forward a couple of feet from the floor.

I laughed. "Those were the days, for sure."

We fidgeted in silence a few seconds.

Lorrie crossed her arms and smiled. "Where's that tall, good-looking hunk of a man you're married to?"

I focused on the wall behind her, frowned, and cleared my throat. She laid a hand on my arm.

"Oh, my," she whispered. "Has something happened? Is Monty okay?"

A smile crept across my face. "Oh, yes, Monty is...okay." I shook my head. "He's so okay that he's rented himself a new little place in Ellicott City. It came with a twenty-five-year-old and divorce proceedings."

Lorrie's crinkles disappeared from the corners of her eyes and reemerged on her forehead. Her hands flew to her cheeks. "Oh, no! Olivia, I'm so, so sorry. What can I do?" She patted my arm with one hand, the other one, like a frail bird, perched on my shoulder.

I shrugged. "I don't know, Lorrie. I kind of take one thing at a time. It feels so... " I struggled for the right word, "alien, y'know?"

Lorrie nodded. "I do know. Been divorced ten years. Just up and left one day, without a good reason. Said we'd gotten 'stale.' Can you believe that? We'd been married thirty-six years." Her wise, weathered blue eyes regarded my anxious hazel ones.

"Oh, Lorrie, I had no idea," I mumbled.

"Over and done with now," she said. "Point is, you learn. You learn to keep goin'. To do without 'em." She shrugged and pondered my face. "Not the end of the world. You'll survive, girl. Every day will get better. Just know you can call me if you need anything, okay?" She dug into her pants pocket and pulled out a business card. "It's got my cell. Don't you hesitate to call."

I nodded and dragged my palm across my wet cheeks.

She pulled me into a hug. "Anytime, day or night, y'hear?"

* * *

I stirred awake with the words "Anytime, day or night, y'hear?" scrolling through my mind on a loop. My nose twitched. Smells of bacon, eggs, and coffee. I burrowed contentedly into the mattress, reluctant to leave the beach, reluctant to leave the kind woman who said she'd help me, but I scrambled out of bed anyway, my sole intent to find notepad and pen before the dream faded.

Eventually, all the dots would connect.

Chapter Twenty-One

The connection failed again. His internet had been balky and undependable all day. Monty snapped his laptop shut in disgust.

"Kirsten! Get the techs up here. The computer is not working."

He heard the scrape of a drawer closing, the squeak of a chair, and light, brisk steps. His door opened.

"You don't have to yell," Kirsten said, then dropped her voice, "baby."

Monty glared at her in spite of the burnished mahogany hair falling provocatively over one eye, and in spite of the form-fitting, short dress she wore. He looked away and through clenched teeth said, "Don't ever call me that here. We've talked about this."

Kirsten laughed. "I know." Her eyelids lowered. "No one is around, honey."

He blew out a long sigh. "Look, we can't afford to let anyone know, okay?"

She put her hands on her narrow hips. "Even though you've already moved out? Even though all my friends know? Even though your daughters have talked to my sister at the pool—"

Monty held up his index finger. "If you want to keep this job—"

"*My* job? I thought you were going to find another position at a different firm."

Monty walked to Kirsten, reached behind her, and closed the door to his office.

He put his arms around her and stared into the chocolate eyes that had reduced him to an unfaithful mound of Jell-O.

"I've been meaning to talk to you about that," he said gently. "Leaving this company isn't an option. They've promised me another project manager position, at a ridiculous rate. I—*we*—would sacrifice too much money if I walked away."

Kirsten's lips pressed together. She crossed her arms and wiggled out of Monty's embrace.

"So what does that mean?" she asked. "That I should start putting out my résumé?"

Monty shrugged. "It just means we should be cautious."

"Fine." She turned on one heel, jerked the door open, and slammed it behind her.

Monty walked to his window and looked outside. He needed a break from hysterics. The backdraft from his intention to divorce Olivia had caused enough feminine drama to last a lifetime. Did he have to go through it with Kirsten, too? He walked behind his desk, bent down, and pulled out a drawer. Underneath the framed pictures, he pulled out one of Olivia. Strange how different she was. More...interesting? Intriguing? He couldn't quite put his finger on it.

Something had changed.

He frowned, replaced the picture in the drawer, and slid it shut. Maybe he should pay a visit to Olivia and the girls. Sometime this week.

"Kirsten, get the techs up here!" She yelled that she would.

Chapter Twenty-Two

Olivia

I 've gotten used to the feel and sounds of the house, I realized as I brushed my hair and tried to pull it into a band. It was almost long enough now, and I left it in a low, short ponytail at the nape of my neck. Foraging through my dresser, I found a short-sleeved, light-blue V-neck cotton pullover and pulled it on over my jeans, which nearly fell off me before I found a belt. As I trotted downstairs, I mentally added "shopping for clothes" to my growing list of things to do.

The floor above me squeaked as Sophie—*Mom*—padded around the bedroom, packing. I stood in the kitchen staring at nothing, listening to the sounds she made in the guest bedroom above, already missing her.

"This old house definitely has a voice," I said as I plugged in my coffeemaker and poured in water. Except for the panic attacks every so often that I didn't yet understand, I was beginning to enjoy being here. Still, I was grateful Mom had stayed an extra week.

Riot had finally warmed up to me. As I stooped to pet him he wrapped himself around my ankles. His fur felt silky, and a purr rumbled in his throat. A stranger in my own home, but being here was beginning to feel familiar, as if long ago I had seen the movie but forgotten the plot. And the cast. And the ending.

Memories flared up like hives, then vanished. I'd experimented with different areas of the house—sitting first in one chair, then another, walking in and out of rooms and focusing on certain objects. Sometimes I'd stand still and quiet in the center of a room, trying to smell and taste and hear the past. Had I been a quiet woman? A boring woman? An interesting woman? Had my girls careened through the house, laughing and yelling as little girls do? Had Monty been a good dad? An involved dad? I frowned, thinking about this. How could he have been if he'd been such a horrible husband? Had he really been horrible, or was my mother just exaggerating?

I sipped from a yellow-and-brown-striped cat mug that had become my favorite. Its tail curled around the handle, and on the bottom were the words *To Mom, Happy Mother's Day, Serena.* The mug made me smile. Sunshine spilled through the window, highlighting the room's fussy wallpaper. I couldn't picture myself picking out a single thing in this kitchen, especially the wallpaper—a ghastly hash of flowers divided by pastel borders. Had my tastes changed?

The squeaks and creaks above my head moved to the hall, then the staircase—the wheels of luggage thumping down each step. I ran to assist.

"Let me help, Mom."

"It's okay, honey, not that heavy." She bounced to the bottom step with a gasp. "It just sounds like I'm dying because I need to quit smoking," she said, her voice matter-of-fact. She wore a flaming orange top and white capris. Gold hoop earrings hung to her shoulders, peeking from carefully finger-combed curls. Bracelets jangled at her wrist, as usual. She wore a locket necklace—gold with delicate antique whorls engraved on its face.

She picked up the locket, opened it, and slanted it toward me. "Remember this?"

I stepped closer. Two adorable little girls in matching yellow swimsuits. "Serena and Lilly?"

"Yes. Do you remember the day we took this picture?"

I thought a minute. Nothing.

"That day," she continued, "we were at Hilton Head, your family's normal spot on the beach at Palmetto Dunes."

I tried to picture it.

"You ran to the unit to grab some snacks. Monty had the umbrella all set up." She paused. "Blue with white edges." An exercise we'd utilized all week. She would talk about a joint activity and stop every few minutes to let my brain catch up. Sometimes it worked, and I had a flash of memory. She continued, "I had taken a walk on the beach, and Monty was supposed to be watching the girls."

My palm flew to cover my mouth. "Oh, no. Did the girls have an accident?"

She nodded. "They grabbed the raft and headed straight into the water. It was a windy day, waves were really crazy." She paused. I saw an old pain crease her features. "The sweet little things just disappeared in the blink of an eye, I guess."

I gasped.

"I yelled at Monty, 'Where are the girls?' and he yelled back he thought I had them…" She groaned. "We nearly had heart attacks, of course. The lifeguards went crazy."

My mind turned somersaults, trying to remember. When a memory tugged at me, my breathing sped up, my heart beat faster. I began to pant. My mother patted my arm.

"This might be a tough one," she said, and waited.

My mind spun back.

Huge waves crashing. Screams slicing the air. I raced like a wild thing from our unit onto the beach. Monty crying. My mother's arms flailing. I flung myself into the waves, screeching the girls' names. Salt water seared my lungs. I couldn't make any progress; the waves were too strong.

I spied them then, two tiny yellow blots on an endless ocean, their rubber raft an impossible distance away. Miraculously, instead of floating out to sea, the raft had bobbed toward shore. I screamed at Monty and pointed. It seemed like an eternity until his strong, panicked strokes reached them. Once his fingers touched the raft, he waved a frantic victory wave.

I remembered everything clearly, as if it were yesterday.

"Oh. My. God," I whispered.

"Exactly," my mother replied. She closed the locket with a snap. "I keep this photo of that day in memory of the miracle God did for us. I will never forget it." She smiled and poked me with her finger. "And neither will you."

* * *

On the way home from taking Mom to the airport, I left Dr. Sturgis a voicemail to thank him for releasing me to drive. I relished the feel of a steering wheel under my hands again and was thankful for my mom's help with the insurance payout on my missing Ford Escape and the purchase of another car before she flew home.

I sighed.

Without Mom's sweet distractions and help with memories, I felt lost. It wouldn't last forever, this feeling, but in the meantime I struggled to pull more memories into place, marveling that I remembered day-to-day things—like driving, or how to adjust a GPS or the importance of a seatbelt—but could not recall names of my girls' friends, carpool parents, teachers.

I pulled onto my gravel road. My first drive had been a rousing success.

A breeze fluttered the leaves. Staring at the towering storybook arch entwined above me, I nearly smashed the front of my car into a tree. I stomped the brake. The car idled, the front bumper inches away from a mammoth oak.

Through the trees, I saw the back of a black SUV in my driveway. My pulse raced. My throat constricted. I breathed in tight, panicked gasps, thinking about the darting shadows I'd seen. Maybe it hadn't been my imagination. My mother's cautions rotated through my mind. *Lock the doors, be aware, just be careful.* What if my mystery attacker waited for me around the edge of my house, his small-caliber gun cocked and aimed at me as I got out of my car? What if he had a knife? I shook my head and blinked. *Calm down, Olivia.*

As if on a reconnaissance mission to scout out dangerous territory, I tiptoed from tree to tree, hiding behind each one. By the fourth tree, I could see a man sitting in one of my rocking chairs on the porch. I recognized him immediately. *Monty.* I groaned and stalked back to my car. As I pulled into my garage, he waved and smiled. I ignored him. Who shows up on the porch of a recovering coma patient—much less a soon-to-be ex—without calling first?

I walked through the annex that connected my garage to the rest of the house, dropped my keys and purse on the kitchen table, and grabbed a banana. I took my own sweet time about eating it, too. He could wait. Stuffing the last of the banana in my mouth, I closed my eyes and tried to put Monty and I together in this house.

Nothing.

My eyes sprang open, and I almost choked on the darn banana. What if this whole experience—the assault, the holes in my memory—what if he'd been involved? Maybe my mind was protecting me from the truth.

I stalked to the front door and opened it, leaving the screen door latched.

Monty approached the door. He wore jeans and a Baltimore Ravens jersey. Neither of us said anything. I crossed my arms and watched him, his face neatly pixelated into little squares by the screen.

"Olivia, it's good to see you."

"What do you want?" Divorce pending and who knows what preceding it, I still had a lot to figure out, and I was in no mood to hear his version right now.

The smile vanished. He didn't speak for several seconds.

"What?" I barked.

He peered down and around me, at Riot settling inside the doorway. "I'm just a little surprised, that's all."

"That makes two of us. Why didn't you call first?"

He grimaced. "Wow."

I sighed. "Look, I'm…I'm having a pretty good week, and I don't think I'm ready to talk about…ahh…an *us*…or the divorce, or any of it. Not yet."

"Could we at least go over a few things," he pointed, "inside?"

"No."

"No?"

I shook my head.

He rolled his eyes. "Okay." He nodded at a wicker chair. "Can I sit?"

"A little while, Monty, that's all."

After a tug at my conscience that I'd actually considered grabbing a knife and sticking it in my back pocket, I went outside and sat in a chair across from him. Riot regarded Monty through the screen with his steady, amber gaze, silent and solemn as a sphinx.

"Could we at least have afternoon tea?" Monty asked. "Like we used to?"

"No."

He nodded, took a deep breath, and leaned forward. "Olivia, I wanted to apologize for not coming by the hospital, um…earlier."

"Okay."

"That's it? Okay?"

I nodded. "Why?"

He pulled his chin into his neck. "I'm having trouble getting used to the new you."

This piqued my curiosity as nothing else.

"Tell me about the old me."

He rubbed his chin. Strands of dark hair lifted in the breeze. If I was honest, on a purely physical level, he was a solid nine. But I trusted him about as much as I trusted one of those reporters who had shoved their microphones down my throat. I wouldn't let him in the house if my life depended on it.

Monty cleared his throat. "I'd say the old Olivia—the one I've been married to for twenty years—was gentle and kind. A good mother." He turned and looked at the yard. "A gardener and lover of flowers."

"Good things. What else?"

"She was very anxious to please."

"Really? How?"

His eyes narrowed. "To please her husband."

Now *my* eyes narrowed. "To please…you?"

"Yes."

I stroked my cheek thoughtfully, and studied his face, trying to remember our life together. Had I had no life of my own? Had I given him so much power over me? Being here with him stirred all kinds of emotions, and I couldn't seem to bottom-line any of it. But in the next heartbeat, memories crashed through.

* * *

I'd made it through grocery shopping in Piggly Wiggly without falling apart, and by the time we pulled into our complex's parking lot, the sun hung low in the sky. I allowed a few seconds of self-congratulation for actually getting us to Hilton Head Island—without Monty's help—in one piece. I stared at the familiar landscaping, the lush green of the grass, the manicured walkways. Maybe keeping the same unit had been a bad idea, but it seemed easier to plod along the same path. Besides, I'd never made a reservation in my life.

"Finally," Serena declared, unbuckling her seatbelt. "After we got lost for two hours and drove almost to Raleigh."

I sighed and thought about how hard the last few months had been on the girls.

"How was I supposed to know the GPS goes off every time the car does? I thought I was going the right way, or it would've said something," I responded, striving to keep irritation out of my voice.

"It's okay, Mom," Lilly placated. "Really. We're glad we're here. Aren't we, Serena?"

I switched off the ignition. Serena leaned over the front seat and whispered to Lilly in the back. They both giggled. I was too tired to address whatever joke they'd had at my expense, an all-too-common occurrence since their father's absence.

"C'mon girls, let's get the groceries inside and go for a walk on the beach."

They whooped, dashed out of the car, and ran, legs pumping with adrenaline and youth. I watched them run toward the beach, leaving me to unpack the car. Their father would have never allowed it, would have insisted that they help out, but I was too numb to care. I lugged the groceries up the stairs and wrestled with the lock. Dumped seven plastic sacks on the kitchen table in a heap, then retraced my steps and locked the front door.

The unit smelled musty. My flip-flops squeaked across the tile floor. In a rush of fabric and a flurry of dust, I pulled aside the curtains covering the balcony access, then unlocked the glass doors. The metal handle felt cool and smooth beneath my hand. Before I could slide the door open, I heard Monty's condescending voice, saw the downward curving lips of his disapproval. "It is important to develop good habits, Olivia," he said as he closed and locked the door. He liked everything locked down, but I longed for access to beach breezes and an open door. I'd watched him lock us in, a smile painted on my face. An endearing eccentricity, I'd convinced myself—proof that he loved me, loved the kids. Wanted what was best for us, to protect us. Then he'd led me to the bedrooms and illustrated locking the windows as well. I'd kept the windows and doors shut and locked at all times, like an obedient child, even if we longed for the sound of the ocean at night or the feel of a soft breeze on our skin during the day.

I stared at my hand on the door. The impossible blue of the sky. Approximately half a city block from where I stood, pelicans hurtled like feathered missiles into the water. Sea oats waved a cheery hello from sand dunes, surf curls crested and withdrew. A few people bicycled on the hard-packed beach. Seagulls clamored and swooped. A pelican exited the water with lazy flaps of its wings, a fish dangling from its beak.

I flung the door wide open and left it that way.

I blinked. The memory faded, but I desperately hoped I would remember enough to add it to my notebook scribblings. My takeaway from the episode: the guy I'd been married to for twenty-odd years sitting on my porch and glaring at me was a creepy guy. What else had he demanded of his family? And why had I allowed this type of behavior?

I asked Monty to repeat what he'd just said.

Irritated, he repeated, "You were anxious to please your husband."

"And did this kind of...precipitate...the divorce? The fact that I was gentle, kind, a good mother, and wanted to please you?"

Monty ran his hand through his gel-stiffened black hair. "I wouldn't put it that way."

"How *would* you put it?"

"More like we just kind of...grew apart. And, I don't know if you remember, but—"

Bells rang in my head, deep tolls like ancient church bells in European steeples on Sunday mornings. "A *woman*. You got involved with a younger woman, right? And you took me out to dinner..." I squinted, forcing myself to remember. "...and it didn't go well?" I stared at him.

He frowned. "What the hell does that have to do with anything? It was just…dinner."

I'd had enough. I rose from my chair. "Well, this has been fun, but I've got a life to get back to remembering."

He sighed and stood.

I folded my arms across my chest. "I'll call when I'm ready to talk, okay?"

He mumbled a goodbye, got in his car and roared down my beautiful lane trailing clouds of dust and irritation. I brushed one palm against the other and walked into the house.

Chapter Twenty-Three

Detective Hunter Faraday pushed the *up* button. He calculated each detail of his surroundings under lowered eyelids as he stood waiting for the elevator on the first floor of one of Richmond's grand, old, redbrick office buildings. A scant eight floors separated him from Niles Peterson, person of interest in the Callahan case.

The doors slid apart. A crush of office-dwellers mobbed him in. They stood silent as stones, shoulders almost touching. Every floor was punched, a vertical row of neon-white circles. Hunter, patient and still, breathed in the smell of coffee and morning showers as he briefly scrutinized his elevator companions, an old cop habit. He tugged each cuff of his starched, yellow shirt to the requisite inch that was supposed to show at the end of his tan sport coat sleeves. A worn leather bag slouched from one shoulder. The elevator's dings for each floor registered dimly in his mind, but he was laser-focused on his approach to the interview. Should he be gracious and friendly? Distant and routine? Hunter felt the weight in the elevator decrease each time its doors opened and closed, and by the time he reached the eighth floor, the elevator had emptied and he had made his decision.

* * *

"Detective Faraday," Niles' assistant announced as she eased open the door.

Niles Peterson rose and extended a hand over his desk. "Morning, Detective. Please have a seat."

Hunter smiled politely and sat, pegging the man's demeanor as somewhere between angry and skittish. "This shouldn't take long, Mr. Peterson."

"Please, call me Niles. Take all the time you need." Niles shrugged and lifted his palms. "I don't know if I have anything worthwhile to offer, though."

Hunter pulled a small notepad from his inside pocket. As he scribbled on the pad, he said, "We're just following up on all contacts Ms. Callahan had within a three-month period, to see what shakes out. Routine."

Hunter patted his coat pockets and produced a phone, purposely giving Niles a glimpse of the gun he wore under his armpit. He held the phone up questioningly, noting Niles's face had paled. "Don't mind if I record, do you?"

Niles shook his head, leaned in, and put his elbows on the desk. His movements were jerky and indecisive.

Hunter punched the record button. He wondered if Niles realized that all cops were fluent in body language.

"Let's start with how you met Olivia." He leaned forward and mirrored Niles's position.

"As I told you, a brief meeting on the beach. She'd been on an early morning run and I gave her some water."

Hunter waited, quiet and watchful.

Niles fidgeted. "We talked a little."

"About what?"

"Nothin' in particular, just dumb stuff a guy says to a pretty woman on the beach." He quipped, chuckling. Mutual man-joke.

After staring thoughtfully at Niles for a few seconds, he bent his head down and scribbled on his notepad.

Niles loosened his tie.

"Can you be more specific?"

"We talked about why we liked Hilton Head."

"Mm-hmm. What else?"

Niles shrugged. "That was it. Then she went back to her place, and I went back to mine."

"Did you see her again?"

Niles cocked his head and thought a minute. Hunter noticed moisture beginning to dampen the man's forehead.

"Yes, I seem to recall, that…on the beach, the next day, I was riding my bike and saw her. I said a few words and moved on. Just 'Hi, how are you today?' That kind of thing."

Hunter checked his phone and replaced it in the same position directly beneath Niles's chin. "Okay. What else?" He lifted his eyebrows. "Were you at the beach alone?"

"My son and myself."

"Married? Separated? Divorced?"

"Divorced."

Hunter scribbled.

"I saw her another time, at a restaurant," Niles added helpfully. "The Boat House. She was at the bar alone, so I said hello."

Hunter contemplated that. "You attracted to her?"

"Who wouldn't be? But she was going through a divorce and—actually, not quite divorced, so…"

"So your conversation with her was a little more intimate than you originally thought?"

Niles reddened. "Maybe I forgot—"

"Maybe you did." Hunter placed his pen on his small tablet, leaned back, and crossed his arms.

Niles looked away. "It's been a couple of months."

"I understand," Hunter murmured, careful to keep his expression neutral. "What else?"

"That's it. Except for a chance meeting on the beach the day she left."

"Just happened to be walking by?"

"On a bike. I said goodbye and told her it had been nice meeting her."

Hunter let the silent seconds tick by.

Niles blinked. "That's it, I swear."

"Okay." Hunter shrugged, picked up his phone, and pressed the screen. He rose from the chair and shook Niles's hand, his mind churning with the next steps to pin down this guy's story.

"That's all I have for now, but stay close, okay?"

"Uh, okay, but…am I, uh…"

"I'll be in touch, Mr. Peterso—Niles."

Hunter picked up his notebook and pen and stuck them in his pocket. With a smile, he dipped his head and left.

Chapter Twenty-Four

Olivia

I stared at Serena's anguished expression without a clue how to respond. Unraveling my life had been difficult at best, but talking to my daughters, well...I figured we had to hash things out, even if I hadn't recovered completely. I took a deep breath and focused on her words. *My words came more easily now, and I was grateful.* Dr. Sturgis had warned that the post-coma aphasia might depart suddenly, or linger. Mine, happily, was on its way out.

"I know it's been hard on you, Mom, but it's been hard on us too." Serena slid her eyes sideways at her sister sitting beside her on the couch in our den.

Lilly wiped a tear off one cheek.

Serena continued, "You don't remember our friends, who we like or don't like, their moms...it's crazy!" She rose, stalked around the den, and leaned against the wall, as gorgeous as a magazine ad model with her startling eyes and perfect hair.

"I understand. That's why I wanted us to have these regular talks." The strain on their faces broke my heart.

"Girls, I have this...*deep love* for you both. It's *unwavering.* Just because I don't remember specifics doesn't mean I don't remember being your mom." I put my hand on my chest. "I *feel* it. In here."

"But do we have to, like, start over?" Lilly asked. "Like, every day?"

Serena huffed out a breath, walked to the loveseat, and sat. "Of course not," she said to Lilly. "We just have to be patient."

Painful as it was, I needed to get the girls to open up—not only to rebuild our relationship but also because I needed *their* memories to trigger mine.

"Girls, I am hoping you can kind of...carry me for a while. The memories are coming back, but some are stubborn."

"Like what?" Lilly asked.

"Like the dreams I keep having." I shook my head in frustration. "I don't get them at all. But I've figured out that the memories I can't remember are the more...difficult ones."

"Like the divorce," Serena said.

"Probably."

"Like the mean things Daddy's done?"

I looked at Lilly's earnest fourteen-year-old face and wished we didn't have to talk about things like this. "Something like that. I'm sure he wasn't mean on purpose, honey."

Serena frowned. "And he didn't intend to get involved with a twenty-five-year-old slut on purpose, either?"

"Let's leave that alone for now, okay?"

Serena stretched her arms over her head. "Whatever."

"I'm working on a time to get with your father and discuss things."

"Right," Serena grunted.

"Really?" Lilly chirped.

"I'm serious," I said. "It's tough because I do not know what I've done, what he's done, or how we even got to the point of divorce."

"We've *told* you, Mom," Serena snapped. "Over and over. He had an affair."

I sighed. "But what led up to it? We need to have an honest conversation about our marriage. I need to understand."

They mulled this over, one face earnest with the optimism of youth, the other weary and cynical much too early in life. A date popped into my head.

"Serena! Your birthday is in two weeks, right?"

Her mouth dropped. "You remember that?"

"Yes!" I clapped and jumped up. "Yes! Yes!"

All three of us broke out our best happy dance moves right then and there.

Chapter Twenty-Five

The after-work crowd packed the Artful Gourmet Restaurant in Owings Mills until there was barely room to stand, but I managed to snag a corner table in the bar.

I had distinct memories of this place and found it easily. The sticky memories involved relationships, not the lay of the land.

Mom had helped me figure out my options before she returned to West Palm Beach, since apparently, I had been a basic Stepford Wife in my pre-coma life. She'd led me through financial management 101, patiently explaining how things like insurance and paying bills online worked. She also told me that I previously had *no* access to money. Her pleas to get me to change that had fallen on deaf ears, she'd said. Aghast at this tidbit, it spurred me to find out everything I could about a wife's rights in Maryland. My name was on one measly checking account, the one Monty put money in for me every month. When I'd found Monty's old paystubs in the filing cabinet in the back of our closet, I couldn't believe how much he actually brought in. My anger had climbed from simmer to slow boil.

Maybe I've come late to the party, but I still have time to dance on a few tabletops, Monty, I thought with a smile.

The insurance had decided to pay out on my old car—still missing—and through a lovely and fortuitous mistake, the payout landed in my checking account. Maybe I wouldn't tell him. Perhaps it would be better if he were to keep thinking of me as passive and helpless; unable to figure out how to buy her own car. Mom had been my staunch ally at the car dealership, and we'd bought a three-year-old, low-mile Honda Accord.

I grinned. I'd always wanted a Honda, but Mom told me Monty was an 'only buy American' guy.

The girls had been generous with their closets until I could re-stock. *My* closet had been quite the disappointment. Most of it went straight to Goodwill. Before she went home, Mom and the girls had helped me shop for things a little more my style...or what it had become lately.

For this occasion, I'd borrowed gold, dangly earrings from the girls, and a top with a shirttail hem that complimented my fitted, black stovepipe pants. Serena and Lilly had insisted on doing my hair, coaxing my unmanageable corkscrews into loose waves with their curling wands. Judging by the look on my server's face as he wove his way through the crowd to my table, their efforts had paid off.

Five minutes later, Monty powered through wall-to-wall people in the bar to my table in the corner. "Why didn't you let me know you'd be in the bar? I spent ten minutes trying to find you," he complained, jabbing a finger in the direction of the attached restaurant area.

I shrugged. "Didn't know it'd be a big deal."

He scraped out a chair. The server slid my wine in front of me with a flourish and an appreciative, lingering gaze, then asked Monty what he'd like. Monty ordered a Stella. The server disappeared.

I picked up the glass of wine and tilted it toward him. "*Salut.*"

He squinted and crossed his arms. "I have never heard you say *salut* in my life. And you're *drinking?*"

I shrugged. "I hear I wasn't the most exciting woman on the planet."

He put his elbows on the table. "Well, let's just say you were very—"

"Dependable?"

He colored. "Yes. Always."

"Pleasant? Understanding? Patient?"

"Yep."

"I think that particular perception may change."

Monty frowned.

The server thunked the beer in front of Monty and left.

"Okay," I said. "So here we are. What do you suggest we tackle first?"

He cleared his throat. "We need to talk about...well, finalize issues concerning the divorce."

"Of course." I sipped my wine. The server took our appetizer orders. I watched him walk behind the bar.

"Are you listening?" Monty waved his hand at me to get my attention, like I was two years old.

I ratcheted my gaze back, amused. "You start."

He drew a stuffed folder from the black leather bag he'd brought in and shuffled through them. He pulled out two pages stapled together and laid them in front of me.

I scanned them. "This is an Addendum."

He nodded.

"Addendum to what?"

Irritation flashed across his face. "You have the original Motions."

I glared at him. "You mean you didn't bring all the paperwork with you?" I let the document fall to the table. "How am I supposed to know how the Addendum fits if I can't remember the other stuff? Give me a break, Monty."

"Fine." He reached into his bag, pulled out a pile half an inch thick, and tossed it on the table. "There."

I traced the title of the top document with my fingers. The words DISSOLUTION OF MARRIAGE flapped from the page like a flag of surrender, Plaintiff and Defendant in bold Times Roman in a text box. Monty was named plaintiff. I grabbed the Addendum, rolled everything up, and stuffed the wad into my purse.

"I'll have to take this home and read it, Monty. I need to make notes, think about things, and talk to my attorney."

His eyes widened. "You mean you haven't already done that?"

"How would I know? Memories are starting to come back...a little." I drained my wine, caught the server's eye, and pointed at my glass. He scurried over with a refill. "A *little*," I emphasized. "There's still a big, blank space when I think about the divorce. All I know is that you had an affair. I'd like to know why."

Monty's mouth hung agape in that way men have when they are blindsided.

The server brought appetizers. We spent a few minutes munching in silence.

"You don't remember the dinner at Fells Point?"

"Fells Point? What is that?"

He huffed. "An area downtown. Close to where I work."

"O-kaaay...so what does that have to do with anything?"

"Everything!" He pounded the table with a fist. A few people turned around. I pointedly stared at his fist, then his face. A flush of red crawled up his neck. He looked away.

"I didn't know you were, well, so far gone."

I bristled. "I am not *far gone*, Monty, I am recovering from a *coma*. Forget that little detail?"

"No, of course not. It's just that I—"

"This is ridiculous." I hissed, pointing to the cylinder of paperwork sticking out of my purse. "I have no clue where my original copies are, if I ever got copies at all, so I need time to review."

"You had them, Olivia. Why would I—"

"I don't know. That's the point. I don't know enough yet to know why you would do anything. But I am not going to sit here and watch you have a tantrum because my memory has been compromised. I guess this behavior is typical?"

I drained the rest of my wine and motioned the server to bring my check. Monty mumbled that he'd get it. I told him not to bother, and we waited in silence.

I flopped my debit card down and snapped the black folder shut, then handed it to the server. Monty, frowning, kicked back the rest of his drink and crossed his arms. He asked about the girls. I gave him a generic response. We lapsed into another uncomfortable silence. The server scuttled to our table, pointedly thanked me and not Monty, which I thought was awesome, and as soon as I could I flounced out the door. I resisted the urge to turn back and watch Monty's reaction to my abrupt exit. The server winked as I left. I laughed and winked back.

Traffic was light on the way home, fortunately. The brick wall I'd mentally erected for my talk with Monty started to crumble at a long stoplight in Reisterstown. The way he moved his mouth, his gestures...patterns of speech...all wretchedly familiar. Then, in spite of my best efforts, the wall collapsed, and I was lost in the past. When the light turned green and I didn't notice, the car behind me honked. I pressed the accelerator and plowed ahead, through a flood of memories so wounding it threatened to drown me as I drove.

I white-knuckled the thirty-minute drive to Fells Point to meet Monty, my pulse racing. Since I hadn't driven to downtown Baltimore in, well, years, the glut of traffic caused minor anxiety attacks every time I changed lanes. When I finally found a parking place after circling the area like a confused homing pigeon, I breathed a sigh of relief.

Still gripping the steering wheel, I stared at couples walking by hand-in-hand, at the slice of ocean I could see, at the quaint brick storefronts that lined the streets. It was an entirely different world, one I'd almost forgotten, just half an hour from my life in charming, quiet Glyndon.

I peeled my sweaty hands from the steering wheel and thought about Monty's call earlier.

"Um, remember that place we went a few years ago?" he'd asked. "The one downtown? I think it was called Meli or Mezze or something, in Fells Point. I thought I might meet you there tonight."

"Really?" I'd squealed in delight. It had been a long time since he'd asked to take me to dinner. "What time are you thinking?"

"Seven-thirty? Meet me there." He ended the call.

Maybe things were turning around, I thought. Maybe I'd imagined the mysterious late nights, last-minute trips with few details, or all the times he'd missed Serena and Lilly's volleyball games. Maybe, like me, he wanted to hit the reset button on our marriage.

After dropping several quarters in a meter, I carefully picked my way over two blocks' worth of cobblestone streets, bemoaning my lack of foresight. Cobblestone streets might be historical and quaint and all that, but they were a nightmare in heels.

The ponderous wooden door creaked as I pulled it open. My eyes took a few seconds to adjust. The room was darkly intimate. Dark wood floors, dark wood walls, bright brass accents. Four or five men sat on barstools. As one, they eyed me from top to bottom, then turned in the other direction. I looked down, tugging self-consciously at the gauzy top the girls had loaned me for an unheard-of night out with their father. Had I worn the wrong thing? Was it too young for me?

A hostess approached. "Olivia? Right this way," she said with a gracious sweep of her hand.

I beamed like a lighthouse, straightened my shoulders, adjusted the too-snug waist of the tight, black pants I'd borrowed from Serena, and followed her into an airy room populated by round tables dressed in starched, white tablecloths.

Monty rose when he saw me and waved a hand toward the chair across from him. He did not smile. I glanced around the room as I sat.

"This is nice. It's been so long since I've—we've—been here. Nothing looks familiar." I smiled, hooking my purse by its strap on the back of the chair. It promptly fell to the floor. I picked it up, rehung it. I felt my cheeks grow warm. "Am I late?"

Monty shook his head. "No. Just got here."

A waiter approached our table. Young and thin, white shirt, black slacks. Wispy goatee that matched the slacks. He rattled off specials, handed us menus, and took our drink orders. Sparkling water for me. Martini for Monty.

I arranged my napkin in my lap and leaned forward on both elbows. "So. How was work? You said you had to work late?"

"Yeah. New boss. You know how it is."

"No. Of course I don't know how it is." I smiled at my slight joke about being out of the loop on his life. Over the years, he'd stopped talking with me about work.

He did not acknowledge my joke.

I put my hands in my lap and stared at them. The waiter returned with our drinks, silent as a wraith, then slipped away. I reached for my glass, my mind fizzing. What was the matter with Monty? Like me, was he having trouble remembering how to act on a romantic night out? I smiled. That was probably it.

After an awkward pause, we told each other our dinner choices like strangers on a first date instead of a married couple with a twenty-year history. We chatted about the girls, a source of irritation for me since his work hours had nearly eradicated his involvement with them. When our conversation sputtered to a stall, my woman's radar bleeped a warning.

I ignored it.

We nibbled our food like nervous rabbits. The waiter cleared our plates. Monty ordered another martini. I declined a refill of sparkling water.

"Dessert?" Monty asked.

"No, thanks."

Monty slammed back his second martini and gave me a look that I couldn't decipher at all. He cleared his throat. Reached for his water glass and drank. A sheen of moisture dampened his fingers when he withdrew them. He grabbed his napkin and dabbed his hands. Then he meticulously folded it and laid it on the table with a pat.

"Olivia," he began, "I know things haven't been, ahh, quite as they should be between us for some time." His hands death-gripped back to the napkin.

I thought a few seconds about where this train of thought might lead. Maybe an apology? I brightened. "You think so? Maybe you're right. I guess every marriage goes through this kind of thing."

"Well, probably," he agreed. His eyes raked my form, then looked away. "But wouldn't you think a phase shouldn't last quite this long?"

I stared at him a few seconds before speaking.

"Well," I volleyed, "every marriage is different. Don't know that I'd put a clock on how long a phase should be." I didn't know what to do with my hands. They splayed in separate little rooster tails on top of the table.

Monty cleared his throat. He pushed the napkin—now a crumpled heap—aside. He stared at a spot on the wall behind me, the ruts between his eyebrows deep and troubled. A nest of centipedes crawled into the pit of my stomach.

"This is difficult, Olivia, and I ask that you hear me out. Please."

"Oh Monty, it's just a phase," I interjected with a whiff of desperation. "It will pass. We can go to counseling, or schedule in more time for each other, or..." my eyes darted around the room, "Like tonight! We can start dating again." I pried

his locked hands apart and took them in mine. "We could use a fresh start," I said, my voice too bright and too brittle.

He sighed.

"We can turn back the clock." Don't babble, I warned myself. He doesn't like babbling.

"This is so hard." He removed his hands from mine. "So I'll just come out and say it. I've met someone. I want a divorce."

I went completely still, the words registering with a slight delay. One at a time they pegged like a ball-peen hammer tapping in rivets. I've. Met. Someone. Three small words that had no right to represent such a noxious mix of desertion and lies. Impossible, my mind insisted. After twenty years? This happens to other couples, but not us. I felt tears welling and blinked them away. The crawling sensation in my stomach edged up my throat. I politely excused myself and walked to the ladies' room. I made it to a stall and closed the door before dinner exploded from my mouth.

I picked myself up from the bathroom stall floor, rinsed out my mouth, chewed an Altoid, and reapplied my lipstick. Focused on the muffled din of restaurant activity and soft jazz playing on the other side of the door. I breathed in slow. Out slow. In slow. Out slow. Scrutinized myself in the mirror surrounded by soft lighting designed to minimize the effects of aging, or in my case, devastation. My eyes, wide and staring, did not blink. Maybe I was in shock. I put a hand on my chest. My heart was not racing. On the contrary, it had slowed to a death march. The fresh lipstick only intensified my ghostly pallor. I grabbed a tissue and blotted.

Did I think fresh lipstick would change Monty's mind?

My thoughts scrabbled about in my head, and my stomach clenched its protest over Monty's admission. What reaction was appropriate? Would a wronged wife leave without a word? Would she stride back to the table and toss a drink in his face? After a while, I left the bathroom and walked back to our table.

"You okay?" Monty asked.

I couldn't answer that.

He reached across the table for my hand.

"Olivia, I can't tell you how sorry I am about this, but it's the best thing. For

115

both of us. This...this isn't a marriage."

I slid my hand from his. "It isn't? Then what is it?"

Monty threw his arms up, angrily. "You know what I mean."

I straightened in my chair, determined not to cry. "I don't, Monty. I don't know what you mean."

He sputtered something unintelligible. "That's the problem. Unless I spell everything out for you, you don't get it. It's hard to define. Like...you are not there, anymore. It's just gone, whatever we had." He placed his elbows on the table and tented his hands. "You're satisfied with this?"

I gaped at him and stuttered, "What...do you m-mean by this?"

He waved his hand around in a circle. "Our life. See? I have to explain freakin' everything to you."

A tear straggled down my cheek. "Why wouldn't I be satisfied with our life? You've never said anything about...never indicated—"

"Why in the world would I have to say anything," he hissed. "It's obvious." He slapped the table lightly and laughed. "To everyone but you, of course."

"The girls..." I paused. What would happen to them? How would I manage? "The girls haven't noticed anything. And our friends..."

He blew out a rude noise. "Our friends? Are you kidding me? Those cows aren't my friends. Their husbands need to wake up and smell the coffee."

"What on earth do you mean?"

"Exactly, Olivia." He signaled the waiter for a check. "My point."

Indignation crept into my voice. "People have to communicate to understand each other. We never even talk." I felt as if I were in a bad soap opera. This wasn't happening to me. To us.

"Think about our sex life." Monty spat the words. Each one felt like a blow. I ducked my chin. "You of all people should realize it's not exactly off the charts."

My forehead furrowed. Hadn't I willingly obliged? Was it my fault he hadn't been interested the last ten months? My head started to pound. I pressed my fingers to my temples.

"Oh sure, act like you don't know what I'm talking about!" Monty reached across the table and pulled my hands down. "I need you to listen to me, Olivia."

I put my hands in my lap.

He groaned. "Anyway, I wanted to do something nice for you before we...well, before we go our separate ways."

The waiter approached and handed Monty the small black folder containing the bill. Monty placed his debit card inside, snapped it shut, and gave it back.

My tongue had glued itself to the top of my mouth. For so long, I'd hoped for more from Monty—more conversation, more affection, more attention, something. But divorce? How long had he been thinking about it? How long had he been seeing someone? My mind was so blown that I couldn't summon a coherent statement. So I sat in my cushioned, trendy chair with my arms crossed, staring at him.

"Well, that's it." Monty pushed back his chair, relief etched on his face like he'd successfully completed a distasteful task.

"I've rented a one-bedroom in Ellicott City for the time being. I'll start moving out this weekend. Until then, I'll sleep in the extra bedroom."

And just like that, my life fell apart.

✳ ✳ ✳

As I turned onto my winding, graveled driveway, I realized I'd been sobbing through the last five miles. I sniffed loudly, wiped the back of my hand across my cheeks, and groped for a Kleenex. "Some stuff I wish I didn't remember," I mumbled with a sigh. I parked the car and spent a few minutes studying my cute house, the jumble of flowering bushes in the front yard, the path leading to the front steps and the coziest front porch I'd ever seen. "What an absolute ass," I declared of Monty, and strode to my porch, my hand resting on the rolled-up divorce documents in my purse. I pulled them out and waved them in the air like a baton. "The pen is mightier than the sword!" I yelled, then wondered what I meant by that, exactly. Still frustrated at the occasional post-coma lapses, I continued, "You'll see what I mean, Monty!" and stormed into the house.

Chapter Twenty-Six

"One thing's for sure," Detective Faraday murmured appreciatively as he drove through Maryland's manicured horse country hills. "It's beautiful out here, where she lives."

He'd called Westminster PD Criminal Investigations, who handled Glyndon's law enforcement, to touch base and let them know he'd be interviewing the victim of a potential crime committed in Richmond. They'd offered to accompany or drive him, but he couldn't think of any reason he'd be in harm's way, so he declined. Now, as he looked out at miles and miles of peaceful, thousand-acre estates, he was sure he'd made the right call. But it was good they knew who, where and what, just in case. He turned right onto a curvy gravel road and parked at the end of the driveway.

The redbrick home—a perfect representation of an 1800s colonial farmhouse—was narrow and spare and bookended by chimneys. A bright-white front porch put him in mind of the southern verandas and mint juleps of his beloved Richmond. An Abe Lincoln split-rail fence surrounded the house.

He grabbed his leather binder and his bag, slapped his khakis a couple of times to get rid of crumbs, and made his way to the porch. A cat balled up on the floor glared at him, rose, stretched, and padded away when he knocked.

A slender woman rounded the corner and walked to the door. "Detective Faraday?"

He inclined his head. "You look completely different from the woman I saw in the hospital. Are you sure you're Olivia Callahan?!"

She laughed. "Please come in."

The screen door squealed on its hinges as she pushed it open. Detective Faraday stepped inside. The entry smelled of melon and raspberry, a result of candles flickering on a narrow table. A framed watercolor print of Baltimore's Inner Harbor hung over the table.

Olivia stretched an arm toward a room on the left, a comfortable den. "Please, Detective, find a seat. Would you like tea?"

Her face glowed in the candlelight, framed by vibrant, coppery-red, wavy hair. Her lips, full and lush, parted slightly, waiting for his answer. She was lovely.

He stared, covering his amazement with a cough. "Sure. Thanks."

Detective Faraday sat in an oversized wingback chair. Olivia returned with a serving tray and sat it on the table between them.

"Sugar?"

"Sure," he said. She daintily picked up two cubes with silver tongs and dropped them into his cup, then poured piping hot tea over them.

"Cream?"

"No, thanks. Never been much for cream."

"Okay," she said, smiling, and prepared her own tea.

They sat, quiet and sipping. Hunter felt a little ridiculous with the ornate teacup, but he did his best. After a few minutes, he put his phone on the table between them and pulled out his notebook.

"I'll be recording. You ready to start?"

"Define ready," she quipped, putting down her teacup.

He chuckled. "This would've already been done if you'd been—"

"If I'd been able to talk or move or remember?" she interjected.

He studied her. "Your situation is very positive, considering."

She cocked her head. "Considering?"

"Considering that you were left at a *hospital*, and we aren't trying to find a dump site right now. That you survived a massive head injury. Now all we have to do is find who did this. Not outta the woods yet."

Olivia fell silent.

"Okay if I begin?"

She nodded and straightened.

Detective Faraday referred to a page in his notebook. "So let's start with who you were visiting on the weekend in question?"

Olivia paused. "Can't remember. I'm getting memory back, but it's limited to places and things. Relationships...people, memories are still shaky. I know I told my mother I was going away, and apparently I visited an old friend for that weekend, but I have no recollection of who or why."

"Okay. It's safe to assume you stayed in Richmond, since that's what you told your mother, and, obviously, that's where you ended up. I don't want to rule other locations out, though." Detective Faraday pried his eyes away from her and focused on his notes.

"Try smells. Close your eyes and think back to the weekend." He paused. "Put yourself in the car. What smells can you identify? What sounds?" After a pause, he added softly, "We'll have a follow-up appointment. No pressure today. Just try."

Olivia concentrated for several minutes. Detective Faraday studied her. Coppery curls fell to her shoulders. So thin he could see jutting bones where soft shoulders should be. She wore loose denim shorts and a pink T-shirt.

She grinned and opened her eyes. Hazel.

"Chicken."

"Excuse me?"

"I smelled chicken." She squinched her nose. "Clear as day."

"Hm. Could be a restaurant." He scribbled in his notepad and looked up. "Anything else?"

"I tried to see more, but it was foggy." Olivia shook her head and shrugged. "It's always foggy. But...I think I smelled something else, too."

Detective Faraday waited.

"Doesn't blood have a distinctive odor?"

Chapter Twenty-Seven

Olivia

The screen bounced shut behind us after a forty-minute interview. I watched Detective Faraday trot down the stairs to his car. He turned, smiled, and saluted me with two fingers. I waved goodbye as he sped off. Riot padded to the door and sat, tail twitching.

"No," I said. "You cannot come out. You wanna get eaten by a fox?" I plopped into my favorite chair and checked the time. Four o'clock. The girls would be home soon.

Detective Hunter Faraday had been a surprise.

When I'd stood beside him, the top of my head had only reached to his broad shoulders. I'd found myself wondering what was underneath the blue button-down, oxford shirt he wore. He'd even worn a tie but loosened it when he sat—such a sexy move, I'd almost giggled. The crease in his khakis was so crisp that it looked like it would have cut my finger if I'd touched it. I'd examined his strong, capable hands as he set up his phone to record. No wedding ring. He'd sat proud and tall, those amazing shoulders aimed at my pitifully scrawny ones.

I stared at my bony wrists and encircled one with my fingers to see how much my thumb overlapped. Definitely too much. While Detective Faraday had taken notes, he'd kept slapping an unruly cowlick of thick brown hair off his forehead. Laugh lines around his eyes—kind of amber, I thought—suggested he enjoyed life when he wasn't tracking down attackers.

He'd smiled easily and often and made me feel safe.

My brow furrowed. Did feeling safe seem foreign to me? Why? Being with Detective Faraday was like being with the ever-protective Dr. Sturgis, except he was closer to my age and crazy hot. I laughed out loud. Who was I kidding? He probably had a girlfriend, and besides, I could think of no worse time to start something.

The scrape of steps and breathless panting interrupted my thoughts. My girls raced into the yard, the gate squealing shut behind them.

"Hey, Mom!" Lilly bounded up the stairs and sat across from me, cheeks rosy from running.

Serena dragged behind, slowing to a plod.

"How'd it go today?" Lilly asked.

"Interview."

"Oh, yeah."

I sighed. "I wasn't much help. He tried to get me to tell him about the weekend I was gone, but I don't remember yet."

"You will," Lilly said.

I smiled at her. "I believe that."

I watched Serena plod through the gate and up the stairs.

"So, what's up, honey?"

She shrugged.

"Any birthday thoughts?" I smiled. "Just name it. What do I usually do for your birthday?"

She stared at the floor. "We used to have a big party at the pool. With you and Dad and..."

I nodded. "Okay. Is that what you want?"

Serena's fists clenched by her sides, and her eyebrows jerked together. "That's just it. You should *know* what I want!" She stalked into the house and ran upstairs. Riot scrambled out of the way.

Lilly watched her sister's retreat. "Mom, she's just stressed."

I smiled. "That makes two of us."

"Serena's been weird. She'll get over it, Mom."

I ran my fingers over my shorts. "Sure hope so. Is anything going on with her that you know and I don't? That maybe I should know?"

Lilly's bouncy curls swayed as she shook her head. "Nope."

"You'd tell me, right? I'm not sure I'd recognize if something's wrong..."

"I'd tell you, Mom," she assured me. "What's for dinner?"

"Haven't thought about it."

"Well, *that* hasn't changed, Mom."

"Very funny," I said, thinking about their tongue-in-cheek comments that referred to my inadequate cooking ability. "But you and your sister like to cook, right? That's a good thing."

Lilly laughed. We walked to the kitchen together.

It was getting easier with the girls, but Detective Faraday's words loomed on my fragile horizon like a gathering storm.

Not outta the woods yet.

* * *

The next morning, I woke to the sounds of rain pinging my roof and a day as chilly and gloomy as I felt. After I'd dragged on a sweatshirt and leggings, I fixed breakfast and tried to call Mom, but the call went to voicemail. Disappointed, I put the phone on the counter and made sure the ringer was loud enough to hear in case she called back. Through the front door, I watched trees tussle with the wind. Thunder grumbled in the distance.

I walked around the house, aimless and squinting, trying to remember rainy days of yore. What did I do when I couldn't get outside? I went in and out of rooms, touched things, peered out windows, stared at ceilings. Conjuring up elusive ghosts of the past was exhausting.

The doorbell chimed. I breathed a sigh of relief and ran to the door.

A pair of twinkly black eyes shimmered up at me from underneath a raincoat hood.

"Hi, Olivia." The short, plump woman grinned.

I waited for her to continue.

She shifted her weight. "I wanted to bring you, well..." She thrust a dish forward. A casserole, still warm.

"How sweet." I pulled open the door and took the casserole from her. "Please. Come in."

"I meant to come sooner, I did, really, but I've been so busy, the kids and everything, and housework, and the carpool committee had to meet and we had to think about things, because you know—well, maybe you don't know—Samantha's car is in the shop, and anyway, Johnny and I had to get in a vacation *sometime*, and…you know how it is." She paused to shrug out of her coat and hang it on a hook in the foyer which led me to believe she'd been here before.

"It's okay." I smiled. "I'm sorry, but I don't remember much, and you are—?"

"Oh gosh, I'm sorry." She stared at me for a heartbeat, then continued. "Callie. I'm Callie, one of the carpool moms? Our girls are good friends?"

I beamed at her. "I'd hoped I'd start meeting some of you so that I could maybe…ahhh…prime the pump."

Callie smiled. Her dusky blond ponytail swished back and forth as she talked. Judging by her tan, she was a regular at the 'Y' where the girls worked. She wore capris, sparkly flip-flops and a diamond the size of Delaware.

"I was just horrified, Olivia, to hear about what happened. Positively horrified. That's why it's taken a couple of weeks for me to get over here. I figured you needed time to adjust."

"I'm still pretty confused." I chuckled. "On the bright side, I *am* grateful I'm still alive and kicking."

Callie laughed. She crushed me in a hug which I stiffly endured. We walked to the kitchen where she pulled out one of my three stools and sat at the island that doubled as a breakfast bar. I put the casserole in the refrigerator, leaned over the island and hesitantly asked, "So, pardon the question, but were we—are we—good friends?"

Her eyes grew round. "So you really *have* lost your memory." A pause. "Wow," she whispered, and continued. "Pretty close friends, I think. We used to talk on the phone a couple times a week. We'd go out for coffee once in a while, do walks around the neighborhood, that sort of stuff."

I took that in, studying her, trying to remember. "You live close?"

Callie pointed a manicured finger, her nails blinding in their pink. "Yeah, a couple of miles down, on the right."

I played with my hands, wishing I had painted my nails.

"It's been hard trying to patch together my past. I feel like I'm so...*rude* or something...not getting in touch with people I used to know."

Callie reached out and patted my shoulder. "Hon, we all know you need time. We are here for you whenever you want to talk." She grinned and popped her eyebrows up and down. "I'll be glad to fill you in on whatever you want to know."

"That would be great." I laughed. "Where do we start?"

*　*　*

The rainy afternoon passed in a pleasant mix of girl talk and giggling and lots of tea. The picture Callie painted dovetailed with the information I'd gleaned from my daughters and mother. Boring, predictable, dependable Olivia.

It made me sick.

Callie, whose stream of information gushed endlessly, paused. "Okay, your turn. Tell me what's going on with you. I'll talk all day if you let me."

I thought a few seconds.

Callie leaned forward.

"Listening to your description of me...I seem so *different* now."

Her eyebrows raised. "What do you mean?"

"I'm not the same." I stared at the ceiling. "For instance, I love practical jokes. I'm a morning person. Apparently, I've been really rude to Monty..."

Callie's mouth hung open. She snapped it shut. "Totally weird. You wouldn't pull a practical joke on anyone if your life depended on it. Olivia, you would sit in one place an entire evening if you thought you could avoid a conversation with someone you didn't know. You're shy."

I shook my head. "I'm not."

She whistled softly. "Whoa."

"Yeah. Monty doesn't know what to do with me."

Callie's plump shoulders shook with laughter. She laughed so hard tears came. "Oh, my! Ohmigosh! I'm—"

I waited, puzzled.

"Olivia," she said, struggling to catch her breath, "oh, gosh girl, you don't know how long I've waited to hear you say something like that." She breathed a huge, deep breath. "All of us. We felt so bad for you with that idiot—oh, sorry, I mean—"

"It's okay. My mom has been quite vocal in her character assassination of Monty."

Her nose crinkled in disgust. "Well, I'd imagine so. And to top it off, he's bonking his assistant. Are you kidding me? The guy deserves no mercy."

"I'm kinda getting that."

"Good for you, Olivia. So, what's happening with the divorce? All we knew was he'd filed and moved out. You isolated after that. We were worried."

I shrugged. "Memory's gone."

"So you have no recollection of…anything?"

"I get hazy images, or bits and pieces. When I focus on them, sometimes a whole memory emerges, like a piece of a puzzle. I also remember locations—how to get there, that kind of thing. But when I met with Monty yesterday—"

Callie startled. "Wait." She put a finger on my forearm. "You met with Monty? *Yesterday*? What happened?"

I detailed our discussion. The laughing jag picked up where it left off.

"I love it." She flung both arms above her head and applauded. "You go, girl."

I laughed. "I guess. But I don't know how I *was* before. I am being myself the only way I know how."

Callie put a hand on her chest and exhaled. "Olivia, I cannot wait to tell the girls. We've got to do dinner soon, okay?"

I nodded. "That would be great. Would you tell them, though, that I'm not being rude if I do not remember them, or the carpool, or whatever? It looks like it'll take some time."

She assured me she would, promised to call, then dashed out the door and to her car. As she pulled away, she was already on her phone.

Chapter Twenty-Eight

onty struggled to get comfortable on a stool crafted to look like a human hand—his butt in the palm, his back resting on four erect fingers. He glanced around in disgust. How could she have suggested this lousy place? He decided that sitting in an oversized, orange, lacquered palm was kind of creepy—especially in dress slacks and shirt and tie—and slid off. A server seated him at a table. Where was Kirsten? He'd been looking forward to talking about his issues with Olivia all week; to get a woman's insight and understanding. He sighed. She should've been here thirty minutes ago. He crossed his arms and glared at the door.

Eventually, Kirsten walked in with two stringy-haired, stubble-bearded young men wearing pants a couple sizes too small and a couple of girlfriends whose skirts barely covered their backsides. He gripped his mug angrily and downed his beer. She could've mentioned that she was bringing friends. Monty signaled his server for the check, hoping she'd not see him so he could get the hell out. He didn't have patience for this.

Too late. She flung out an arm and waved him over. Frowning, he walked to the bar where they each sat on the creepy barstools.

"Hi, baby." Kirsten ruffled his hair.

He caught her wrist and pulled her hand from his hair.

She giggled and introduced her friends. They smothered him in a boozy group hug.

"Good to meet you," he said, masking his disgust at the smell of musk oil one of them—or maybe all of them—wore. He made a quick decision. "I appreciate that you want me to join, but…something has, uh, come up that

I need to take care of, so catch you later?"

Kirsten flashed her irritation at him. He kissed her cheek. She pulled away and focused on the bar.

"Look," he whispered in her ear, "I think we need to talk."

Her elbow jutted him aside. "Yeah, we do," she said. "Soon as possible."

"Okay. Where and when? The office is not an option."

"Don't care. You pick," she hissed, and turned her back on him.

A black anger puffed his chest. *Who needs this?* He grabbed her arm and turned her toward him. "You don't just turn your back on me, you little—"

"Hey, man, chill out!" The two dudes gawked.

Kirsten jerked her arm away. "Yeah, chill out."

Her grating laughter tipped him over the edge.

He thought of all he'd given up, the sneaking around the office, the depressing apartment in Ellicott City.

"I think we need to talk *now*," he whispered.

Kirsten ignored him.

"Kirsten!"

Monty's rage built as he faced the bent-knuckled back of her stool.

He shoved it around with such force that her drink flew from her hand, hurtled to the floor and shattered.

Kirsten screamed. "What. The. *Hell?*"

Monty widened his stance and held his ground. Kirsten's friends muttered amongst themselves, and with anxious glances toward Monty, they told her they'd see her later. She made mewling noises, but they left anyway.

She jerked toward him. "What is the matter with you?"

He threw some bills on the bar and gripped her arm. "Get your purse. We are going to talk. Now."

She huffed, stooped for her purse, flung the strap over her head and across her chest. "Fine. Night's ruined anyway."

He walked her, terse and stiff, to the courtyard. A street musician played a banjo and sang for quarters and dollar bills. Couples huddled on benches nuzzled each other. Snatches of laughter floated around them. He pointed to a bench. Kirsten sat ramrod-straight, lips clamped together.

The salty scent of Baltimore's Inner Harbor flavored the breeze around them. He was quiet, trying to get a handle on his temper. Kirsten studied her ever-present pink phone nestled in her lap.

"I'm sorry, Kirsten."

"You should be," she muttered.

"Well, I am," he said. "But you don't realize—you have no idea—"

She turned toward him. "That's where you're wrong, Monty. I *do* realize. I realize a lot of things. One, you are too old for me. Two, this is just... *wrong*. I don't know why I ever agreed to go out with you in the first place. It's so *totally* not working." She crossed her arms tight across her chest.

Monty studied the revealing, flimsy top Kirsten wore, the cheap, tight pants, and the hair pulled into a messy bun that spiked in all directions from the back of her head. She looked so different at work. Tonight, the way she was dressed reminded him of his daughter Serena. All resolve to make peace evaporated in the wake of his frustration. The black anger returned. Pent-up stress of living away from home and being away from his girls floated to the surface, along with anxiety about his mounting debt accumulation—not to mention that dating her could cause him to *lose his job.*

All that sacrifice for *this?*

"So, it's not working for you?"

"No," Kirsten mumbled, staring at the ground. "Not."

He thought of the jewelry he'd bought for her. Dinner checks he'd picked up. Clothes he'd surprised her with, from Nordstrom's. How he'd had to dumb down his conversation. His breathing quickened. The stars glinted like a thousand accusatory eyes in a black sky. *Calm down, Monty. Calm down.*

Kirsten alternately glanced at him and her phone, which lit up every few seconds. He ripped the phone from her and threw it on the cobblestone courtyard where it splattered pinkly into pieces.

"Ohmigod!" She jumped up. "That's it, Monty. We are so done. *Done.*" She turned to leave, muttering, "What a crappy start to my weekend."

Monty shot out his arm and grabbed her by the shoulder. "Oh, we are so *not* done," he said, pulling his arm back as far as he could, before letting his open palm fly, full force, into her cheek. She stumbled, then fell backward onto the grass. He watched as her cheek turned the color of her phone. "Now we're done."

He spun on his heel and strode away.

* * *

Monday morning, Monty stormed into his office early, slamming the door behind him as hard as he dared. Yet another sleepless night on the rock-hard mattress of his tiny twin bed in his tiny apartment. He walked to his desk, pulled out a drawer, and rummaged for something to staunch his headache. He found a bottle of ibuprofen and gulped down four of them with a dry swallow. He put a palm on his forehead and squeezed.

Something has to change. Monty wrenched his eyelids apart and walked to the window. Baltimore's Inner Harbor stretched before him, far below. Sailboats rubbed elbows with huge tankers, drays buzzed back and forth from Federal Hill, and water taxis trolled for passengers. A bevy of dragon paddleboats bobbed expectantly in the marina which would soon be populated by tourists and throngs of professionals. Around eight a.m., the homeless would show up to man the posts they militantly guarded like ragtag soldiers.

He liked the peace and quiet of early morning before the crowds came, but his thoughts were on Kirsten and their argument, and his early morning arrival provided no peace. Not this time.

How could I have been such an idiot? He wondered if she would even show up for work. She would be bruised and swollen. Assault. That's what she'd stick him with. How would that affect his record? The first thing she'd do is register a complaint with Human Resources, which would spur an investigation. He could hang his head and offer an apology. Grovel. That's what his life had become. A series of grovels.

Maybe he should just quit now, avoid an investigation. Or maybe he should head it off at the pass, go and deal with it before Kirsten said anything.

What if she doesn't go to HR? What if…he shook his head. *This is insane.*

Olivia had always listened to him with an understanding smile. Olivia had been gentle and kind. Intelligent. All things he'd taken for granted. He frowned at the memory of their chat at the Artful Gourmet. Maybe she'd had an off day. Maybe he had. He shrugged, pulled his cell from his pocket, and scrolled to her name.

He had no one else, he realized, that would even care.

Chapter Twenty-Nine

Olivia

"What's up?" I answered the call in the same tone I'd use for a pesky telemarketer call. I sipped my coffee and looked at the morning sun shining through the trees. The birds crowding the feeders. The porch was fast becoming my favorite spot. Maybe it had always been.

"Olivia?" Monty's voice sounded strangled at first, and then he sobbed.

I held the phone at arm's length, my mouth open. Why in the world would he be blubbering in my ear? *I'm the victim here, I think. Not you.*

After a few seconds, I put the phone back to my ear. "What's happened?"

He sobbed so hard I wouldn't have been surprised if the phone leaked water down my arm. I waited.

He drew in a shaky breath and blew it out. "I'm in trouble, Livvy."

Livvy? The man calls me Livvy?

"What do you mean, Monty?"

He blew his nose. "I smacked her."

My eyebrows shot up. "Smacked? As in *hit?*"

"She fell on the gr...ground." Sniff.

"Who, Monty?"

Pause. "Kirsten."

"Who is that?" I asked, though I had an idea.

He was silent.

"The one you had—are having—an affair with?"

"Yes," he whispered.

My eyebrows drew together. "Why on earth would you smack—um, hit her?"

I heard a tissue pull out of its box, and a honk.

"Just couldn't take her crap anymore."

I was silent.

He inhaled, exhaled. "It's over, Livvy."

"Well, that's good to know," I said. "And why are you calling me Livvy?"

"That's what I called you when...when we were happier."

I thought about that.

"I don't remember it," I said.

"That figures," he said. "Been a while since we were—*I was*—happy."

"I'd imagine so. Can't say, myself."

He was silent a few seconds. "Maybe this was a mistake."

"What? Calling me?"

"Yeah."

I struggled to hear my mother's voice and her endless references to appropriate scriptures, because I sure as heck didn't know how to respond to this situation. After a few seconds of deliberation, I cleared my throat and said, "Well, you want to come sit on the porch and talk?"

A heartbeat of silence. "You mean it?"

"Yes."

"I'll be over in thirty minutes," he said, and ended the call.

I stared at my phone, then lay it gently on the wicker side table. Had I done the right thing?

* * *

The shiny, black Lexus SUV threw gravel all the way up the driveway where it slammed to a stop a few feet from the garage. In a nod to civility, I'd donned a collared shirt and clean jeans and tennis shoes. I stood and attempted a smile as Monty erupted from the car.

"In a hurry?" I asked.

He took the stairs two at a time. "Yeah." He smoothed his hair, plopped into a chair and loosened his tie. "How about some tea?" He studied me, then looked away. "Like we used to."

I crossed my arms and stared at him. *We used to have tea and talk on the porch?* Finally, I murmured, "Back in a minute."

I warmed up the pot, replaced it on the tray I'd already prepared, and took it outside.

I plunked two sugars into his cup, poured tea, added cream, stirred. I paused in realization, holding the spoon motionless in midair. "I remembered how you like your tea, didn't I?"

Monty smiled. "Yes, you did." He leaned forward and sipped. "Delicious."

A rush of familiarity overwhelmed me. Tangles of memories suddenly shook loose. Monty sharing war stories about work, Monty hugging the girls, Monty mowing the yard. Monty grabbing my butt playfully.

Clear and compelling memories.

"Olivia? What's the matter?" He put his cup and saucer on the table.

I blinked. "To remember," I muttered, "is an interesting process."

He frowned. "I can imagine. I guess my being here is a trigger."

I nodded. "Obviously. I never know what's going to pop up," I said with a wry grin. "It's not pleasant."

"How does it feel?"

I shrugged. "You know, it was tough the first few days. Like I was in a dark tunnel on a runaway train. Had no control, nothing. Then…"

"Then?" Monty asked, intently watching me.

I studied him. Other than what I might feel for a casual acquaintance, I had no feeling one way or the other for this man.

"I'm different now, Monty."

He snorted. "No kidding. You are *way* different, you—"

I shook my head. "Yeah, I get that, but I'm not talking about the personality change. I know it sounds weird, but…I'm *really* different now. A new person. It's incredible. I cannot explain it."

"Oh, God," he muttered. "Sophie finally got to you, didn't she?"

I laughed. "Maybe. But I don't feel…don't feel *afraid* anymore."

"Afraid? Of what?"

I thought a minute. "I think I was afraid of everything. Life. Responsibility." I stared into his somber, black eyes. "*You.*"

His chin pulled in as if dodging a blow.

I sighed. "You don't have to understand, Monty. You don't even have to approve." I picked up my teacup and sipped. "Now, what about this… situation you're in?"

His stress lines softened. "I just needed someone to talk to."

"Okay."

"The first name that popped into my head was yours."

I was silent.

"I've…" He cleared his throat. "I've been a jackass, Olivia."

"So I've heard."

He squinted.

I continued, "Seems you've been a jackass, and I've been blind, deaf, and dumb."

He whooshed out a long breath. "Yeah, okay. I needed a friend, and I think you are probably the best one I've ever had."

I sipped, clinked the cup back into its saucer, and fiddled with it. Finally, I said, "I figured if it were me, I'd need a friend, too. That's why I invited you over."

Monty leaned back in his chair, arms hanging limp down each side. "I miss you, Olivia."

"I will try being a friend," I said, the words marching out before I really thought them through.

"Good enough," he said.

He talked through another pot of tea and beyond. Since I didn't recollect much of our life together, I found detachment helpful, my comments objective and unburdened by history. When he left, I felt a little sorry for him, like I would feel sorry for a neglected puppy. I couldn't quite figure out how or what I *should* feel, but at least I didn't hate him. As his taillights disappeared down the drive, my shoulders sagged in relief.

I opened the door. Riot raised his head and blinked at me, his version of a kitty-kiss. I picked him up and hugged him, hard, against my chest.

Chapter Thirty

Monty glanced at his watch again. Talking with Olivia had helped, but to face his accuser was something else altogether. Kirsten was due in the office any minute.

"This is what I get for dating my own assistant," he muttered, slapping a palm on his brown trousers and re-tucking his checked dress shirt. He rose from his chair, heaved out a great sigh, and walked to the window. Dark clouds had moved in. White caps chopped the water in the Inner Harbor. He pressed his cheek against the pane, craning his neck to see farther. Yachts bobbed and strained against their moorings along the marina, and very few people were out. A smattering of moisture dotted the window, and the sky grew darker. Within minutes, a driving rain spiked the glass.

He stepped away.

Kirsten arrived. He heard her quietly putting her purse away, the scroll of her chair's wheels on the carpet.

It's time to face her. He clutched his chest at the stirrings of a panic attack. "What have I done?" he whimpered.

Kirsten knocked softly on his door and pushed it open. Monty tried to straighten his shoulders and face her like a man, but it was no use. He was scared.

Her eyes widened when she looked at him. "Monty, what's wrong?"

He gawked, his carefully rehearsed reaction delayed. Anger, accusations of assault—even a lawsuit, or a cleaned-out desk, a summons, maybe. He'd anticipated these things, but concern? What was this about? He groped for his desk and sat on one corner.

Kirsten walked to him and put a reassuring hand on his shoulder. "Is this about the other night?" She shuddered. "Monty, I kind of...blanked that night. Whatever happened between us, I'm sorry." Her eyes puddled. "I have to control the drinking. I *have* to." Tears spilled down her cheeks.

Monty brightened. He could not believe his luck.

His shoulders straightened. He puffed out his chest, stood, and pulled her into a brotherly hug. "It's okay, Kirsten. We all have our challenges. Forgiven, forgotten."

She untangled herself from his embrace, wincing and patting the yellowish-gray bruise on her cheek.

Monty pasted on a concerned expression. "What happened?"

Kirsten shrugged. "I'm not sure. All I remember is landing on the ground. I remember you walking away at some point, and—"

"Yeah," he said. "I just couldn't handle, you know..."

She nodded. "I'm sure. I can be obnoxious when I'm drunk. Did you see someone, um, *hit* me?"

He feigned shock. "No! Of course not. Is that what happened?"

"I guess. I'm not sure how I ended up on the ground, but it probably had something to do with what happened to my face."

Monty leaned in and inspected Kirsten's cheek. "It'll be fine."

Kirsten cleared her throat. "I seem to remember a conversation we were having..."

"You do? What about?"

Kirsten squinted at him. "About us. About it not working?"

"Right. *That* conversation." He weighed his words. "Yeah, well, we ended it on a good note, don't you think?"

Her palm rested against the wounded cheek. "Guess so-o-o-o," she said, drawing out the word as she thought about that.

Monty beamed. "Take the rest of the afternoon off if you'd like, Kirsten. Hell, take a few more days."

"No kidding?"

"Absolutely. Go home and take care of yourself."

She grabbed her purse and shot down the hall.

Chapter Thirty-One

Detective Faraday dashed into the coffee shop ten minutes late with an apology ready, looking for Monty's little-thing-on-the-side. *You better stop calling her that,* he admonished himself, *or it'll come out of your mouth in this interview.*

He looked around the room, half-filled with patrons guzzling overpriced lattes, some with computers open, some with their phones pressed to their ear, others with earbuds. The rich smell of coffee and the sounds of obscure jazz put him at ease. He smiled and shifted his leather bag to a different spot on his shoulder. Couldn't beat Starbucks as a calm, neutral setting. His eyes landed on a beautiful young woman with thick, dark hair. She held her phone in both hands as if she was afraid someone might snatch it and blinked rapidly as she watched him. Gotta be her, he thought.

"Kirsten?"

She jumped up and extended a hand.

They shook hands. Hers was as cold and clammy as a dead fish. "I'm Detective Faraday. So sorry about the delay. Sit, sit." He gestured at her chair, smiled, and continued. "Can I get us both coffee?"

Kirsten dropped into her chair, laying her phone down on the table. Her hands shook a little, and she was dressed ultra-conservatively: navy pantsuit with white silk shirt. "Yeah. Make mine a triple-shot soy latte, no foam, extra hot."

He nodded, ordered their drinks at the counter and returned to the table.

"This won't take long, Kirsten. I appreciate you making time to meet with me."

She cleared her throat. "I, uh...sure hope everything turns out okay with, um..."

"Olivia," Detective Faraday finished for her. "I know this might be a little difficult, given the...situation."

Kirsten smiled. "Kind of a cliché, huh? Assistant dates married boss." She shrugged.

"It happens." Faraday rose at the sound of their names being called and returned with two steaming lattes.

"He didn't love her," she stated flatly, as if it justified the affair. She picked up her latte.

Detective Faraday smiled. "Could be." He pulled out his pad and pen.

"How long have you two been seeing each other?" He sipped his coffee.

"About nine months, I think. Romantically, anyway. I've worked for him a couple of years." Kirsten's focus darted to the door and back. Detective Faraday knew he'd need to make it quick; she was already planning her getaway.

"I assume you knew he was married..."

She nodded, both hands gripping her cup. Her long nails had little birds painted on them. "But he was miserable. She was...she wasn't right for him."

"In what way?"

Kirsten rolled her eyes and touched her phone like a security blanket. "For one thing she wasn't very...interested in sex."

Hunter wrote that down. "What else?"

"She was boring, he said. And shy. Monty is confident and successful. She couldn't keep him happy."

"But you can?"

She frowned and stared at the table. "Yes."

As she turned her head, he noticed the bruise on her cheek. "Something happen?" He pointed.

Her hand flew to her cheek. She blinked. "I'm an idiot," she murmured, her eyes pinned to the floor. "I can't even remember how it happened." She shrugged. "I run into stuff all the time."

Uh Oh. Here it comes, Detective Faraday thought. The wrinkle. It typically arose about one-third of the way into an interview.

"Okay, so to the point. I wanted to see you in person to ask this question: were you with Monty on the night that Olivia was dropped off at Mercy Hospital?" He recited date and time.

Kirsten picked up her phone and played with it. "Yes, Monty told me you'd probably ask that, so I looked it up."

Detective Faraday waited while she found a date on her calendar.

She giggled. "It was a Saturday." She wiggled the phone at him to prove it. "Monty got us a room downtown close to the office. The Four Seasons in Harbor East. We were there all weekend."

He wrote it down.

"Do you want the details?"

Detective Faraday stopped writing and looked at her. She grinned at him under hooded eyes. She was young enough to be his daughter, he realized, and he felt a pang of sympathy. An old story, but he wished Monty could have spared her the heartbreak.

"Not necessary, Kirsten."

She drank the rest of her latte. Was it his imagination, or was her whole body quivering from three shots of espresso? So far, he registered nothing but pity for the young woman. She didn't seem the type to be involved in an assault on the wife of her lover, or sharp enough to act innocent if she had. Kirsten seemed exactly as she represented herself: a young woman trying to make her way in a sex-driven world riddled with false promises and a warped view of real love. He sighed, focused on his notes, and resisted hating Monty Callahan.

He closed his notebook and put it back into his pocket. Kirsten straightened in her chair and smiled.

"We done?"

"Just about." Detective Faraday leaned in on his elbows. "How would you describe the current status of your relationship with Monty?"

Her perfectly arched eyebrows pulled together. "Good. Why?"

He studied her. She'd nested her phone in her hands, and her shoulders had rounded into a tense hunch. She was lying.

"I have a suspicion he's the reason you have a big bruise on your face."

Kirsten blanched. Her eyes darted wildly around the room. "He's not! It was an accident or something. *I can't remember,*" she yelped.

So much for avoiding a public meltdown. "Calm down, Kirsten. I'm not the enemy. Just trying to gather facts."

She crossed her arms and looked away.

"Are you sure you've told me...*exactly* what's going on between you and Monty?"

After a few seconds, Kirsten whooshed out a breath. Detective Faraday watched as relief relaxed her body. It happened when people needed to amend their stories. He could always tell. It was a gift.

"The truth is, Monty and I had a little...misunderstanding last weekend. But he didn't do this. He...he didn't see what happened, and I was too drunk to remember."

Of course he didn't. "So, what did he tell you happened?" he asked softly.

"Some random guy must have slapped me and pushed me down." She held up her phone. "Had to get a new phone. When I fell it broke. I barely remember." She paused. "He's a good boss, though. He gave me a bunch of days off after it happened."

An admission of guilt if I ever heard one. "Okay, Kirsten. We're done."

Kirsten grabbed her purse, threw her phone inside, and rushed out. He lingered over his coffee, pulled his pad back out, and started jotting down his thoughts.

* * *

Olivia's shady gravel road caused the shocks to squeak. The official Richmond PD-issued vehicle probably needed new shocks. He sighed and thought about his interview earlier in the day with husband's little-thing-on-the-side. She had corroborated Monty's alibi the night of Olivia's assault. He would follow up and verify their hotel stay, but he knew in his gut she told the truth. The cheek injury, though, had been problematic. Definitely pointed to aggression and battered wife stuff but, unfortunately, Kirsten's injury may not be verifiable. Who would believe that had been an accident? He felt the line between his eyebrows deepen. A victimized woman, that's who. One used to being treated poorly. Could Monty have lost it with Olivia, too? His mood and demeanor darkened with each question that raced through his mind.

He braked hard when he nearly rear-ended a parade of SUVs and vans notched between the trees along Olivia's lane. He shoehorned his car between them and walked the rest of the way.

Laughter and high, girlish voices trilled from the front yard. As he drew closer, he saw long tables placed in an L-shape, every inch covered with cake, paper plates, drinks, and gifts. Bits of ribbon and discarded crumples of wrapping paper dotted the lawn. A yellow balloon had unmoored itself and floated serenely toward the clouds. Olivia sat in the middle of a group of yakking women on her porch. Teenage girls chatted in clusters around the yard.

Detective Faraday frowned. Had she forgotten their appointment? His steps crunched on the gravel. Female heads turned, one by one. He decided to walk a few more feet and stop. Politely waiting in the middle of the driveway was a better strategy than inserting himself into a bunch of women and teenage girls.

Olivia shaded her eyes, jumped up, and scrambled down the driveway toward him. As she drew near, she slowed. Detective Faraday's steps crunched in tandem with hers. He stopped within a foot of her.

"Hi. Is there—" Olivia's puzzled look yielded to regret. "Oh, no." She clutched her hands in front of her chest like a penitent nun. "I must have forgotten our appointment! I'm so sorry."

"Guess I should've confirmed first." He glanced at the festivities. "Looks like a good party."

Detective Faraday's gaze slid appreciatively down the floral sundress she wore. He watched her blush. "So, reschedule?"

"Of course not. You've driven all the way from Richmond." She patted her cheek thoughtfully. "How about hanging out until the party's over? Things are winding down."

He walked behind Olivia to the porch and up the stairs. Noticed the warning look she shot at her friends in response to their amused glances.

Olivia turned toward him, then addressed her friends. "Um, this is Detective Faraday. We had an appointment." The women smiled at him, dipped their heads, and murmured niceties. "I forgot about it, so I've asked him to wait inside until the party is over."

Detective Faraday grinned. Apparently squashing rumors would be high on Olivia's list of things to do for the next few days. She led him down the hall and waved toward the den. Den on the left, formal living room on the right, kitchen at the end of the hall, he noted, checking his memory of the layout of the house from last time. Family portraits dotted the staircase wall. Bedrooms upstairs, he guessed. Olivia turned. Her cheeks were still flushed. "Can I get you something? Piece of birthday cake? Water?"

He picked a spot on her comfortable leather sectional and dropped his shoulder bag on the floor. "No thanks. I'm good."

She nodded. "Okay. I'll be back...um...when—"

"Take your time. You're my last appointment." Detective Faraday stretched his arms across the back of the couch and crossed his legs.

Chapter Thirty-Two

Olivia

I waved from the porch until every last vehicle left. Serena's party had been a success, but I was glad it was over. Hunter's arrival had been a surprise. I wondered if they'd bought my explanation, and decided there was nothing I could do about rumors. Let them think what they wanted.

As I headed inside to meet with him, tires raced up the driveway and skidded to a halt.

"Olivia! Is the party over?"

I stifled a grimace and turned around.

Monty trotted up the stairs with a wrapped gift. "Hey, sorry I'm late."

"No problem," I said stiffly. "I'll get Serena."

He scowled. "I know where her room is, Olivia."

"Rather you wait out here."

"Are you serious? I can't go into *my* house for *my* daughter's birthday? Come on, Olivia."

I moved between him and the door. "Rather not."

"We'll see about that," he said, and shoved me aside. Hunter stepped out quietly.

"Monty, Detective Faraday. Detective Faraday, Monty," I managed, so relieved I almost passed out.

The men shook briefly.

"Monty is, um, here for the party," I added,

I forced a smile at Monty. "I'm sure she'll be happy to see you. I'll get her."

Without a word, still looking at Monty, Hunter opened the door for me. Monty grunted and stalked to a chair on the porch.

Once inside, I let out the breath I'd been holding.

"These things are never easy," Hunter assured me as he stepped in after me and closed the door behind us.

I plucked at my dress. "And I'm not exactly…uh…*myself* yet."

"Should we pick another time?"

"No," I hissed. "If he has a problem with you being here, well, that's his problem, not mine."

"Understood."

Serena clomped down the stairs. I told her to talk to her father, *outside*. She tossed her head angrily and went out. Hunter followed me into the den.

I fell into a chair. "So sorry about that, really."

He was quiet.

"So where shall we start?" I asked.

"With tea?"

I laughed. "Coming right up."

* * *

An hour into the interview, I felt the blood in my body drain from each extremity to the point that my fingers and toes grew cold. "I think I—I don't know but, the room, it—" I rubbed my hands together and stamped my feet to get the circulation going.

My awareness shifted to the leaves rustling outside the open window. Birds chirping. Riot quietly bathing himself on the floor beside us. How, I wondered, could such calm exist when my mind thrashed and twisted like this? I moaned.

"Keep going," Detective Faraday urged.

I began shivering. I wrapped my arms around myself. "A man—I think I was at his *house*…"

147

"Good, Olivia. Keep your eyes closed. Tell me what you see."

Tears ponded, then spilled.

"You can do it," he said, his voice soft.

I hiccupped a sob. My forehead crumpled from the force of my concentration. Like the end of a carousel ride, the whirling figures in my head slowed and stilled. A man—the recurrent shadow in my dreams—loomed in the forefront. I watched in horror as color seeped from his edges and slowly filled him in. Mechanically, I recited what I saw. "Dark hair. No. Lighter. Curly. Pressed shorts, khaki." I squinted in confusion. "A blue towel?"

"Good," Detective Faraday said, nodding his encouragement. "What about the room? What do you see? What do you smell? Feel?"

I squeezed my eyes shut and pulled back the image. "Smooth. Shiny." In my thoughts, my hand trailed along the top of something smooth and gleaming. I struggled to identify it. "Um...stainless steel...a *kitchen*. It's a kitchen. Granite counters and stainless-steel appliances." I gripped Detective Faraday's arm. "Ohmigosh, I saw it!"

He put his hand over mine. "Congrats. Looks like you're on your way to a full recovery."

"I am. I am!" I fell back against my chair, my heart flapping like a wild bird in a cage.

"Good job, Olivia. Progress." He turned off the recorder and put it in his leather bag. "Don't want to overdo it. You're shaking. You need to rest."

A harsh knock at the screen door interrupted us. After an apologetic look at Detective Faraday, I walked to the door. Monty frowned at me through the screen. I'd sent Serena out more than an hour ago, and she'd already gone back upstairs. Why was he still here?

"Sure taking a lot of time in there," he muttered.

Detective Faraday cleared his throat and walked down the hall toward where I stood.

"That will do it for today, Olivia. We're getting there," he said, louder than necessary.

I shot him a grateful look. "Good. I appreciate your time."

CHAPTER THIRTY-TWO

Monty's frown deepened.

Detective Faraday paused, and cocked his head. "Left my bag in your den. Be right back..."

I stepped outside. Monty moved aside, but not much, like a disgruntled child in line that didn't want to give up their spot. His jaw clenched.

"How'd it go with Serena?"

He shrugged. "Okay. She's hard to get along with lately."

I said nothing.

He stared at me. I crossed my arms and held his gaze. Two could play this game.

Eventually, I sighed and blurted, "What?"

He nodded toward the house. "A little cozy."

"What do you mean, Monty?"

"Just sayin'."

"Just *sayin'* what? For God's sake, Monty, I can't figure out this... *doublespeak* thing that you do."

His eyes darkened. Menacing, flat. Like a shark.

"Still my *wife*," he seethed.

"Whatever." I turned to go inside. "It's time for you to leave, Monty."

He gripped my upper arm and spun me around. His breath was sour with alcohol or rage—or both—and my arm hurt from the force of his grip.

Detective Faraday exploded from the foyer, grabbed Monty's arm and twisted it behind his back.

Monty blanched. "What the hell, man! That hurts!"

He gentled his hold. "We all calmed down?"

Monty panted and looked away.

Detective Faraday released him. Monty brushed his shirt into place, rubbed his shoulder, scowled at us, and strode to his car. Fired up the engine. Gravel spurted in little gusts under the tires as he left.

"I could've handled him," I muttered, rubbing my arm.

He chuckled. "Yeah."

A breeze riffled through the trees. I sighed and looked at the sky. "I don't remember him, really. How he was, how he treated me, anything."

A chittering chickadee swooped down and landed on one of my feeders. "All I know is what I've been told, and it's not all that hard to believe after what just happened." As the words came out of my mouth, my mind tried to reconcile the sobbing and sorrowful Monty on my porch just days before with this threatening, angry Monty. What kind of man had I married?

"I'd be careful," he said. "Have you had your attorney file a restraining order?"

I thought about that. Had I needed to do that before my world had narrowed to a hospital bed? I shook my head. "I'll check."

"I'd get one as soon as possible."

I sighed and agreed. The red flare of a cardinal zipped past us to one of the bird feeders. The cardinal snagged a sunflower seed, chirped in triumph, and flew away.

"How close are you two to finalizing the divorce?"

"I've been putting it off."

"Maybe you should move it up your priority list."

"It appears so."

He was quiet a few seconds, then continued, "Put my number in your phone."

"It is."

"Good. Anything happens, I can put things in motion pretty quick."

I rubbed my arms self-consciously. "Thanks. I think he has a temper, but I don't think he'd actually...*do* anything."

"That's what they all say."

I blinked. Had I become a statistic? Just another assaulted woman who tried to believe the best of an abuser? That gave him chance after chance and didn't learn anything?

I closed my eyes and shook my head. Smiled at him. "I better go catch up with the girls. Thanks for everything."

We shook hands. "You're welcome. I'll be in touch. Call me if you have more revelations, okay?" He held my hand a heartbeat too long. "Keep your exterior lights on at night." He walked to his car, paused, and turned back. "Do you have a baseball bat?"

Chapter Thirty-Three

Olivia

I tossed off the comforter in frustration. Another confusing nightmare. The moon cast a silvery glow, and the reassuring night symphony of frogs and cicadas floated into the room. I stretched, then rotated my neck, still thrilled and grateful for the simplest physical movement.

The images in my dream faded. I rolled onto my back and slapped the mattress angrily. As much as I wanted to sleep, the dream might be important. I squeezed my eyes shut and concentrated.

The house smelled faintly of used cat litter. The neighbor I'd lined up to take care of our cat had dropped the ball, I guessed. Riot walked toward me, stuck his tail straight up, and walked away.

I laughed. "You're mad we left. I get it. I'll give you some space to pout."

The girls had disappeared into their rooms upstairs and I could hear them putting things back in drawers, shoving them shut, emptying suitcases. They'd slept most of the drive home.

Had I taken a trip? Where? I slowed my breathing and put myself back in the scene.

I saw my rambling old house, a two-story Maryland farmhouse, circa 1885, before we'd restored it. Good bones, the realtor had said. Really, really old bones, I'd thought.

We'd bought it twelve years ago. Close enough to the city to make a good living, Monty had said; far enough from the city to avoid getting shot. I saw us scraping and repainting molding, replacing crystal doorknobs, unsticking, stripping and re-caulking windows.

I opened my eyes. So, once upon a time, Monty and I had been happy and content, remodeling the house, working together. When had things taken a turn for the worse? Like storm clouds, memories floated across my mind.

We'd remodeled the bedroom closet. Rows of neatly hung suits and color-coordinated, starched shirts hung on his side, and the handy niches we'd designed as drawer space held his socks and underwear, all facing the same direction, all folded just so.

I smiled. His side of the closet long-empty now, I thought about *my* things, all stuffed and jammed in. No wonder I had been uneasy in my cavernous closet. He had probably neat-freaked out about my sloppiness over and over.

A breeze sighed through the window. Riot, curled in a tight, fuzzy ball at the end of my bed, lifted his head, licked a paw, and put his head back down.

My eyes fell to the dresser that flanked the wall. Ancient, claw-legged, and marble-topped, I wondered if it was one of the many antiques Monty and I had restored. I stared at the dresser for several minutes. The memories tugged at my brain. I closed my eyes and waited.

I saw a crisp, white rectangle with black lettering—a business card. I picked it up with a smile, my fingers caressing the letters. Niles Peterson, Heritage Fund Group. Richmond address. I laid it carefully on the dresser in the empty space where Monty's caddy had been before he'd moved out.

My eyes popped open.

Niles. My mother had told me about that business card, but her call had been a dead end. A random meeting on the beach that I didn't remember. Had Detective Faraday interviewed him?

I pushed my hair off my face. Why would the thought of that business card cause stress and...some other feeling I couldn't explain? I rose from the bed, pausing to grab my fuzzy robe and the notebook and pen in my nightstand. I wanted a cup of tea and my porch. Passing by my daughters' bedrooms, I heard their soft breathing and smiled. Wee-hours house noises and squeaky stairs whispered in the dark. I paused and listened intently, thinking about the shadow in my yard I'd seen—or thought I'd seen—sneaking around. After a bit, I relaxed my shoulders and continued into the kitchen.

I fixed chamomile tea and carried it outside. The moon shimmered behind a billow of clouds. By the time I took a couple of sips, the clouds had parted, revealing a full and brilliant moon. I burrowed into my chair and listened to the frogs. Then I wrote down everything I could remember.

* * *

"I clearly saw this guy's business card in my dream. Why would that be?" I asked, sipping my morning coffee.

I heard the creak of Detective Faraday's chair through the phone. "I'm not ruling anything out. But your memory is unpredictable. Maybe he was looking for clients, maybe he wanted you to contact him for personal reasons. Do you remember what he did for a living?"

A chill zipped through me. "No, but my mom called him when they couldn't find me. He's an investment advisor."

"She told you that?"

I was quiet.

"So, don't you think you remembered his card through her, rather than—"

"Maybe," I blurted, irritated. "The experience just seemed so…well, intimate."

He paused, then I heard him rap his desk with his knuckles. I barely heard him when he whispered, almost to himself, "We'd need to move quick."

"Move quick on what?"

He cleared his throat. "Are you up for a trip to Richmond?"

I was quiet. My heart shimmied in my chest.

"I know it's a lot to ask, Olivia. It's just a crazy idea."

"So—if I had flashbacks or something? And then—"

"And then we'd call for backup and an investigative team to snoop around. They would be on alert and ready."

"Detective, I—"

He groaned. "Would you call me Hunter, please?"

In spite of the tension, I laughed. "Hunter, I—what an incredible name for a detective. Did you ever think about that?"

He sighed. "No one lets me forget."

"I like names, I—" A thought gripped me. I clapped my mouth shut.

Hunter's voice softened. "What's going on, Olivia?"

"Let me call you back."

* * *

Some memories dangled just beyond my reach, like that last juicy peach high on the tree, and some stabbed and prodded like thorns. This one was about to cut my finger off.

"Niles." I waited. "Niles…Niles." I clutched at what I'd said to Detective Faraday about how I liked names. *Something about names.* What was it about Niles's name? I pounded my fist on the wicker arm of the chair in steady rhythm, as if I needed a cadenced backdrop to remember things. I slowed my breathing.

I heard the rushing of the surf, smelled it. A beach. Sand beneath my feet. Running. *Running had been in one of my dreams.* Was I a runner? Sand, hard and firm, beneath my feet. Bending over, hands on knees, breathing hard. Someone handed me a bottle of water. *Niles?*

My eyes popped open. *No! Don't interrupt this!* I closed them and pulled the scene back into place. Beach. Niles. Our words bounced around like an echo in a cave. A close-up of lips in slow motion formed the word *Niles.* Niles. Dabney.

I snapped to attention in my chair. *We'd talked about names on the beach.* Sweat beaded my temples.

"Name's Niles."

I shook his hand. "Niles?"

He repeated his name. "I know, I know," he said. "My mom must have been enthralled with all things British." He shrugged. "And no, I am not from 'across the pond,' as they say."

I chuckled. "Caught me off guard. Niles is a great name."

154

"I'm okay with it. The kicker is the middle name."

My eyes grew round. "She didn't give you a...more, um, sedate middle name?"

He nodded. "You'd think, but, no. It's Dabney."

I blinked. "I cannot imagine...no, I won't...can't possibly ask—"

"My last name?"

I drank from the water bottle in my hand to mask a giggle, choking in the process.

He smiled and wiggled his eyebrows. "I'll tell you that next time we meet on the beach. Now, your turn."

I twirled the empty water bottle. "Olivia. Olivia Rosemary Callahan. At least for now."

Niles's eyebrows rose.

I sighed. "In the middle of a divorce. Don't know if I'm going to keep the last name. You might say my mother was a fan of all things Elizabethan." I shrugged. "My maiden name was Pellegra."

Niles laughed. "Keep Callahan, for gosh sakes. And you thought Niles Dabney was bad? Olivia Rosemary Pellegra? Wow."

A squirrel fell off one of my bird feeders and scampered away. I jumped.

Chapter Thirty-Four

"It's complicated," I said.

Lilly, wearing flowered leggings and a T-shirt, sat at the kitchen table. Her cheeks bulged with Raisin Bran. I watched with a smile. Sun dappled the kitchen through the window.

"So?" Lilly prodded, looking exactly like a human hamster with springy red curls. The word came out "sho"?

Serena stood in front of the open refrigerator, bored and staring. She'd been standing there for five minutes.

"Close the fridge, Serena. Pick something and close the door," I said absently, thinking about Lilly's innocent question: *Are you and Dad getting back together?* No words had come at all. None with which to answer her. "Just not time to answer that question yet, honey."

Serena nodded. "Yeah, I get that."

She pulled out a chair, carefully peeling a banana and smashing it with a spoon into a bowl of cottage cheese.

"Ewwww." Her sister eyed the unappetizing mound.

Serena shrugged. "Healthy."

Lilly grunted. "But disgusting."

"Whatever." Serena dug into her concoction.

"Seriously, Mom," Lilly persisted, "...is there a possibility?"

I sighed. "Honey..."

Serena chimed in. "Stop bugging her, Lilly."

"Girls, I don't know. I'm not ruling out anything. There's always a possibility."

"I'm kinda used to Dad not being around, actually," Serena said.

I stared at her. "You are?"

She shoved a spoonful of cottage cheese and banana into her mouth.

I continued, "That's the problem, I don't know yet what I'm used to and what I'm not. It's coming, though."

"You are *really* different, Mom," Serena declared, after she'd swallowed.

I smiled at her. "So I keep hearing. It's peaceful in this house with you girls. Memories are starting to come back already." I thought for a minute. "The traumatic stuff seems to be what I can't tap into."

"Maybe you're not supposed to remember that stuff," Lilly said.

"Maybe not," I agreed.

"Sure be easier to get back together with Dad if you didn't." Lilly stuck her tongue out at her sister.

The girls finished and put their dishes in the sink with a clatter. I hugged them goodbye. After they left, I felt lost. Bored. Frustrated. Faithful Riot curled around my legs. I knelt and picked him up, burying my nose in his soft fur. Serena's words rang in my ears: *Kinda getting used to Dad not being around.* I tried to patch together a picture of Monty being around, and how I would have approached life after he left us. Nothing presented itself but a murky rumbling in my head. I put Riot down and walked outside onto the porch. I heard an unfamiliar screech, shaded my eyes against a buttery sun, and looked up. A seagull swooped and cried high overhead. "Lost? Ocean is that way," I said, pointing in the general direction of downtown Baltimore's Inner Harbor.

And that's all it took. I ran inside, grabbed a comforter and fell into a chair in my den. The memories washed over me.

* * *

The girls were in their PJs, nodding off in front of a movie. A half-eaten tub of popcorn rested on the floor between them. Soft sounds of seagulls getting ready to bed down and the rush of surf drifted through the patio screen. My daughters wouldn't miss me, I thought. No one would know.

I wiped the kitchen counter, dried my hands on a tea towel, and stepped into the bathroom to look in the mirror.

Freckles had popped out on my cheeks and across my nose. I turned to one side and pushed my breasts together, bemoaning the weight loss that had stolen any hope of cleavage. Still, within spitting distance of forty, I wasn't such a bad-looking woman.

I popped out of the memory with a start. Clear memories of one of our vacations. One without Monty? Settling deeper into the chair, my hands clutching the armrests, I closed my eyes and dove back in.

Should I do this? I've been separated nearly half a year. I shouldn't feel guilty, right? The thought gave me goose bumps, but maybe it would be a good thing to try to socialize without Monty—to enjoy a lively bar scene and talk to people with a glass of wine in my hand. I'd always wanted to, but he'd barely let me drink alcohol, let alone talk to strangers in a bar.

Yes, a little voice inside me whispered, you should absolutely do this. It'll be fun!

With a glance at the girls, I walked to my bedroom closet and peered inside. Five changes of capris and five mom-tops. Not a single thing that I could classify as sexy.

Fifteen minutes later, I walked to the kitchen, a vision in tan capris and floral top. I'd borrowed a pair of sandals from one of the girls' closets instead of wearing my typical flip-flops. Not exactly sexy, but cute in a soccer-mom sort of way.

"Hey, going to hit the shops before bed. Think you'll be all right?"

They turned and blinked at me in surprise.

"What time is it?" Serena asked, squinting. "Do you have make-up on?"

"Seriously?" Lilly chimed in. "You're usually getting ready for bed by now."

I shrugged. "Just feel like it, that's all."

"We'll be fine." Serena waved her hand.

I felt dizzy with liberation. One little white lie wouldn't hurt.

* * *

I pulled into the parking lot and watched happy family units streaming into the restaurant—the same one our family had enjoyed for the past fifteen years. I swiped at my ever-present tears. Maybe this hadn't been such a good idea, to test drive my singleness.

I sniffed the rich smell of grilled seafood. A heavy bass line thumped from the band in the outdoor bar. Stars had begun to prick the soft, purplish twilight.

I breathed in a lungful of air like a big dose of courage and stepped out of the car. Alone.

To a bar. For the first time in my life.

I walked past the long line of people waiting for tables inside and made my way to the outdoor bar along the waterfront. The lights strung along the pier and encircling the bar blinked once, twice, then flared. A huge Live oak, heavy with Spanish moss beckoned me. I walked over and nonchalantly leaned against the tree, a direct countermove to the impulse I was feeling, which was to run back to the car. Without Monty, I had no idea what to do.I studied people. Watched how they acted with each other. One of my mother's patented nuggets of wisdom ran through my head: 'A decision to do nothing is still a decision, Olivia.' I adjusted my shoulder on the comforting sturdiness of the tree and pushed out my chest, proud of myself. For better or worse, at least I'd made a decision.

In retrospect, life with Monty hadn't required me to make many decisions. He took care of things. Wasn't that normal in a marriage? My eyebrows drew together. My mother told me I didn't have a 'normal' marriage.

What was normal?

"Stop it," I hissed to myself.

A couple sitting on a nearby bench stared at me. I smiled at them and squared my shoulders. I could do this. I took a tentative step toward the bar. Then another. The band appeared, picked up their instruments and asked the crowd if they were fans of the Rolling Stones.

I laughed. Monty would absolutely hate all this, but here I was, lapping it up. Voices all over the huge outdoor deck yelled encouragement. A raspy-voiced lead vocalist screamed "Brown Sugar" and they were off. People got up from tables to dance. A small, wizened man, his back bowed with age, shuffled around, bouncing out a percussive beat on a small tambourine. The back of his T-shirt said, "Life's Better High."

I took another step. A couple slid off stools and walked, arm in arm, into the restaurant. I made a beeline for one of the vacated stools, clutching my purse like a teddy bear. On one side, a man sat with his back to me, knee-deep in conversation. On the other side, the empty stool. The slightest relief zipped through me that I wouldn't need to talk to anyone just yet.

Three young female bartenders—wearing impossibly short shorts—worked the bar. A blur of motion, one of them stopped in front of me long enough to ask me what I wanted to drink. I ordered a glass of the house red and a water. An older, plump woman squeezed into a strapless sundress claimed the stool beside me. I smiled at her. She ignored me.

The bartender brought my drinks and left. I'd just settled into people-watching mode and taken a sip of wine when I felt a gaze from the other side of the bar. I scanned the sea of faces.

He waved.

The man who had given me a bottle of water on the beach, Niles. He'd made me laugh. His eyes had been the color of the sky.

I panicked. Should I wave back? I wasn't sure.

I waved.

He struggled off his bar stool and waded through the crush of people. Apparently, a wave meant that he should join me.

"Hey! It's nuts here tonight," Niles laughed.

I glanced at the seat Niles had vacated, already filled.

"It is." He wedged himself sideways and leaned against the bar. We shouted at each other, roared over the crazy-loud music.

He tilted his head back and swigged a bottle of beer. Dos Equis. "Where are your girls?"

"Home. I thought I should take the bull by the...ahh..." I couldn't remember the rest. Tail? Nose? My nerves were messing with my words.

"Horns," he completed for me. "So you're by yourself?"

Niles ordered another beer. He shouted something. I pointed at my ear and shook my head. He pointed to another seating area with a question in his eyes. Carefully juggling my wine glass and my purse, I slipped off the stool and followed him.

We walked through a quarter acre of beach and picnic tables and found an *empty table near the water. I sighed happily. Letting Niles take the lead felt like slipping into a well-worn glove. The music throbbed in the background. Out of habit, I silently asked myself what Monty would think about this, then told myself not to think about Monty.*

"At least we can hear each other now." I cleared my throat awkwardly. "The band is great."

"Amazing," he agreed.

"Amazing is a good word." A huge, Lowcountry moon gilded the gentle waves hitting the dock. Sailboats bobbed, their masts tilting left, right, left.

"You seem happy," Niles said.

I turned toward him. "I think I am."

"You think?"

A thin ghost of a cloud drifted across the moon. A smattering of stars glinted in the darkening sky.

"Well, yes, I think so."

Niles shook his head. "Don't you know?"

I couldn't tear my eyes away from the moon. "Kind of in between." I laughed and warned myself to keep things light. "Did I...did we talk about my upcoming divorce?"

"A bit. You've got a lot on your mind, I'm sure." He shrugged and drank his beer. "I've been there. You'll get through it."

"I'm not sure about getting through anything at this point," I murmured.

"Yeah," he whispered back. "I understand." He leaned in and touched his lips to mine. Gentle. "You are gorgeous, you know."

The feel of his lips, the smell of him, so disconcerting, so foreign. I inched away. My hands drifted to both cheeks and stayed there. "I'm sorry," I mumbled, keeping my gaze on the ground, trying to sift through my feelings.

He laughed, teasing. "Really? What for?" He scooted over and closed the gap I'd created. "I just kissed a beautiful woman. Why should you be sorry? I'm the one that's sorry. I may not see you again after this week."

I stared at the boats. Life was so simple for boats. "What am I supposed to do now?" I whispered to this man I barely knew, articulating aloud my inability to respond like a perfectly sane woman being hit on by a gorgeous man.

"Excuse me?" Niles raised his eyebrows.

"Nothing." I ratcheted my gaze to the moon and kept it there.

He smiled and drained the last of his beer. Niles twisted his body around so that he had a clear line of sight to the restaurant. "Sorry, but I gotta get goin'. I just dashed in for a quick drink and to listen to the band until Casey was ready to go." He turned and pointed toward the restaurant where his son had appeared with a couple of other boys. Niles waved at them. Casey began walking in our direction. "Enjoy your night."

I rose from the picnic table and dug around in my purse for my keys. Talk about confusing. Why had he kissed me if he had other plans? A simple kiss does not a commitment to an entire evening make, I told myself. Does it?

I cleared my throat. "Thanks. Good to see you again."

"Good to see you too, Olivia Rosemary. You drive safe, now. I'll probably see you at the beach tomorrow."

I stood on rubbery legs. A man besides Monty had kissed me. I touched my lips and smiled.

* * *

Pounding.

Incessant, insistent. Where was it coming from? I threw off the comforter and struggled out of a weird disorientation. As always, when memories struck, they left me with a hangover of sorts—an exhausting mental numbness that mimicked a headache, but wasn't. More like a vacuum had just sucked out my brain and hidden it somewhere. I slowly got up. More pounding. Front door. Okay. I could walk to the front door. One hand on my forehead, I stepped into the foyer and looked through the peephole.

For a moment, I couldn't move.

Two men stood on the porch, one playing with a toothpick in his mouth. They both wore aviator sunglasses. I inched the door open. They stared at me through the screen. The one with a shaved, shiny head removed his sunglasses and regarded me with watery, blue eyes. His nose, a bulbous mass, had been broken at some point and leaned slightly to the right. He sniffed and crossed his arms.

"Yes?" I squeaked as I edged back from the door.

The bulbous nose jutted in my direction. His lower lip stuck out a little with a wad of chewing tobacco.

"Mornin', ma'am. We're lookin' for Monty Callahan."

I blinked. These guys knew Monty?

"I'm sorry, but I have no idea where he is. He has not lived here for—"

Think, Olivia! What if they kick open the door and assault you because you told them there's no man around? What happens when the girls come home? I coughed, tried to bring my frontal lobe back to clarity. "I mean, he hasn't been here in a while. I do expect him at some point, though."

The nose bobbed in understanding. "That's fine. Are you his wife?"

I nodded. He dug into the pocket of tattered jeans and pulled out an envelope. He lifted it in preparation to slide it inside the screen. "Mind?" His scraggly eyebrows arched.

"Of course not," I said. I watched in fascination as huge, blunt fingers with dirty nails nudged the envelope through the crack. It dropped to the threshold. I was determined not to open the screen, and they seemed okay with that. He withdrew his hand and stuck it into his pocket. An elaborate skull tattoo adorned his bicep.

"Tell him we're sorry we missed him." Both men laughed about that.

They shuffled off the porch toward a faded blue vehicle of indeterminate age and reliability. I tried to memorize height, weight, race, distinguishing characteristics, and plate number so that I could tell Hunter. After the car disappeared, I retrieved the letter, slammed the door shut, and shoved the deadbolt home all in one panicked, fluid motion.

Five minutes later, I held a steamed-open, gummy envelope from which I extracted a letter written on lined notebook paper. I unfolded it and smoothed it out.

To Monty Callahan,
You know what you owe Horseshoe Casino and we been sent to collect. If you don't we can't be responsible for conseqwences.

This amount includes interest and you must pay us in person $100,000 in 10 days.

Sincerly,

WE WILL BE BACK

I stared at the words. A phone number and today's date had been scrawled at the bottom like an afterthought.

Had my husband been involved in something illegal? Had I known about it? I thought about the shadows I'd seen stealing across the yard. Hiding behind bushes. Maybe that hadn't been my imagination. Carefully, I folded the note, put it back into the envelope and pressed the flap down.

It would be better if Monty didn't know that I knew.

Chapter Thirty-Five

H er inhale was slow, and her exhale even slower.

Some memories returned subtly, like this one: listening to my mother blow out long plumes of smoke during marathon phone conversations. And me, jabbering like a blue jay until she interrupted to insert an appropriate scripture.

"I wasn't sure when to bring this up, honey, but since two thugs appeared on your doorstep...well, it's time to tell you." Long drag. Exhale.

I groaned and tucked my unruly hair behind one ear. It immediately sprang back. "What, exactly, is it time to tell me about?"

"While you were gone that weekend—"

"Richmond? Or, um...supposedly Richmond?"

"Yes. While you were gone, I needed something to write on. A drawer fell out of the sideboard in the kitchen when I looked for paper. Something was taped to the bottom which I thought odd, so—"

"So you had to check it out."

She paused. "Guess what was in there?"

"Mom. Seriously? How the heck would I know?"

"Fifty thousand dollars."

I blinked. "Excuse me?"

My mother was quiet.

"How is that possible? I mean, from what my lawyer's told me, he's got everything tied up in stocks, bonds, the house. There couldn't be that much cash lying around, could there? Do you think that maybe I—"

"No," she said, firm. "Not about you. There was a little slip of paper with a phone number on it, too."

I held my breath, thinking about the note. Was it the same number?

"You should call." She waited.

"I should?"

Silence.

I groaned. "What's the number?"

She recited a number with a Maryland area code. I entered it into my contacts. "Fine. I'll call."

"Good. Let me know."

The call ended. I stared at the phone, then tossed it on the carpet as if it were infectious, and pounded the arms of my chair like a child. "How much more," I screamed to my empty house. *"How much more can I stand?"* I demanded again, of whom I wasn't sure. God, maybe.

I stared at the phone, grabbed it and put in the number.

"Horseshoe Casino," a chirpy voice answered. "How may I help you?"

I thought a minute. "I'm looking for Monty Callahan. Someone gave me this number."

After a few beats of silence, the voice, considerably less chirpy; continued, "Mr. Callahan is banned from this casino. Who is this?"

I felt the blood drain from my face. I ended the call. My mind raced. The creepy guys? Does this involve them? Of course it involves them. What else could it be? Did I gamble, too? I shook my head. No way. I wasn't that type of woman. Was I? Maybe I had a dark side.

I couldn't breathe. Somehow, I needed to avoid a full-on panic attack. I found ibuprofen in the bathroom, took three of them and stared at my reflection. Pale as a ghost, my freckles stark and pronounced, hair springing wild. Even I couldn't stand to look at myself.

I ran to get the creepy guys' note. Sure enough, same number. My palm felt cool against my forehead as I pressed it there, thinking. I went outside. The simple act of sitting on my porch and staring at my little plot of land comforted me.

I called Mom.

"Wow, I had no idea. *Gambling.* Did you know?"

166

"Mom," I said patiently, "I repeat, how the heck would I know?"

"Well, things are coming back."

"Yeah, but in pieces. Not much makes sense yet."

She paused, then said, "I'm betting the envelope taped underneath the drawer was his gambling stash."

I felt dizzy.

"Are gambling debts a spouse's liability if—"

"Don't know. We need to find out."

My hands tightened around the armrests of my chair.

"Time to go see your attorney. When I get there next week, I can go with you."

"So you're still coming?"

I heard the flick of a lighter, sharp intake of breath. "Yes. And Dr. Sturgis is coming too, by the way."

I blanked. "What?"

"He's been very kind to help me know how best to...handle things." She blew out.

I thought about that. "I see."

"He thinks it's a good time to, ahh, to drive up and see how you're doing in your home environment."

Pause.

"Are you kidding? Doctors do that?"

Mom laughed. "This one does."

"Mom...what are you not telling me?"

She ignored the question. "He's booked a hotel. He'll be staying in Hunt Valley and, well, he'll be around all weekend."

My mind was officially blown. When had this happened?

Mom trilled, "It will be fine, honey. I will do everything. Let's focus on you. I'll be available to you, and so will he. Can you make an appointment with your attorney?"

"I will," I told her.

After our conversation, I started to schedule the appointment, but paused, thinking.

Guys like the ones that showed up at my front door didn't really care where they got their money. They just wanted the money.

What good would talking to Earl do? If Monty couldn't pay, would they come after me?

Chapter Thirty-Six

I ran up the stairs with a load of fresh sheets and dumped them in Lilly's bedroom, which doubled as a guest room when Mom visited. After a blissful, crisis-free few days, Mom and Dr. Sturgis were due to arrive any minute.

I heard steps on the porch, then the screen door banged shut.

"Mom! They here yet?"

Serena and Lilly trooped into the kitchen as I walked downstairs.

"House looks great, Mom." Serena grabbed an apple and bit into it.

Lilly opened the refrigerator and stared. I rolled my eyes. "Pick something and close the door!"

"Pool was crowded today," Serena said, chomping a crater-sized bite from the apple. "And the gym."

Lilly looked exhausted. She closed the fridge. "*That's* why the nursery was overflowing. We had so many kids, I couldn't keep up. Need a nap," she mumbled, yawning.

I laid my hand on her springy hair. "Go take one. And while you're up there, change the sheets on your bed. Your Grammy is sleeping there tonight. I just put fresh ones out."

Lilly groaned and went upstairs.

I went into the den and switched on the classic jazz station. *Done,* I thought, and ran upstairs to do my hair. I wanted the house perfect, and for Dr. Sturgis to see me complete and whole in my own environment. In regular clothes instead of a hospital gown. I needed to hear him tell me I was okay.

I swished on blush and tore my hair out of the all-day ponytail and fluffed it.

Fifteen minutes later, the screen slammed again.

"Olivia," my mother called, "we're heeeee-re."

I heard heavier footsteps and the sound of luggage rolling across the floor. I took a last glance in the mirror and ran to the landing.

"Hey!"

Mom smiled up at me. "Hi, honey."

"Your luggage can go in Lilly's room, Mom," I said, trotting downstairs. My mother tapped Dr. Sturgis on the shoulder, who picked up two bags, and started up the stairs.

"She got you trained already, Dr. Sturgis?" I joked as we passed each other midway.

He laughed, balanced the luggage, and pulled me in for a hug.

"Olivia, it's great to see you. You look *wonderful*."

I smiled, more than a little self-conscious greeting my neurologist on my turf and not his.

"So, where am I going?"

I led him to Lilly's closed bedroom door, nudged it open, and stuck my nose in—she was asleep with a pillow over her head. To her credit, she'd changed the sheets.

"Let's leave it outside the door. She's taking a nap," I whispered.

We went downstairs, where Mom gathered me into one of her trademark lung-smashing hugs. I commented on her new look. She smiled and said she didn't think West Palm sundresses would go over very well in Baltimore. I told her it didn't matter. She was quiet. My gaze slanted to Dr. Sturgis, whose entire focus had shifted to my mother. *Oh*, I thought. *Of course.* Guess it had been a long time since I'd seen my mom in full dating mode. Had I *ever* seen her in full dating mode?

* * *

Dr. Sturgis whistled as he transported six chicken breasts to the grill. He'd drowned them in an orange-chipotle marinade he'd whipped up. The fact that he was a hobby chef delighted me because now I would have to cook even less over the next few days. My mother followed him around like a puppy, exclaiming over every little thing he did. I found the whole situation darkly humorous. I poured myself a glass of wine and stepped onto the porch. The jazz I'd turned on earlier undergirded a glorious sunset, and I could hear my mom and Dr. Sturgis chatting as they babysat the chicken.

Serena sat on the porch stairs, texting. I sipped my wine and watched her. She slipped the phone into her back pocket and put tan arms around tan knees. Inwardly I sighed and outwardly, I smiled and sat beside her. My older daughter's convoluted thoughts left me off-balance, and I didn't yet know how to give her what she needed from a mom. But I had to try.

"How'd your day go, honey?"

"Fine," she said.

Silence.

"Just fine?"

Silence.

"What's up, Serena? You've been kind of distant," I murmured.

She laughed. "Distant? You're one to talk."

"True. But my distance is unavoidable. I'm trying. It's coming back, Serena."

"I know," she mumbled, her head dipping. "I just miss, well, how it was."

"How it was?"

"You know, when you and Dad..."

I drank more wine.

She twisted toward me. "You and Dad were happy once."

I waited.

"Lots of good memories, Mom. Not all that long ago."

I sighed. "I wish I could remember that."

"Dad just got stressed out at the end."

"Explain."

Serena twisted a piece of her hair. "He got mad easier."

I thought about that and tried to pull a memory from her words. Nothing

171

happened. I drank more wine.

She continued, "Gotta say, he was really mean for a while." She thought a minute. "I know he put you through a lot."

"Could you give me a specific situation?"

"Well, once, in the kitchen, he grabbed your arm. You cried, so we knew he'd hurt you."

I looked at the trees, a deep summer green now. Chickadees flitted around the birdfeeder hanging from a tree branch. "Why would he do that?"

Serena shook her head. "Not sure, but I think you guys were talking about money." She grunted. "Always."

"We fought about money?"

"Well, *you* didn't. I think Dad gave you a certain amount to buy us stuff, take care of the house, whatever...but he got mad when you asked for more."

"I didn't have enough?"

"I guess."

I thought a minute. "What else did we fight about?"

"Mom, it was only the last year or two before Dad left. The rest of the time, everything was fine."

I doubt that. "This is good, Serena. This helps me. I need to put together what life with your dad was like before things fell apart." I thought a few seconds about whether I really wanted to wade into this muddy pond any deeper. I took a deep breath and blurted, "Anything else?"

"He started sleeping in the guest room," she mumbled. "Things went downhill fast after that."

"That's probably when he met..." I said slowly, thinking out loud, before I realized I should not verbalize these thoughts. I pressed my lips together. Not a conversation a teenage girl should have with her mother about her father. "Thanks, honey," I said, ending our discussion with a smile. "That helps so much."

Serena stood and arched her back. "Guess I'll go see what Grammy and Dr. Sturgis are doing. Can you believe they're dating, Mom?"

I smiled. "I'm beginning to believe your grandmother is capable of anything at this point."

Serena laughed and went inside. I thought about the things she'd said. It made perfect sense that we'd fought over money if he'd been gambling it away.

Had I known?

* * *

The girls had set the dining room table with candles, placemats, and silverware. The room shimmered. Mom carried in the salad I'd prepared and divvied it up into bowls. I stared at her. She'd arranged her hair in a French twist and wore a simple pearl necklace and pearl earrings. Pretty stunning.

"Mom, what have you done with my mother?"

She stole a glance at the kitchen. "Gotta keep 'em off balance, you know."

"By wearing a business suit?" I took in her pale-blue, tailored jacket, the cream-colored, V-neck blouse, the matching pencil skirt. And heels. She'd worn heels for a dinner at home and seemed perfectly comfortable with it.

She shook croutons on each salad. "Mm-hmm. And he definitely likes it."

My jaw dropped. Had I known about the man-eater lurking inside? Her hands stopped moving. She squinted at me.

"What's the matter?"

"You just look too good, Mom." I gestured at my jeans, T-shirt, and flip-flops and spread my hands.

She put down the can of croutons and hugged me. "You have never looked better in your life."

Dr. Sturgis appeared in the doorway. "Am I interrupting, ladies?"

Mom gave me a final squeeze and walked back to her croutons. "Of course not. Chicken ready?"

He held a platter up. My mother smiled and pointed to the table. I leaned over one of the chairs, admiring his efforts. I breathed in a savory breath, and that was it. Images struck so fast I could barely take them in.

A platter held under my nose. A man's lips speaking. Glasses of wine. Someone pushing in my chair, seating me at a table. Mahogany—no—black table, all precise edges. Chairs with white cushioned seats. Slurred words. Blurred vision. A man smiling. Me on the floor, something had drenched the white carpet. My head, the side of my head, wet and heavy on the floor in something slick.

The room tilted. I gripped the back of the chair.

Dr. Sturgis walked around the table and held out a hand. "You okay, Olivia?"

I put my hand in his. My eyelids fluttered, and then…nothing.

* * *

I blinked once, twice, then woke to four anxious faces riveted to mine. I felt fabric. Birds cheeped. A cool breeze wafted over me. I focused on the white, slim, painted boards on the ceiling. *I'm on the loveseat on my porch.* I struggled to sit up. Gentle hands held me back.

"What happened?" I whispered.

"Can you hear me, Olivia?" a male voice asked from far, far away.

A penlight flashed. I squinted against the brightness. Dr. Sturgis turned it off.

He continued, "We were hoping you could tell *us* what happened. How's your head?"

Dr. Sturgis knelt before me on one knee, holding my wrist. My mother hovered, wringing her hands, crying a little. My daughters sat across from me, silent and still as stones. My heart ached for them.

"Girls, I'm okay. Just fainted." I thought a minute. "Didn't I?"

Dr. Sturgis nodded.

I gulped in a huge lungful of air and held it, then blew it out. "How long have I been out?"

"Ten minutes, give or take."

I sat up. Dr. Sturgis supported me with his arm. I rubbed my face and shuddered. "I'm sorry, guys." I rubbed my head, careful to avoid the healing wound. "Memories come at me at the oddest times. *Pieces* of memories," I clarified. "This one was intense."

* * *

After dinner, Serena and Lilly bounced out of their chairs like sweet angels to clear the table and clean up. This puzzled me beyond words. Mom leaned over and whispered, "See? If you faint occasionally, they'll do whatever you want without arguing about it."

I laughed. Dr. Sturgis eased his chair back. "How about a quick exam, Olivia?"

"Now? But—"

Mom replied, "*Now.* I'll go help the girls with the dishes."

Dr. Sturgis picked up a bag he'd tucked in the corner.

"Feels very familiar, Doctor," I quipped, as he followed me into the den.

"It does, doesn't it?" He smiled. "Don't worry, Olivia, you have far exceeded any expectations."

I stood in the middle of the room and extended my arms to each side. "Okay, now what?"

He held up a stiff hand sideways. "Follow my hand."

He dragged out a stethoscope and checked me, then hung it around his neck and checked reflexes. "Okay, good. Now walk for me."

I walked.

"Turn around, stand on one leg."

I flapped like a flamingo on one leg. "Ha!" I crowed. "Pretty good for a woman who's had two glasses of wine…and a coma."

He laughed, then gave me a series of memory questions. Ten minutes of brainteasers later, he pronounced me "almost" back to normal.

Mom walked in holding plates of carrot cake with cream cheese frosting. "We done in here?"

Dr. Sturgis grabbed one of the plates. "We're done. Olivia is now officially a miracle."

"I've known that since the day she was born." Mom smiled and gave me the other plate.

"I bet you were a great mother," he said to her.

"She's still a great mother," I protested.

Mom chuckled. "He meant when you were growing up. Needed more mothering then."

I stopped chewing and swallowed. "Never needed a mom more than right now."

Mom teared up. Walked over and put an arm around me.

My cell jangled. "Excuse me," I mouthed, and walked outside. The dusky purple sky had sprouted a few stars. It smelled like rain was on the way.

"Hi, Olivia, it's Hunter Faraday."

A happy smile spread its bright little wings at the sound of his voice.

"Am I interrupting?"

I updated him on our evening and my excellent medical report.

"Sounds great," he said. "Wish I could've..." He paused.

"I guess you want to know...if I've remembered more?"

He cleared his throat. "Yep."

"I've got company now, so can I call you later? I've had...quite the afternoon."

"Okay, that's fine. And one more thing..."

I listened to him breathe.

"Niles Peterson? Remember, I paid him a visit a couple of weeks ago? What I didn't tell you is that we got a judge to grant us a request for his phone records."

I couldn't move my mouth to ask the next question. *Why?*

"Olivia," he said, "Be careful. We're doing everything we can, but the media is champing at the bit to get your full story out. If you remember specific details, call me immediately. Do not talk to the media and under no circumstances tell *anyone* about our potential drop-in date with Niles next week."

* * *

Later that evening, Mom and I waved and watched until Dr. Sturgis's taillights were out of sight.

"He's only a few minutes away, Mom," I said in response to her deep sigh.

She stepped out of her heels, which made her two and a half inches shorter. "Yeah, I know."

The dark-velvet sky cradled a three-quarter moon. We stood shoulder to shoulder. I hated to break the spell, but I needed input.

Hunter's admonition not to tell anyone shouldn't include my mother. Should it? I needed direction, and my mother was fast becoming the best compass I had. "Mom, Detective Faraday wants me to pay a surprise visit to the guy in Richmond. Next week."

She furrowed her brow at me and crossed her arms. "Niles Peterson?"

I nodded.

"For what purpose?"

"A trigger. To see if any memories surface, and to see *his* reaction when I appear without any warning." Quickly, I added, "You can't tell anyone."

Mom's mouth dropped open in disbelief.

"I'm not sure what to do," I said, twisting a piece of my hair around my index finger. "Hunter—Detective Faraday—says he'll have backup close."

She smiled and cocked her head. *"Hunter?"*

I shrugged. "Whatever."

"Don't you think that could be dangerous?"

"That's why I am asking."

She was quiet, thinking.

"You'll have the detective with you?"

I nodded. "And officers outside."

"Does this man live alone?"

I shrugged. "Don't know."

"Well, how do you feel about it?"

I stared at the sky. A breeze whispered through our hair. How could my life have become so complex, I wondered? Had it been full of secrets? How had I ended up dumped outside a hospital? Why? Who would do that? I pushed the questions away. I would have answers when I was supposed to have answers, but I couldn't shake the feeling that the trip would reveal the tip of a huge iceberg.

I blew out a long breath. "I trust Detective Faraday. This guy Niles wouldn't be dumb enough to pull something while I'm there with Richmond's finest." I stared intently into my mother's anxious blue eyes. "Would he?"

"I wouldn't think so. But we have no idea what is going on in people's minds. He might be...right on the edge."

"Yeah," I agreed. "Well, so am I."

Chapter Thirty-Seven

Mom and I sat in matching leather armchairs before my attorney's ponderous desk, waiting for him to show up. Snatches of morning sunlight, bleary and weak, quavered through a window. It had been raining off and on. My mother's fingers played with the arm of her chair. I crossed and re-crossed my legs, slight puffs of impatience escaping my lips. Mom stretched out a placating hand and placed it on my arm, her bracelets gently chiming.

"He'll be here, honey. Something must have come up."

"How much are we paying this guy again?"

My mother sighed. "I know."

The door opened and his assistant's head peered around it. "Comin' down the hall now. Sorry for the delay." She left the door open and returned to her desk.

I glanced at my watch and sighed. "Thirty minutes?"

Mom shrugged.

Earl Sorenson III strode into the room, shoulders hunched, face drawn, the gray mane atop his head limp from one hundred percent humidity. He plunked a heavy briefcase on the floor beside his chair and turned his palms up.

"Judges. What are you gonna do?"

My mother straightened in her chair. "Tough day at the office?"

"You might say that," Sorenson squinted at her. "Who are you?"

My mother stood and extended a hand over his desk. He shook it. "Olivia's mom, Sophie."

"Glad to meet you, Sophie." His bushy eyebrows waggled. "And how are you, young lady?" he asked me.

"Tired of waiting."

Sorenson's smile was thin. He slid out of a dark-green sport coat, hung it on a hook, and rolled up his shirtsleeves. "Sorry about that. Nothing I could do."

I re-crossed my legs.

Sorenson slapped the top of his desk, startling us. "Okay, let's proceed." He picked up a file from a stack on one side of his desk. His assistant came in with a steaming cup of coffee. "Thanks," he said, scanning the contents of the file. He removed his reading glasses and looked from me to Mom and back again. "Anyone offer you coffee?"

We shook our heads. He eyebrow-waggled at his assistant, who politely inquired of us, and we accepted. I studied Sorenson's eyebrows, shaggy clumps that hung over deep-set eyes. I checked out his ring finger. Naked, as expected. No wife would allow her husband to walk around with eyebrows like that.

The assistant brought us coffee. He watched her perky posterior as she left before turning his attention back to my file.

After a few minutes, he stroked his chin in our direction. "Tell me what we need today."

"What *we* need," I said through clenched teeth, "is to fill you in on what's going on and ask for your legal opinion."

He nodded. "You haven't called in..." he glanced at the paperwork, "in a matter of months. Or made an appointment, though it appears we've tried to contact you."

I cleared my throat. "Mr. Sorenson, I—"

He waved dismissively. *"Earl."*

"Earl," I repeated, "I've been a little distracted with a life-threatening head injury. I've only been out of the hospital three weeks and my priorities were learning to walk and talk again, stuff like that."

Sophie shot her daughter a warning glance.

Olivia rolled her eyes. "We are ninety-nine percent sure that I was

180

assaulted. It put me in a coma for over a week. I'm lucky to be alive."

Those crazy eyebrows shot straight up, the fleshy jaw dropped. "I'm sorry. I had no idea, no idea at all—"

I frowned. "It's been all over the news. Anyway, I have coma-induced aphasia. Need you to bring me up to date. I'm remembering things here and there, but it'll take a while to get back to normal."

Sorenson's big, black chair squeaked as he leaned back and rocked, his fingers clasped over his belly. Heavy-lidded, basset hound eyes bored into mine. "You don't think your husband had anything to do with this, do you?"

My mouth dropped open. "Of course not." I crossed my arms and tried to ignore the pangs of doubt that crept into my mind. "I...I cannot imagine," I amended.

He shifted his gaze to Mom. "What do you think, um..." He concentrated on the ceiling as if it would disgorge her name. "Sophie?"

She shook her head. "No way. He can be a scumbag, but I don't think he is capable of—would never—"

"Okay." Sorenson shrugged. "Had to ask. Because if so, it would definitely complicate things. Not to mention a criminal charge. In that case, you'd need a criminal attorney, and that's not me."

Mom crossed her arms, gave me a sideways glance.

"I don't think any of that's my concern right now. I need to be updated on what's going on with the divorce, plus there's an additional issue."

I proceeded with questions about a wife's responsibility for a husband's gambling debts. Ten minutes later, mesmerized by Earl's ability to recite case number after case number plus legal precedent without actually answering my questions, I interrupted him.

"Can you fill me in on our earlier meetings?" I lay a hand on Mom's arm to stop her from telling Sorenson where he could stick his case numbers and precedents. Her shoulders relaxed. "Can you read me your divorce notes? At this point, I've been reading copies of things my husband has, but I don't really understand how those decisions were reached."

"Okay," he murmured thoughtfully. He looked at me over his reading glasses. "We were on a real peaceful course, here." He looked at his notes, a thin stack of pages. "You were very amenable, Olivia. Let's see…you agreed to sell the house and split the proceeds with Monty. You agreed to share custody of your daughters."

My lower back tightened. I leaned forward.

"Monty asked for help with the child support, and you were fine with that."

"What does that mean, 'help'?"

Earl rattled off a monthly sum, then told me I'd agreed to reduce it. By half. Then he added that I'd agreed to let Monty keep the investments with his financial firm until I'd proven I could run a household by myself.

I stared at Mom. Her face was a blank slate. How could I have agreed to these ridiculous demands? I never even wanted the divorce. Did I? Plus, had I even known what our monthly expenses were at that point? The coffee swirled in my stomach in a noxious mix of heartburn and disgust. I must've been a complete idiot. This was my future we were talking about. His *daughters'* futures. I had to think clearly.

Suddenly, I couldn't bear to listen to his droning, monotone voice any longer.

I held up my index finger. The voice stopped. His mouth dropped and his eyebrows drew together as if he were irritated at the interruption. The reading glasses perched on his long nose accentuated the bags under his eyes.

"Earl, you can throw those notes in the trash, or hang onto them, I don't care. But we're going to start over, you and me. I agree to none of those things. And if you want to continue to represent me, *find out what my rights are concerning those damn gambling debts!*"

Mom, for once, was speechless.

Reluctantly, Earl found a notebook and started writing down what I wanted. I did most of the talking, and he answered my basic questions. To my growing horror, I learned I'd been the most clueless woman on earth.

Thank God I wasn't that woman anymore.

I couldn't wait to see Monty's reaction to the barrage of paperwork he was about to get hit with.

Chapter Thirty-Eight

Monty unlocked the door to his apartment, loosening his tie with the other hand and juggling the stack of mail he'd grabbed from his mailbox. He threw the pile of envelopes on the breakfast bar and put his keys and sunglasses beside it. A cold beer would go a long way right now, he thought.

When he heard light knocking on his door, his forehead crinkled in surprise. No one ever visited him here. Standing at the door, an earnest young man held a fat manila envelope. His dark, short-sleeved uniform shirt bore the words *Security Courier Service.*

"Special delivery, sir," he said, and handed the envelope to Monty. The messenger dipped his head and left.

Monty read the return address—Olivia's attorney.

"Perfect," he grumbled. "Just what I need after this crappy day." He ripped open the envelope and pulled out a stack of papers. Monty squinted at them, then reached into his pocket for reading glasses and put them on. "Request for Deposition. Request for Temporary Spousal Support. Request for Temporary Child Support. Answer to Custodial Issue," he recited, growing angrier by the second.

He threw the sheaf of papers on the floor, ignoring them for the moment. Another smaller envelope caught his attention in the remaining mail, addressed in Olivia's familiar script. He tore it open and withdrew a smaller, unaddressed envelope.

Monty eyed it suspiciously and placed it on the breakfast bar, squaring its edges with the corner. Glancing every few seconds at the legal documents on the floor in disgust, he got a bottle of beer from the fridge and took a long gulp. The pile on the floor represented more money slipping through his fingers, and the reason his head now throbbed with brutal force above his left eyebrow. He balled the smaller, unopened envelope in his fist and dropped into his chair. When the beer was gone, he took aim and threw it toward the trashcan. The bottle fell short, hit the wall, and dropped to the linoleum. Monty watched it roll around on the floor until it stopped.

Frowning, Monty smoothed the envelope he'd fisted and inspected the flap. Olivia had obviously opened and resealed it. He flipped the envelope open with his thumb and extracted a piece of lined notebook paper with a message that could be summed up in four words: *pay up or else.*

Monty cursed, thought about the money he'd taped to the underside of a drawer in Olivia's—*his*—house, and how it had been his insurance against this very thing. A get-home-free card. What he'd squirreled away would have been more than enough to buy him some time to pay the full amount. He thought about other options to get the money. But he'd promised himself he wouldn't dig into his "other resources" unless it was life or death. There had to be another way.

Monty went to grab another beer. He thought about the hold Olivia's attorney had put on his checking accounts and the thousand or so deposited in her personal account each month. As he rolled the cold bottle over his forehead, his cell vibrated.

"Monty, you told me this thing was going to be easy," his attorney groaned. Monty was silent.

"Do you know I got slammed with a mountain of motions just now?"

"Yeah," Monty said. "Got mine, too, Greg." He chuckled and swigged his beer.

His attorney's voice shrilled, "You realize we got a *fight* on our hands now?"

"Yeah," Monty admitted.

"What happened?"

"Olivia's waking up."

Greg was quiet.

"She's turned into a barracuda." He slapped the arm of his chair and shrieked with laughter. "Freakin' barracuda," he repeated.

"How did that happen?" Greg hissed.

Monty told him about her accident, or whatever the Richmond PD was calling it now, surprised his attorney didn't already know about it.

"I heard something about that. I just didn't know it was *your* Olivia."

"All mine, all mine," Monty sing-songed.

Greg cleared his throat. "Gonna cost a bundle."

"Already has," Monty mumbled.

"What does that mean?"

Monty sighed.

Greg told him to be at his office the following day at noon, then hung up on him.

Chapter Thirty-Nine

"Yeah, she's on her way now," Detective Faraday said, his fingers tracing patterns on his notebook. He listened to his captain's voice, nodding. "Right. I'll immediately alert if I need the backup team to move in." He ended the call, propped his elbows on his desk and tented his hands. A young female officer appeared in his doorway. "Olivia Callahan is here."

Detective Faraday nodded and began rolling down his shirtsleeves. "Okay, be right there," he told her as he reached for his sport coat.

He'd wondered if Olivia would make it this far. In the week since they'd talked, he'd often wanted to call her and tell her the jaunt to Niles's home had been called off. She was, after all, still recovering from massive brain trauma and he didn't want to push it. "Out of my hands, now," he muttered, and walked to the front counter.

"Hey," she said when she saw him, smiling half-heartedly.

"Hi, Olivia, come on back."

He watched Olivia register the scrape of quick steps, people disappearing into various offices, muted phone conversations, uniformed officers chatting at glass windows. Detective Faraday tightened the knot of his tie and buttoned his top button as they walked. At one of the many doorways, he touched her arm and pointed.

"This is me."

Olivia nodded, entered the small office, and dropped into one of the worn, olive, pleather chairs in front of the desk. Her eyebrows drew together as she studied the armrest and rubbed its cracked surface. Detective Faraday walked behind his desk and sat. Conflict billowed off her like smoke-signals.

"Look, I know you're nervous, Olivia. That's normal."

She gripped the purse in her lap and looked at the floor.

"The back-up team will move in at my instruction if necessary."

Olivia straightened. "How? Are you wearing a wire?"

"Yeah. That's standard." He shrugged. "Not that we'll need them," he added hastily after glancing at her expression. "It's a precaution. Here's the plan." He grimaced. "I call it a plan, but we're not sure how it will play out. Here's the *loose* plan."

Her purse fell to the floor. As she bent to pick it up, Detective Faraday noticed the revealing slit in the back of her blouse.

"We'll have two cars on either side of the block, listening. We'll approach and knock on the door. His reaction should tell us a lot. I'll flash my badge, tell him I've got a few questions, ask if he remembers you, say I thought it'd be good for us to go through events together—very routine, cop-interview stuff."

He paused and leafed through notes. "With me so far?"

"I guess."

"Hang in there, okay? You'll be safe."

Olivia frowned. "Last time I had a rush of memory, I fainted, remember?"

"Yeah," he agreed. "But if that happens, we can use it to our advantage." He thought a minute, then snapped his fingers. "It's a great way to get you to one of his other rooms, like a bedroom. The only specifics you recall are in a kitchen, right? Either way, it could tell us a lot if we could get you into more of the house."

"Glad you're so excited about this," Olivia quipped.

His expression softened. "I know this is tough, but you can do this." He paused and drummed his fingers on his desk. "Your memories seem to return via triggers, so this should be interesting. We have all kinds of safeguards in place," he said. He lightly slapped the arm of his chair. "Reminds me." He stood and picked up a bulletproof vest from the top of a filing cabinet. "Put this on under your shirt." He pointed to the hall. "Bathroom's to the right. I'll wait."

Olivia held the heavy, gray vest at arm's length like it was a rotting piece of garbage, gave him a dirty look, and disappeared.

When she reappeared a few minutes later, Detective Faraday stopped scribbling on his notepad and scanned her form. "All set?"

"I feel like I have on one of those dental X-ray shields, but yeah, I'm as set as I'll ever be."

"They're heavy, I know. But your vitals are protected, and that's the important thing. You're so thin, can't even tell you have anything on."

"Not by choice," she groaned. She held her pants out to each side—a good two inches too big. "Stress."

"We can fatten you up after this is over. Ready?"

She took a deep breath. "Let's do it."

He patted himself, checked his gun, notepad, badge, then paused and concentrated a few seconds. His mind stalled on the word "we." Had he really said that?

He strode out of his office without a word, assuming Olivia would follow. When she didn't, he glanced back at the door to his office. "Coming?"

"Yes." Olivia stepped into the hall, squared her shoulders, and lifted her chin. "Lead the way."

He smiled.

Showtime

* * *

"There," he pointed from the car. "That's the one. That's Niles's townhouse."

Before them, a squat, white fourplex surrounded by manicured hedges, four perfectly symmetrical driveways, red tile roofs. Olivia balled her hands into fists and squeezed in an effort to focus.

She sighed. "Nothing," she said.

Granite-faced, jaw set, Detective Faraday pulled into the driveway and killed the engine.

"It's time," he said, with a sideways glance. "Let's go."

Olivia nodded but didn't make a move to get out of the car.

Detective Faraday walked around and opened her door. He held out his hand. "Breathe."

After a few seconds, she let herself be pulled out of the car and followed him to the front door.

The house number on his notepad matched the number on the door. He turned to Olivia and gave her a reassuring smile. He rapped five times and waited.

Rapped again.

"Who's there?" a voice eventually called from inside.

"Richmond PD," Detective Faraday said, pressing his badge against the peephole. "Just want to talk for a few minutes."

"Not a good time," the voice mumbled.

"Just a few minutes is all we ask, sir."

Detective Faraday glanced at Olivia and shrugged.

Finally, the door edged open. Olivia's arms involuntarily snaked around her ribs.

The door opened further, halted by a security chain. Niles drew back, then placed his head carefully underneath the chain to eyeball us. Satisfied, he slid the chain out of its socket and opened the door wide. Niles wore a gray polo and jeans. He crossed his arms and looked at each of us in turn, standing directly beneath the glare of his blinding porch light. In spite of the curly, brown hair and light-blue eyes, the shadows gave him a corpse-like pallor.

"Oh yeah, I recognize you. Detective Faraday, right?" Niles grinned as if they were best buds. He turned to Olivia with a quizzical look, stroked his chin for a few seconds, then said, "And you're the woman I met on the beach, right? *Olivia.* Come on in."

They stepped inside the small foyer and into the larger living area. Olivia's hands started to shake. She folded them together, and stared at the black couch. The chrome and glass. A picture of a young man...his son? Detective Faraday gave her a look.

Olivia nodded. Yes. She remembered.

Niles offered the couch and sat in a chair opposite, carefully avoiding looking at Olivia too long. The conversation lagged.

Niles shot Olivia a quick glance. "So…I've heard all about your troubles on the news, Olivia. How are you, anyway?"

Something innocuous fell out of her mouth. Detective Faraday said nothing.

"So, what's all this about?" Niles continued. "I thought we'd finished my, um…interrogation."

"Olivia is having trouble piecing things together. Thought it would be good for you and Olivia to chat, see if talking helps her remember anything." Detective Faraday smiled. "Sure appreciate your cooperation, sir."

Niles nodded. "Anything for the Richmond PD. Glad to help."

Olivia cleared her throat. Niles stared at her. Detective Faraday glimpsed fear there, but it was quickly doused. He looked pointedly at Olivia. They'd discussed who would do what, and it was her turn.

"Niles. Niles Dabney, right?"

He paled. "Yes. How did you remember that?"

"I seem to remember we talked about names. About how weird they were."

His rubbed his pant leg nervously. "Now that you mention it, we did. I remember now. You thought my name was funny, and when I said my middle name—"

"When you said your middle name, I lost it."

He nodded. "You did."

"What else did I do, Niles?"

He paused.

"You drank the water I gave you, we talked about five minutes, and that was it."

Olivia snapped her fingers as if suddenly remembering. "I saw you later on the beach when you were riding a bicycle."

"Uh, maybe, yeah."

"I am certain of it. We talked awhile. I remember you sat beside me and we watched our kids. You have a son, right?"

He colored. "Okay."

Beads of sweat flared on Niles's forehead.

CHAPTER THIRTY-NINE

"You know what would help?" Olivia asked, the picture of innocence.

Detective Faraday smiled. She was good at this.

Stress lines formed little parentheses around Niles's mouth.

"Would you show me your place? It feels like...I've been here before." She fluttered her eyelashes, in spite of her nerves. Must be some kind of primal female instinct. Men were suckers for helpless women.

Detective Faraday made a show of pulling out his notebook.

Niles's eyes widened. "Um...sure," he said, and rose. "Where would you like to start?"

"In the kitchen," Olivia said.

She followed him to the door. Detective Faraday lagged behind, watching Olivia struggle to control her shaking hands. He remembered her description of this in one of her dreams—no mistaking all that stainless steel and black. The professional oven, the black dishes arranged in symmetrical rows behind glass cabinet doors. She grabbed the doorframe to steady herself.

Niles watched her with a quiet intensity.

Detective Faraday edged closer, his gaze bouncing to Niles, then Olivia and back again. "Everything okay?"

"I'm a little dizzy," she said.

"Want some water?" Niles asked, walking across the kitchen and pulling a bottle out of the fridge.

"Sure, thanks."

Detective Faraday sat on stool by the kitchen counter and crossed his arms. Olivia drank the water, but seemed distracted. Worried.

"Maybe she should lie down," he suggested. Olivia smiled weakly. "She's still has these...episodes. Where's the nearest bed? Just for a few minutes, maybe."

Niles looked uncertain, then pointed. "Bedroom's that way."

Detective Faraday put an arm around Olivia's waist and tugged her arm over his shoulders.

"I'm remembering," she whimpered when they were out of earshot. "This hallway. How helpless and limp I was."

"I've got you."

The reassuring hump of the gun in his shoulder harness dug into Olivia's side.

"This the bedroom?" he called over his shoulder.

"Yeah," Niles called from the kitchen doorway.

"You mind staying put? We'll be out in a few minutes," Detective Faraday told him.

"Sure. I'll just be in the kitchen."

He slid Olivia on the bed, left the door ajar a bit. She glanced at the en suite bathroom.

"Here it comes," she whispered, gripping the sides of the bed, eyes wide.

Chapter Forty

Olivia

I stared at myself in the mirror of Niles's guest bathroom, my hands gripping the sink, my body tense. Seems I needed to take the obligatory shower he'd suggested after our bike ride, but first I wanted to think about why he would have black-and-white prints of naked women cavorting beside a lake on the walls of the guest bathroom. Tasteful photos, but still, were they appropriate for a guest bathroom? I studied the women. Caught unaware by a photographer with voyeuristic instincts and a penchant for full-bodied women, their eyes flirted with the camera, heads swiveled over plump shoulders. I squinted at the title of the photos scrawled in pencil at the bottom next to the print number. "Caught skinny-dipping."

I involuntarily shielded my breasts from imagined prying eyes and stepped into the shower, turning the water slightly north of scalding, trying to burn away the images in my mind. "To each their own," I muttered as the water cascaded.

As a precaution, I pulled the shower curtain aside to check if I'd locked the door. Nope. I stepped out, dripping, and locked it.

Toweling my hair after the shower, I walked to the dresser and found something to wear.

After a final check in the mirror at my hastily made-up face, I took a deep breath, opened the door, and walked down the hall, past the bedrooms, past the main bathroom, and into the living area. Empty. I walked past the black couches, past the ebony bookcases, and into the kitchen. No Niles.

The smell of his chipotle chicken in the oven filled the kitchen. A small gift lay on the counter. Shiny, white wrapping paper with a simple red ribbon tied in a bow. I simpered like a little kid.

I swiveled my head. "Niles?" I returned to the living area. "Niles?" Probably on his third shower. The guy loved showers.

I went back to the kitchen and read the tag: "To Olivia. Thanks for visiting me. Affectionately, Niles Dabney." A rush of warmth exploded in my chest. Monty had never been one for gifts. He'd never been one for compliments, either. Package in hand, a goofy grin spread across my face. Would it be rude to open it without Niles? Yes. I replaced the package on the counter.

"Found my little gift, I see."

I jumped.

Niles leaned against the kitchen entry, a light blue towel knotted around his waist, his chest flushed and red from a steamy shower or two. I looked away.

He glanced at himself and chuckled. "Oh. I just took a break from getting ready. You don't mind, do you?"

I shook my head. Of course I didn't mind. But I did. I minded. I stared at the floor.

Niles laughed. "Oh, yeah. Shy."

I kept my gaze on the floor. Light-gray tile with dark-gray grout.

"I'll get dressed in a minute. Go ahead and open the box." He padded beside me.

He smelled like soap, which under different circumstances would have been pleasant but unnerved me now. Is this what men did on a first-weekend-together date with someone they barely knew? I picked up the box.

* * *

I emerged from the scene to Hunter hovering over me, his forehead furrowed with concern. I tried to reassure him I was all right, but the image shifted, and in the space of a heartbeat, Hunter morphed into Niles. Then, memories began to scroll through my mind, slowly at first, then faster and faster. I squeezed my eyes shut, held up my hands as if I could hold them off. Hunter grabbed my hands.

"I'm here, Olivia," he whispered, glancing over his shoulder at the bedroom door. "Go with it. I've got you."

* * *

Niles had not let me help with after-dinner cleanup and told me to stay in the dining room and enjoy the candlelight. Glancing at my wine glass, I'd watched its curve distort the moon as it rose outside the window, listening to the comfortable clatter of dishes being loaded in the dishwasher. The wine had been very helpful in allaying any concerns about an illicit weekend with a handsome man I'd met on the beach that I'd told no one about, thank you very much.

I lifted my third glass and sipped. I told myself to be cautious with alcohol since I didn't know Niles very well, but caution had sailed out the window an hour ago.

"The chicken was amazing, Niles," I said as he returned to the dining room with two slices of cheesecake.

"Glad you enjoyed it," he said. "That recipe is always a winner." He lifted the small plates. "I hope you like cheesecake."

"Who doeshn't like cheesecake?" I laughed at the accidental slurring. "Oopsie," I sang, toasting him with my wine glass.

He laid the plate down and bent to kiss me. His hand drifted to my shoulder, then inside my blouse. I tried to push it away, but my arms lay in my lap like pieces of wood. I couldn't deny that I was getting hammered.

"Niles, please," I whispered. I couldn't seem to make my voice work. I tried again. "I like you, but we don't really—"

"Can't blame a guy." He withdrew his hand. "You look amazing tonight, Olivia."

He walked around the table to his chair and sat. At least I think he sat. As I watched, he split into three of himself. I blinked and promised myself to lay off the wine.

"Thank you," I responded to the compliment. The cheesecake in front of me, like Niles, had also split into three images. I aimed and stabbed at it with my fork, hitting the table instead of the dessert plate. Niles laughed. I squinted at him.

"Niles, I'm so shorry, but..." I paused. Had I really drunk that much? "I think I'm going to have to...to..." I placed my fork on the table, which melted right before

my eyes. I stared at the place my fork had been.

"Too much to drink?" His expression was confusing, and as I watched in horror, his face melted.

What was wrong with me?

* * *

"What do you see, Olivia?"

"I was here," I whispered. "He fixed me dinner. I remember thinking I'd had too much to drink, but then my legs, my arms, they were wobbly and wouldn't work." I put my hand on my throat and closed my eyes. "I can't be sure yet," I told him, apologetically. "The images…are confusing."

Hunter patted my shoulder. I breathed in deep and breathed out slow. *You can do this.*

Niles called from the kitchen. "Need anything?"

I shrank back involuntarily. Hunter shot me a warning glance.

"She's doing better. Be right out."

I ran my hands through my hair, smoothed my shirt, and sat up. "I'm okay now. I'm going into the bathroom, see what happens in there."

Hunter nodded. "I need to get back out there and keep an eye on him. You sure?"

I nodded.

"Look, we don't know what happened yet, but you shouldn't be alone with this guy. I'll come back and get you, okay? Lock the door when I leave."

I closed the bathroom door behind me, locked it, and promptly had a meltdown. I stifled my sobs, clinging to the sink, trying to reel in a memory of struggle, a *specific* memory of Niles…on the bed…with me…but I couldn't. It just wouldn't come. I ran water and splashed it on my face, then sat on the commode to think. I noticed the framed prints of nudes on the wall, a confirmation some of my memories had sprouted accurately. He'd prepared me dinner—I saw him in his kitchen, his mouth moving, his smile, flirting. I'd been excited. I'd driven to Richmond, to his house, and hadn't told a soul. I clutched the edges of the commode and steeled myself for another onslaught.

* * *

I'd begun measuring time by Niles. Three weeks since I'd met Niles. Fourteen days since I'd talked to him.

My cell jangled. The number displayed made me smile. "This is Olivia," I cooed.

"Hey. Niles here. How are you?"

I murmured that I was fine.

"Sorry I haven't picked up the phone."

I laughed. "That's okay," It wasn't, though. Not really. A few texts—that had been the extent of it. Most of my time had been spent fantasizing about when he would call and the next time we could be together. And now I could barely string words together.

"Look, I've been thinking...why don't you spend a couple days here? You'd have your own bedroom and bath at my place, wouldn't have to spend a dime, and you'll fall in love with Richmond. Ever been here?"

"Ages ago." I desperately hoped my voice sounded sexy.

"My son's at his mom's for the summer. I'd love to show you my town and get to know you better. Think about it?"

I fist-pumped the air and stifled a giggle. "I will."

Pause.

"Two weeks?" he asked.

I opened my laptop, clicked on the calendar. "Should be fine." The thinking had taken exactly ten seconds.

* * *

I palmed my cheeks in disbelief. Okay, so we'd accomplished the trip's objective...the memory of dinner and candlelight, even the dinner menu—all clear in my mind. And now this, an accurate memory of a conversation that could pin down the timeline. Wouldn't that be enough to search his place? That's all Hunter needed, right?

Suddenly, all I wanted was *out*.

I tiptoed into the hall. A wall clock ticked, the huge refrigerator hummed. *Where were they?* "Detective Faraday?" I called. His brisk steps strode from the kitchen to the hallway.

"Better?" he asked, which I took to mean as: *Did you remember more?*

I nodded.

Niles stepped out of the kitchen and walked down the hall to the front door. "Are these your guys?" he asked, looking at Hunter and pointing outside. "Official-looking SUV hanging around at the end of my driveway."

I squeezed past Hunter in the narrow space.

He whispered, "You okay?"

I stood uncertainly in the hall. Both men walked past me and went outside.

I stepped on the porch and struggled to see what was happening, but it was dark. Hunter glanced at me. "Be right back." He trotted to the end of the driveway.

I found it beyond awkward to be alone with Niles on his front porch. My eyebrows drew together. Did Hunter do this on purpose?

I stifled a shudder.

"So…" Niles began. "Hope you've gotten what you need, Olivia. It was nice seeing you again."

Get it together, I told myself. He doesn't know you know. Does he? No. There'd be a tip-off of some kind.

I shrugged. "Maybe. It seems a lifetime ago, but it feels familiar here."

He regarded me for several seconds. Watching him, my unpredictable subconscious brought back the memory of Niles in a towel.

"I think the mind is a strange thing," Niles murmured. "Perhaps you thought you were here, but you were *never here*, Olivia."

"Well, *somebody* dumped me at Mercy Hospital. Maybe I had an accident, and someone found me. But why was I in Richmond?"

"Maybe you weren't."

I was quiet.

"You had a brain injury. Is it possible that you assumed you were visiting someone here because you were found at Mercy?" He shrugged, stuck his hands in his pockets. "Maybe someone found you on the highway and drove you."

His smile didn't quite reach his eyes. A cold sweat broke out on my chest and crawled down my arms. What the heck was Hunter doing? Niles' cologne triggered a quick lurch of my stomach. I avoided throwing up by jogging down the drive to join Hunter. Their shadowy shapes materialized. I heard soft metallic sounds and angry, hushed voices. To my horror, Hunter had a guy cuffed against the SUV.

"Detective Faraday," I sputtered, "what on earth?"

With a weary look at me, he spun the man around.

I gasped.

Monty?

Fuming, Monty glared at me. "Tell him to take these cuffs off!"

"Stay," Detective Faraday commanded with an outstretched arm as he walked over to me.

Speechless. That's what I was. Out of words. Was there no end to this man's insanity?

After making sure Niles was nowhere near us, Hunter whispered, "Monty must have followed us. Don't ask me how he knew about this. Now he's impeding an investigation. Had to do something."

"You have got to be *kidding* me," I yelled at Monty. In spite of Hunter's protests, I stalked within spitting distance of Monty, so angry I didn't trust myself to get any closer, or I'd punch him.

"What in heaven's name do you think you are doing, Monty?"

He scowled. "Taking care of *my wife*."

I glared at him. "Monty, this is ridiculous, we—"

"You have no business coming down here with this man."

I jutted my chin. "And what I do is *none of your business*."

Monty fought to get his breathing under control. "Get me outta these." He turned and lifted his cuffed hands slightly behind his back. "And who's the guy on the porch?" he mumbled, staring at the ground. Detective Faraday chimed in. "Need to know basis, Monty."

"For your information, this is part of the investigation," I hissed through clenched teeth. "Which you have just screwed up."

His eyebrows shot up. "How could I have known that?" he bellowed.

He lost all interest in me when he watched Niles walk further down the long driveway. The two men seemed to study each other. It was unsettling. Like they were locked in some kind of mental showdown.

I spun around in disgust and joined Hunter as he stood halfway between Monty and Niles.

"I assume you have a plan B?" I whispered.

He ran his fingers through his hair. "Like I said, *loose* plan. This one's sprouted two heads." He nodded toward Niles's front door. "What happened while I was dealing with Mr. Stalker, here?"

I told him about my innocent act. "Not sure, but I don't think he suspects I remember anything. I did my best."

He grinned. "Good job. I got enough for a warrant, anyway."

"He's denying I was there at all."

"Yeah, well, everything about his reactions says that you were. That, and the fact that you do remember a few specifics, is enough for a search."

"What are you going to do with *him*," I asked, tilting my head at Monty, who stared morosely at the ground.

He rolled his eyes. "I doubt he'll tail you again."

I didn't agree, but said nothing.

"I'll let him off with a warning. Let's wrap up. You ready?"

"*So* ready," I said.

Chapter Forty-One

I talked Hunter into letting me go home after we got back to the police station. I was too wound up to sit there and answer questions, so we agreed to do it by phone. After I checked in with the girls, I thanked Hunter and jogged to the parking lot. Even though it would be three a.m. before I made it home, I didn't care. My body's PTSD jitters, or whatever they were, lasted the first hour of the drive, then abated. The image of Niles in a blue towel kept popping into my head like a bad game of whack-a-mole.

I wondered if Dr. Sturgis would have approved this little jaunt. Probably not. Good thing I hadn't asked him.

If Niles had been so inclined, a gun could have complicated things. After we'd gotten back to the station, I'd gladly turned the body armor over to Hunter with a sigh of relief. Maybe I'd live to bounce Serena and Lilly's children on my knees after all.

At the thought of my daughters, my grip tightened on the steering wheel. My pulse sped up. Another memory. Why now? I groaned and looked for a place to pull off. I exited I-83 onto Shawan Road and pulled into Wegmans' brightly lit parking lot in Hunt Valley. With a sigh, I laid my head back and closed my eyes.

My mom looked up at the sound of my luggage rolling. "Hi, honey. All packed? A weekend away with a girlfriend will do you a world of good. Get your mind off things." She unfurled her arms from the girls and started up the stairs. "Here, let me help you with the suitcase—"

"No thanks, Mom," I protested. "Got this."

"Who did you say you were visiting again?"

"You wouldn't remember her," I lied. "A girl I went to college with. We've reconnected."

"Oh, okay." Brow furrowed, she tilted her head and searched my face.

I hoped with all my heart she'd believe me. Liars cannot hold a steady gaze. They break eye contact and look to the left. Or was it the right? At any rate, mine was steadfast. Proof of sincerity.

To my enormous relief, she smiled and nodded. "Well, I guess if we need you, we have your cell. Make sure you keep the sound on."

"I will," I assured her. "How about if we all do Starbucks when I get back? You can tell me about your adventures."

"Sounds good," Serena said.

"We work until three, though, remember?" Lilly groaned.

Serena pulled at her hair and shrugged. "No big deal. We can go after that."

"Probably won't be back before then anyway. Three it is." I turned toward Mom, who still looked like she was missing something but unsure what.

"Now, where is it you're going? Somewhere in Virginia?"

I nodded. "Richmond." Guilt percolated in my gut like indigestion. At least I'd told her the truth about location. I'd convinced myself that not telling them about Niles was in the best interests of everybody.

Especially me.

I gasped. I'd made a conscious decision to lie about the guy.

My thoughts veered toward Monty. I'd been flattered that he'd followed us, much to my horror. According to, well, *everyone*, he was the biggest loser on the planet. The fact that he'd thought I was involved with Hunter—had been bothered by it—confused me. Why did he care? He'd filed for divorce, not me. And for that matter, why had he sought me out that day to vent about his young conquest? It felt good to believe he still needed me, wanted me. I shook the thought off. *Ridiculous.*

Still…

I sighed. Hunter had directed the backup team to leave quietly. He'd already put in a request for the warrant. It wouldn't be long now, I tried to reassure myself. They'd figure it out, and everything would fall into place. How much more is a person expected to endure, anyway? I needed a break.

My cell jangled.

"Hey, honey."

"How'd it go?" My forehead wrinkled. Serena's voice sounded odd.

"Fine. I'm at Wegmans. What are you doing up so late?"

"Uhhh..."

I frowned. "What did you guys do for dinner?"

Silence.

"Serena?" I heard voices in the background. "Who is that?"

She cleared her throat. "It's Dad, Mom. He just got here."

I blinked. My voice rose. "Why is he there?"

"Don't know, Mom. He just stopped by."

How did he beat me home?

"Is your grandmother awake?"

"She's still out with Dr. Sturgis. He picked her up."

My brain hiccupped. "Your dad isn't supposed to be there unless I'm there, or Grammy."

"Mom," she whispered, "he's here with some really gross-looking guys. Can you hurry?"

* * *

I rocketed the final half-mile to my house, slammed my car to a stop, and flew to the porch where the girls were waiting for me.

"What's going on?" I demanded. "Where's your dad? Whose car is that?" I asked, pointing to a decrepit blue car. My heart sank. I recognized the stupid car.

"Mom, Dad's in the kitchen with those guys I told you about," Serena's voice was brittle. "They showed up right before Dad did, and Dad let them inside."

Lilly yawned sleepily and rubbed her eyes. "They were arguing. It woke us up. We came outside to wait for you..." She buried her face in my shoulder.

I pulled Serena into my opposite shoulder and hugged them both. "Wait here."

I inched the front door closed behind me and tiptoed through the den, into the hall, behind a half-closed door where I could hear without being seen. A thousand tangled thoughts ran through my mind, not the least of which was what the *hell was Monty thinking*? How could he bring this monstrous situation into our—*my*—house? How much trouble was he in, anyway? I exploded into the kitchen. "It's three o'clock in the morning!" I gritted my teeth. "Monty! What. The. HELL?"

In the harsh overhead light, the two grimy men were less threatening, more pathetic. Unless, of course, they produced a gun or a knife, in which case I would re-evaluate. I glared at Monty.

He cleared his throat. "Olivia, I didn't know," he jerked his thumb at the men, "*they'd* be here. I just wanted to come before I went home and apologize for my inappropriate—"

"Ma'am, excuse us, but we've been lookin' for Monty for some time..." The man with the skull-adorned forearm interrupted. When he grinned, I saw that one of his front teeth was gold.

"Does that mean you've been *watching* my house?" Rage clawed its way to my shoulders and stayed there.

The man looked from me to Monty. "Well, you *are* married...he had to come back sometime."

"HE DOESN'T LIVE HERE."

The man's mousy companion blinked. "He don't?"

"No! Plus, he's violating a restraining order." The men looked at each other uneasily. My hands balled into fists at my sides. "Get out of my house, all of you, before I call the cops!"

Monty puffed his chest and walked two paces closer. "Now see here, Olivia..."

"No! *You* see here! The girls are scared to death, and you had no right. You think because Detective Faraday let you off with a warning you can still do this stuff? Unbelievable." I pulled my cell from my pocket.

The men edged toward the door.

"Olivia." Monty's voice was soft as butter. "This is a special circumstance. Surely you can see that"

"Wrong." I scanned recent calls and pressed Hunter's number. "Watch this." I put it on speaker and held the phone out for Monty to hear.

Monty's eyes slitted. He crossed his arms, waiting. The men skulked into the hall to wait.

Hunter answered on the first ring. I machine-gunned events for him and ended the call.

"Police are on the way. *Restraining order*, remember?"

Monty pinned me with his stare.

I pointed at the men. "Get them out of here," I demanded, my voice shaky with exhaustion and fear. I mustered one last shriek. "NOW!"

He cursed, then stomped through the house. I followed, tried to hear, but couldn't quite make out the words as he talked to the two men. Soon, Monty's SUV roared to life and sped away, followed by the other vehicle, sputtering and backfiring. I slumped into one of my porch chairs.

Serena and Lilly stepped out of the shadows. Lilly's index finger was in her mouth and her face was red. Serena leaned in close. "All clear, Mom?"

"All clear, girls. Sorry you had to hear all that."

"We hid in the dark over there." Lilly took her finger out of her mouth, wiped her cheeks, and pointed to a cluster of azaleas bushes. "What *was* that?"

"Yeah, Mom, what was that about?" Serena tossed her hair over one shoulder.

I ran a hand through my hair. "Your dad has over-extended himself."

They looked at each other.

I thought a minute. They were old enough to deal with adult situations. My talks with Mom and the girls had given me an idea of how much I'd shielded them from the truth about their father. How long had I allowed them to think this stuff was right and normal? What did that do to their idea of what good and appropriate men should act like?

"Mom?"

I chewed my lower lip. "Girls, your dad has a gambling problem. He owes a lot of money that he hasn't been able to pay, and those men met with him to get the money."

"Wow." Serena frowned.

Lilly grabbed her hair and looked away.

"This is his problem, not ours." I stabbed the air with my finger. "What he did was wrong, and he cannot bring the consequences into our home."

Lilly's expression cleared. She sniffled. Serena's frown grew deeper.

"Go on to bed," I urged, motioning upstairs. "My gosh, it's so late. Everything's fine. We'll talk tomorrow."

They trudged upstairs.

I doubted I would sleep this night.

* * *

Just as my heartbeat finally slowed, Mom and Dr. Sturgis drove up and parked. They kissed longer than I thought necessary, then disentangled and told each other goodbye. I watched with interest as Mom opened the gate, humming. A nice contrast to my nightmarish evening.

She spontaneously danced from the gate to the porch, then ran up the steps, catching her shoe on a stair and falling smack on her love-struck hiney. She giggled and pushed herself upright, stopping short when she saw me sitting in the dark—like a teenager caught out past curfew.

"What happened to your makeup, Mom?" I teased. "I bet you had some *on* when you left."

She blushed and sat in the chair across from me.

"What a wonderful evening." She sighed.

"Apparently." I chuckled. "I watched you guys nuzzle each other."

"No!" Her hands flew to her cheeks. "You watched?"

"Couldn't tear myself away."

"Me either."

We laughed. I laughed long after she did and stopped when I realized I was becoming slightly hysterical. Maybe I was in delayed shock. She cocked her head at me.

CHAPTER FORTY-ONE

"How did it go in Richmond today?"

I blew out a long breath.

"Oh no."

"It's complicated. When I walked into his house, I had this...I don't know... weird courage. I was a lot braver than I thought I could be."

She recited, "Be strong and of a good courage—"

I held up a hand. I really wasn't in the mood for scripture quotes.

"Sorry." She folded her arms. "So you definitely feel that is who you—"

"No. I had sporadic memories, but I know I was there." I turned toward her. "I lied to you about it."

Sophie nodded. "When I found that man's card...well, I wondered. She shrugged. But he didn't...he wasn't...cooperative?"

I stared into the blackness of my yard, the shadowy shapes of the trees. Birds had started to chirp in anticipation of sunrise. "No. He's trying to hide that I was ever there. How could I have been so stupid?"

Mom leaned toward me. "Honey, you can't blame yourself for that." She paused, seeming to flash back to her own choices. "You made a bad choice. So have I. We learn and move on."

"Maybe." I thought a minute. "But I *did* know it was wrong, Mom. That's why I couldn't tell you the truth. I told you where I was going but—"

Mom shook her head. "Don't even go there, honey. Forgiven."

"But how could I...why did I...do that?"

She sighed. "Olivia, when you were young, I married for all the wrong reasons. I tried to make the best of things, but all I ended up doing was managing crisis after crisis and protecting you from the truth." She sighed. "Maybe I should have been more honest. I didn't know what to do but survive the relationships. Hope that you wouldn't notice how strained and awful they really were. Try to pretend like nothing bad was really happening."

She entwined and un-entwined her fingers in her lap. "I really didn't grow a backbone until well into my forties, and by then you were grown and on your own."

I squinted. "But you never..."

She grimaced. "No, I never let on that anything was wrong. So you apparently figured things were just peachy. And subsequently married a man like Monty."

My eyebrows drew together. "Yeah, but did I have a choice?"

"What do you mean?"

I hesitated, crossing my arms, thinking about a memory I'd not yet fleshed out:

A woman walked down the aisle of a quaint, small church, dressed in a floor-length wedding gown. An older woman walked with her. The older woman relinquished the bride to a dark-haired man once they arrived at a podium and stepped away. Her posture as she took her seat did not convey joy, but regret. Sorrow. Something.

The people didn't appear to be anyone I knew until the bride turned to take her groom's hand and stepped in front of the minister to take her vows. I gasped at the little jig my heart performed upon noticing.

The baby bump was unmistakable.

"Was I...pregnant at my wedding?" I whispered, a furrow forming between my eyebrows.

Mom's eyes widened. "You remember that?"

Okay. It was an actual memory.

Mom went silent.

"Was I happy about the pregnancy?"

She signaled me to wait until she could speak, pressing palms against her eyes. "You didn't know what to think, and I didn't know what to advise. We could've cared for that child—you and I. There were other options besides getting married. But...I just kind of let things work themselves out."

I frowned. "That's what women do, right? Get married if they love the man who got them pregnant?"

"Sometimes it's not the right thing to do. But in this case, I wasn't sure what the right thing to do was."

I thought about that.

"I guess...abortion wasn't discussed?"

Mom smiled, but her eyes were sad. "Monty argued long and hard for

208

that. I stood my ground about not having an abortion, and you listened. You were so *young*. You were scared to death, and you did every little thing Monty told you to do." She shrugged. "I felt so helpless. But in the end, you had the baby."

I thought about Serena. Willful, stubborn, wild-child Serena. How often I'd wished I were more like her. Like her hard-fought entry into the world, she still carried that chip on her shoulder. Maybe in a way, she sensed that her birth had been preceded by a struggle about whether it should happen.

"That's...surprising about Monty."

She frowned. "Monty controlled your every move. You couldn't even have friends unless you snuck around. No way was I letting him talk you into a decision that you might regret your whole life."

I was silent.

"I prayed that something would happen—that you'd wake up and see what he was doing. But you never did." She paused. "You became more passive, less able to voice an opinion, or even know what you wanted. It was all about what *Monty* wanted. And I wondered how deep his controlling behavior went. I asked you if his temper ever became dangerous, but you wouldn't say. Until now..." she said, her voice thoughtful.

I changed the subject. "Those weird men were here tonight."

Mom's eyebrows shot up. She thought a minute, then squinted. "The gambling debt guys?"

I nodded.

She gasped. "You weren't here? What about the girls? They didn't let them in, did they?"

"No, *Monty* was here. I guess they'd been watching my house. Maybe they called him and he agreed to meet them. Don't know. I walked in on a couple of terrified daughters and a shouting match in the kitchen."

Mom slumped in her chair. "I didn't think being gone a few hours would be a problem...the girls were fine when I left, and I thought you'd be back earlier. I'm so sorry, honey."

"Mom, you couldn't have known. It's okay."

"What happened?"

"I ran into the kitchen and freaked out on them."

Her mouth dropped.

"My gosh, I have a restraining order! Monty tried to debate the issue, as usual. I called Hunter, who said the police—"

Both our heads snapped around at the lights flickering up the drive and the sound of crunching gravel as a police cruiser coasted to a stop in my driveway. A uniformed man and woman got out and walked to my gate.

"Olivia Callahan? We had a call about a domestic disturbance. Everything okay here?"

Chapter Forty-Two

"We've kicked up a real firestorm, young lady," Earl Sorenson said a few days later as he pushed a pile of paperwork toward me. "You ready for this?"

I thought about the envelope containing fifty thousand dollars that I'd slid inside a book buried in the deepest, darkest corner of a bookcase. Cozy little security measure.

"Yeah, I'm ready." I smoothed my black skirt and folded my hands in my lap. His "firestorm" paled in comparison to what I'd been through the last few months.

Sorenson's scruffy, gray eyebrows agitated as he riffled through documents. "Hearing's scheduled for next week. You'll need to review all this and get back to me with your responses."

"Why can't we do it right now?"

He pulled at the toupee atop his head, thought better of it, and lowered his arm. "Now?"

"Just give me a few minutes," I said, and scanned each page. I might not be ready for the war yet, but I was ready for the first skirmish. I threw the first motion on his desk. "No way I'm giving him shared custody. I want full custody until I know what our life was like before my accident."

Sorenson pulled the motion closer and scribbled something on it. I assessed the division of assets, his suggestion of an allowance, and groaned. I explained about the gambling issue. I'd already told him about Monty's affair. Sorenson scribbled notes.

"We'll put that in our response. Judge won't like that at all," he said.

We spent another forty-five minutes discussing options. We decided to finalize a formal separation agreement with split assets until I could get my ducks in a row. Monty would throw a fit. I doubted he was used to pushback from his quiet, cautious wife of twenty years. How things had changed.

"Okay, that should hold us for now," Sorenson said. He laid his pen on his desk and folded his arms. "Have you thought about what you want, Olivia, after these stopgap measures are in place?"

I leaned back in my chair and fiddled with what I'd come to believe was my good-luck charm, the heart necklace. "I'm taking it one day at a time. My goal is to have my full memory intact before pursuing something, well... final." I shook my head in frustration. "According to my doctor, we don't know when that will be. So I guess you could say I'll know when I know."

He smiled. "As good a strategy as any. I'll get these typed up and filed today or tomorrow." He stood and stuck out a hand. I stood and clasped it. "I think you're doing a good job with this, Olivia."

"Thanks."

He stuck his gnarled hands in his pants pockets and continued, "Most folks get too emotional to use their common sense. What's important here is what's good for the children and the family as a whole, not getting even."

I was quiet.

"What I'm saying is, you are approaching this in a level-headed way, and it works out better for everybody."

I smiled. "I don't have a lot of memories of our marriage, either. Working to my advantage?"

He laughed. "Probably."

I chatted with the receptionist before I left, who complimented me on my longer hairstyle and new "look," and it made me wonder if I'd not worn makeup or attempted to maximize my feminine collateral before...before what? No one was really sure what had happened to me. As I walked down the hallway, I thought about what a different woman I must seem to everyone but myself.

Outside, the typical humid heat of a Maryland summer had receded. I reveled in the cooler temps, the lush green of summer plumping all the trees. The girls were at their jobs at the YMCA, Mom had returned to Florida, and Dr. Sturgis had returned to Richmond.

All was right with the world. Kind of. I still felt a little insecure on my own.

I approached my car. Reached for the door handle. The reflection of a man behind me crawled up the window. I ignored it—merely someone passing by. But the reflection hovered just behind my right shoulder, unmoving. My hand stilled.

I turned slowly. My jaw dropped. *Niles.*

"Wait...wait, I'm not here to do anything—"

Tremors of fear zipped through me, but a righteous anger batted them away.

"I'm sorry for all this. I never meant..." His voice trailed off.

"Never meant what?" I demanded.

He sighed and shifted his weight from one foot to the other. "I misread the signals, maybe...and, well, Olivia, I shouldn't have done what I did. I'm sorry."

I blinked. How to respond? Certainly he can't know I'm still mixed up about the whole thing, that I'm still piecing it together. But obviously he's in pain about it. Should that make a difference? I frowned. When would I get all my damn memory back? Did I even want to remember? Maybe it would be a mercy...*not* to remember.

"Cops turned my condo upside down." He had trouble looking at me and fastened his gaze to the ground. "They found your prints, hair...more." He shrugged. "Got nothin' to lose by begging. I'm charged with third degree attempted sexual assault." His voice dropped to a whisper. "Askin' you to find it in your heart to...talk them into a lesser charge."

I listened in stunned silence.

He continued, "It'll be in the papers any day, all over TV. I've already had to resign from my firm; my clients have been reassigned."

"How are you...why are you..." My words sputtered and stopped.

"I know," He groaned. "I'm not supposed to be anywhere near you. Like I said, nothin' to lose. I might get outta this with my bicycles." He scrutinized me with red-veined, defeated eyes, and tried to smile. "We had a good time that day, didn't we?" His shirt had a stain on it and his jeans could stand up on their own. Three days' worth of beard stubbled his face.

I tensed for another onslaught.

"Okay, all set."

Niles smiled and rose from the black sectional. "Great! I'll give you a tour of the place." He put his arm around my waist and guided me to the kitchen. "This is where I spend a lot of time. I love to cook, y'know."

"I remember you saying that. I don't, as you know."

He laughed. "Yeah, I get that. Single mom."

His kitchen was a photo shoot from 'Better Homes and Gardens.' Dark wood cabinets, black granite countertops, stainless steel. Two sinks.

I smiled. "Wow, amazing kitchen!"

He moved to the refrigerator and opened the gargantuan Dutch doors. Pulled out a tray with flesh-colored blobs floating in some sort of herbed sauce.

"Looks delicious."

"Hope you like your chicken a little spicy." His forehead creased in concern. "You do, right?"

I nodded, amused. "Yes, that sounds wonderful."

Niles slipped the tray back into the refrigerator with near reverence. I chuckled. He shut the refrigerator and turned to me. "What's funny?"

"Oh, I don't know. Just not so involved with food." He frowned. "Doesn't mean I don't appreciate you cooking for me," I added hastily. His face relaxed. "I just don't get into the art of it, that's all. When I cook, it's a chore, not a joy. I'm sure I'll love the chicken."

"For a minute there I thought I might have to send you packing," he joked.

I winced. A bit too Monty-esque.

He slipped in behind me, propelling me forward. "Okay, gotta see the rest," he said.

He directed me to his bedroom, which, unlike the rest of the house, was warmed by yellows and golds and a thousand pillows on the king-size bed. Less glass, more pictures.

We continued to the master bath, a monstrous affair with a tiled, doorless entry.
"This is what sold me on the condo," he boasted.

I smiled dutifully, thinking no one needed a shower this big. No one. "Beautiful.
I don't think I've ever seen a shower this, um, extravagant."

"My safe place," he said with a sigh.

"Safe place?"

"I like to hop in this shower and soak. It has a blaster of a showerhead. He
wiggled a hand for me to look inside. Monstrous, indeed. Several mini-blasters
lined each side. "It's like therapy," he whispered. "After a hot shower under that
thing, I feel reborn."

I stepped back a pace or two.

He continued, "Sometimes I take two or three a day."

My eyebrows rose. The only man I'd lived with was Monty, and one shower a
day was enough for him.

Niles led the way to the living area and extended his hand toward one of the
black couches. Obediently, I sat.

Niles blurted, "You like bikes?"

"Well, yes, if you mean the non-motorcycle kind."

"I have two. You up for a bike ride right now?"

My gut started fizzing. I clutched at it.

"Sure," I agreed.

He waved his arm around the space. "Only cost me forty thousand dollars to
furnish. After my wife left, she got the house and the furnishings in the divorce,"
he explained. "Not a bad deal, huh?"

I obligingly inspected his furnishings. Forty thousand dollars seemed a small
fortune.

"My ex handled our finances. I never knew the exact price of things—he took
care of all of it. I picked stuff out, but he paid for it."

Niles laughed. "Things are sure different for you now, aren't they?"

I decided no response would be the wisest response. A beat of silence passed. I
cleared my throat. "Should I go change, then?"

Niles nodded. "Yeah, let's go for a quick ride. Then we can come back, take a shower, and have a few drinks before dinner."

That shower thing again. I smiled at him, rose, and walked down the hallway. I closed the door to my room behind me and locked it. I marched to the dresser, jerked out shorts and a T-shirt. I should've gotten to know this guy a little better before I committed to an entire weekend. But I was determined to have a good time. Even if it killed me.

* * *

I re-focused on Niles. Everything in me wanted to jump in my car and speed off, and yet...had we really had a good time that day?

"Richmond PD is probably putting out an APB on me right now, but I had nowhere to go. Only thing I could think of was staying somewhere safe and cheap. Somewhere I could maybe talk to you, and where they wouldn't look for me."

I backed away.

Niles held his palms up in surrender. I flinched. "Okay, I'm outta here. That was all I had. Please...just think about it." He took a few steps, paused, and turned back. He gazed at my chest and smiled. "I'm glad you kept the necklace."

I clutched the gold heart in horror. As he walked away, I ripped the necklace from my throat, threw it on the sidewalk, and ground it into a mangled mass of metal beneath my shoe.

Chapter Forty-Three

The car in front of him jerked to a stop. Detective Faraday slammed on the brakes, his seatbelt nearly giving way with the force of it. He cursed.

"That's what happens, dude," he whispered to himself as he waited for Richmond's rush hour traffic to start moving again. "That's what happens when your mind is on a woman instead of the road." He draped his arm over the steering wheel and fumed. It would be at least seven p.m. before he made it home.

A call appeared in the display. He pressed the button on the steering wheel. "Yeah? Faraday here."

"Detective Faraday?" an aging voice warbled. "This is Father Henry. You don't know me, but I have some information that may interest you."

"Excellent," he quipped. "I'm stalled in traffic, and who knows when I'm gonna move again, so you have my full attention."

The older man laughed. "It has to do with the, uh, 'Mercy's Miracle' case, I believe."

"Okay."

"Are you familiar with the name Niles Peterson?"

Hunter jerked upright. "What about Niles Peterson?"

"He came by my church a few days ago, and I just got off the phone with him. He's definitely a tortured soul, that one."

"Go on."

"This is not within the realm of a confessional, you understand..."

"I understand, Father. Go ahead."

"He walked into my church, had confessional, and I was so concerned I asked him to stay afterward. He's lost his family, and the publicity about the case has isolated him. His job is gone now too. I'm afraid he's at risk."

"Yeah, well, he's a person of interest, you know, in Olivia Callahan's assault."

"I do. And I can't share anything about that one way or the other, but I can share what he told me that's public knowledge. His parents died in a tragic fire when he was a boy, and he lost everything but an old photo album and a stuffed toy. He was fostered after that. Terrible experiences that scarred him for life."

"That's sad, Father, but I don't see how it has any bearing on whether he committed a crime or not."

"That's not what I'm concerned about. Niles has had one tragedy after the other. I'm concerned about his state of mind and whether he wants to live." After a slight pause, the older man said, "He gave me the stuffed toy and photo album. Said he wouldn't need them anymore, then he went through a box of Kleenexes as he sat there."

Detective Faraday was quiet.

"I can't say anything definitive about what he's done or not done, but I can assure with all confidence that he has repented of his sins. However, he's holding on to guilt and shame and it's eating him alive. I don't know what he is capable of."

"Can I have those artifacts, Father? I will return them."

"You don't have to return them," Father Henry told him. "Perhaps he will want them later—if he survives the trauma he's going through."

Detective Faraday nodded thoughtfully. "Thanks, Father. Can you drop those things by the police station?"

The man laughed. "Well, I would, but aren't you in Richmond, Virginia? I'm in Maryland."

He briefly flashed on Olivia's face, her full lips, her delicate hands. "I'm sure I'll be back there soon." He frowned. "Wait...Niles was in Maryland?"

"Yes, I'm not sure that he still is. But when he walked in, I knew he was a man in trouble. Let me know when you're back in the area and I'll get the articles to you. And, Detective Faraday, one last thing…you should be aware that he does own a gun."

Chapter Forty-Four

Olivia

I glanced around the table, clutching my iced tea glass as if it were a life preserver in a sea of unknowns. Our animated group sat on the patio at Hunt Valley's Oregon Grille, a lavish affair with intricate, landscaped paths and lights strung overhead. The lights reminded me of something, but I couldn't remember what. Callie had insisted on a girls' night out, and I figured I had to get back to my life sometime, so I agreed. Now I wondered if it had been a mistake. Of the seven women, I only knew Callie, even though they all had "Olivia" stories to share.

Loudly and with great flourish.

Callie raised her glass, which held a frothy, peach concoction. "Hold up a second, ladies. Let's toast! Welcome back, Olivia."

The six other women shouted their approval and lifted glasses. We clinked. The others had ordered mixed drinks, but I—I guess out of habit—had ordered iced tea.

My eyebrows drew together. These women knew me as wallflower; cautious, go-along-with-whatever Olivia. The mousy wife who had allowed Monty to grind her opinions to mush. The wife who'd had an *allowance*, for God's sake.

I plunked the tea on the table and signaled our waiter.

"Martini, please."

He smiled and disappeared.

Callie gawked at me.

One of the women blurted what everyone was thinking. "Olivia, you don't drink anything but a glass of wine about once a month."

"I do now," I said.

They shrieked with laughter, and two martinis later, so did I.

* * *

Cushiony and lubricated and strewn with song, the drive home was a complicated one. I struggled to stay awake.

"Must've been a reason you didn't drink mixed drinks," I muttered as I chugged up my driveway, vowing to never drive after two martinis again. Ever.

My car jerked when I turned it off in front of the garage, which I thought strange. On closer examination, I'd forgotten to put the car in park. I giggled.

I got out of the car and snugged my arms around me against the night chill. How I loved this place, I thought, looking around as the night sounds croaked and bleated. A canopy of stars twinkled in a dark, clear sky. Staring upward, scenes flashed through my mind: miles of strung white lights, families at picnic tables, sand. Sailboats bobbing. A marina. Full moon. *Stay with it.*

A name jigged and jagged into my consciousness. *Niles.*

I'd been with Niles at a familiar...wait...The Boat House? Yes. That was right. We'd been there often as a family, hadn't we? I concentrated, and saw Monty herding us into the restaurant, his voice shrill and commanding. Resignation reflected in my daughters' slow steps. Heat flushed up my chest. *Stay with it.* Monty had been more interested in accomplishing an agenda than enjoying his family.

The images faded in murky wisps, like the afterglow of Fourth of July fireworks. I exhaled and ran upstairs to check on the girls. I watched them sleep for several minutes, then padded downstairs to the porch and plopped into my favorite chair, eyes closed against the dizziness two martinis causes

221

a non-drinker. *Former...*non-drinker. I smiled.

Seconds passed. Minutes. My breathing paced with the night, rising and falling. Images whirled into focus. In my car, driving. Singing. On my way to...where? A driveway. My forehead pulled together. A man helped me out of the car. Or was that into a car? I'd walked through a house.

Go with it, Olivia. I rubbed my shoulders, willed myself back into the memory.

The images accelerated, whizzing by, an out-of-control carousel. I desperately snatched at details as the images blurred together in my mind: wine glass. Full moon. Candlelight. Out of focus. *Out of focus?* My speech... slurred. I rose from a table; no, I was lifted. Lifted from my chair. By whom? *Niles.* Niles had his arm around me, helping me to a bedroom. My legs... my arms...wouldn't work. I groaned, unable to stop the onslaught. I pulled my legs up and curled into a ball.

* * *

"I'm not sure," I told him, forcing out the words, slow and deliberate. "Only had a couple." I pointed to my wine glass, half full. "Shee? Barely started on my third."

I pawed at the glass, my movements mysteriously clumsy. It crashed to the floor. Niles jumped up in slow motion and his form seemed to float to the floor as he picked up broken glass and mopped up liquid with his napkin. Each of his motions left a rainbow trail which had me mesmerized.

"Well, it seems you are done for the night, young lady." He pulled me from my chair.

My legs collapsed under me. "Whoopsie," I sang.

"Easy." He laughed and helped me up.

He carried me to the guest room and put me on the bed. I fought to stay conscious. Through a fog, I watched Niles undress. Why would he change his clothes? I struggled upright on an elbow, but the room started to spin.

I lay back down. "Niles, I'm okay." My speech sounded flat, elongated, as if from a great distance. "You don't hafto shtay..."

Nothing made sense. Why didn't my body work? I opened one eye to see if the world had stopped spinning, and forced myself to focus. Niles stood there, in all his naked glory, smiling. Why would he do that? I thought about the nude women prints on the wall in his bathroom. I couldn't seem to stop giggling. Maybe he thought sleeping with me would help.

"It's shweet, Niles, to think you should stay, but I just need to...need to—"

Then hands were everywhere, unbuttoning, unzipping, pulling off my shoes, insistent. Alarms clanged through every dulled sense.

"No!" I pushed him away, but it was like pushing through wet cement. "No!" Niles backed up, laughing. His head seemed too big for his body, and all I could see was this huge face, mocking me. As I watched in horror, Monty's face appeared on Niles' body. I tried to scream but all that came out was a squeak.

I clung to consciousness and scrambled backward off the bed and fell to the floor with a thump. My body was useless and weak and wouldn't obey. I begged my arms to work. Work, dammit! Nauseated and dizzy, I shifted my weight until I rolled over, then struggled up to hands and knees, bleating like some sort of wounded sheep.

* * *

My arms flailed at the air. The night enveloped me in its comforting darkness. Breathing hard, I stared at the moonlit trees lined up along the drive like sentinels. Felt the familiar fabric of my chair cushions beneath my hands. Slid my feet across the sturdiness of the porch flooring. *You're safe, Olivia. Safe.*

"Ohmigosh," I whispered, "It *was* him." My forehead creased in concentration. "It had to be." But why had Monty entered at the last minute?

I left my chair and sat on the top step. The leaves on the trees shimmied with the breeze. A stray cat bounded from behind a hedge. The cat hesitated, one paw in mid-air, when it saw me. I clapped my hands at him. He ran away.

Chapter Forty-Five

I yawned and glared at the antique alarm clock on my nightstand, buzzing like an angry, oversized bee. In the background, pounding assaulted my front door. Fumbling for the alarm switch, I managed to turn it off and hastily pulled on T-shirt and jeans. I walked to answer the door, finger-combing my hair.

"Who's there?"

"Hey, girl, it's Callie. Is this a bad time?"

I quickly opened the door, irritated at how jumpy I'd become. "Of course not, come on in."

Callie squinted at my just-out-of-bed face. "Really tied one on last night, eh?"

I laughed. "I think we all did."

We walked to the kitchen where Callie placed her ample bottom on one of the bar stools and palmed her chin, watching me make coffee. "Need help?"

"Nope," I said pleasantly. As the Keurig did its thing, I bent over the island and planted my elbows.

"So I was mostly a teetotaler, huh?"

She grinned. "Well, you were not one to go out and just...drink for *fun*." She paused and thought about that, then continued, "You drank once in a while just because everybody else did." Her eyes twinkled. "But last night you were the life of the party."

I laughed. "I must've been a blast before."

Callie shrugged. "We loved you anyway."

I pulled two mugs from the cabinet, poured coffee, and put cream and sugar onto the island in front of us.

"I'm dying to know how things are going with Monty—and that cute detective..." Callie wiggled her eyebrows and jiggled her shoulders.

I laughed. "It would make a great soap opera."

My cell lit up with a text from Serena. I texted back that I was fine, slept in. She texted that she and Lilly had tried to say goodbye before they'd gone to work, but I'd been asleep.

"Sorry," I said.

Callie nodded. "Don't change the subject."

I grinned and sipped my coffee.

"Let's just say Monty is probably having a long, hard talk with himself right now."

Callie whooped and threw her arms up. "Hallelujah."

"I wouldn't celebrate so soon. He just got hit with a ton of stuff from my attorney."

"Yeah? Oh. My. Gosh."

"I'm sure he is not rejoicing in his tent."

She looked puzzled. "Excuse me?"

"A happy camper," I explained with a sigh at my lingering verbal misfires. She chuckled.

I folded my arms on the granite countertop. "I am not sure how he will react. I know it's killing him, since I never stood up to him before. One thing I'm hoping is that I'll see the real Monty." I sighed. "I cannot remember how we—how *he*—was before the coma. It's just not there."

Callie snorted. "I can fill in those blanks for you, dear."

I was quiet.

She continued, "Let's see if I can come up with a few words to describe Monty." She tilted her head back and forth, ponytail waving like a flag. One plump finger touched her chin. Her nails had been painted bright purple. "Angry. Controlling. Dismissive." She paused. "Condescending, that's a great one." She picked up her mug and drained it.

I picked at a strand of hair and curled it around my finger. "Even when he was trying to be...well, trying to act normal?"

"Even when he was trying, it was...it was so obvious. You could tell it was fake. And all of us," she emphasized, "knew that you couldn't make one move without his approval. Not one." She sniffed. "We tried to talk to you, but you always shut us down. We gave up."

I considered this. "What words would you use to describe me?"

"Well, not *now*, of course," she trilled. But before...you were just...kind of there. Not saying much. Smiling and patient and...always courteous... kind."

I frowned.

Callie fluttered her hands. "All that was just fine, but we couldn't get you to...open up. It didn't seem like you had much fun, actually." She chuckled, shaking her head. "To say that we're shocked at the transformation is an understatement.' We'd love to be flies on the wall when you stand up to him."

I traced patterns on the counter with a fingertip. "I'm just being myself." I whooshed out a long breath. "At least I think I am."

Callie reached out to pat my hand. "We are *relieved.* We were afraid his anger would escalate, that you would disappear. Isolate. You showed up a couple times with a black eye, or a huge bruise on your arm. And there was nothing we could do about it."

I gasped. "I had no idea he was abusive."

"We suspected. We never knew for sure. You never said he did it."

I thought about that. "So words to describe me now are?"

"Straightforward. Decisive." She paused. "Fun. In the moment." She snapped her fingers. "That's another thing: you were always distracted, like you were waiting for something, or someone, to bust you." She leaned toward me. "That is totally not there anymore. It is awesome to see you bloom like this." She walked around the island and enveloped me in a hug. She smelled like roses. "You're coming back to life, and we are *so* excited for you."

I mumbled into her soft shoulder.

She released me and said, "Pardon?"

CHAPTER FORTY-FIVE

"I never even knew I was dead."

* * *

After Callie left, my cell vibrated. Hunter. I let it ring once. Twice. Three times before answering.

"Hey. How're things?"

"Good," I said.

He cleared his throat. "I called to check on you and see if anything new…"

"Has popped up," I finished.

"Yep." I heard his office chair creak as he rocked.

"Actually, I was going to call you."

"Of course you were," he teased.

"I was."

"Okay."

I paused. "I had more memories of…that night."

The creaking stopped. "You did?"

"I think my brain is slowly piecing together all of it, but it's shaky."

"Did you write it down?"

"I'll email it to you."

"Good," he said. "I interviewed a friend of his here in Richmond—or correction, *former* friend. Niles used Rohypnol on her, Olivia."

I gasped. "Is that what happened to me?"

"I would stake my badge on it. Said she'd testify. Said it was Niles and someone else."

I was silent.

"Are you ready to press charges?"

I sighed, grabbed a lock of my hair and coiled it around my finger. "And ruin a man's life? What if it wasn't him?"

Hunter grunted. "Chances are ninety-nine percent that it *was* him. If we want to press charges, we need to make sure he's still around. Niles is a perfect candidate to disappear."

What would happen if I pressed charges? So far, I hadn't remembered things with any huge, convincing clarity and I'd been pretty smashed. Was that enough to convict? The story would drag through the media for weeks, maybe months. My phone would blow up with requests for interviews, mics shoved in my face every time I left the house. The girls would be hounded as well. And my mom—what would it do to her relationship with Dr. Sturgis? Everyone would be in the spotlight again. But…he'd done it before. Someone had to hold him accountable.

"Olivia? You still there?"

"Yeah," I muttered.

"Listen, I know it's a tough decision. A lot of women don't press charges." He sighed. "Sad thing is, when guys like this walk, they get empowered or something. Statistics say most of 'em do it again."

"I realize this is serious. I'll have an answer soon, I promise."

"Okay. In the meantime, how's our friend Monty doing?"

"My attorney just dumped a bunch of motions on him. I imagine he's not doing very well."

"Yeah?" Glee leaked into his voice. "Watch your back with that guy. When a man gets mad enough, stressed enough, he's capable of—"

My brow furrowed. "Let's change the subject." Why didn't I want to talk about this? Was I defending Monty? Ohmigod, why would I do that? Did I not want to believe I'd married someone capable of abuse? Pushing the thoughts away, I silently reminded myself that I was not that woman anymore.

Hunter let out a breath. "Okay."

My gut fizzed a little.

"Olivia, I don't know if this is appropriate or even—"

"Responsible?"

"Yeah."

"I'm sure it's not."

"How do you know what I'm talking about?" he joked.

My cheeks grew warm.

"Your call," he said. "But you need to understand that until my involvement in this case is over, we can have no personal, uh…involvement. It'd be my job, so..."

I traced tiny patterns on my jeans. "I understand. How about if we just... meet for coffee?"

"For interview purposes, that's fine." He paused. "I'll be in touch. Have a nice night, Olivia."

I stared at my phone for a full minute. What on earth had just started?

My cell vibrated in my hand. My breath caught in my throat, but then I realized it was Mom. Thank God. I needed her insights right now.

"Hi," she answered. "How's it going today?"

I blurted what Hunter had shared with me about Niles and the ongoing investigation.

"Wait...what was the last thing you said? Niles did what?"

"He approached me the other day."

Mom went quiet. I heard the flick of a lighter. An intake and outake breath. "I'm sure you called your detective, right?"

"He's not *my* detective, Mom. And I thought about it but, I don't know whether it would help or hurt."

"Olivia Rosemary, that man is *dangerous*. You need to tell him!"

I sighed. "Mom, he wanted to apologize. He said he had nothing to lose, that he'd already lost everything, his kids, his work—basically everything. He said he'd do anything to make it up to me. I don't know... this is so confusing. I can't even remember everything that happened, and I felt sorry for the guy. If I get Hunter involved, he'll be violating his bail or something, and I just don't want to see him—look, what if he didn't do it? Or what if it was an accident?"

"That man should be in prison! The least they could do is get him off the streets."

"Well, someone put up bail."

I heard mom's bracelets clinking, and pictured her thoughtfully smoking the last of her cigarette. The silence between us lengthened.

"Mom, I'm trying to figure out what to do."

"I know, honey." She groaned. "But this man—do you not understand that he is a significant threat?"

"Is he? What if he's just a broken man trying to get fixed?"

"Olivia, you have a brain for a reason."

"Well," I retorted, "then should we just ignore that scripture that you keep saying about loving your enemies?"

Sophie was silent.

"Mom, I'm not saying I'm going to snuggle up with the guy. I'm just saying that sometimes mercy is better than judgment."

Sophie snorted. "Mercy doesn't mean *stupid*, honey."

Chapter Forty-Six

The more he thought about the mess the divorce had become, the more he fretted. He still wasn't certain he wanted to reconcile with Olivia, but anything would be easier than this blasted divorce. He couldn't seem to make the simplest decisions anymore. Monty stared down at Baltimore's Inner Harbor from his office window. A few seagulls screeched past his window. A yacht drifted into the harbor, its horn blaring yacht-language at other yachts. Kirsten knocked and peeped around the door.

"Monty? Remember your eleven o'clock."

He didn't respond. She took a tentative step into his office.

"Monty?"

He focused. "What?" he barked.

"Your appointment…be here in a few minutes."

"Yes, thanks." He smiled, apologetic. "Thanks, Kirsten."

"No problem," she said, then left.

Monty sat at his desk, carefully patting his hair to make sure it wasn't sticking up anywhere, and decided the last thing he needed for this appointment was to put on his sport coat. He didn't want to look *too* successful. His starched, white dress shirt and ridiculously expensive tie should suffice to intimidate.

He wasn't looking forward to it, but in desperation he'd invited the thugs to his office. Maybe the professional environment would enhance credibility, buy a little time to get the money together. He frowned. Olivia must have found that money, but he was loath to ask. Maybe *she* hadn't found it, but somebody had—he'd checked the sideboard. Fifty thousand would have been a down payment on a few months', maybe even a year's delay. In the meantime—he dug his fingers into the armrests—all he could do was punt. He'd thought about taking the money from some of his investments he'd had his advisor scatter abroad for tax liability purposes, but he didn't want the tax burden and regulatory questions when a large sum of money from overseas landed in his bank account. No, he had to keep all that separate, and continue to let it grow, unless he wanted to subject himself to lengthy legal conversations and massive IRS tax hits. The cash in the envelope he'd saved had been his hedge against this situation, and it pissed him off mightily that it was gone. Was it gone, though? His scowl deepened. It better not be. He laid his head on the back of his chair and covered his eyes with his hand.

He heard Kirsten greet someone, the squeak of her chair as it wheeled back, the soft steps as she walked to his door.

"Your appointment is here." Her nose wrinkled in disgust.

Monty quickly covered the space between his desk and the door. To their credit, they'd dressed for the occasion and looked less like drug addicts and more like door-to-door salesmen. One had greased his hair back and wore an actual button-up instead of a T-shirt. The other had traded tattered sandals for slip-ons. Both wore baggy polyester slacks that bunched around their feet.

Monty closed the door and gestured to the two chairs in front of his desk. The men obediently shuffled to the chairs and sat. The smell of cigarettes drifted in with them. Monty coughed and sat behind his desk.

"You work *here*? Seriously, man, you shouldn't have trouble payin' the measly hundred grand," the thinner, shorter of the two said.

"I need more time," Monty said, tenting his fingers, staring earnestly at each man.

The men snickered.

The one with the gold tooth extended his hands to each side. "The boss told us to tell you we're all outta time."

"I'm working on it, okay? You'll get your money."

The smaller man warbled, "We got our orders, man."

Monty glared at him. "And I have my reasons. Look around you," he said, waving his arm. "You can tell I'm good for it."

"No dice, man," Gold Tooth said as he reached behind his back and slowly slid a Glock 19 pistol from his waistband, racked the slide, and held it in his lap. "You might say we're very serious."

Monty stared at the gun. The men stared at Monty.

Gold Tooth laughed and said, "*Seriously* serious."

The smaller man leered, his eyes overbright. His pupils had pinned.

Monty pulled at his collar and cleared his throat. "Now, c'mon guys, you can't—"

Gold Tooth rose, strode to Monty's side, and placed the barrel of the gun against Monty's head. "Yes, we can."

He heard a gentle knock.

"Monty?"

"Answer her," Gold Tooth hissed and moved slightly so his back would be toward Kirsten if she entered. He eased the gun off Monty's temple and pointed it at his chest.

"Yeah," Monty croaked, then cleared his throat. "Busy in here, Kirsten."

"Okay," she said through the door. "You have a lunch date with your daughters. They are in the waiting area."

He paled. The man holding the gun frowned. He nudged Monty's chest with the muzzle.

"Okay, Kirsten. Tell them I'll be there in a few minutes."

"Will do."

Her steps receded. Monty blew out a breath.

"Now, that could be real handy," Gold Tooth said. The other man snickered.

Monty's heart jackhammered. "You touch my daughters and I'll...I'll..."

"You'll what?" The man's finger moved closer to the trigger.

Monty looked down. Tears leaked from his eyes. "Please," he begged. "Please don't do this. I'll get it. I will."

Gold Tooth flipped the gun muzzle-up up with a flourish. "That's all I needed to hear, man." His bleary, blue eyes disappeared beneath parchment-thin folds of flesh as he smiled. The man returned the gun to its holster, then sat in the chair in front of Monty's desk.

Monty hands shook. He laced his fingers together.

"Need a date," the man blurted.

"How much time can you give me?"

"A week."

After a drawn-out staredown, Monty agreed.

Kirsten trotted in the minute they left. "What was that all about?"

"Get back to work, Kirsten," he said, his back to her as he looked out his window.

A beat of silence. "Fine. But your kids are waiting."

She slammed the door on her way out.

Chapter Forty-Seven

Olivia

Wiping my hands on a tea towel after loading vegetables in the soup stock to simmer, I covered the pot and set the burner to low. I pulled the band out of my ponytail and walked into my bedroom to trade my comfy leggings for jeans, and my cooking-stained T-shirt for a clean one. *Who says I can't cook*, I thought smugly. I refreshed my pink lipstick. The soup would be ready in about an hour, and the girls would be surprised I'd cooked…but where were they? I'd been happy to drop them at their father's office for lunch, but five hours seemed a long time for a simple lunch downtown. I grabbed my cell and texted.

Waited.

Nothing. I tossed the phone on my bed in frustration.

I needed tea.

As I walked downstairs into the kitchen, I heard the muffled *ching* of a text. I ran back upstairs, dove onto the bed, and scooped up my phone. Lilly. They were on their way. Good. I slid the phone into my back pocket.

Thirty minutes later, Monty's car raced up the drive. I shook my head. Why couldn't this man drive like a sane person? The girls hopped out, followed by their father. I sat rocking and wating on the porch.

Monty spoke first. "Sorry about the delay. I should have called."

"What took so long?"

Serena and Lilly traded guilty glances. I tried to quench a growing sense of doom.

"Dad had some, uh, business to take care of," Serena said.

Lilly's curls bobbed in agreement.

"Yeah? And it took all afternoon?"

They were quiet.

"I dropped them at my gym while I took care of a few things," Monty mumbled.

I glared at him. "Your *gym*? You mean the one by the freeway, right across from the *prison*?" I felt the familiar pounding at a pulse point in my temple that occurred mainly when Monty was around.

"It's perfectly safe, Olivia."

"Whatever! Nothing's safe down there." I turned toward the girls, who were edging toward the front door. "How did it go in there, girls?"

"Fine. Great, Mom," they chorused. Their expressions begged me to let it go.

I told them to go inside. The screen slapped closed behind them. Riot rearranged himself inside the door. I waited.

Monty groaned. "I guess I need to talk to you about this."

I winced. "About what?"

"Can I sit?"

I nodded. He sat, loosened his tie. I resumed rocking my chair. Nice and slow, staring at him.

"Remember the men that were here, and you, um—"

"Told you to get the heck out and take them with you? Yeah, who could forget that?"

He scowled. "Still can't get used to the new you."

"Get used to it," I fired back.

He sighed. "I have a problem, Olivia, and I owe some people money."

"No kidding."

He studied me. "You found the money."

I said nothing. The wicker rocker made pleasant, crunchy sounds on the floorboards as I rocked.

"Olivia, the men came to my office today and threatened me. With a gun."

I stopped rocking. "What have you done, Monty?"

He waved a dismissal. "You know I like to gamble a bit. And I've, well, taken a little too long to pay them back, that's all."

"How much?"

Monty pulled the knot out of his tie, slid it from around his collar, rolled it carefully, and lay it beside him—a silken, rainbow-colored, cinnamon roll.

"How much, Monty?"

"A hundred thousand. Maybe more by now." He shrugged.

The tension in my gut percolated up to my mouth. I thought about the note I'd snuck out of its envelope, then resealed and sent to him. At least he'd told me the truth. I struggled to control the words that wanted to fly out. In a brief moment of sanity, I threw up a silent prayer. The tension eased a little. I smiled and shook my head.

"What?" he asked

"Nothing," I said. "This is *your* problem. It has nothing to do with me. I suggest you fix it."

"Kinda hard to fix it. Thanks to you, there is a hold on our accounts. Can't pay anything but routine bills."

"Good," I said.

"You don't understand, Olivia."

I waited.

"These guys know where I live…they know I have daughters." He looked at me. "*We* have daughters. What if they, what if…?" He paused.

I felt drops of perspiration break out between my shoulder blades and trickle slowly down my back. My mind raced to Hunter. I'd ask him what to do. Instant relief saturated my mind. When I looked at Monty now, all I felt was hatred. Loathing.

"That you would put me and the kids at risk like this…it's…it's *unthinkable.* You're on your own with this one. Unless you want to talk to Detective Faraday."

"Right," he spat. "Be a cold day in hell before I talk to that bast—"

"Hold on a second. He's a good guy to have on your side."

He snorted. "Definitely not on *my* side."

I shrugged. "I'll talk to Hunter about the situation. In the meantime, you need to abide by the restraining order."

"*Hunter?*" Monty's voice sliced the air like a knife.

"Detective Faraday."

"Ah. Got it."

Monty had a knack for making me feel guilty, even when I'd done nothing wrong. But when had I started thinking of Detective Faraday as Hunter? It had just popped out. Natural as you please.

I glared at Monty.

Monty twisted his mouth enough to leave no doubt as to his opinion of the detective. He stalked angrily to his SUV. Any shred of hope I might have had for reconciliation evaporated.

I glanced at the chair he'd been sitting in. He'd forgotten his tie, still rolled and sitting pertly on the side table.

I picked it up and called out.

When he turned, I threw it as hard as I could. It unrolled itself at his feet like a snake in the grass.

Chapter Forty-Eight

I couldn't get past the irony.

A covert weekend with my alleged attacker had led me to Detective Faraday, and now he was spending his off-duty weekend in Maryland, ostensibly to interview me, but I think there was more to it than that. It felt like a Hallmark movie. A really bad, dark, and twisty Hallmark movie that had not ended yet.

"Mom! Did you hear me?" Serena's voice chided.

I shook my head and turned toward her.

She sighed. "Listen much?"

"Sorry, honey," I said, wiping down the counters. "Thinking."

Lilly's eyelids dropped to half-mast. "I bet I know what..." she sing-songed. "You didn't dress up for *us*, Mom."

"Whatever. He's just here to interview me in a casual setting." I looked down at my white pants and pink, sleeveless top, smiling. They were right, I'd even worn my good gold hoop earrings and spent time on my hair.

The girls shoved bites of cereal into their mouths at the breakfast bar.

"Sure, Mom," Serena said, winking at her sister. They laughed.

"What time do you guys go to work today?"

Serena pressed her phone to look at the time. "In an hour. He coming over now?"

I nodded.

"You fixing him breakfast, Mom?"

I smiled at Lilly. "Least I can do."

"I like him," she said, matter-of-fact.

239

"Me too," Serena said, slurping the last of the milk from her bowl.

I told her to use her spoon and, as usual, she ignored me. I grabbed the bowl, rinsed it, and stuck it into the dishwasher. "So why don't you guys catch me up on stuff?"

Lilly grabbed a tendril of hair and wrapped it around her finger. Serena rubbed her phone thoughtfully. I wiped my hands on a tea towel and waited.

And waited.

I sighed. "Lilly, you start. How's work?"

She glanced at her sister. "It's good. I mean, nothing really exciting, just lots of kids and yelling." She went quiet a beat, then lifted a finger in the air. "A group of us want to go to Artscape downtown next weekend. Just so you know."

"Okay, honey. Let me know details when you can and we'll figure it out." I turned toward Serena.

"What about you? How's work?"

Her sun-kissed hair fell to one side as she looked at me. She tossed it over her bronzed shoulder. "It's fine. Boring. I just sit there and watch the pool." She stuck out an arm. "At least I'm getting a tan."

I murmured the usual sunscreen admonitions, which she tuned out. I had to admit, she was stunning with that dark skin and long blond hair. I wondered what was really going on in her head.

"How's, um, what's his name?" I asked.

"Joseph."

"Yes. How's Joseph?"

"He's good. We just hang out sometimes. Not serious." She shrugged, walked out of the kitchen.

Wistfully, I looked forward to remembering what my daughters' expressions and reactions meant; looked forward to an existence devoid of secrets and lies and crisis. I longed for closure...or a fresh start. Something. For now, all I wanted was for my girls to know I loved them.

I finished cleaning the kitchen, set out eggs, a frying pan, griddle, and pancake batter. Maybe he liked blueberries. I grabbed some out of the refrigerator.

My pulse quickened. I wiped sweaty palms on my pants. My mother used to say she had premonitions. Her palms would sweat and her pulse would speed up just before something crazy happened.

Great, I thought. I needed less crazy, not more.

I poured a cup of coffee and went outside. The girls had planted themselves in the porch swing, apparently to wait for Hunter. The swing creaked comfortably from its hinges in the ceiling. A morning breeze whistled through the trees. Birds swooped to the feeders in the yard.

"There he is, Mom," Serena said, pointing.

We heard a car crunch up the driveway on the gravel.

But it wasn't Hunter's car.

It was Monty's.

I groaned.

The black SUV pulled in front of the house and stopped. Monty erupted from the car, all smiles. "Morning, everybody."

The girls stared at me. I stared at Monty. Had I missed something? Forgotten a planned meeting? He shouldn't be here, right? *Right.*

He walked up the stairs.

The girls whiplashed from him to me and back again.

"Why are you here, Monty?" I nearly choked on the words.

He took a step toward me. I jerked my head toward the front door. The girls skedaddled into the house.

He spread his hands. "Listen, Olivia, I've been thinking. Hear me out."

I glared at him. "Monty, you should have called. Why would you…just show up like this? Especially after all that crap with those disgusting men? Are you out of your mind?"

A shadow passed across his face. "It's my house too, Olivia."

"Court order says you are to stay away, Monty. And you've been ordered out of the house for the time being."

"Screw the court order," he sputtered. "This is ridiculous. We're still married."

"Separated." I stood and squared my shoulders. "Almost divorced."

"That's what I wanted to talk to you about." His eyes were dark marbles.

241

"Let's go back to...the way things were. Forget it ever happened."

I glared at him. "Are you serious?" I pointed a finger at his car. "Leave!"

Monty crossed his arms and planted his feet.

My stomach churned.

Monty stared at me, set his jaw, and didn't move.

My eyebrows drew together. What was this, a dare? Were we three years old? Why was he still on my porch?

Monty scowled. "Didn't you listen to all that stuff your mom used to preach to us about marriage? What about *forgiveness?*" He drew within ten inches of me, punctuating the words with his large hands.

My mom's words sprang to my mind. "Forgiveness doesn't mean *stupid*, Monty."

Oops, I thought, too late.

His lips pressed together in an angry scowl. He sprang at me, one arm drawn back, fist aimed. I flinched and put my arms up, trying my best to push away the cascade of images he'd triggered, but it was no use.

His scorched breath and angry words made me back away. When he clenched his fist and knocked me to the floor, I barely saw it coming. I put my arms up, but his were strong and hard and mine were soft and thin. The shock I exhibited made him even angrier. He shoved me to the floor. I tried to pick myself up and got onto my hands and knees before he kicked me back to the floor. My mind ran in crazed, panicked circles. This was the man I loved. He couldn't possibly be doing this to me. But he was, my mind insisted. I drew my legs up and encircled them with my arms, rocked to my side in a fetal position and ducked my head—that way he couldn't hurt the baby. "Please, don't hurt the baby," I sobbed. "Please, please—"

As the horrific images receded, my delayed reaction was pure rage. Monty paled at my expression and let his fist fall to his side. Then, his expression vicious, he shoved me, hard. I fell awkwardly onto the end table between the chairs. The flimsy table gave way, and I crashed to the floor. Serena screamed, then exploded through the door and pushed her dad out of the way to get to me. Lilly's terrified sobs broke my heart. Serena's strong, young grip pulled me up and, over Monty's shoulder, I had the immense satisfaction of watching the best witness to the whole thing that anyone

242

could hope for dash to the porch.

Monty spun around. Hunter bounded up the stairs. I rubbed my aching backside and tried to comfort Serena. He took it all in—me, the SUV, Monty shaking and angry, Serena defiant and defensive, Lilly weeping quietly inside the front screen.

"You okay?" he murmured, urging me to back away from what he had obviously identified as a dangerous situation. He opened the screen and gently moved Serena and I inside with Lilly. Then he planted himself between us and a red-faced Monty, breathing fire on the porch.

His voice calm, he said, "Thought you were not supposed to be here unless prearranged."

I watched as Monty took in Hunter's casual attire. "Don't think that's any of your business. Between *my wife* and me."

"I agree. Not my business. Unless there's a threat involved."

I tried to shoo the girls out of earshot, but they wouldn't budge. Serena jammed her arms across her chest and shook her head. Lilly inched closer to her sister and stared at the floor.

"Looks like a threat to me." Hunter glanced at me through the screen. "Olivia, you can press charges, you know."

Monty clenched his hands at his sides and dropped his head like a snorting bull with the matador in his sights.

"You'd better think long and hard before you proceed," Hunter told him. The words were clipped and precise. He balanced lightly on the balls of his feet, his hands relaxed and open by his side.

Monty's jaw tightened. He looked past him into the house, where I waited, horrified, for the outcome of this nightmare. "Olivia, that unfortunate gambling issue has been cleared up. That's why I came over, to tell you." He continued, "I could have won it all back and then some in two hours with that fifty grand you hijacked."

"Ease up, man," Detective Faraday warned.

"I just want her to know, okay? No bank would touch me. But I did what I had to, Olivia, to keep my family safe. I got the money." With a black look at Hunter, he added, "*Legally.* Those men won't be bothering you anymore.

I'm sorry, okay?"

"Okay, Monty." I said, through clenched teeth.

The picture of penance, he clutched his hands, sighed, then addressed Lilly and Serena. "Girls, I'm sorry you had to know about this little...incident with your mother. I'll call you later, okay?" Lilly gave him a forlorn look. Serena stomped past me to the door and graced him with an obscene hand gesture.

Monty laughed at that, got in his car and roared away. I wondered if this had been a "normal" family episode for us, back in the day. Lilly, her first two fingers firmly implanted in her mouth, trudged upstairs.

Detective Faraday flexed his hands and put them in the pockets of his khakis. "What happened?"

The door squealed and slapped shut with a bang as I stepped onto the porch. "He just...showed up."

"Just showed up? No notice?"

"He wants things...like they were before. Like none of it ever happened. Perfect timing, by the way."

"No problem. Wish I'd come sooner. I didn't really see everything, just his back and you getting up off the floor. Did he hit you?"

"He didn't hit me, just kind of...pushed me down." I sighed. "Like he couldn't risk actually hitting me with everything going on, but he could 'accidentally' shove me. If you hadn't shown up when you did, I'd probably have a black eye or a broken jaw."

He shook his head and blew out a breath. "What a freakin' idiot. The more I know about him, the more I think he's the one that needs to be locked up. Please file a police report, just to have a record."

I asked about Niles.

"I heard he was going to plead out, not go to trial," Hunter said.

I smiled weakly. "That's a relief. I just want to put it behind me."

Detective Faraday frowned. "Olivia, sometimes you have to confront. Monty could have—"

"I know." I crossed my arms and looked at my yard.

"Anyway, it doesn't look like you are going to have to testify. The guy's apparently had a big change of heart. At least he says he has." Silent a few seconds, he continued, "We've had a tip which our background check corroborated. The guy lost his parents in a fire when he was eight. Watched his house burn with his parents in it. Rough start, for sure. Bounced around as a foster kid."

Somehow, I'd known something horrible had happened to him. Niles wasn't a monster; he was a poster child for trauma, acting out what had happened to him, or what he'd seen, maybe. "I think…I think I want to talk to him."

He squinted at me. "Why would you want to do that?"

"Look, Hunter, I appreciate everything you're doing to get to the bottom of this…assault, attack, whatever…but people can change. He has a son. An ex-wife. A life. I'm not even sure what happened! My memories are still foggy and confusing."

He was silent.

"I don't know. I just can't get the poor man out of my head. What you've told me confirms why."

A beat of silence passed between us. "I need to tell you something else."

His caramel-colored eyes watched me steadily.

"I've decided to press charges."

Hunter widened his stance and crossed his arms, waiting for me to go on.

"I…I think it is important that he have consequences. But that doesn't mean I don't…won't forgive him."

"Lots of people have a horrible past, Olivia, and manage not to assault women." He smiled thinly. "I'm glad you're pressing charges."

"Maybe he can get a lesser…"

"I can talk to the judge. It is kind of strange, he has no record of this kind of thing."

"Good." The word was a sigh.

"He approached me," I whispered.

"He what…*when?*"

I gave Hunter the condensed version, editing out the necklace, still too raw to think about.

"You should've told me immediately," he barked.

"Some people just never have a chance, you know?" I murmured.

He sighed. "I'll see what I can do about a face-to-face." He pointed a stern finger. "But only with me. Not alone."

"Fine." I smiled, my growling stomach a reminder that I needed to eat. "Can I fix you breakfast?"

With a guarded grin, he agreed. "Casual interview."

"Got it," I said.

* * *

Later that night, like a starry-eyed kid, I relived every detail of the 'interview' in my mind. Turns out he *did* like blueberries, and scarfed down the pancakes. We talked about the case over my kitchen table. After he left, I spent Saturday doing normal stuff that normal people do. People who have not been stalked by crazed ex-husbands or assaulted by pathetic, emotionally crippled individuals. I allowed myself to fantasize—my life returning to... what? What was "normal," anyway?

Chapter Forty-Nine

The next morning, my heart did a little flip when I heard Detective Faraday's car drive up. I dolloped the last of my mascara, dragged on lip gloss, scrunched my hair and sprayed it one last time, ran downstairs, and threw the door open.

"Morning," I said, all breathless and wide-eyed and coy.

"Morning." Callie eyed me. "You must be really glad to see me."

I gasped. "Hi, I...oh, *gosh*."

She fluttered plump fingers. "Forget we were going to the Farmer's Market in Hunt Valley this morning? It was *Sunday*, right?" She swept past me to the kitchen. "Coffeeeeee?"

I closed the door and turned, slapping my forehead. "Callie, I totally forgot."

She laughed. "Understandable. Not like you don't have anything going on."

I quickly stuck a mug under the Keurig spout, got out cream and sugar and a spoon, and put them on the island. "It's just that, ahh...I have company this weekend, and..."

Her eyes almost popped out of her head. "Company?" She stirred cream and sugar into her mug. "Who?"

I didn't know what to say.

"No!" Her smile widened. "Seriously? That detective?" She pointed toward the second-floor bedrooms. "He here?"

"Of course not! He's in a hotel. It's about the case."

She chuckled, took a sip of coffee. "So, where is he, that gorgeous specimen of law enforcement?"

"On his way."

She sipped. "Ahh. That accounts for your reaction when you opened the door." She laughed. "Should I leave, then?"

"No. I'd love you to meet him. But can we reschedule the shopping?"

"Oh yeah. And of course I'll stay a bit. I wouldn't miss meeting this guy for all the homemade pies and fresh produce in the world."

I laughed. "He's just a normal guy, trust me."

"Right," she said, with a roll of her eyes. Rapping sounded at the front door.

"Stop it." I laughed and trotted down the hall.

My smile faltered when I opened the door. Hunter looked like he'd lost his best friend. He opened his mouth, started to speak, then closed it and looked away.

Tension rippled up the back of my neck. "What is it?"

He took a deep breath. "Niles is dead. I just got the call. Westminster PD alerted me and want me to collaborate with the investigation. I'm headed there now."

The words went in, I was sure of it, but they swam around in my head like sharks, circling and circling. I pointed at Callie, speechless, then turned back. "I wanted to...I was going to..." I pounded a fist into my hand in frustration. The words would not come.

Callie drew closer, widening her eyes. I don't think she even knew who Niles was. Had I told her? Or had I just given her the generic version of why my face had been splashed all over the news?

"What is it, Olivia?" she asked, softly.

"I wanted to give him...to tell him...I was going to tell him I forgave... give him a chance to..." I went all quiet and soft. My old friend, Oblivion, stretched out his arms. I shook my head. *No.*

Hunter introduced himself to Callie. "Sorry to have to ruin the morning. Look, you guys have a good day. I don't know how long I'll be, and I'll let you know when—"

"I want to see him," I blurted. "I *need* to see him," I insisted with a defiant lift of my chin.

"Not a good idea." He spread his hands. "Crime scenes are not fun places. This one is messy."

I stared at him. "What does that mean?"

"Trust me, you don't want to know, Olivia."

"I do. I want to know."

Callie's face went pale. She edged away from us.

"Can't share details. Look, I gotta go."

I snagged his arm. *"Please."*

After a few seconds, he frowned. "Okay. You can come, but you have to stay in my rental car. Got it? It'll be my badge if I let the victim into a crime scene. Are you sure?"

Olivia nodded.

"Get your purse. Don't know how long it'll take to process the scene before the coroner gets there."

I darted into the house and returned. Callie gave me a quick hug. "Can I do anything? Need me to be here for the girls?"

I blinked. The girls! They'd be getting up soon. Had Monty heard? If he had, would he come charging over here with some kind of wild accusations? "Yes! Please, that would be a great help." After a pause, I added, "If Monty shows up, do not let him in the house. I have a restraining order. If he won't leave, call the cops. And Lilly and Serena cannot go with him, if he asks."

If possible, Callie's face paled even more. I put a hand on her arm. "Look, I doubt he'll show up. This is just in case, okay? Don't worry. Feel free to take them to your house if you're concerned."

"Come on!" Hunter called from his vehicle.

I jumped into the car and off we went. I wasn't sure why I needed to go, but I did.

* * *

Fifteen tense minutes later, we pulled into the small parking lot of an aging, but well-maintained hotel named The Westminster Inn. Police had scrolled yellow tape around the cracked asphalt lot, and unhappy guests were demanding to be let into their rooms. A few uniforms stood around the perimeter, explaining that no one but qualified personnel were allowed, and no, they had no idea how long it would be, thank you for your patience and no details were available at this time. An ambulance sedately exited the lot and somber-faced, uniformed personnel inside the tape walked in and out of one of the rooms. I lowered the passenger window. Hunter reiterated that I stay in the car, then got out of the car and showed his badge.

One of the cops nodded and lifted the yellow tape.

Feeling numb and cold in spite of the warm day, I settled in to observe. One man handed out booties. A coroner's van pulled into the lot. Tears leaked down my cheeks. The main memories I had of Niles were happy ones; completely at odds with what I experienced when Hunter and I had gone to his house. So now, I felt such regret that I hadn't been able to connect with him before this...this...what had it been? Suicide? Maybe. Probably. I thought about how he'd talked about his son on the beach. So proud.

I swiped the tears away. He'd drugged and assaulted me, or at least tried to. Maybe he'd tried to kill me, I didn't know. But part of him was good and kind. Questions rammed my mind. I pushed them away. I trusted that I'd know things when I was supposed to know, and I needed to leave that there. In God's hands. I smiled a tight, sad smile. I sounded like my mother.

I craned my neck to get a better look inside the room, but I was too far away. As I hung out the window, I saw a portly man in black. We locked eyes. He smiled and walked toward the car. I saw that he wore the white collar of a Catholic priest. This reassured me somehow. Maybe Niles's family had been contacted and they'd asked for someone. I frowned at the thought. From what Niles had told me, his wife and son wanted nothing more to do with him, so no, that couldn't be it. The priest stood beside the car and looked down at me. "A sad day, this one."

"Yes," I agreed and looked up at him. "Did you, um...know the deceased?"

He extended his hand. "Father Henry."

I took his hand and shook. "Olivia."

After a heavy sigh, Father Henry said, "The young man inside—Niles is... *was* his name—wandered into my church one day. After the confessional, we sat and talked. I was troubled about him. As desperate a man as I'd seen in a while."

My eyes widened. "When was this?"

The priest named a date. The same date I'd been to see my attorney, just a few days ago. My shoulders sagged. I closed my eyes. He'd been staying at this modest, hole-in-the-wall hotel because it'd been close to my attorney's office where he figured he'd run into me.

I started to speak, but nothing came out. Helplessly, I stared at Father Henry, an apology in my eyes. My words had stalled. It still happened, especially in stressful situations.

His gaze intensified. "It's you! The one I've seen on TV that lost her memory." His forehead furrowed in concern. "And you should probably be at home getting your life back rather than here."

Struggling with my stubborn vocal chords, I watched Father Henry contemplate this information and make the connection. Niles, the attacker and me, the attacked. I coughed, cleared my throat. "I don't remember everything, but I wanted to..." I sighed. "Maybe it's ridiculous, but I wanted to tell him I forgave him."

The kind priest smiled. "You think maybe God wanted you to know? To release you from that burden? I can tell you with all confidence that he found forgiveness, Olivia."

Tears sprang to my eyes. "I think that may be part of it, Father."

"Do you understand what's happening?" he asked.

I shook my head no.

"Well, the paramedics had to first check to verify whether a life could be saved or not. Since the coroner is here, obviously not. Now they'll conclude the investigation of the scene and either release it, or keep investigating." After a pause, he continued, "I'm sorry you've gone through all this."

"Thanks," I said, distracted. Out of the corner of my eye, I watched Hunter stride toward us. I excused myself and got out of the car. "What's going on?"

He gave me a hard stare as he swept past me to talk to someone who'd just arrived. "Get back in the car. Just be glad you didn't go in there."

The coroner's team came out of the room, walked to their van and got a gurney. Solemnly, they pushed it into the room. Coiled like a spring about to explode and break into a thousand pieces, I had no sense of time as I waited for them to come out. When they did, the gurney held a black body bag. I suppressed the insane urge to dash to the gurney and rip open the bag to make sure it was Niles. I tried to get in touch with what I felt. Was it relief? Anger? Sorrow?

No.

It was that excruciating, frustrating numbness I experienced when I was in a coma, and it scared me to death. Rooted to one spot on the sunbaked asphalt, my feet and arms like lead, I forced my feet to move just enough to convince me that the haunting paralysis of the coma had not returned.

The men threw open the van's back doors, and grunted as they lifted the gurney and collapsed its frame to slide him in. Then they slammed the doors shut. A horrible, final, clanging sound. Behind me, a low-voiced conversation. I turned.

"You okay?" One man asked another who knelt as if worshiping a plot of grass. He rose slowly, wiping his mouth.

"Yeah."

"It'll get easier."

The man who'd gotten sick, apparently, hissed, "When the hell does that happen? This is the worst yet. Maybe I'm not cut out for this."

I got out of the car and edged closer to hear. No one seemed to be babysitting me, or caring too much about people outside the perimeter. These men were outside the yellow tape, anyway, so fair game. I took a few more steps.

"But did you see him, man? Did you even look?"

The other man shrugged. "You learn not to look too close. We're in there to do a job, then we leave. Get prints. Process, bag and tag. Take pictures of everything in sight. It's automatic after a while, and you don't even look at the victim as human. It's just a dead puzzle to figure out." He shrugged.

"The rest is up to the investigators. This is just the training phase, man, it'll be okay. Don't be too hard on yourself."

"But is this normal? Half the guy's head was blown away. For Chrissakes, his *eyeball* was hangin' out." The man covered his face with his hands. "His brain was all over the floor, like chunks of vomit. I'll never get that outta my head."

I felt blood drain from my face, my hands. I inched closer. Though I knew this couldn't be good for a post-coma, aphasic, recovering victim of assault, I listened anyway.

"Blood around his head was way extreme. Spatter pattern was definitely unusual," the other man ticked off teaching points on his fingers. "Autopsy'll show more when they dig out the bullets. Two entry points. If I had to guess, and we definitely *cannot* do that, you understand me? But if I had to, I'd say the guy didn't off himself."

"How could you tell?"

"His gun wasn't in the right hand. So there's that. How do you shoot yourself with your left hand when you're right-handed?" He shrugged. "Did you notice that he was right-handed? Watch on the left arm, wallet in his right back pocket..."

The other man nodded thoughtfully.

"And his body was all twisted toward the door. Like he was trying to get away."

I closed my eyes.

"But that's not what got me," the teacher-mentor continued. "What got me was what was in his right hand...did you see that picture?"

The other man nodded. "His son, someone said."

I slid away slowly, before my own chunks of vomit decided to hurl. The mentor-teacher finally noticed me and yelled, "Hey! Can't be this close to the scene! Are you authorized?"

I scuttled back to the car and jumped inside. As horrific as the description had been, it wasn't Niles I was thinking about, it was me in his bedroom, laying on white carpet saturated with blood. I could still smell it, feel it; slick and warm, and it was coming out of me.

I felt the bed give with Niles's weight as he lay beside me. Then his hands were everywhere. I kicked both legs as hard as I could, but they had turned to mush. Exerting all my will and strength, I slid away from him and landed on the floor. In slow motion, I managed to pull myself to my hands and knees, but before I could struggle to my feet, Niles jerked me up.

"You're supposed to be unconscious," he said, his breathing labored as he tried to hold me upright. "I sure hope you don't remember any of this," he whispered. Had he drugged me? My mind wound through a labyrinth of possibilities and settled on one thing: you have to get away from him. Focus on that.

He held me by the armpits, leaving my hands free and his occupied. I took a deep breath, pushed both arms up, and connected with his chin. His head snapped back. His grip loosened. Twisting away, I tried to run, but my legs would not obey. Niles gripped my shoulders. I clawed at his cheek and drew blood. He yelped and shoved me with all his strength.

The front of my head connected with the solid, sharp corner of his dresser. My last thought before I blacked out was lying to my mother. "I'm sorry, Mom," I whispered as I fell to the floor, blood streaming down my back, my chest; convinced I'd be drawing my last breaths on Niles' snowy white carpet.

I clapped both hands over my mouth. It was true, then. Niles had done it, but the injury itself—the incident that landed me in the hospital—was unintentional. If that was the case, then he'd saved my life because I had to assume that he was the one that took me to the hospital. After he'd drugged and attempted to rape me. I shuddered. There'd been no evidence of rape, the nurses had told me. And there had been no proof he'd drugged me, either.

What a mess.

And now he was dead. Would I ever know what happened? Did I need to know?

It had been *my* decision to visit a total stranger, *my* decision to throw caution to the wind, *my* decision to not tell anyone I was going. What had I been thinking? And now...my choices had ended someone's life and almost ended mine.

I choked back a sob, dropped my face into my hands, thinking about the picture he must've grabbed when he knew he was dying. *His son.* Had he even had time to say goodbye to his only son? That was it. I shattered then, and I was gone.

As if I were still held prisoner by a coma, my soul simply left my body. Higher and higher it floated, gliding up to the shimmering sun until, like Icarus, I thought I might burst into flames. I was floating, floating, floating... above the carnage. Above trying to figure things out. Above the guilt I felt, the fear, the shifting moral dilemmas. Above everything, I couldn't bear to think of anymore. It was safer that way.

As if from a distance, I watched the coroner's vehicle drive off with its sad cargo. Slow, like a funeral procession.

I huddled into my little corner of the sky and looked down on my corkscrewed form in the car.

Hunter walked toward me, shoulders hunched and hands deep in his pockets. How could he approach me here next to the sun? Could he fly? Could I? He walked closer, frowning. Anxious. A chill shivered through me. I rubbed my shoulders, and with the movement, sadly, drifted to earth. He leaned into the open window, tried to talk to me, but his words were garbled. I put my hands over my ears. Father Henry approached and asked if he could talk to me.

No.

I sat stoic and still.

Hunter got in the car and drove.

I looked out the window as we drove. Felt the wind hitting my face, blowing back my hair. We pulled in front of my house and just sat there.

Somehow, we ended up on the porch swing. Hunter rocked us gently with one foot as he talked to someone on his cell. He kept glancing at me. It took too much effort to speak, so I didn't.

I stared at my beautiful yard with its flowers and bird feeders and all the things I'd planted through the years. It failed to bring solace, or closure, or anything at all. I watched Hunter's leg moving with the motion of rocking us. The squeak of hinges where the swing was affixed to the ceiling became irritating. I wanted it to stop.

It seemed like an eternity before he spoke, and when he did, it was only to tell me something I already knew.

"It wasn't a suicide, Olivia."

* * *

I looked at Mom for a long time. Cotton-candy wisps of pink fluff, my thoughts disintegrated the moment I sank my teeth into them. I felt the planes of her face with my fingers, a face I remembered, now. The past not completely patched together, but at least the puzzle was close to being finished. Just a few pieces missing now.

The girls had come to wake me earlier, but I'd groaned and pushed them away. They'd hugged me, kissed me, and left. Sweet. I had such sweet girls. I didn't deserve them. A chickadee fight drew my attention to the bird feeder. I needed to fill that bird feeder, didn't I? I did. I needed to do that.

My mother cleared her throat. "Honey, what are you thinking?" She picked up my hand. "Detective Faraday called yesterday, and I got on the next flight. I'm here to help. Whatever you need."

I would not tell her about the cotton candy. Nothing made sense, anyway. The chickadees made their peace. A cardinal swooped, cheeped, and landed. The chickadees exploded off the feeder. The cardinals always won.

"Honey?"

Why was she here? She hadn't told me she was coming so soon to visit again, had she? No matter, I was glad. My head began to pound. I put my fingertips on each temple.

"I'll get you something, Olivia," Mom said, and ran into the house.

I pressed my fingertips harder against each side of my head. The pounding increased.

The door banged behind her as she emerged with two white pills and a bottle of water.

"Dr. Sturgis is on the way, Olivia."

I opened one eye. "Why?"

"Yesterday was hard for you."

256

CHAPTER FORTY-NINE

"Yesterday?"

"Yes, honey. Traumatic."

I nodded slowly. "I guess so."

We sat and rocked in silence.

Chapter Fifty

"Wait, wait, slow down..." Monty pulled off his reading glasses and put them on his desk as he listened to Lilly's staccato version of what had happened.

"Yeah, Dad, it's the guy that hurt her that killed himself. Remember, his name was—"

"Niles," Monty finished.

"Yeah. Anyway, gotta go, Dad, get back to work. I've gone over and over this with you, that's all I know. Maybe you can call Mom..." Lilly hesitated. "Maybe not, since she's not doing so good."

"It's going to be all right, kitten. Have a good day, okay? Tell your sister I said hello."

"Dad, you know she doesn't want to talk to you."

Monty grunted. "She will, eventually, sweetie."

Monty tucked his cell back into the pocket of his black dress slacks. His fingers tapped random rhythms on his desk. He almost yelled for Kirsten before he remembered she'd gotten another job and he was assistant-sharing with another department for the time being. His project for the State of Maryland had wound down and would soon end. No sense hiring another assistant at this point. He formed a tent with his hands. The rich mahogany sheen of the desk reflected his palms.

Monty thought about his wife. Their meager beginnings. The pregnancies. Time he'd invested in training and molding her. She owed him. Without him, she'd be a poverty-stricken single mother living with that religious nutcase, Sophie. He stood and stretched, then appreciatively surveyed the luxurious office he'd had for two years. He would miss it. It had been a good run for an IT consultant, but it was over. His recruiting firm would just have to get used to the fact that he had decided to work at what was still *his* house for the next few weeks, until they found him something new.

Olivia needed him. She'd see that now.

Chapter Fifty-One

Detective Faraday sat on the edge of a floral couch in a house on the outskirts of Richmond, scribbling notes on his ever-present notepad. Niles's son gazed out a window and waited for the next question, ramrod straight, thin, and pale.

The woman who sat next to the boy glared at Detective Faraday. "You can see he is not up to this."

Detective Faraday nodded. "I understand, ma'am, but it's procedure. The sooner the better."

She shrugged. "You want water?"

"No, thanks." Detective Faraday studied Niles's son. Lanky and tan, brown, curly hair like his father. The beginnings of a decent beard. Sixteen, just had a birthday. *Some birthday present.* He flipped the page over. "When was the last time you talked to your father, son?"

The boy slapped at a tear that threatened to fall. "About a week ago, I guess."

"What'd you talk about?"

"Not much. He'd gotten really depressed about everything. Couldn't hardly talk to him about stuff." He sniffed. "Shoulda thought about what he was doing." The boy's mouth twisted. He frowned at his mother. She turned away.

"Anything out of the ordinary stand out? Things that he said that he didn't normally say? Things that he did that he might not typically do?"

The boy's eyebrows drew together. His mother warned him with a look.

Detective Faraday wondered what was going on. "Something you're not telling me?"

The boy sighed. "Last time we talked, Mom was in the room with us." He glanced at her. "It was the only way she'd let him see me since the...since it happened."

"What did he tell you happened?"

The boy stared at the floor and tapped his feet. "Didn't have to tell me nothin'. Read the whole thing online."

Detective Faraday made a note. "How did that make you feel?"

He grunted. "What do you think? Like crap."

"I'm sure," Detective Faraday murmured. "Did you, uh...talk to him about what you'd read?"

"Sure," the boy spat, "like I wanted details." He gestured angrily toward his mother. "She's the one that let him have it."

Detective Faraday's eyebrows rose. He turned toward Niles's ex-wife. "Ma'am? That true?"

She turned her haggardness toward him and crossed her arms. "Well, what would you do? Hasn't my son been through enough? Haven't we given that man chance after chance? He didn't deserve our *pity*, for goodness' sake."

"And you said to him?"

"I told him to go to hell, where he belonged. To leave us alone. That I wished he'd never been born."

Detective Faraday scribbled. "Anything else?"

She sighed. "I told him there was no hope for a man like him. Guess he agreed with me."

He flipped his pad shut. "Okay, that should do it." He gave Niles's ex-wife his card. "I apologize for the trouble. I am truly sorry for your loss. Call me if you think of anything else."

"No big loss, that's for sure." She shot a guilty glance at her son.

The boy's lower lip trembled. He rose from his chair, hands clenched at his sides.

"For your information, Mom," he choked out, "Dad talked to a *priest*. He wanted to change. He apologized to me about a hundred times." The boy spun around and left.

Detective Faraday thanked her again for her time. As he walked back to his car, he thought about all the ways people cripple each other. Almost felt sorry for the guy.

Almost.

He started his car and drove away.

Chapter Fifty-Two

Gray's car roared up the gravel road in a huff of dust. He burst from his car and ran up the stairs where Sophie waited on the porch.

"How is she?"

"Don't know, Gray. She's not saying much. Glad you're here."

He put an arm around her and pulled her in for a hug. "I'm glad we could be here for her together. Let's go see her," he whispered into her hair.

Olivia sat on a stool at the kitchen counter, nestling a cold cup of tea. Gray snapped open his medical bag and retrieved a vial of mild, low-dose relaxants and a sleeping pill prescription. Olivia stared at the items.

He laid a hand on her arm. "Olivia?"

She turned toward him. "Yes?"

"Do you know who I am?"

Her eyebrows drew together in concentration. "Of course. Dr. Sturgis. Dr. Grayson Sturgis."

"Do you know where you are?"

"In my kitchen."

"Olivia, what day is this?"

"Sunday."

Gray glanced at Sophie. It was Tuesday morning. "Olivia, what are you doing right now?"

"I'm sitting in a car," she whispered, her voice dreamy and slurred. "It's a beautiful day. My friend is with me."

"Who is with you, Olivia?"

"Detective Faraday. A good friend."

"Can you look at me, Olivia?"

Like a child, she obeyed. Gray checked her eyes with the focused beam of the penlight, held up his hand, and asked her to follow it.

"All her reflexes appear normal," Gray murmured. "Delayed, but not bad."

Sophie waved to get his attention. Gray followed her pointed index finger to the hallway that led to the front door. Sophie moved closer to Olivia.

He saw a man standing at the door, shifting his weight from side to side. After he thought about it, he realized that this was Monty, Olivia's estranged husband. He frowned. Olivia and Sophie had been through enough without this guy intruding. Gray stood inside the door. "Yes?"

"Been knocking for a while. You guys deaf?"

Gray stepped onto the porch. "Monty, right?"

Monty stopped short. "I know you?" He squinted. "Wait, you're Sturgis, right? The neurologist?" Monty's eyes widened. "Is she okay?"

"Let's sit over here, Monty." The men settled themselves on two facing chairs, elbows on knees, leaning in toward each other. Sophie walked down the hall and listened through the screen door, careful to avoid being seen. She kept one eye on Olivia.

"It appears that what happened Sunday put Olivia in a, um…fragile emotional state. I take it you've heard about what happened."

Monty was quiet.

Gray continued, "Due to Olivia's prior head injury, I am not able to foresee the physical or mental implications. She could go one way or the other."

Monty paled. "You mean she could go…back into a coma?"

"It's possible that stress can delay her recovery, yes," Gray admitted.

"So, what now?"

"I've given her a routine exam. For the time being, all I can do is watch and wait. Maybe offer her a sedative, but I don't want to do that yet. I want to hear her speech patterns."

Monty's face contorted. "I need to see her."

"I wouldn't advise it."

Monty glowered. "She's still my wife."

"Wife or not, Monty, she's fragile. We don't want to push her into—"

"Yeah, but what if my presence would kick her out of it…this shock or whatever it is that's happened because of that whack job shooting himself?"

"How did you know that?" Dr. Sturgis's eyebrows drew together. "That's not been confirmed at all."

"People talk."

"But—" Dr. Sturgis began, then stopped.

Sophie glanced at Olivia in the kitchen. She sat peacefully on a stool, staring off into nothing.

Gray's voice was somber. "Did you know she insisted on being at the crime scene?"

Monty sighed. "No," he said, twisting his hands and looking into the distance. "No, I didn't."

"My best guess is that it threw her into a mild catatonic state. Kind of like shock. She's numbed herself as a means of protection. Sometimes people numb themselves to the point that their minds shut down."

"Oh, God," Monty cried, "this can't be happening again. I just can't… won't…NO!" He jumped up, eluded Gray's hasty grab, and ran to the front door.

Sophie darted back into the kitchen and placed herself as a shield. Monty's footsteps slammed down the hall.

Sophie held her arms out to each side like a human fence when he entered the kitchen. "Not now, Monty. You could do serious damage. Please don't."

Monty skirted her arms.

He leaned down until his nose was inches from Olivia's and looked into her vacant eyes. "Olivia," he whispered, "I'm here to take care of you, honey."

Chapter Fifty-Three

I blinked. "Monty?"

He smiled. "Yes, I'm home, Olivia. Home with you."

"But where did you go, Monty?"

"I made a mistake, Olivia. It's all over now."

I smiled.

Dr. Sturgis walked in. He looked upset.

"Monty, are we going to get married?" I didn't feel my lips move until after the words came.

Monty glanced at Dr. Sturgis. "Yes, honey, yes, we are."

My hand drifted to my stomach and rubbed. Blurry memories crashed against themselves in my confused brain. "But what about the baby? You said we wouldn't get married unless I...unless I..." Tears coursed down my cheeks. "I love this baby."

With a glance at Sophie, Monty swore softly. "That is all behind us now, Olivia."

I whimpered.

Monty patted me on the shoulder. "I've arranged everything, Olivia. You don't have to worry about a thing."

"No!" I screamed. "I won't abort my baby! I'll raise this baby alone if I have to!" I was a young woman again, covering my rounded belly protectively with my arms.

Monty shoved his hands in his pockets and looked away. "Olivia, you must be imagining things. I always wanted that baby. That baby is our Serena."

"You are lying! You never wanted *this* baby," I hissed.

Dr. Sturgis hovered, pacing in a tight circle around us. My mother begged Monty to leave the house.

Images blasted through my mind. Suddenly, the images slowed and marched one by one in perfect order. I pounded the breakfast bar for each word: "You. Never. Wanted. This. Baby."

Monty patted my shoulder, his lips curved in condescension. "Of course I did, silly."

I turned on him, lit with an unholy fire. "You kicked me," I whispered, my eyes wide, watching the scene play out in my mind. "I was *trying* to reason with you. You wouldn't listen. When I had the opportunity to pour out my heart, that I was pregnant and scared..." I choked on the words, then continued, "you went crazy!" I could hear the whispers of the past as clear as a mountain stream. "*My fault*, you kept saying...it was all my fault. I was *sixteen*," I hissed. "Sixteen, Monty! I barely knew what sex was, let alone how not to get pregnant."

Fluttering his hands, Monty beseeched me, "You don't remember at all. You're wrong." He gave me a pitying look, and is if playing to an audience, turned and spread his hands. "She really doesn't remember. An early miscarriage, that's all it was, and I thought it best to spare everyone the sadness." He shrugged and turned back toward me.

My arms drifted across my belly. "You were furious," I murmured thoughtfully, then gasped. "You kicked me in the stomach! Grabbed me, put your hand over my mouth." My hands involuntarily rose to my throat. "You choked me!" I stared at him in horror. "I must have passed out." My forehead knotted, remembering. "The next day, I woke up in a hospital and my baby was gone. Gone!" A gnawing anger coursed through me. I glared at Monty as the reel spun out and the memory came home to roost. *Panic. Intense abdominal pain. Pressure. A river of blood. My cheek on the wet carpet after I fell. The smell—my own blood.*

"You told me I *lost* that baby, that it couldn't be carried to term, but... that's not what happened." My face crumpled in disgust. "You told me I miscarried. That I'd had a nightmare. It was *real*." I stared at him. "You killed our baby—the one before Serena, Monty. The one no one knew about."

Monty's complexion mottled. He scowled at me with contempt. My whole world narrowed to a familiar twenty-year fear. My shoulders slumped as if I'd caved in on myself. I looked at Dr. Sturgis on one side of me, Mom on the other.

His tone subtle and thick, the words slithered into my mind: "Olivia, everything I have ever done was for your good...for *our* good...as a family. You've always been fragile. You needed me to guide you." He pointed at my arms still crossed over my stomach. I slid them off and let them hang at my sides. "See? Even now, you confuse yourself. How could you accuse me of those things?" He stroked my shoulder, my hair. "You need me. You know that now, don't you?"

"Get away from her!" my mother shouted. She shoved Monty as hard as she could, then tucked me under her arm and herded me out of the kitchen.

Monty shot her a hateful look. Dr. Sturgis pulled out his phone. An uncertain look crossed Monty's face then he bolted down the hall and out the front door. Dr. Sturgis ran after him, barking Detective Faraday's name into the phone.

I couldn't believe it.

My mother was so pale I was afraid she might faint. "Honey, why didn't you tell me?"

Memories, like candles, lit up the darkened corners of my mind. "You were going through a divorce my senior year in high school. I could've gotten away with anything and you'd never have known about it," I recited, wondering at the continuing memory download, amazed at the evolution of my healing brain. In a way, the injury had kickstarted a healing of more than my brain.

Mom was quiet, her hand swiping away tears.

"Then when I got pregnant again, nothing mattered but the baby and Monty's proposal."

My long sigh bounced off the ceiling. "I think I've known for some time something was wrong." The words felt stiff and uncomfortable, but right. "Why was I never able to make decisions or take care of things? Monty was…he was like a *dictator*, and I didn't try, or didn't know how, to stop him. Now I know why. I *know*." I thought a minute and said, "I didn't, I couldn't…" I groaned. "I couldn't tell him no. About anything." I slapped away the wetness on my cheeks. "Mom…he…he was so furious when I wouldn't end the first p-pregnancy," I stuttered, looking down and lightly stroking my abdomen. Grief crept into my voice. "When I tried to stand up to him, he went ballistic…slapping and punching…I must have shut down my emotions, or…" I tried to slow my heartbeat. "I don't know, really. But right now, this moment…it feels like the first time I've remembered."

Mom stroked my cheek. "Oh, Olivia," she murmured, crushing me in a hug.

"Maybe there are other things I've suppressed," I muttered. "Mom, I don't know how much more I can take of this." My throat felt gravelly, and the floor rose and fell beneath my feet like a ship in a storm. Mom led me to a chair and told me to take deep breaths.

"This is crazy. Niles and Monty must have been all jumbled up in…my mind…uh oh—" I squeezed my eyelids together and waited.

The man's arms that carried me were hard and strong. His movements were determined, his breathing labored. Through a haze, I watched a towel slip off me. It was blue. The scene shifted and Niles stood in his kitchen with the same towel knotted around his waist. With a smile, he walked over to me and clasped a delicate gold chain around my neck, and gently turned me around, but when I looked up at him to thank him, Monty's mottled, angry face had replaced his, and Monty's hands gripped my shoulders and threw me to the floor.

I'd been so sure. Niles had tried to rape me. But had he?

"What is it? Olivia! What's wrong? I'm here, honey. I'm here." Mom shook my shoulders gently. "Olivia! Stay with me."

I struggled through an anxious desire to escape. To forget it all, make it go away. Like I always had. Just dive into my old friend, Oblivion. I frowned. This time, I told myself, I would look at the past in specific detail. Whatever I could remember, I wanted to remember. Somehow, I had to fix this. And turning over rocks was a good place to start.

"I need to be alone," I whispered to my mother. I looked into her stress-lined face and wondered if I'd ever really appreciated how much she loved me. Supported me. "Would you mind if I kind of…disappear for a while? I have a lot of sorting out to do." After a beat, I added, "You don't know how much I appreciate you, Mom."

She smiled and wagged an index finger at me. "I'm not leaving this house until you work through all this."

I shot her a grateful glance, walked to my bedroom, and closed the door.

Chapter Fifty-Four

Two weeks later

My cell lit up with Hunter's number. I smiled. I needed a break from journaling, anyway. Plus, I'd missed his voice.

"Hey."

"Hi there. Interested in an update? I think I may have a better picture of what happened, now."

"Sure." My fingers tightened around the phone.

"I interviewed Niles's ex and his son. I think she might've been the final nail in the coffin."

I winced.

"If he was already on the edge, which he was, talking to her would've pushed him over." He paused. I heard the shuffling of pages. His notebook, I thought. "Also, he told his son that he had seen Father Henry. Remember, that was the priest that came over to the car at the crime scene? The son seemed to have hope for his dad."

Tears welled in my eyes.

"But we're not rock solid on homicide yet. It's still an open case."

I thought about the strange premonition I'd had. "He was there," I blurted. "Monty."

He paused a beat, then asked, "How can you know that?"

I ignored the question. "Do you think Monty following us to Niles's place in Richmond was random?"

Detective Faraday sighed. "Perhaps your daughters overheard your conversations with your mom?"

I definitely could see the possibility of the girls listening in, but something in me balked.

"No," I insisted. "He knew Niles. They *knew* each other." I thought about Monty and Niles connecting on the driveway. I'd thought it odd, but now... had they planned something together?

"We do suspect that is true, but," Hunter cleared his throat, "we can't find anyone who can put them together."

I tilted my head, thinking. "Could they have been gambling buddies? Or known each other through work?"

"We're trying to pin down what happened. Monty's lawyer won't let him say a word." He paused. "We did find Monty's number in Niles's phone, but no recent calls. We have enough blood spatter patterns to nail down the angle of the shot, though, and it isn't consistent with a suicide." More shuffling of pages. "But that's it so far. If it was a homicide, they knew what they were doing. We can't find a stray hair, a single print, nothing."

I sucked in a breath. "Do you think, well, that Monty hired him to...to... " The thought that my husband would hire someone to kill me was too ghastly to articulate.

"Maybe," Detective Faraday said gently. "Maybe not. I have my opinion, but not a shred of evidence to hang it on." He paused. "Olivia, we don't have to talk about this anymore."

I was quiet a few beats. "If ever I needed justification for the divorce"

"I'm sorry Monty wasn't a better guy, Olivia."

"I was seventeen when we got married. Just a kid. I thought he was the greatest thing that had ever happened to me."

"I get it," he said. "And your mom was distracted...single moms usually are."

I nodded. "Yeah, and she was going through her big life change. She went to church all the time, on top of her job and trying to take care of me."

"She didn't get you in church at that point?"

"No," I said flatly. "My religion was Monty."

We both went quiet.

"You can still prosecute for the abuse, you know."

My brow furrowed. "Monty?"

"Yes."

I shook my head. "Just *knowing*...that's what needed to happen. After the coma, when I started patching things together, I could never figure out why my friends painted a picture of me that I didn't relate to at all. The girls and Monty said the same kinds of things: passive, shy, accommodating. I've heard those words over and over again, to the point that I never want to hear them again. My counselor told me it was a classic pattern of behavior—young girl in a single-parent home, a mother who had a lot of distractions...vulnerable to men like Monty." I shook my head. "But I had no idea that he was any different from *other* men. How would I know? My mom didn't marry the best role models. So, I think, in a way, life with Monty felt...familiar. Safe." I chuckled. "Isn't that sickening?"

He was quiet.

"I think...what he'd done—that whole first pregnancy thing, was so horrible, so unthinkable...my mind just...swept it away."

"I'm so sorry, Olivia—"

"Don't be sorry," I snapped. "This is a process. I'm working through it. I am so tired of people telling me how *sorry* they are."

He waited.

I moaned softly. "Didn't mean to bite your head off. Realizing this stuff... it's taking a toll." I grunted. "Counselor tells me I'm going through the grief stages. This anger thing is taking a lot longer than it should, maybe."

"No problem."

I paused. "How could I have ever loved someone like that?"

"Maybe you didn't. Ever think about that?"

No response to that one.

"I think you've got a lot to look forward to," he continued.

"Hope so."

"I miss you, you know."

I smiled.

Chapter Fifty-Five

Sophie ended the call with a grunt of disgust and poured herself a cup of hot, black coffee. She tapped a cigarette out of a pack, grabbed a lighter, and walked to the porch.

"Last one until two o'clock," she told the cigarette, and lit it. She inhaled, blew out, and held it aloft. "I'll miss you when I quit." She sighed. "Whenever that is."

The third call about a book deal and movie rights. Local media had gone nuts with Olivia's story, still unfolding. How these people managed to get her number she didn't know, but she was glad her daughter had taken her advice and changed her number so that she could have some peace.

Her cell lit up again.

She answered it without speaking.

"Sophie?"

"Sophie isn't here."

Gray laughed. "Right."

She exhaled a plume of smoke.

"Quit yet?"

"Almost. Down to three a day. It's horrible."

"I got an e-cigarette. You should try those."

She shrugged. "I'm doing okay."

"How's Olivia today?"

"Fed her breakfast, and she disappeared with her journal. She's been like a monk for days."

"How's counseling?"

"Great. They meet twice a week." Sophie pushed a lock of hair off her forehead and stubbed out her cigarette. She drew her legs up into the chair and wrapped an arm around them.

"Monty should have gotten a finalized copy of the divorce to sign a few days ago. He's got no choice but to sign. Life as he knew it is over, thank God." She grunted. "Hopefully, he will be arrested soon. He's charged with violating a protection order, stalking, and is a suspect in that awful man's murder. At least they think it was a homicide. Then there are assault charges when she was sixteen. And who knows, they may consider the murder of an unborn child when he caused her to miscarry."

She listened to Gray breathe.

"It's been a long time coming," he said after a few seconds. "It's devastating, but it's over. Olivia will be okay, Sophie. All blue sky from here."

"Let's hope."

She lit another cigarette.

Chapter Fifty-Six

Three months later

The smell of grilled burgers floated through the condo. Mom and the girls sliced tomatoes and onions, and I gathered silverware, counting as I pulled from the drawer: Gray, Mom, Serena, Lilly... Hunter would be arriving soon. Callie and her husband and their daughter. Nine including me. I put the settings on the counter and sorted them into piles of forks, knives, and spoons, then grabbed a fistful of napkins and put them beside the plates.

I walked to our third-story balcony and watched the ocean swallow the sun, pink trails of glory shooting through the clouds. A few gulls swept so close I could almost touch them.

It had been Mom's idea to reinvent our Hilton Head vacations. A celebration, she'd said, of a new chapter for our family. She'd rented a condo for a week on the opposite side of the island from the one Monty had always rented. As usual, my crazy, wonderful mother was right, and the change helped. I didn't feel Monty's ghost lingering around every palm tree anymore.

"Perfect," I whispered to myself, watching the surf swell further onto the beach. A few people biked or walked together, silhouettes in the waning light. "Just...*perfect*."

"What's so perfect?" Hunter turned me around and pulled me in for a hug. I took in his bloodshot eyes. "You made it!"

"Barely. Last-minute stuff before I could get to the airport." He shrugged and sat. I scooted in beside him. He raked a hand through his hair. "Let's not talk about the case. It's closed now, anyway. How are you?"

"I *want* to know what happened. It's okay."

After a searching look, he bent down and dug around in the bag he'd plopped on the floor. He pulled out an old iron cross and extended it. Puzzled, I took it, feeling its heft, running my fingers over the dents and scars. Inlaid lilies curled around its edges. The initials *N.D.P.* had been scratched on the back. I dropped the cross like a hot coal. It bounced once, then clanked to a stop on the balcony's concrete floor.

"Found it in his desk at his office. We traced it back to one of his foster families."

I bent to pick it up.

"We contacted the son. He wanted an old photo album we found, but not this cross." He paused, leaned forward, elbows on his knees. "When we interviewed the woman who gave him the cross, she went ballistic. Said he'd grabbed the cross off the wall and attacked her with it. Her standard M.O. when he wouldn't do exactly as she asked was to force him to kneel and pray to that cross." Hunter let out a frustrated sigh. "Not a very friendly environment for a boy."

The battered bronze cross reflected scraps of dulled pink from the sunset. I rubbed the lilies around its edge. A damaged, terrible beauty that hinted at hellish pasts and betrayal, but new beginnings, too. "After he lost his parents, he was shuffled from one terrible experience to another."

"Something we see a lot." Hunter frowned. "Sometimes the foster families just want the check. Poor kids get messed up."

"He tried, though." I thought about Father Henry. "Can I have it?"

"Why I took it." He smiled.

Lilly bounced outside, told us the burgers were ready, then skipped away.

After dinner, Hunter and I walked to the balcony. The ocean below made gentle shooshing noises, and a few gulls squawked on their way to bed for the night. I could just make out silhouettes of cyclists pedaling down the beach, blurred shapes in the dusk. Stars dotted the darkening sky. Hunter and I leaned over the railing and watched the cyclists disappear.

"You like to ride bicycles?" he asked.

I felt my eyebrows pull together. My breathing sped up.

Hunter sprang into action. He'd seen this before. "Over here, Olivia. Sit."
He pulled me to a chair and sat beside me to wait it out.

* * *

Niles had one speed—fast. He also had the perfect spandex outfit, including color-coordinated helmet and shoes.

I pedaled as fast as I could, embarrassed at my own outfit—my shorts and worn Nikes a sad contrast to his stem-to-stern matching bodywear. My T-shirt was plastered to my back with sweat, and I puffed like mad trying to keep up. It had taken me a while to figure out the gears and adjust my butt on the hard, tiny seat of the bike, but I was getting there. The helmet he'd insisted I wear was too small and perched on my head like a neon yarmulke. Niles finally noticed how far behind I was and whizzed to my side.

"You okay?" He spun his lighter-than-air bike around and stopped beside me.

"I'm dying. So not used to this humidity. And...look at my hair!"

He reached out and touched the curls springing from underneath my helmet.

"Not into this, are you?"

I gave him a rueful look. "I think I had a different idea of how this would go," I said.

Niles stared at me a few beats too long. "So did I."

I tensed. Perhaps this weekend adventure had been a mistake, after all. A huge, dumb mistake.

"I want to apologize in advance, Olivia," he whispered, and looked away.

I cleared my throat. "What do you have to apologize for, Niles?"

He shrugged. "Let's just say sometimes we don't make the best decisions." Irritation flashed across his face.

I thought a minute. "Do you think having me visit is a bad decision?"

He grinned. "It was a horrible decision."

I had laughed.

CHAPTER FIFTY-SIX

* * *

"He was serious," I whispered, as the memory drifted into the background. "He tried to warn me."

Hunter frowned. "Who?"

"Niles," I said. "I just had a memory of us riding bikes." I spread my arms. "It was fun, normal. Then he changed—his demeanor, the way he phrased words...something changed." I groaned in frustration and sank back into my chair. "Will there ever be an end?"

"Yes," Hunter stated flatly. "There will be an end. But right now, it's helping to solidify the facts. What else did you see?"

"It's not what I saw, it's what he said. He told me it had been a horrible decision for me to visit him, like it was a joke, but...he tried to *warn* me about the assault, I think."

Hunter nodded. "He wrestled with things mentally, I bet. Probably all of his life, after his parents died. Not so unusual for someone to have a good side and a bad side."

"What must that do to a child? To lose both parents, then have to live with strangers?"

"Yeah," Hunter said, his voice thoughtful.

I shuddered. "After such a horrible thing, I'd be numb."

"Or mad as hell," Hunter said.

Chapter Fifty-Seven

Monty adjusted his elbows on the sand dune behind a cluster of sea oats. The binoculars had become heavy after an hour of surveillance. Olivia and her detective had been on the balcony quite a while before they'd gone inside. He put the binoculars down and rolled onto his back, cradled his head in his hands, and looked up at the sky. Twilight draped the beach. Stars popped out, and the moon was on the rise. The rolling surf had picked up. Tide was coming in.

His thoughts turned to his hearing in a few days. They still hadn't been able to nail down enough evidence to arrest him, and his lawyer thought they had a solid defense strategy worked out. He sighed and stretched his arms over his head. "It'll never get to trial," he muttered to himself, glancing at the starry sky. "I'm that good. Right, Niles, ole' buddy?"

He picked up the binoculars again. Hunter had returned to the balcony and leaned on the railing, watching the moon rise. Monty grinned behind the lenses. He pointed his fingers as if they were a gun, and whispered, "Boom."

As he started back to his rental car, he saw a shadowy form walking toward him in the distance. With a start, he recognized Olivia's gait and her curly hair bouncing in the breeze. He froze, his eyes darting left, right in panic. Only a couple of sandy humps and sea oats between them. He dove behind a neighboring sand dune, hoping she couldn't see clearly in the dusk. The soft shushes of her steps in the sand drew closer.

Closer still.

He held his breath. The steps stopped. He heard her call back to her detective, "Come on down. The waves are breathtaking tonight."

Monty swore silently. No doubt that imbecile would arrive within minutes. Beads of sweat broke out on his forehead. By being here, he'd not only violated the restraining order, but the mandate to stay in the state of Maryland until the hearing as well. He snaked into the sand, heedless of sand crabs or biting sand fleas, still as death.

"You're right." He winced at the sound of Detective Faraday's voice in the distance a few minutes later. "Waves are incredible. Let's walk in the surf. I'm taking my shoes off."

Olivia giggled. "Me, too!"

Monty felt as if his head would explode with rage. Had she forgotten all he'd done for her, all he'd *lost* because of her? Three years of dating and seventeen years of marriage earned him a degree of ownership, divorced or not. A bellow of rage climbed up his windpipe, and he almost—but not quite—stifled it.

He grimaced at the sound he'd made and inched as far into the sand as he dared, hoping it would not collapse with his weight. The sea oats above him seemed to announce his hiding spot with manic bobs of their straw-colored, spikey heads. Monty heard the muffled ding of a cell notification. Hunter remarked that he had to take a call. Steps padded in the other direction. Olivia was alone now.

He listened intently for several minutes. Had they both gone? The wind had grown stronger, and waves crashed in a thunderous roar. The cramps beginning to form in his arms and legs were taking a toll.

Chapter Fifty-Eight

Olivia

My heart sinking, my nerves as raw as if they'd been peeled with a knife, I recognized the nasty, guttural growl distinctive to Monty. With frantic hand motions and hushed sounds, Hunter and I made a plan.

Now I had to do my part. I hesitated, then glanced over my shoulder at Hunter. He gave me a thumbs-up and flapped his palm forward. *Go now.*

I took one tentative step. Two. *Hunter told me he had my back. Trust him.* Three steps. Four. I stared at the sky. My heart battered my rib cage, and a numb hysteria gripped me at this endless nightmare that once—I'd been convinced at the time—had been a happy marriage. If Monty *had* killed Niles, what would he do to me? Five steps. Six. Seven. Eight. I saw a foot. My mother's voice inserted itself: *You've got this, honey.*

Nine steps. Ten. A calm surged through me.

"You can get up now," I said.

I watched his back and arms relax. He abandoned his foothold in the sand and turned, dusting himself off. "Fancy meeting you here."

I turned on my phone flashlight. "I see you brought binoculars to the party."

"Yeah, I was hoping you'd bring the champagne. Divorce being final, and all that." Monty stood and craned his neck. "Where's your fine detective?"

"He got a call," I lied smoothly. "What are you doing here, Monty?"

He frowned. "What I've always done, Olivia. Help you see what's best. Protect you."

I stared at his dark eyes, the arrogant lift of his chin. "Actually, you've *never* wanted what was best for me."

His jaw clenched, and he crouched slightly, as if expecting a fight. Flashbacks of similar situations raced through my mind. I pushed the images away. He couldn't hurt me now.

I took my flashlight off his face and blurted, "What you wanted is to *own* me, like a dog...or a faithful servant. Isn't that what you wanted, Monty? Isn't that what you want now? Not a wife, but a servant? You know, like a hooker with benefits."

Monty shifted his weight in the sand and dropped his crouch lower. The sane part of me told me to run, but the calculated, logical part of me told me I was carrying out Hunter's plan just fine. "Tell me the truth, Monty. You and Niles knew each other, right?"

He cursed. "All that idiot was supposed to do was keep an eye on you. That's what I paid him for. Keep me updated, give me reports."

"What? Why?" I sputtered. "When we were separated?"

He frowned. "But he...instead he enjoyed it too much."

My thoughts went crazy. I'd felt someone was following me for a while. I'd seen dark shapes in the front yard, but written it off to wildlife or my imagination. How long had Niles been watching me? He'd been paid! Had the trip to Hilton Head and the accidental meeting on the beach been orchestrated? *Of course it had.* I'd been so damn clueless.

The beach breeze whistled through my hair. I stood, stark and confident, every sense on high alert in this moment of truth. This awful man, one I'd trusted with my life, had never, not one second, been worth it.

I continued, "You told Niles to keep up with me because I was still your *property* even though you deserted your family for some...some immoral, boob-enhanced bimbo!"

Monty's breathing came out in harsh, shallow gasps, and his body language warned me he was about a minute away from losing control. I heard a shift in the sand behind me. Hunter had quietly moved closer. *Keep pressing his buttons.*

"You couldn't even help me with stuff around the house after you left, you arrogant sonofabitch." I spat the words. "But I'm *glad* you left, Monty. Or I'd never have figured out what an abusive, controlling animal you were. *Are*," I amended quickly.

Monty balanced on the balls of his feet, as if he were in a boxing ring. His eyes darted back and forth. His smile was forced, almost evil. "You still haven't learned, have you? You don't have what it takes to be a successful person, Olivia. How much clearer does it have to be? You've never had the ability to keep even an *animal* like me interested." He cursed. "You think that detective is going to take care of you? He can't even figure out what happened to..." his voice trailed away. He squinted at me. When he spoke again, his tone was speculative. "But you figured it out, didn't you?"

"I'll tell you what I figured out," I shot back. "You killed our firstborn and lied about it, made me feel like I had no worth as a human being, and gave me an allowance. An *allowance*, for God's sake! In short, I was your slave." I barked a laugh. "I don't want you to come within a mile of me ever again. Plus, you can stay away from the girls, too." I paused, and quipped, "Oh, wait—there's already a legal order in place. You're *supposed* to do that. You know, that little thing you ignore constantly?"

He drew close. Too close. His arm muscles tensed. "Try it," I urged.

"I mean it, Olivia. Stop."

I thought about Niles' remorseful attempt at reconciliation the day he approached me after my appointment with my attorney. The picture of his son he'd clutched in his hand in death. All of the events colored by Monty's shadow. It occurred to me in a split second that he'd been the backdrop to most of the bad stuff that had ever happened to me.

I prayed for words that would spark a confession. "It was *you*," I hissed. "You killed Niles, didn't you?"

"Of course I killed Niles, you stupid bitch," he growled. "I swear all I hired him to do was tail my family and report back. Take a few photos. But when I confronted him, the sniveling liar told me the whole story. He roofie'd your wine on your little romantic getaway, did you know that? Do you know what he was trying to do, you dimwit?"

I blanched. It was all true. "Drugged my wine?"

Monty spat the words, "The guy was going to *rape* you, and the drug he used causes amnesia, so you'd have never even known."

I sucked in a breath. It made sense now. Niles's cryptic apology, his haunted expression. My mixed memories that made no sense. His visit to the priest.

"You should be glad I killed him," he shouted, loud enough for all the world to hear.

Mission accomplished.

Fortunately, I had the presence of mind to jump back before Monty's right hook landed on my jaw. At the same time, Hunter leapt from behind the closest sand dune and wrestled Monty to the ground—no small feat, as Monty outweighed Hunter by about fifty pounds. Riding Monty like a human bull, Hunter grabbed one of Monty's beefy arms and twisted it behind his back.

"Remember this move, Monty? You just don't learn, do you?"

Monty bellowed a string of profanity, thrashed like a man possessed. Hunter lost his hold. He arced through the air and landed on his back, taking out a row of sea oats and the fragile top of a sand dune. I scuttled away sideways, like a crab. Monty's head whipped around. His glare landed on me. I got up and ran, slipping and sliding in the sand, his heavy steps and obscenity-laced screams at my heels. I looked back.

Hunter whipped across the sand like a human tornado. Monty had gained on me. I thought about his hands. Those hands could snap my neck like a twig. I ran faster.

Who was this guy? How had I not seen this?

I easily beat him to the condos and jumped in the middle of a shadowy thatch of palmettos. Parting the fronds, trying to get my breathing under control, I watched him jerk to a stop and swirl around, looking for me. His face was a red mask of rage. I shuddered. If he ever got Hunter in his sights—wait, did Monty have a gun? Frantically, I tried to remember if I'd seen one in his pocket or stuffed into his pants. I didn't think so, but I knew we had one locked in my safe at home. I couldn't rule out the possibility that he'd snuck in and gotten it at some point.

Seconds passed. Monty gave up trying to find me, thank God. Instead, he ran toward the pool.

To my immense and heartfelt relief, I heard sirens. And they were getting louder.

In minutes, red and blue lights coated the resort's parking lot. Panicked, Monty looked for an escape route. I parted my palm hideaway's leaves in another direction, but I didn't see Hunter anywhere. Where was he? A wrought-iron fence surrounded the pool area and on each side, stairs led to locked doors only accessed by guests with hotel keycards. Behind Monty, miles of beach. The only way out was back to the beach, and Monty knew it. He took off. The police had doused the sirens, but the lights kept circling. I hunkered down in my hiding spot to wait it out. Six cops got out and shone flashlights around the pool. "Beaufort County Sheriff's Department! Monty Callahan! Show yourself."

Hunter exploded from the shadows and stopped Monty in his tracks with an uppercut that lifted him off his feet. Monty stumbled and fell backward into the sand. The uniforms poured in from around the pool and took aim. Hunter lifted his badge and pointed. A deputy raised his chin in acknowledgment, then muscled Monty to his stomach and straddled him until one of the deputies could slap on cuffs.

Rubbing his knuckles, chest heaving, Hunter left Monty to the uniforms. He walked a few paces, then stopped. "Olivia?"

I popped up, but the palmettos held me in the grip of their huge thorns. I ddin't even know a palm could *have* thorns.

"Olivia!" Hunter called again, louder.

"Over here!" I yelled as I wrenched free. "Here!" I shouted, waving one hand high in the air. He wheeled around and ran toward me, relief etched across his face. He slowed as he approached, then put his arms around my waist. We looked at each other. Seconds ticked by. I heard the rush of the waves, felt the sweetness of the breeze on my face.

"You really should warn a guy what he's in for when he wants to take you out, Olivia."

I hugged him hard and long.

Chapter Fifty-Nine

As I enjoyed a cup of afternoon tea on my porch, the clouds darkened. I tugged my sweater more tightly around me. Occasionally, I still had fits and starts of memory-dump, but the tragic ones had stopped. Forever, I hoped. Some memories shouldn't be unearthed.

Serena and Lilly had accepted the fact their father might spend the rest of his life in prison, but the emotional backdraft would take a while to sort out. Dr. Sturgis had recommended therapists in the Baltimore area, and their appointments started next week. Serena stalked around, furious most of the time, and Lilly said little. I hoped the therapy would help them. For now, I answered their questions as best I could, thankful they'd been spared the sight of their dad being dragged away by a small army of cops. They'd been in their bedroom in the condo, watching a movie through the whole thing.

I sighed and drained my tea. "It's over," I declared, jabbing a fist in the air. "I think I can stop holding my breath and waiting for the other shoe to drop," I told Riot, who, as usual, looked like a golden, furry donut just inside the door. He raised his head and looked at me through the screen at the sound of my voice. Tires crunched up my driveway. I froze. Then I rolled my eyes. I had to quit being scared to death every time someone drove to my house.

When the maroon sedan gently rolled to a stop, I couldn't tell who it was. The door squealed open and Father Henry stepped out and waved. I smiled and jogged down the stairs with hands extended. He met me and took them in his own.

"I hope this isn't an imposition on your day, young lady," he said.

"No, of course not, Father. Would you like to sit a bit?" I extended an arm toward my porch.

"Sounds good," he said. Slow steps clomped up the stairs behind me. "Not as spry as I once was," he quipped, sinking into one of my rockers.

"Me either," I joked, but it was the truth. My steps were heavier now. But lightness was on the way. I looked forward to it.

"Tried to call, but no answer."

I pulled out my phone. Sure enough, three calls from a local area code. "Sorry, it's been on silent. Plus, I don't answer numbers I don't recognize anymore.

"I can well imagine."

Father Henry tapped his long fingers on his legs as he rocked thoughtfully in one of my rockers. I figured there was a good reason he showed up, so I waited for him to speak when he was ready. Words were overrated, I'd decided. I used less and less of them lately. I wasn't sure what was going on with me, but I think it had to do with grieving. Grieving a lot of things. Kind of like a funeral in reverse, I hoped both the figurative and literal corpses would stay buried.

He cleared his throat. "I've thought at length about this, and don't know if I should say, but after prayer I decided to come out with it." He shrugged. "I'm not aware of all that's transpired, Olivia, but this may be important." His eyebrows rose slightly, and he continued, "It may not be."

"Okay," I said, straightening.

"Niles and your husband...did you know that they knew each other?"

"Yes." Where was this going?

"Did you know that Niles was your husband's financial advisor?"

I frowned. "No. I should have, I guess." My mind raced. Why didn't I? Wouldn't Hunter have uncovered that piece of crucial information?

"They were friends at a critical time, apparently," the old priest coughed. "He didn't get specific, but he told me they'd done some awful things. Formed this, well, unholy alliance."

"Wait..." my mind stalled. "Are you saying Monty...that he and Niles...

289

what did they do?" My voice rose an octave. I stood. Had he been controlling Niles like he'd been controlling me? Why?

Father Henry flapped his hand. "Doesn't matter. Long time ago. They met in college, I think it was. And Monty had apparently twisted Niles's arm for insider trading tips, once the poor man became a financial advisor." He paused. "Are you sure your detective didn't tell you all this?"

"He's not *my* detective," I said vacantly, my mind trying to make sense of this fresh bit of news.

"I don't know how it fits into what happened, but..." Father Henry pulled a sealed envelope from his shirt pocket. "Here. Niles wanted me to give it to you in the event of his death."

Rubbing his hands together nervously, he added, "I hope I'm not risking God's wrath or my collar by giving it to you." He smiled. "You can do what you wish with the information."

I thought about the Power of Attorney Hunter had insisted Monty sign over to me before he got trotted off to jail. "Does anyone else know?"

The old priest stroked his chin, thinking. "What's his name again? The detective?"

My eyebrows shot into my hairline. "Hunter Faraday?"

The priest nodded. "Yes."

My mind spun furiously. I'd told Hunter ten days ago I thought we should take a break until I'd sorted myself out. He'd been pretty upset. Why hadn't he told me about this, if he knew?

"That's all I had. Anything else was privileged." Father Henry rose. "I wish you all the best, Olivia." He walked down the stairs, to his car, and turned. "I hope the letter brings you a little closure. He was a tortured soul, that one."

After he'd gone, I stared at the letter in my hand. It was light. Probably just one page. I slid my thumb under the flap, slid out the paper, and unfolded it. It was dated the day before Niles's body had been found. I sucked in a breath.

Olivia,

If you're reading this, then Monty must have made good on

his threat to kill me. He broke into my hotel room a couple of days ago. I think he's convinced I told you about the accounts he's been hiding from you for sixteen years. You may know by now that I've been his (reluctant) financial advisor, and he leaned on me to give him information I wasn't supposed to. Let's just say, he had enough dirt on me from our younger days to force me to do "investment favors" here and there, which resulted in an impressive balance in an offshore account. Olivia, I want to apologize again for everything, and I hope the information in this letter will help you start over. I guess I'm free of him now. I hope you are too. Forgive me. Niles

At the bottom of the page—handwritten in decisive, bold strokes—were passwords, account numbers and contact information. My hand shook so violently, I dropped the letter. A chilly gust of wind blew it into the yard. I ran after it, scooped it up, and went inside.

I called the number. The young woman who took my call told me in a British accent that the accounts had been emptied and closed a week ago. She was very sorry, and asked if I wanted to talk to her manager.

Monty had been in jail a week ago.

I stumbled out of my den, into the kitchen, my thoughts rattling around my brain like a pair of dice.

It had been *Hunter* who insisted on the Power of Attorney, and he'd been quite forceful about it. It had been *Hunter* who insisted that there was no evidence to convict Monty of the murder. It had been *Hunter* who held my hand, and eventually my heart, through the whole process. In fact, he'd been so attentive before I'd suggested we take a break that it had made me cautious. It had been *Hunter* that pumped me for personal information about Niles and Monty. What if Hunter had learned about these accounts early on? Why would I think I should trust him? Because he was a detective? Did that make any difference at all?

I called Richmond's Chief of Police, managed to get him on the phone, and summarized my dilemma. He told me he'd follow up and call me back.

Then I texted my friend Callie for her cousin's number. A well-known attorney, she'd told me he was mean as a snake in court. He would suit just fine. *This time,* I thought, *I will be prepared.*

I pictured Hunter's piercing look, and his mouth falling open when I'd suggested we take some time apart. Then I pictured the same expression when my attorney and I dinged him for the missing two million bucks he thought I didn't know about. My eyebrows pulled together so hard I was afraid the rut between them would become permanent.

How much had Monty been willing to pay to keep this quiet? Maybe Hunter had negotiated a lesser charge in exchange for a fat paycheck. I wiped away hot tears.

Look at the bright side. Once this is all out in the open, Hunter and Monty may get a chance to rekindle their relationship. Behind bars.

My cell rang. I jumped.

"Hey."

The familiar voice sent a shudder through me now.

"Hello," I said, my tone so cold, it should've given him frostbite.

He paused. "Got a minute?"

"Of course."

"Something the matter?"

"Why don't you tell me what's on your mind, and then I'll tell you what's on mine?"

I pictured the puzzled look on Hunter's face, the caramel eyes darkening, thick brows pulling together. I sighed. I'd have to forget all that, somehow.

He cleared his throat. "Olivia, I haven't been quite honest with you."

No kidding. "You haven't?"

"I didn't want to tell you until I had proof, but Monty and Niles didn't just happen to casually know each other; they'd been friends for years, and Niles was actually Monty's investment guy."

"Really," I said, my voice dripping with already-knew-that disdain.

Hunter went silent.

I continued, "Had an interesting conversation ten minutes ago."

"With who?"

CHAPTER FIFTY-NINE

"Father Henry."

He was quiet a few breaths. "So what'd he tell you?"

"You first."

"Okay." He cleared his throat. "Brace yourself." I heard the squeal of his desk chair wheels as he pulled closer to his desk. "Monty had approximately two million in offshore accounts that we recently discovered. We had him bring it back to the U.S. and told him he had to put your name on the accounts, as per asset laws in a divorce. There's 1.8 million in a local account—well, actually we had him spread it over several accounts for safety purposes. And there's two hundred thousand dollars in a trust for Niles's son, since his dad was the reason that account had grown so large. Well, that, and the fact your ex shot him."

"Wait. What?" He repeated what he said. The words fell like healing rain, sinking deep into the cracked, dry ground of my suspicion. *He hadn't known about the money from the beginning, and he hadn't used me to steal it.* Had he? My brow re-furrowed.

"Why didn't you tell me?" I demanded.

He sighed. "Offshore accounts are tricky things. We had to lure the information out of him, so I gave him the impression I'd take a bribe. It was a risk to tell you. The slightest look or tone variance could've tipped the scales, so we kept you in the dark on purpose. When he took the leap in a private meeting with me, we had him. He still thinks I'm working on reducing his sentence, I think." Hunter cleared his throat. "He wouldn't have moved the money unless he thought he'd get something huge out of it."

Could it be? Is it really true? I bit down hard on my lower lip.

"We have all the signature cards ready for your...wait." A pause. "Did you think...that I..." He laughed. "Olivia, if I did that, I'd not only lose my career, I'd be in prison, too. Look, I know you've been through so much it's hard to trust anyone, but you can trust me."

A tear straggled down my cheek. "It's hard," I whispered.

"I understand," he said.

Cell clasped tight against my ear, I stepped out onto the porch, walked down the stairs and into my yard. My shoes rustled the leaves as I walked.

The leaves were nearly all off the trees now. The bright sun in a hard, blue sky warmed my face. A chill in the air hinted at snow flurries later, and two brilliant-red cardinals swooped to my empty feeders. How long had they been that way? I would fill them immediately.

Hunter cleared his throat again. "Any idea when you might, um…lift this separation boundary you've set up between us? Just wondering."

I pictured the glint in Hunter's eyes and the uplift of the right corner of his mouth as he waited for my response. For the first time, I felt equipped to make an informed decision about whether or not I wanted, or even needed…a relationship.

"I'll let you know," I said.

He told me he was okay with that, but I knew he wasn't. When we ended the call, his voice had a testy edge.

And the funny thing, the *amazing* thing…was that it didn't matter. If we were meant to have a relationship, it would work out. But first, I would make sure I was emotionally healthy and whole.

Finally.

I thought about Callie. I thought about Mom. They would be so proud.

I looked up. Felt God smiling.

Or maybe it was Niles.

Acknowledgements

When I first became a writer, I had no clue how much persistence, patience, and thick skin were involved. As I look back, it is hard to think about, but in a good way—like exercising and getting sore afterward as proof of the hard work. A lot of people held my hand and heart as I trudged through multiple edits, blistering critiques, five different endings, and a host of naysayers.

The life lessons are profound. I've become less impatient and more teeth-grittingly persistent. I've become a better writer. Offenses at every little comment or manuscript change no longer have the power to paralyze me. I respect those who have helped me along the way, and they are many.

First, and foremost, I want to thank my first editor, Heather Andrews. Thank you, Heather, for being a believer from the beginning, and for your awesome editing skills and heart of gold. The time you spent honing my book was invaluable, and your sense of humor and professionalism made it easy to 'kill my darlings'.

Second, I want to thank my daughter, Bonnie Miller, a Navy-trained journalist, for her sharp wit and deep insights as a beta reader. Her input has been significant, and she's spent long hours reading my efforts in addition to maintaining a family, finishing her undergrad degree, and serving in her church. Thanks, honey. Additionally, to my husband, Jim, I'm grateful for your long-suffering patience and support of my many treks to writing conferences, events, and meetings. If I didn't have the foundation you provide, this wouldn't have happened. Thank you.

I'd also like to thank the wonderful authors I've met along the way, and specifically those from Killer Nashville Writer's Conference. To Clay Stafford, Joseph Borden, and Susan Crawford, thank you from the bottom of my heart. You believed in this book, and helped refine it further.

To Brian Thiem, author of the popular Matt Sinclair series and my favorite retired homicide detective and go-to person for cop stuff, my gratitude is boundless. Thanks for the time and constant encouragement you've given me. Many thanks, as well, to the Beaufort County Sheriff's Department for producing and presenting a free Citizen Police Academy—an entire week of fascinating presentations by law enforcement professionals on the front lines. This was both informative and inspiring, and I hope you keep it up. Also, warm regards to the author I met at an author event for my first book at the Hampstead Library in 2014 in Hampstead, MD. Little did she know how intriguing I found her personal experience with life-after-coma, and it became the catalyst for The Deadening's storyline.

To my publisher, Level Best Books, and Harriette Sackler, my editor, thanks for your faith in the manuscript and your final edits and insights about how to polish it even more.

To my readers, endless thanks for your encouragement, support, and patience as you waited on the next book.

About the Author

Kerry's publishing credits include a popular newspaper and e-zine humor column, "The Lighter Side," (2009—2011); and her debut novel, *The Hunting*, women's fiction/suspense, Pen-L Publishing, released in 2013. Before starting to write full time, she spent twenty-five years in advertising as an account manager, creative director, and copywriter. She is past chapter president of the Maryland Writers' Association and a current member and presenter of Hilton Head Island Writers' Network, and the Sisters in Crime organization. Recently, she worked as editor and contributor for Island Communications, a small, local publishing house. Her magazine articles have been published in *Local Life Magazine*, *The Bluffton Breeze*, *Lady Lowcountry*, and *Island Events Magazine*. *The Deadening* is the first in the Olivia Callahan Suspense series. Book Two will be available in 2022, and Book Three in 2023. Kerry is the mother of four adult children. She lives in Hilton Head Island with her husband and three annoying cats. She has a bunch of wonderful grandkids who keep life interesting and remind her what life is all about. Find out more about Kerry here: https://www.kerryperesta.net .

CPSIA information can be obtained
at www.ICGtesting.com
Printed in the USA
FSHW011719140221
78583FS